HOGGING
The Holidays

DEDICATION

To Christmas cheer, which is absolutely not responsible for any of the decisions made in this book—unlike my pastor husband, who listened to every unhinged biker idea I pitched and still didn't schedule me for counseling. A Christmas miracle, truly.

TRIGGER WARNINGS

Before you dive into this Christmas biker adventure, here is your friendly seasonal heads-up. Think of this as the literary equivalent of someone whispering, "Maybe don't let Grandma read this one first." This book may contain heavy subjects wrapped in holiday lights, so please take care while reading.

Violence: Includes fights, rough moments, and at least one incident where someone's holiday spirit gets knocked sideways.

Domestic Abuse: Depicted seriously and without humor.

Physical and Mental Abuse: Characters deal with harmful past experiences that linger longer than fruitcake.

Life After Divorce: Emotional rebuilding, reevaluating, and the search for new traditions.

Attempted Sexual Assault: Addressed with seriousness. Please proceed with caution.

PTSD: Characters carry significant trauma, with attempts at healing throughout.

Religious Trauma / Church Trauma: Includes harmful church experiences, misbehavior by religious authority figures, and the realization that sometimes the church caused more damage than the biker gang ever did.

Holiday Shenanigans: Contains tinsel misuse, questionable decisions, and at least one moment when someone really should have asked, "What would Santa not do?"

Biker Behavior: Includes leather, loud engines, and emotional issues that absolutely cannot be solved with duct tape, though you know they will try.

PLAY LIST

O Come, O Come Emmanuel - Skillet
Ho, Ho, Ho, and a Bottle of Rum - Jimmy Buffet
Carol of the Bells – Trans-Siberian Orchestra
Run Rudolph Run – Lemmy Kilmister
Northern Lights – Thirty Seconds to Mars
Blue Christmas – Elvis Presley
Underneath the Tree – Kelly Clarkson
I Won't Be Home for Christmas – blink-182
Yule Shoot Your Eye Out – Fall Out Boy
Last Christmas – Halestorm
Santa Claus Is Back in Town – Elvis Presley
Mistress for Christmas – AC/DC

CHAPTER 1

CECE

THE WORST PART about coming home with your tail tucked between your legs isn't the pity—it's the way everyone pretends they're not giving it to you.

I drag my suitcase up the front steps of my childhood home, the wheels catching on every crack in the concrete like it's protesting this whole mess as much as I am. The yellow paint on the porch railing is peeling worse than I remember, curling away in long strips that remind me of my marriage. Something that looked fine from a distance but fell apart the moment you got close enough to really see it.

"Cecelia Marie!" Dad's voice booms through the screen door before I even reach for the handle. He must have heard my car in the driveway—he always does, like he's wired into the damn gravel. He's been waiting; I can feel it in the sharp edge of his tone. "Get yourself in here before Mrs. Henderson sees you and starts running her mouth."

Too late for that, catching a glimpse of our neighbor's curtains twitching back into place. The San Salona gossip network moves faster than wildfire in August, and I've just given them premium fuel. Divorced daughter crawling back home at thirty-two with nothing but a beat-up Honda and enough emotional baggage to fill a storage unit. To be honest, I'm surprised the local paper isn't here taking my photo for a front-page news story. It's not every day that the preacher's daughter and the mayor's son get divorced.

"Hi, Dad." I let the screen door slam behind me, wincing at the sound. Some things never change. Like the way this house makes me feel twelve years old again, all scraped knees and disappointment.

He's standing in the hallway wearing his best attempt at a welcoming smile, but I can see the worry lines around his eyes have deepened. The last time I saw him, I was still pretending my marriage was just going through a rough patch instead of a total demolition.

"You look thin," he says, which is Dad-code for *I'm worried about you but don't know how to say it.*

"Divorce diet." I force a smile. "Very effective. Might write a lifestyle book about it."

He doesn't laugh. Instead, he takes my suitcase from

me, his weathered hand brushing mine. "Your room's all ready. Didn't change a thing."

That's exactly what I'm afraid of.

I follow him up the stairs, each step creaking in the exact same places they did when I used to sneak out to meet my first boyfriend, Jake, behind the high school bleachers. Jake, with his motorcycle, leather jacket, and the smile that promised trouble worth having. The town bad boy who ended up becoming a dentist in Tallahassee. Life's funny that way. Apparently, marrying the born to be successful mayor's son wasn't as safe of a bet as I had originally thought.

"I made pot roast," Dad says over his shoulder. "Figured you'd be hungry after the drive."

My stomach growls in response. It's been nothing but gas station coffee and stale donuts since I left Boulder this morning. "Thanks."

The room is exactly as I left it fourteen years ago when I left for college. Floral bedspread. Faded posters of bands I pretended to like because the cool girls did. Cheerleading trophies I earned to make my parents proud more than myself. The whole room is like a museum exhibit: *Teenage Dreams, Circa 2010.*

I drop onto the bed, and the mattress squeaks in protest. "How long before the whole town knows I'm back?"

"Oh, honey." Dad sits heavily in my old desk chair, making it spin slightly. "They already know. Mrs. Patterson called as soon as you crossed into the city limits."

She would. I can practically see her perched at that lace-covered window of hers, phone already unlocked, waiting for the exact moment my Honda's bumper touched Maple Street. She lives for this—information delivered like a prayer request.

"And?" I brace myself.

"Well, she wanted to know if you'd gained weight. I told her you looked beautiful as always." He clears his throat. "She also asked if it was true about Ethan and his secretary. She called her something else, but it doesn't bear repeating."

Even a hundred miles away, Ethan managed to humiliate me in my hometown. "It wasn't his secretary."

Dad raises an eyebrow.

"It was one of the flight attendants for his company's private jet. Well, the current one, anyway. Before her, it was his yoga instructor. And probably half the women at his country club, if I'm being honest." The words taste bitter, but there's relief in finally saying them out loud. "I was the last to know, apparently. Very cliché of me."

"Cecelia—"

"It's fine, Dad. Really." I lie back on the bed and stare at the ceiling, at the glow-in-the-dark stars I stuck up there in seventh grade. Most of them barely hanging on now. Kind of like me, and my sanity.

Dad sighs and I can hear everything he's not saying. The disappointment that I didn't try harder to save my marriage. The unspoken "I told you so" about marrying into the Kincaid family in the first place. He's too good a preacher to say it, but I know he's thinking it.

"You ready to eat?" he asks finally, changing the subject in that classic Montgomery way. Feelings are messy, whereas pot roast is straightforward.

"Starving," I admit, though the knot in my stomach suggests otherwise.

We eat in near silence, just the scrape of forks against plates and the occasional "pass the salt" breaking through. Dad tries to keep things light, updating me on church gossip—Mrs. Daniels' fight with the choir director, the youth group's car wash fundraiser that turned into a water balloon fight. The women's group has been protesting a movie they want to shoot in town. Normal, safe topics that don't venture anywhere near my failed marriage or uncertain future.

It's when we're clearing the dishes that he finally breaks.

"You know you can stay as long as you need," he says, rinsing a plate. "But what's your plan, Cecelia?"

The million-dollar question. The one I've been avoiding since I signed the divorce papers and realized I had nowhere to go but backwards.

"I don't know yet," I admit. "I've got some interviews lined up at the elementary school. They need a substitute teacher." I've never taught a day in my life, but a job is a job. Back in Boulder, I had my floral shop and high-end boutique, but I lost half of it in the divorce. Thankfully, Ethan had agreed to sell his share along with mine. I just need to find a buyer first. Until I do, I am stuck.

Dad's eyes narrow slightly, the way they always do when he thinks I'm not being completely honest. "Substitute teaching? With your business degree?"

"It's a job, Dad. And last time I checked beggars who've been financially gutted by their ex-husbands can't be choosers." I wince at my own tone. "Sorry. It's been a long day."

"I understand." But his tight smile says he doesn't, not really.

I dry the last plate and hang the dish towel on the oven handle. "I just need some time to figure things out. The shop back in Boulder is being sold, and once that's done, I'll have a little cushion to rebuild with."

"The Lord provides," Dad says automatically, and I fight the urge to roll my eyes. The Lord didn't provide, my lawyer did, after fighting tooth and nail to keep Ethan from taking everything. And all that providing just bought him a nice new vacation house after his fees.

The truth is, I don't have a plan beyond surviving each day without crumbling. Without calling Ethan and begging him to take me back, dignity be damned. That's why I drove twelve hours to get here—to put enough distance between us that I couldn't make that mistake. That and the thought of spending Christmas alone hurt more than it should have. Ethan and I always took a trip after the holidays. Just the two of us. When we first got married, we'd put places we'd like to visit in a fishbowl and pick until the very last piece. Last year, we spent New Year's Eve in Rome. The year before that Bora Bora, on the prettiest white sand beach I'd ever seen.

"Your mother would be proud of you, you know." Dad dries his hands on a dish towel, his gaze not quite meeting mine.

The mention of Mom hits me like a sucker punch. She's been gone for fifteen years, and her absence still feels fresh sometimes. "Would she? Or would she be disappointed that I couldn't keep my marriage together?"

"Cecelia." His voice takes on that pulpit tone.

I stack the plates into the plastic drainer. "I ignored the red flags. I believed him every time he said, 'it won't happen again.'"

Dad sets down the dish towel and turns to face me. "Red flags don't make the person who ignores them responsible for someone else's choices, Cece. Ethan chose to betray his vows. That's on him."

I want to believe that. God, I want to believe it so badly it makes my chest ache. But the voice in my head —the one that sounds suspiciously like Ethan's mother —keeps whispering that maybe if I'd been more attentive, more interesting, more something, he wouldn't have needed to look elsewhere.

"I should probably get some sleep," I say instead, because this conversation is heading somewhere I'm not ready to go.

Dad's shoulders slump slightly. "I have to go into

the church early tomorrow. The annual toy drive starts in the morning, and Jillian can't make it. She took it over last year, but her husband has been in the hospital. If you're interested in it, I sure could use the help."

"I'll think about it." I kiss his cheek—stubble rough against my lips—and head upstairs. The floorboards creak their familiar song as I make my way to the bathroom to brush my teeth. In the mirror, I look exactly like what I am. A woman who's been through hell and is still picking gravel out of her knees.

My phone buzzes on the nightstand as I'm pulling on an old college t-shirt. For one terrifying moment, my heart jumps, thinking it might be Ethan. But it's just a text from my best friend Maya back in Boulder.

How's the homecoming going? Scale of 1 to 'I'm running away to join the circus'?

> Somewhere between 'drinking wine in the bathtub' and 'googling witness protection programs.'

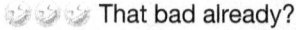 That bad already?

> Mrs. Henderson was watching from behind her curtains. Dad made pot roast. My bedroom still has the N'SYNC poster I swore I took down before college.

So basically time travel to your most
awkward years. Perfect healing
environment.

I smile despite myself. Maya always could make me laugh, even during the worst of it—like when I found the earring in our bed that definitely wasn't mine, or when Ethan's credit card statement showed dinner for two at restaurants I'd never been to.

At least you have good timing. You're
missing the first snow of the season.

Boulder's probably a winter
wonderland by now.

It is. Ethan's car got stuck in it this
morning. He posted on social media
offering to pay someone $1,000 to pull
him out if they could be there in fifteen
minutes or less.

My stomach clenches at his name.

Please don't tell me things about him.

Sorry. Old habit. How long do you think
you'll stay there?

I stare at the ceiling, at the faded glow-in-the-dark stars.

Until I figure out what comes next. Or until someone kidnaps me. Whichever comes first.

Call me if you need me. Seriously. I will drop the boys off at my brother's and run.

I love her for the offer, but this is something I need to figure out on my own.

I set the phone aside and pull the covers up to my chin. The house settles around me with all its familiar sounds—the furnace kicking on, the old pipes groaning, the grandfather clock in the hallway chiming eleven times. Sounds that used to comfort me, back when this place felt like home instead of a retreat.

Sleep doesn't come easy. Every time I close my eyes, I see Ethan's face when I confronted him about the earring. The way he tried to gaslight me, making me feel crazy for asking questions. "You're being paranoid, Cece. It's probably yours from months ago." As if I couldn't tell the difference between my simple gold studs and someone else's gaudy diamond hoops.

I roll over and punch the pillow into submission. Tomorrow I'll have to face the town properly where everyone will stare and whisper. The thought makes my skin crawl, but I can't hide in this house forever. Well, I could, but that would give them even more to talk about.

CHAPTER 2

CECE

I'M STANDING outside the First Baptist Church at eight-thirty in the morning, clutching a cup of Dad's nuclear-strength coffee and wondering if volunteering for the toy drive was a mistake. The December air bites through my sweater, and I'm already regretting not grabbing a heavier coat. But after tossing and turning all night, I figured I might as well make myself useful instead of hiding in my childhood bedroom like some tragic heroine.

I take a deep breath and steel myself for what's coming. Just get the toys sorted, avoid eye contact, then escape. Simple.

But I barely make it to the bottom step when they descend like vultures spotting fresh roadkill.

"Cecelia Montgomery!" Mrs. Whitaker's voice cuts through the morning air, sharp as a straight razor. She's leading the charge, a flock of church ladies in sensible cardigans and judgmental smiles right behind her.

They surround me before I can retreat, forming a circle that feels more like a trap. I'm caught in a perfume cloud of White Diamonds and barely concealed curiosity.

"Oh, honey, we've been just dying to see you," says Barbara Fletcher, her hand squeezing my arm with false sympathy while her eyes catalog every detail of my appearance. "How are you holding up?"

"I'm fine, thank you." I try for a polite smile that probably looks more like a grimace.

"We were all just devastated to hear about...well, you know." Linda Peterson leans in, lowering her voice to a whisper that could probably be heard in the next county. "Such a shame when a man strays. Was it really with three different women?"

My coffee sloshes close to the rim of my cup. "I wouldn't know the exact count."

"Your daddy says you're staying indefinitely," Mrs. Whitaker says, emphasizing the word like it's a terminal diagnosis.

"That's very generous of him to share my personal business."

The women exchange meaningful glances, the kind that communicate volumes without words. I've been on the receiving end of these looks my whole life—whenever I got caught sneaking out, or when I chose the state university over the fancy Christian college they all thought was more appropriate.

"Well, we just want you to know that we're praying for you," says Margaret Hutchins, patting my shoulder like I'm a wounded bird. "And if you need anything at all—a casserole, a listening ear, help finding a nice Christian man to settle down with—we're here."

"I just got divorced three weeks ago." The words come out sharper than I intend. "I'm not exactly in the market for a replacement husband."

Their collective gasp could power a small wind farm.

"Not at all, dear," Mrs. Whitaker recovers first, her smile tightening at the edges. "Though you know what they say—the best way to get over one man is to get under another."

I nearly choke on my coffee. Did the head of the church ladies' auxiliary just give me sex advice?

"I think you mean 'the best way to get over someone is to find someone better,'" Barbara corrects, looking scandalized.

"That too," Mrs. Whitaker says with a wink that makes me question everything I thought I knew about this woman. She'd been married to the same man since she was in high school. She is the least qualified person to offer me dating and sex advice.

I'm searching for an exit strategy when Dad appears at the top of the church steps like an answer to a prayer I didn't know I was saying.

"Ladies," he calls out, his pastor voice carrying

authority even in that single word. "I hate to interrupt this reunion, but I need to borrow my daughter. We've got donations that won't sort themselves."

The circle parts reluctantly, "We were just welcoming Cecelia home," Mrs. Whitaker says, smoothing her cardigan.

"And doing a fine job of it, but duty calls."

He motions for me to follow him, and I've never been so grateful for his interference in my life. I give the women a tight smile and hurry up the steps, coffee clutched to my chest like a shield.

"Thank you," I whisper when we're safely inside.

"I recognized that trapped animal look," he says. "You used to get it at every church potluck when you were sixteen."

The fellowship hall has been transformed into donation central, with folding tables lined up end to end. But as I scan the room, my heart sinks. The tables are mostly empty, with only scattered piles of toys and a few boxes of canned goods. I walk along the tables, running my hand over the sparse collection of dolls, trucks, and board games. The emptiness is jarring—last time I'd helped with this event, back in college, we could barely see the tabletops under mountains of donations.

"Dad, this can't be all of it. What about the business donations? The fire department's collection? The high school drive?"

He shakes his head, shoulders slumping slightly under his pressed shirt. "This is everything. The fire department's bringing their collection this afternoon, but they warned me it's less than half what they usually get."

"What happened?" I pick up a well-loved teddy bear that's clearly someone's hand-me-down, its fur worn thin in places.

Dad's mouth tightens into a grim line. "Between losing one of our biggest donors and the economy being what it is, we're looking at a pretty slim year."

I don't have to ask who the donor was. The Kincaid family had always made a show of their generosity, especially at Christmas. Ethan's father would roll up in his Range Rover packed with toys, making sure everyone saw him unloading it all himself. The local paper always ran a front-page photo.

"So they pulled their donation because of..." I can't bring myself to finish the sentence.

"They said they're focusing on other charities this year." Dad's tone makes it clear exactly what he thinks of their decision.

"Other charities," I repeat, tasting the bitterness of the lie. "Right."

Dad runs his hand through his silver-white hair, a gesture I've seen a thousand times when he's troubled. "It's not just about us, Cece. We've got families counting on this drive in Millbrook, Pinecrest, even out in Riverdale."

"I thought those communities had their own churches doing drives."

"They do what they can, but..." He sighs, leaning

against one of the empty tables. "San Salona has always been the big brother. You know what this town is like."

I do know. San Salona is basically a country club with a zip code—the kind where you're either born into membership or pay dearly for the privilege. Growing up, I never realized how sheltered we were from the realities just beyond our pristine city limits. The surrounding communities might as well be on another planet compared to our manicured lawns and luxury cars.

"Last year we provided Christmas for over three hundred families in the tri-county area," Dad continues. "This year, we've got nearly four hundred on our list, and..." He gestures to the meager pile of donations.

"That's not even enough for half," I finish for him.

"Not even a quarter." He picks up a worn box of Candy Land, its corners frayed and taped. "The Kincaids usually cover at least thirty percent of our donations. I've been trying to talk to the other businesses in town, but they're not taking my calls."

I sit my coffee down on the nearest table before I drop it. This is my fault. All of it. The Kincaids aren't just punishing me—they're punishing hundreds of kids who have nothing to do with their son's inability to keep his dick in his pants.

"They're doing this because of me. This is their way of getting back at me for the divorce. For making their precious son look bad."

Dad starts to protest, but I shake my head.

"Don't. We both know it's true. They're making sure

everyone knows exactly who to blame when Christmas morning comes, and there aren't enough presents." I pick up a threadbare stuffed rabbit, its floppy ears worn with love. "The great and powerful Kincaids, showing the whole county what happens when you cross them."

"Cecelia, you can't take this on yourself."

"Why not? It's obviously meant for me." I gesture at the nearly empty tables. "This is classic Marilyn Kincaid. Remember when I was sixteen and broke up with Ethan before prom, and suddenly the youth group funding for the mission trip disappeared?"

Dad winces. "That was different."

"Was it? The Kincaids have been weaponizing their money since before I was born. I just never thought they'd stoop to punishing children." I pace the length of the table, anger and shame battling for dominance in my mind. "They're doing the same thing on a much grander, public scale."

I hate them for this. I hate how petty and vindictive they're being, using children as pawns in their revenge game against me. My chest tightens as I imagine disappointed faces on Christmas morning, parents having to explain why Santa couldn't bring what was promised. All because I had the audacity to leave their precious son after he humiliated me.

"The Lord works in mysterious ways, Cecelia," Dad says, coming to stand beside me. "Remember Proverbs 3:5-6? 'Trust in the Lord with all your heart and lean not on your own understanding; in all your ways submit to him, and he will make your paths straight.'"

Scripture is Dad's solution to everything—broken hearts, empty toy tables, global warming. "I don't think the Lord arranged for the Kincaids to punish hundreds of innocent kids because I divorced their son, Dad."

"That's not what I—"

"I know what you meant." I soften my tone to hide my annoyance. "But Bible verses aren't going to fill these tables."

He places his hand on my shoulder, squeezing gently. "Sometimes we need to trust that solutions will present themselves in unexpected ways."

Before I can respond, Mrs. Whitaker appears in the doorway, her face pinched with importance. "Reverend Montgomery, there's an issue with the nativity scene. Jimmy Henderson says someone's stolen baby Jesus and replaced him with what appears to be a...well, an adult toy." She blinks rapidly, clearly scandalized.

Dad's face flushes. "Good Lord, not again." He turns to me with an apologetic look. "I need to—"

"Go," I say, waving him away. "I'll start sorting what we have."

Mrs. Whitaker clears her throat. "Actually, Reverend, I think you should come immediately. Mayor Kincaid is out there threatening to call the sheriff if we don't remove the...offensive item...before the children's choir arrives for practice."

At the mention of Kincaid, my stomach knots. He's here—loud enough, dramatic enough, that I don't even need to see him to know he's already causing trouble.

"Cecelia, I'm sorry—" Dad starts.

"It's fine. Really." I force a smile. "Go save baby Jesus."

Mrs. Whitaker practically drags him out the door, her sensible shoes squeaking against the linoleum as she launches into a detailed explanation of exactly which anatomical features the offending item possesses.

And just like that, I'm alone with nothing but empty tables and my own spiraling thoughts.

I trace my finger along the edge of one table, the silence of the room pressing in around me. This is so much worse than I imagined. It's not just that the Kincaids pulled their donation. They've made sure everyone else has too. I can picture Ethan's mother on the phone, her manicured nails tapping against her designer desk as she calls every business owner, working through her list of country club contacts. "You simply must reconsider donating to the church toy drive this year. The Montgomery girl is back in town, and you know what she did to my Ethan..."

The thought makes my blood boil. I've spent my entire life in this town, watching the Kincaids throw their weight around, but this is a new low. Using children as collateral damage in their vendetta against me.

I'm reorganizing the sad little pile of stuffed animals when the fellowship hall door swings open again. Mrs. Whitaker bustles in, her face flushed with excitement.

"The Reverend asked me to tell you he'll be tied up for a while. The mayor is absolutely beside himself." She lowers her voice dramatically. "Apparently, someone took pictures."

"How terrible," I mutter, not even trying to sound sincere.

Mrs. Whitaker studies me like I'm a suspicious paragraph in a romance novel. "I suppose you think this is amusing."

"A dildo in the manger? Kind of, yeah."

Her gasp could suck the oxygen from the room. "Cecelia Montgomery!"

"Sorry," I say, not sorry at all. "I forgot where I was for a moment." Before she can lecture me, Barbara Fletcher appears in the doorway, flushed and breathless.

"Judith!" she calls to Mrs. Whitaker. "You need to come quickly. The mayor is threatening to cancel the Christmas parade if someone doesn't remove that...thing...immediately!"

Her eyes go wide. "He wouldn't!"

"He most certainly would," Barbara says, glancing at me with undisguised accusation, like I personally placed a sex toy in the manger scene. "He's saying it's a deliberate attack on Christian values."

I snort before I can stop myself. "Christian values? That's rich."

Mrs. Whitaker's lips press into a thin line. "Well, I never—"

"Judith, please!" Barbara interrupts, grabbing Mrs. Whitaker's arm. "Reverend Montgomery is asking for you. He says you're the only one who can reason with the mayor."

Mrs. Whitaker straightens, puffing up with self-importance. "Well, Richard and I have known each other since high school. I suppose it falls to me to talk some sense into him."

She shoots me one last disapproving look before bustling out, Barbara in tow, leaving me alone.

I sink into a folding chair and stare at the empty tables. I don't know if I could hate the Kincaids more than I do at this very moment.

The fellowship hall door creaks open, and I tense, expecting another church lady with an update on the Great Manger Scandal of 2025. Instead, I'm surprised to see Jillian peering in.

"Cece? Is that really you?" She bustles toward me, arms outstretched. Before I can respond, I'm enveloped in a cloud of lavender perfume and wrapped in a hug that threatens to crack a rib. "Oh, honey, I've been meaning to call since I heard you were back!"

"I thought you were at the hospital with your husband," I manage once she releases me. Unlike the vultures outside, her smile is genuine. She taught my Sunday School class when I was little and always slipped me extra cookies when Dad wasn't looking.

"I just had to stop by to check on things," she says, glancing around at the empty tables with a frown. "Oh my. This is...concerning."

"That's one word for it," I mutter.

"Your father mentioned the Kincaids pulled their donation, but I had no idea it was this bad." She shakes her head, clicking her tongue. "Shameful."

I feel a rush of gratitude that at least someone sees this situation for what it is.

"I've been trying to help from home, making calls to some of my contacts," she continues, "but it's been difficult with Harold still in the hospital. My nephew who lives in Carlsbad is trying to pull some strings to help. You remember him, don't you? Brayden?"

"Brayden Cole?" I can't hide my surprise. The last time I saw Jillian's nephew, he was a lanky teenager with a perpetual scowl and a habit of disappearing whenever adults entered the room. "I didn't know he was still in touch with you."

"Oh, he tries to pretend he's too busy for family, but that boy calls me every Sunday like clockwork. Works with some club now, doing...well, I'm not entirely sure what. But he's got connections, he says."

I try to picture teenage Brayden as a grown man. All I can conjure is a taller version of the same sullen kid who used to smoke behind the church during potlucks.

"That's nice of him to try."

"He said he might be able to help with the toy situation." She pats my hand. "Don't you worry, Cece. God provides."

I force a smile, not wanting to dampen her optimism. "I'm sure we'll figure something out."

"That's the spirit." She glances at her watch. "I should get back to the hospital. Harold gets cranky if I'm gone too long." She gives my shoulder a squeeze. "It's good to have you home, honey. Don't let those vultures get you down and don't you work yourself too hard," Jillian says, giving my arm a final squeeze. "And tell your daddy I'll be praying for that...situation...out front." With a knowing wink, she bustles toward the door, her floral perfume lingering in the air behind her.

I watch her go, feeling oddly comforted by her brief visit. At least someone in this town doesn't blame me for my marriage falling apart.

Once the door swings shut, I force myself back to the task at hand. The pitiful collection of toys won't sort itself. I separate them into piles by age group—a depressingly quick job given how few items there are. The dolls have seen better days, their hair matted and clothes stained. Most of the board games are missing pieces. I find myself wondering if the kids would even want these cast-offs, these physical reminders that they're an afterthought.

I check my watch—only ten-thirty. Dad's still outside dealing with the anatomically correct nativity scandal. I decide to take inventory, grabbing a notebook from Dad's office to make a list of what we have versus what we need. The numbers are grim. Three hundred and eighty-seven families on the list, and we have maybe enough decent toys for thirty kids, if I'm being generous.

The hours crawl by. I answer a few calls from people asking about drop-off times, arrange the canned goods by expiration date, and try not to think about strangling the entire Kincaid family. I'm lugging the last box of donations from the fire department's truck when my arms start to tremble. Their collection was better than expected—not great, but at least enough to bump us up to maybe fifty kids covered. Fire Chief Donovan apologized three times while we unloaded, mumbling something about "unusual pressure this year" that we both knew translated to "the Kincaids got to us too."

"That's the last of it," I call to him, forcing brightness into my voice. "Thanks for everything."

He gives me a quick nod, clearly eager to escape before anyone connects him to the Montgomery charity disaster. "Wish it could've been more, Cece."

The fire truck pulls away, leaving me standing alone on the church steps with sweat dampening my back despite the December chill. Inside, the fellowship hall still looks pathetically empty, even with the fire department's contribution spread across the tables. I've spent the entire day organizing, counting, and trying not to cry from frustration.

I'm about to start labeling age groups when I hear it —a steady, rhythmic rumble that seems to vibrate through the floorboards. At first, I think it might be thunder, but the sky outside the windows is clear blue. The sound grows louder, a mechanical growl that can only mean one thing.

Motorcycles. Multiple motorcycles.

I move to the window, curiosity overriding my exhaustion. A procession of bikes rolling into the church parking lot—not just a few bikes, but over a dozen of them and a small box truck.

The engines cut off one by one, leaving an almost eerie silence in their wake. For a heartbeat, I just stand there, blinking at the sight of so much leather and chrome glinting in the afternoon light. Helmets come off, revealing everything from shaggy beards to a shock of pink hair. The box truck door slides open with a metallic clatter, and I catch sight of wrapped toys stacked to the ceiling.

My jaw drops.

A laugh bubbles up from my throat, part disbelief and part relief, because—well, you don't see that every day in San Salona.

Somewhere behind me, I hear the creak of the fellowship hall door and the sharp gasp of one of the church ladies. No doubt she's already clutching her pearls so hard they'll need to be pried loose with the jaws of life.

CHAPTER 3

BRAYDEN

"REMIND me again why we're playing Santa Claus to a bunch of uptight rich assholes?" Domino grumbles, killing his engine beside me. He scratches his beard, eyeing the pristine white church like it might burst into flames at our approach. Or maybe he's hoping it will.

I swing my leg over my bike, boots hitting pavement with a solid thud. "Because some rich assholes screwed over a lot of kids, and my aunt guilted me into fixing it."

"Your aunt could guilt the devil into going to church," Skelly laughs, pulling off his helmet. His pink mohawk springs up like it's been waiting for freedom all morning.

"Tell me about it," I mutter, rolling my shoulders to

work out the kink from the hour ride. "She played the 'your uncle's heart condition' card. It's the equivalent of Danny Kaye using his old arm injury against Bing Crosby in White Christmas."

Domino stares at me blankly. "What the fuck are you talking about?"

"The Christmas movie? With the—" I stop myself. "Never mind." No point explaining that my aunt has been making me watch it every year since I was a kid. Some things the club doesn't need to know about.

"Still don't see why we had to haul ass across here for some church toy drive," Domino continues, eyeing the building suspiciously. "Plenty of kids need help in our own backyard."

"Because I promised," I say simply, running a hand through my hair. It's gotten too long again, hanging past my shoulders. "And because my aunt said this town's big donor family pulled out to spite some woman who divorced their son."

"Rich people drama," Skelly snorts, stretching his arms overhead. The movement makes the skull tattoos dance across his forearms. "My favorite kind of bullshit."

I scan the parking lot, noting the gleaming SUVs and luxury sedans parked in neat rows. San Salona— the kind of place where people judge you by your zip code and family name. The kind of place I couldn't wait to escape fifteen years ago.

"Let's just get this done," I say, nodding toward the truck where our prospects Rabbit and Velcro are already unloading boxes. "In and out, minimal interaction with the locals."

"You afraid they'll recognize you?" Domino grins, slapping me on the back. "What was it your aunt called you? Bray Baby?"

"Call me that again and I'll make you eat your own colors," I threaten. The guys have been ribbing me about this "charity mission" since we left Carlsbad.

"You sure you're one of us, Cole?" Big asks, leaning against his bike with an expression that makes me want to rearrange his teeth. "Because this—" he gestures toward the pristine church and manicured grounds, "—seems far more fitting for you."

"Fuck off," I growl, but that only eggs him on.

"No, seriously." He nudges Domino, who's already chuckling. "All this time I thought you were slumming it with us, when really you're just a rich boy playing biker."

The other guys start hooting, and I feel heat crawling up my neck. This is exactly what I was afraid would happen when my aunt called in her favor. The past I've spent fifteen years burying is suddenly right on the surface.

"Where you been hiding your silver spoon, Bray?" Skelly joins in, eyes glinting with amusement.

I step into his space, close enough that our cuts almost touch. "That silver spoon is about to be relocated to your ass right next to your head if you keep it up."

This gets a chorus of "oohs" from the prospects, who quickly shut up when I turn my glare on them.

"I grew up dirt poor with a single mom who worked two jobs until she dumped me onto my aunt and took off when I was sixteen," I fire back. "My aunt married into money. I didn't. The only silver I've ever owned is the knife in my boot and the rings on my knuckles."

The laughter dies down, but I can still see the questions in their eyes. Fair enough. I've never talked much about where I come from, and showing up at some fancy church in rich-boy territory isn't exactly helping my case.

"Look," I say, lowering my voice. "My aunt is the only family I've got left who gives a shit whether I live or die. She asked for help, so we're helping. End of story."

Domino nods slowly. "Respect for family. I get that."

"Good. Now can we unload this truck before some church lady calls the cops on us?"

As if summoned by my words, the church's front door opens and a woman in a floral cardigan peers out, her face a mask of barely concealed horror. She takes one look at our cuts, our bikes, our general existence, and promptly disappears back inside. I'd bet money she's already on the phone with someone.

"Friendly place," Skelly observes.

"Real welcoming," I agree, grabbing the first box from the truck. It's heavier than expected, packed solid with wrapped toys.

We form a chain, passing boxes from the truck to the church steps. The toys are good quality stuff—none of that dollar store bullshit that falls apart before New

Year's. Video games, bikes, dolls, sports equipment. The kind of Christmas haul that would make any kid's year.

I'm hauling a particularly heavy box when the side door of the church opens, and a woman steps out. Not another church lady in pearls and judgment—this one's different. Younger, maybe early thirties, wearing jeans and a sweater that's way too big for her. Her dark hair is pulled back in a messy ponytail, and there's something about the way she carries herself that catches my attention. Like she's bracing for impact.

Our gazes meet across the parking lot, and I feel something shift in my chest. A recognition that doesn't make sense, because I'm sure I'd remember a face like that—sharp cheekbones, full lips, and eyes the color of spring leaves caught in sunlight. Pretty, but not in the manufactured way of the women who usually populate places like San Salona. This is *real* pretty, the kind that sneaks up on you.

She's watching us with a mixture of surprise and something else—relief? Hope? It's not the usual fear or disgust we get from civilians.

"You the guy in charge?" she calls out, walking toward me with purpose.

"Depends who's asking," I reply, setting down my box on the church steps.

She stops a few feet away, close enough that I catch a hint of her perfume—something light and floral that makes me want to lean closer. "I'm Cecelia," she says, and the name hits me like a punch to the gut.

Cecelia Montgomery. Of all people to greet us...it

had to be her. Fuck. I'm suddenly seventeen again, watching her from across the high school parking lot while she laughed with her friends, all of them wrapped in that golden bubble of belonging I could never penetrate.

"Holy shit," I mutter, the words escaping before I can stop them.

She tilts her head, studying my face. "Do we know each other?"

"Brayden Cole."

Recognition flickers across her features, followed by disbelief. "Brayden? You're..." Her gaze drifts from my face down to my cut with the Heaven's Rejects patch prominently displayed, then back up again. "Different."

I almost laugh at the understatement. The last time she saw me, I was a skinny kid with a chip on my shoulder and a juvenile record. Now I'm VP of an MC that makes cops nervous in three states. Yeah, I'd say I was different.

"Yeah, well. Fifteen years will do that." I gesture toward the boxes. "My aunt said you needed some help."

"Your aunt..." Her voice trails off as she looks past me to the truck still half-filled with toys. "Wait—all this is from you? From your..."

"Club," I finish for her, watching as she takes in the full scope of what we've brought. "Yeah."

The disbelief on her face is almost comical. I can practically see the gears turning in her head, trying to reconcile the scrawny kid she knew with the man standing in front of her. I have to admit, I like the way she's looking at me. More than I fucking should.

"I don't understand," she says, shaking her head. "Jillian said she asked for help, but I never imagined..." She gestures at the truck, at my brothers still unloading boxes. "This is incredible."

"Don't get too excited," I warn, hefting another box. "It's good business for the club. Holiday cheer and goodwill." But even as I say it, I know it's bullshit. "And, well, for the kids."

"Business?" She raises an eyebrow. "What kind of business involves donating toys to churches?"

I shrug, not wanting to explain that sometimes the club does legitimate charity work to balance out the less legitimate activities. "The kind that keeps my aunt off my ass."

She laughs—actually laughs—and the sound hits me harder than it should. It's not the polite twitter I remember from high school, but something real and warm. "Your aunt can be persistent when she wants something."

"Persistent is one word for it. Bull in a China shop is more like it. Where do you want all this?" I ask, nodding toward the boxes stacked on the church steps. My brothers are still unloading, the pile growing higher by the minute.

"Inside, follow me." She turns and heads for the side entrance, grabbing a box from the stack as she passes.

I pick up another heavy one and trail after her, my

eyes automatically dropping to the way her jeans hug her curves as she walks. Fuck. Some things never change. I'd spent half of junior year stealing glances at Cecelia from the back row of English class, watching her twirl her hair around her finger while she took notes in her ornate handwriting. Daydreaming about how that hair would feel threaded through my fingers with her pretty little mouth wrapped around my cock while that shit head of a boyfriend watched me defile her.

Shit. Don't think about that, asshole. The last place you need a fucking hard-on is at a church. Stamp your ticket to hell even harder, why don't you?

I follow her into the fellowship hall, the familiar smell of lemon polish and old hymnals hitting me like a time machine. The room is depressingly empty.

"You can put them anywhere there's space," she says, setting her box down on one of the tables. "We'll sort them by age group later."

She bends over to open the box, and I force myself to look away, focusing instead on the wall of plaques commemorating church picnic winners.

Movement catches my attention, and I glance toward the doorway. One of the church ladies is hovering there, her face pinched with disapproval as she watches us. Her hand clutches at the cross pendant hanging around her neck like she's afraid it might spontaneously combust in our presence. Her gaze flicks nervously between the MC patches on our cuts and the boxes we're unloading.

"Looks like we've got an audience," I murmur to Cece, nodding subtly toward the doorway.

Skelly notices too, flashing the old woman his most unsettling grin—the one that shows off the silver caps on his canines. "Think she's waiting to see if we catch fire by being on holy ground?" he stage-whispers loud enough for her to hear.

Domino snorts. "If that were true, I'd have been a pile of ashes years ago."

The woman's expression tightens, and she takes a half-step backward, like she's genuinely afraid we might burst into flames and take the whole building with us.

"Mrs. Peterson," Cece calls out, straightening from the box she's unpacking. "Is there something you need?"

"I-I was just checking to see if you needed any help," the woman stammers, still staring at Skelly's pink mohawk. "I saw that we had...visitors."

"We're good," Cece says firmly.

"Actually, we could use an extra set of hands," I say, flashing Mrs. Peterson my most innocent smile. The one that makes people nervous because they can't quite tell if I'm being sincere or planning to steal their car. "I've got a whole sermon's worth of toys out there that need saving."

Mrs. Peterson's hand clutches her cross pendant tighter. Cece shoots me a look that's half warning, half amusement.

"Sermon's worth?" she mouths, eyebrows raised.

"You know, like a shitload, but more...ecclesiastical." I wink at her, enjoying the way her cheeks flush pink. "I'm trying to speak the local language."

Mrs. Peterson makes a strangled noise. "I think I hear Reverend Montgomery calling me," she mutters, backing away like we might chase her if she turns too quickly. "I'll just...check on the...situation outside."

She disappears so fast she practically leaves a cartoon dust cloud behind her.

"Situation?" I ask, turning to Cece.

"Someone replaced baby Jesus with a dildo in the nativity scene," she explains with a completely straight face. "It's been quite the crisis."

I burst out laughing. "Holy fuck—I mean, holy..." I search for an appropriate church word. "Holy communion?"

"Not better," she says, but she's fighting a smile. "You're going to get me in trouble."

"This place could use a little trouble," I say, watching the spark of suppressed laughter flicker across her face. Something about her has changed since high school. The Cecelia I remember was careful, controlled—always mindful of her reputation. This woman looks like she's one smart comment away from telling the whole church to go to hell.

I like it.

The door bangs open again as Rabbit and Big haul in more boxes. Rabbit's sleeve rides up, revealing the snake tattoo that coils from his wrist to his bicep. Mrs.

Peterson would probably need smelling salts if she saw that one.

"Where you want these, boss?" Rabbit asks, glancing curiously between Cece and me.

"Anywhere there's room," I tell him, gesturing to the half-empty tables. "We've got plenty more coming."

Cece watches them with something like wonder as they stack the boxes along the wall. "I still can't believe this," she says, her voice low enough that only I can hear. "I pictured maybe a few board games, not..." She waves her hand at the growing pile.

"Disappointed?" I arch an eyebrow.

"Are you kidding? This is..." She shakes her head, and for a second I think she might cry. "This is a miracle."

"Don't let the guys hear you call it that," I warn. "The last thing I need is them calling me Christmas Jesus or some shit like that."

"This didn't like fall off the back of a truck, did it?"

I roll my eyes at her. "We're not the mafia. We're a motorcycle club. Totally different dress code."

Cece laughs again, and something about the sound warms parts of me I thought had frozen over years ago. "I just meant—this is a lot. It must have cost a fortune."

"The club did alright this year," I say with a shrug, not elaborating on exactly how we did alright. Some things are better left unsaid in a church. I glance around the fellowship hall, memories washing over me like high tide. I'd spent countless Sundays in this room, slouched in the corner while Aunt Jillian chatted with the other church ladies. Always the outsider, even when I was technically invited. "My aunt said something about the town's big donors didn't show up this year. Pretty fucking low if you ask me."

Cece's expression clouds, and I immediately regret bringing it up. "Yeah, that would be because of me. Come to find out, when you divorce the biggest donor's son, they stop helping kids."

"What an asshole," I say before I can stop myself.

Her eyes meet mine, surprise flickering across her face.

The door swings open again, and this time it's Domino and Velcro, both of them carrying the last of the heavy boxes. Domino's gaze sweeps the room, taking in the church lady decorations and motivational Bible verses hanging on the walls.

"This place is exactly what I pictured," he says, setting down his box with a grunt. "Feels like it's judging me already."

"That's just your guilty conscience," I tell him, earning a middle finger in response.

Velcro, our newest prospect, is trying way too hard not to stare at Cece. Kid's barely nineteen and still gets tongue-tied around pretty women. I catch his eye and give him a look that says *focus on the job* before he can embarrass himself.

"That's everything," Domino announces, wiping his hands on his jeans. "Truck's empty."

I scan the fellowship hall, and the transformation is incredible. What was a handful of sad, worn-out toys an hour ago now looks like Christmas exploded. Boxes are stacked three high along the walls, and the tables are starting to fill with quality merchandise.

"Jesus," Cece breathes, and I bite back a comment about her language in church. "This has to be enough for every kid on our list, maybe twice over."

"Good," I say, meaning it. The thought of kids going without on Christmas because some rich assholes wanted to play power games sits wrong with me. Always has.

"This is...I don't even know how to thank you."

The fellowship hall door bursts open, and an older man in a clerical collar rushes in, his face flushed and his silver hair disheveled. He stops short when he sees us, his gaze widening as he takes in the leather, the patches, the general aura of trouble.

"Cece?" His voice cracks slightly. "What's...who are..."

"Dad, these are the people Jillian sent to help with the toy drive," Cece says quickly, stepping between us. "This is Brayden—Jillian's nephew."

His stare hardens as it lands on my Heaven's Rejects patch, his entire body stiffening like he's been electrocuted. The warm, fatherly expression he wore for his daughter freezes into something hard and cold. It's the same look he gave me as a teenager when my aunt dragged me to Sunday service against my will. Most preachers would see a lost soul in desperate need of redemption as an opportunity. Not him. Maybe he knew I was a lost cause—or maybe he saw the way I watched his daughter from the back pew. Either way, the only grace he'd ever given me was not throwing me out of the church for soiling his service.

"Jillian sent...these men?" he asks.

I've seen that kind of judgment before—the quick once-over that sizes you up. The kind of look that reminds me exactly why I left this town in the first place.

"Brayden Cole," he says slowly, recognition flickering in his gaze. "Loretta Cole's boy."

"That's right," I reply, keeping my voice neutral even as my jaw tightens. Fifteen years, and he still manages to make my last name sound like an accusation.

"Dad, they brought all of this," Cece gestures around at the boxes stacked high. "They've saved the toy drive."

The Reverend doesn't look impressed. If anything, his frown deepens.

"I see." His tone could freeze hell over. "And what exactly does your...club...want in return?"

Domino lets out a quiet, irritated rumble, and I cut him a warning look. The last thing we need is a fight with a preacher in his own church.

"Nothing," I say firmly. "My aunt asked for help. We're helping."

"Nothing?" The Reverend's eyebrows nearly touch his receding hairline. "Young men like you don't typically do charity work out of the goodness of your hearts."

I feel my temper flaring, that old familiar heat crawling up my neck. Some things never change in San Salona. Once they decide what you are, there's no changing their minds.

"Dad," Cece hisses, her cheeks flushing with embarrassment. "They drove over an hour to bring us all of this."

"It's fine," I tell her, not taking my eyes off her father. "I'm used to it."

The Reverend has the decency to look uncomfortable, at least. "I didn't mean to imply—"

"Yes, you did," I cut him off. "But it doesn't matter. The toys are yours. Do whatever you want with them."

I turn to my brothers, jerking my head toward the door. "We're done here."

"But—" Cece starts.

"Enjoy your Christmas," I tell her, already moving toward the exit. I don't need this shit. Don't need to stand here and let some holy roller make me feel like I'm still that troubled kid who had a thing for his daughter.

Domino follows me without question, the others falling in line behind him. That's the thing about brotherhood—they might give me hell, but they've got my back when it counts.

I'm halfway to the door when she catches up to me.

"Brayden, wait." Her hand lands on my arm, and I stop despite every instinct telling me to keep walking. "Please."

I turn, and the look on her face makes something

twist in my chest. There's genuine distress there, mixed with anger that doesn't seem directed at me.

"You don't have to explain," I say, glancing back at her father who is still standing there like a disapproving statue. "I get it."

"No, you don't." She steps closer, lowering her voice. "My dad is just having a bad day between the dick in the manger and the Kincaids pulling their donation. He's under a lot of pressure."

"You married Ethan Kincaid?" His name scrapes out of my throat like gravel. That golden-boy prick who spent high school doing whatever the hell he wanted and never paid for a damn thing. Teachers drooled over him, coaches worshipped him, and every time he screwed up, Daddy's money swept it clean like it never happened.

I remember him walking those halls like a crowned prince—chin up, smug grin, whole damn place bending around him.

I watch her face carefully, seeing the pain flash across it before she schools her expression back to neutral. It's the kind of practiced move you perfect when you don't want the world to know you're bleeding.

"Yeah," she says simply, redirecting the conversation away from Ethan. "Look, I know my father doesn't seem grateful for what you and your club's done, but I am. How can I thank you?"

"Can you get us some holy water?" Domino calls

out from behind us. "Got some demons that need banishing back at the clubhouse."

"Not even holy water can help you, asshole."

Cece actually snorts at that, covering her mouth with her hand like she's trying to contain the laughter. The sound makes something warm unfurl in my chest, even as her father's disapproval practically radiates across the room.

"I'll see what I can do," she tells Domino, then turns back to me. "Seriously though, how can I repay this?"

"You can tell me what else you need," I hear myself saying, even though every rational part of my brain is screaming at me to walk away. "This can't be everything. Toys are just part of it, right? What about food? Clothes?"

Her expression shifts, surprise flickering across her features like she hadn't considered the bigger picture. "I...we usually get food donations from the grocery stores, but this year..." She trails off, glancing toward her father.

"This year the Kincaids made sure those dried up too," I finish for her.

She nods, looking miserable.

I hold out my hand. "Give me your phone."

"My phone?" Her brows draw together, confusion etched across her face.

"Yeah, your phone."

She hesitates, one hand instinctively moving to her pocket like I've asked for her kidney instead of her cell. "Why do you need my phone?"

"Because I'm not leaving you high and dry with half a charity drive."

Behind me, I can feel Domino's stare burning into my back. This wasn't part of the plan—get in, drop the toys, get out. No lingering, no complications, no getting tangled in small-town drama. But something about the defeated slump of her shoulders, the dark circles shadowing her face, has me ignoring all my better judgment.

"Cece," her father warns from across the room, his voice carrying that paternal edge that probably worked great when she was sixteen.

She shoots him a look I can't quite decipher before pulling her phone from her pocket. "Here," she says, unlocking it before handing it over.

Our fingers brush as she passes it to me, and I ignore the little jolt that runs up my arm. Her phone case is cracked at the corner, and the screen protector is bubbled along one edge. I open her contacts, aware of her watching me intently.

"I'm putting my number in," I explain, typing quickly. I hand her phone back, careful not to let our fingers touch again. "Text me the list of what you need."

Her father clears his throat loudly behind us.

"We should go," I tell her, taking a step back. "Before someone puts boobs on the Virgin Mary and tries to blame us for it."

She laughs. "That's not actually a bad idea. It might distract everyone from penis baby Jesus."

"If you're looking for more ways to scandalize the

town, I've got plenty of suggestions." I back toward the door, my brothers already filing out ahead of me.

"I bet you do." Her smile is different now—softer around the edges.

I give her a nod, not trusting myself to say anything else. If I linger too long, I might do something stupid like offer to help her with the whole damn toy drive distribution. Or worse, ask her out for coffee and watch her try to let me down gently.

"Thank you," she calls after me. "Really."

I raise my hand in acknowledgment without looking back. Some things are better left in the rearview mirror, and the look on her face when she smiles is definitely one of them.

Outside, the December air hits me like a wake-up call. My brothers are already mounting up, engines rumbling to life one by one. I swing my leg over my own bike, feeling the familiar vibration as I turn the key.

"We good to go?" Domino asks, pulling up along-side me.

"Yeah," I say, adjusting my gloves. "We're done here."

"You sure about that?"

The hell if I know.

CHAPTER 4

CECE

I'VE ALWAYS HATED the Brewed Awakening café, with its cutesy chalkboard signs and overpriced pastries, but they're the only place in San Salona that makes coffee strong enough to wake the dead. Which is precisely what my father needs after staying up all night rewriting his sermon about 'moral fortitude in the face of sinful influences.'

The bell jingles cheerfully as I push through the door, the warm scent of espresso and cinnamon wrapping around me like a hug. I'm halfway to the counter when I spot him—the mayor, Ethan's dad, standing with his back to me, surrounded by his usual entourage of *yes-men*. His voice carries through the small café like he's using a megaphone.

"It's an absolute disgrace," he's saying, hands gesturing wildly. "First that...that pornographic display in the nativity scene, and now Thomas is allowing some motorcycle gang to donate to the church toy drive? Has he completely lost control of his congregation?"

I freeze, my hand still reaching for my wallet. Every head in the café swivels toward me like some creepy synchronized movement in a horror film. Even the barista stops mid-pour, her expression going wide with surprise.

The mayor turns, his gaze narrowing when he spots me standing there like a deer in headlights. For a second, I think he might have the decency to look embarrassed at being caught gossiping about my father. Instead, his lips curl into that same smug smile Ethan inherited.

"Well, speak of the devil," he says, loud enough for everyone to hear.

Heat crawls up my neck as every stare in the café pins me in place. I've spent my whole life in this fishbowl, but it never gets easier being the main attraction.

"You know," Mayor Kincaid continues, setting his coffee cup down with deliberate slowness, "I was just saying to the gentlemen here that perhaps it's time for the church board to have a serious conversation with your father."

"About what, exactly?"

"About his...judgment lately." The mayor's look sharpens with malice. "First allowing that obscene display on church property, and now welcoming criminals to donate to a church function? Perhaps it's time for him to consider retirement if he's going to allow such things to happen on his watch."

The café has gone completely silent. Even the espresso machine seems to be holding its breath.

"Those 'criminals' saved our toy drive."

"Saved it? My dear girl, the church may have just helped them launder goods so you can wipe that smug look off your face."

"That's rich coming from the family who pulled donations from a children's charity just to spite me." I step closer, letting the righteous anger that's been building since I saw those empty tables drive me forward. "Do you know how many families were counting on those toys? Or do you just not care?"

The mayor's face turns an impressive shade of crimson, making the veins in his neck bulge like he's about to have an aneurysm right here in front of the pumpkin spice muffins. His little posse of golf buddies shifts uncomfortably, suddenly very interested in their coffee cups.

"Our family supports many worthy causes," he says stiffly. "We simply chose to redirect our generosity this year."

"Right. To 'worthy causes' that don't involve my father's church. I guess that explains why none of your closest friend donated either or that Mr. Miller at the grocery store suddenly changed his mind on his food box donations. You know, the donations his family has made since the store opened in the 1950s."

I don't know what I expected to happen when I challenged him, but it wasn't this. His face goes from red to white to red again, like a patriotic mood ring.

"You have no idea what you're talking about," he sputters, but the guilt written across his face says otherwise. He absolutely did strong-arm his cronies into pulling their donations.

"Don't I?" I take another step forward, and he actually steps back. "Because it seems awfully coincidental that every single business owner in your golf foursome suddenly developed amnesia about their usual Christmas donations."

The silence stretches like a rubber band about to snap. I can feel the weight of everyone's stares, can practically hear them composing their texts to spread this juicy gossip. But for once, I don't care. I'm so tired of being the victim in everyone else's story.

"It's sad, really, that children are paying the price all because I divorced your cheater of a son."

"How dare you," he hisses, stepping closer. "My son made one mistake—"

"One?" I laugh, the sound sharper than I intend. "I stopped counting after his secretary. But please, enlighten me about this mythical 'one mistake.'"

Someone in the back of the café snickers. Kincaid's gaze darts around, suddenly aware of our audience. Nothing travels faster in San Salona than gossip served with a side of public humiliation.

"This is hardly the place to air your marital grievances. Though I suppose discretion was never your strong suit."

"Maybe you should have taught your son how to be discreet. Seems the lack of discretion may run in your family, Richard."

The mayor's face twitches, and I know I've hit a nerve. Rumors about his own affairs have circulated for years, though no one dares mention them aloud. Until now.

"You little—" He catches himself, aware of the audience hanging on his every word. "I've always thought Thomas failed as a father, letting his daughter grow up with such a loose grasp of Christian values. Now I see I was right."

"At least my father taught me that charity isn't a weapon to hurt people with."

"No, he just taught you to welcome criminals into your church," he shoots back, disdain dripping from every word. "Those...bikers are nothing but trouble. Drug dealers, thugs—"

"Those 'thugs' did more for the children in this community yesterday than you've done all month," I cut in, steady despite the tremor in my limbs. "Maybe you should ask yourself what that says about your Christian values."

The café falls into a hush so complete you could hear a sugar packet hit the floor. Everyone here is watching the mayor of San Salona get called out. This will be all over town before lunch.

"I don't have to justify myself to you. The church

board will hear about this," Kincaid snaps at last, anger making his hands tremble. "About your father's poor judgment in accepting donations from criminals, and about your...outburst here today."

"Good," I say, surprised by how steady I sound. "I'll be there to tell the truth, not whatever political spin you try to sell. Bring your popcorn, Richard—I plan to put your 'generosity' on full display."

He opens his mouth, then shuts it. For once, I've left Richard Kincaid without a ready retort. It should feel more satisfying.

"Cece Montgomery, I swear to God—" the mayor manages at last, but it's too late. I've already turned toward the counter.

"Two large coffees, black, and whatever pastry hasn't been contaminated by the mayor's hot air," I tell the barista. Her face goes blank with wide surprise. She nods and hustles off.

My hands are shaking, adrenaline skittering through me like lightning. I can't believe I just did that. In public. With witnesses. My father is going to kill me.

"You'll regret this," Kincaid hisses behind me, the threat low and meant only for me. "Your father's position isn't as secure as you think."

I don't turn around. "Neither is your next run for mayor. Family scandals and all. Oh, the family secrets I could tell, Richard."

The collective gasp from the café patrons tells me my parting shot hit its mark. I shouldn't feel so satisfied, but damn if I don't. Years of playing nice, of turning the other cheek—it feels good to finally bite back.

The barista slides my order across the counter, her expression a mixture of terror and admiration. "On the house," she whispers.

"No, I insist on paying." I make a show of placing a twenty in the tip jar, then grab my coffee and head for the door.

Mayor Kincaid is still standing there, his face mottled with fury and embarrassment. His golf buddies look like they'd rather be anywhere else on earth. One of them—I think it's Dr. Phillips—won't even make eye contact.

"Have a blessed day, gentlemen," I say sweetly, pushing through the door before anyone can respond.

The bell chimes behind me, and I'm halfway to my car when my phone buzzes. A text from an unknown number, but I recognize the name immediately.

Squaring off with the mayor in public, Cece?

Who is this?

Just your friendly neighborhood Santa biker.

I stop walking, staring at the screen. How does he already know? It happened less than five minutes ago.

Another text comes through.

You okay?

I lean against my Honda, balancing both coffees while I type back.

> Define okay. I may have just declared war on the most powerful family in town.

Good for you. They had it coming.

The simple support in those words hits me harder than it should. When was the last time someone took my side without asking what I did to provoke it first?

> My dad's going to kill me when he finds out.

I make a great bodyguard.

I find myself smiling despite everything.

> I think I've caused enough scandal for one day. How'd you find out?

My phone buzzes with another notification. A picture message. I open it and nearly drop my coffee.

It's him, Brayden, leaning against his motorcycle, staring directly at the camera. His dark hair is pushed back, and there's just the hint of a smile playing at the corner of his mouth. But what makes my heart stutter isn't how unfairly attractive he looks—it's what's behind him.

The Brewed Awakening. Their signature blue awning visible just over his shoulder. And if I squint, I can make out a blurry figure in the background who is unmistakably me, standing at the counter not five minutes ago.

Shit. He's still in town.

Across the street. Right now.

I scan the parking lot frantically, but I don't see him anywhere.

> Are you stalking me?

His response comes immediately.

> Just enjoying the show. Your takedown of the mayor was better than Netflix.

My cheeks burn as I realize he must have witnessed the entire confrontation. I look up again, searching the street, and finally spot him. He's sitting on his bike across the way. When our eyes meet, he lifts his hand in a lazy salute.

My phone buzzes again.

> Want to get out of here before the mayor calls in the National Guard?

I stare at the message, my thumb hovering over the keyboard. The rational part of my brain—the part that sounds suspiciously like my father—is screaming that this is a terrible idea. Getting involved with Brayden

Cole would be like pouring gasoline on the fire I just started with Mayor Kincaid.

But the other part of me, the part that's tired of playing it safe and being everyone else's victim, wants nothing more than to climb on the back of his bike and disappear.

> I can't. Dad's waiting for his coffee.

Another message pops up.

> One ride, Cece. When's the last time you did something just because you wanted to?

When was the last time? I can't remember. Every decision I've made for the past decade has been filtered through what other people expected, what would look good, what was appropriate for a my role.

I stare at my phone, the last text message blinking at me like a dare.

The words hit me like a sucker punch because he's right. I can't remember the last time I did something purely for myself. Even my divorce was reactive—a response to Ethan's betrayal rather than my own choice to break free.

Before I can second-guess myself, my fingers are typing.

> Meet me at the church so I can drop off my car.

I slide into my car, set the coffees carefully in the cup holders, and take a deep breath. What am I doing? This is insanity. Pure, reckless insanity.

Yet I find myself starting the engine and pulling onto the street in the direction of my dad's church. I park near the back entrance, hustling inside with dad's coffee. Thankfully, he's not in his office. I carefully put his cup down, chug mine, and head back outside just as Brayden pulls up.

The motorcycle is larger up close than it looked from across the street, all gleaming chrome and matte black metal that seems to absorb the winter sunlight rather than reflect it. Brayden holds out a helmet to me without a word, his eyes watching me with an intensity that makes my stomach flip.

"I've never been on a motorcycle before," I admit, taking the helmet from him. It's heavier than I expected.

"First time for everything." There's that hint of a smile again, just enough to make my pulse quicken. "Unless you're having second thoughts."

I should be. I should absolutely be having second thoughts, thirds, and fourths. But instead, I'm fastening the helmet under my chin with trembling fingers.

"Need help?" he asks, and before I can answer, his hands are on mine, gently nudging them aside. His fingers brush against my neck as he adjusts the strap, and I try not to shiver at the contact.

"Thanks," I manage, my voice embarrassingly breathless.

"Hop on," he says, swinging his leg over the bike

with practiced ease. "Arms around my waist, hold tight, and lean when I lean."

I hesitate for just a moment, glancing back at the church. My father could walk out any second and find me climbing onto the back of a motorcycle with a man in a leather cut. The scandal would eclipse even this morning's coffee shop showdown.

But for once in my life, I don't care.

CHAPTER 5

CECE

I'VE NEVER BEEN good at following directions, but gripping Brayden's waist feels like the most natural thing in the world.

The motorcycle rumbles to life beneath us, vibrating through my entire body in a way that makes me acutely aware of every nerve ending I possess. My arms tighten around his torso involuntarily, and I can feel the solid muscle beneath his leather cut, the steady rhythm of his breathing.

"You good?" he calls over his shoulder, his words muffled by the engine noise.

"Ask me that after you start moving," I call back, echoing his earlier words. The irony isn't lost on me—twenty minutes ago I was buying coffee like any other

Tuesday morning, and now I'm pressed against the back of a man who probably has a rap sheet longer than my grocery list.

He chuckles, the sound vibrating through his chest and into my arms. "Hold on, Cece."

And then we're moving.

The first few seconds are terrifying—the ground rushing past, the wind whipping at the exposed skin around my helmet, the complete lack of walls or seatbelts or anything resembling safety between me and the asphalt. But as we turn onto Main Street, something shifts. The fear transforms into something else entirely. Something that feels dangerously close to freedom.

We cruise through downtown San Salona at a speed that would be reasonable in a car but feels like flying on the back of a bike. I catch glimpses of familiar faces on the sidewalks. Mrs. Henderson pauses mid-sidewalk sweep to gawk at us, her mouth falling open so wide I'm surprised a bird doesn't nest in it. I resist the urge to wave. Let her run to her phone and start the gossip chain. After my verbal altercation with my ex-father-in-law this morning, it's likely already running rampant.

Brayden takes a left onto Maple Street, and I realize he's heading toward the outskirts of town, away from the manicured lawns and judgment-filled windows. The houses grow smaller, farther apart, until we're cruising past farmland and patches of woods that I'd forgotten existed.

"Where are we going?" I shout over the wind.

"Somewhere quiet," he calls back. "Figured you might need a break from the audience."

He's right. For the first time in weeks, I'm not performing for anyone. Not playing the role of the gracious divorcée, the dutiful daughter, or the victim everyone expects me to be. I'm just Cece, arms wrapped around a man who smells like leather and bad decisions.

We turn down a gravel road I don't recognize, trees closing in on both sides until we emerge into a clearing beside a small lake. Brayden kills the engine, and the sudden silence is almost as jarring as the initial roar had been.

"You can let go now," he chuckles.

I realize I'm still clinging to him like a koala. Embarrassment heats my face as I quickly unwrap my arms from his waist, fumbling with the helmet strap.

"Sorry," I mumble, trying to disguise how flustered I am. "Not used to dismounting gracefully."

"I don't mind." There's that hint of a smile again as he swings his leg over the bike and reaches to help me with my helmet. His fingers brush against my jaw, sending a jolt through me that has nothing to do with the motorcycle ride.

When the helmet comes off, my hair tumbles down in a tangled mess. I try to smooth it with my fingers, suddenly self-conscious about how I must look after being wind whipped.

"Don't," Brayden declares quickly. "It looks good like that."

I drop my hands, unsure what to do with this version of Brayden Cole. The sullen teenager I vaguely remember from high school has been replaced by a man who radiates confidence and danger in equal measure. But there's something familiar in his gaze—the same steady intensity that always seemed to see right through me.

"Where are we?" I ask, looking around at the secluded clearing. The lake stretches out before us, its surface rippling gently in the winter breeze. Bare trees frame the water, their skeletal branches reaching toward the sky.

"Old swimming hole," he says, walking toward a fallen log near the shore. "Used to come here when I was a kid. Before my aunt dragged me to San Salona." He sits on the log, stretching his long legs out in front of him. "Not many people remember it's here."

I look around with fresh perspective, trying to picture a younger Brayden swimming in these waters before life carved those scars into his skin and that guarded edge into his expression. It's hard to reconcile the man before me with anyone's past.

"It's beautiful." The lake is small but picturesque. "How'd you find it?"

"Followed some older kids here once. They tried to drown me." He says this so casually that it takes me a moment to process. "I came back anyway. Figured if I was gonna drown, it might as well be somewhere pretty."

I sit beside him on the log, leaving enough space

between us that it doesn't feel presumptuous but close enough that I can still catch the scent of him—leather and something spicy, like cinnamon or cloves.

"That's...a very specific outlook on drowning."

He shrugs. "I've got specific outlooks on lots of ways to die." Then he glances at me, that almost-smile playing at the corner of his mouth. "Sorry. Not the kind of small talk you're used to, I bet."

"I don't know. Ethan's country club friends had some pretty morbid discussions about their stock portfolios."

Brayden lets out a short laugh, the sound rougher around the edges than I expected. "Yeah, I bet losing money hurts just as much as a knife to the gut."

"You'd be surprised how dramatically they react to both." I pull my knees up to my chest, wrapping my arms around them. "Though I suppose you'd know more about the knife part than I would."

He turns to look at me, studying my face like he's trying to figure out if I'm serious or making fun of him. "You really want to know about that?"

"I don't know," I admit. "Maybe? I've spent my whole life in a bubble where the worst thing that happens is someone using the wrong fork at dinner. Part of me is curious about what exists outside of it."

"Trust me, princess. You don't want to know what's outside your bubble."

The nickname should annoy me—it's probably meant to—but instead it sends a little thrill through my chest. "Don't call me princess."

"Why not? That's what you are, isn't it? Preacher's daughter, married to the mayor's wealthy son. I bet you had the biggest house on the block."

"That big house belongs to my ex-husband now. Along with half of everything else I thought was mine."

Brayden's expression shifts slightly, something that might be sympathy flickering across his face.

"It's funny how quickly things can change, isn't it? One day you're someone's wife, the next you're the town pariah."

"I wasn't expecting the divorce to be quite so...public." I dig the toe of my boot into the dirt, watching the small indentation it makes. "In Boulder, I was just another woman with a cheating husband. Here, I'm a cautionary tale."

"Small towns," Brayden nods. "They love to build you up just so they can tear you down."

"Is that why you left?" I ask, genuinely curious about what transformed the skinny, troubled teen into this imposing man beside me.

He's quiet for a moment, staring out at the water. "I left because there was nothing here for me. My mom took off when I was sixteen, dumped me on my aunt. San Salona made it pretty clear I wasn't welcome."

"I remember you in school," I admit. "You were always in the back of the classroom, when you showed up at all."

A sardonic smile twists his lips. "Surprised you noticed me at all, princess."

"I told you not to call me that."

"And yet I'm going to keep doing it." There's a challenge in his gaze that makes my pulse quicken. "What are you gonna do about it?"

The air between us shifts, charged with something I can't quite name. I should move away, put some distance between us, but instead I find myself leaning closer. "I could push you in the lake."

He laughs—a real laugh this time—and the sound does something to my insides. "You could try."

Our gazes lock, and for a moment, I forget to breathe. There's something magnetic about him, something that makes the space between us feel charged. It's been so long since I felt this kind of attraction—immediate, overwhelming, and entirely inappropriate.

"So," I say, breaking the tension before I do something stupid like touch him. "Heaven's Rejects. That's your...club?"

"MC," he says. "Motorcycle Club. And yeah, that's us."

"What exactly does a motorcycle club do?"

His mouth quirks up at one corner. "We ride. We look out for each other. Sometimes we look out for people who need looking out for…"

"And sometimes?"

"Sometimes we do things that good church girls like you don't need to know about."

I bristle at that. "I'm not that good."

"No?" His gaze drifts over me in a way that makes heat bloom across my skin. "What's the worst thing you've ever done, Cece? Forget to put money in the collection plate? Say 'damn' in front of your daddy?"

"I married Ethan," I reply without hesitation. "That's the worst thing I've ever done."

Brayden's expression shifts, the teasing glint replaced by something more serious. "That bad, huh?"

I pick up a small stone from the ground beside the log, turning it over in my palm. "You know what's funny? Everyone in town thinks I'm the victim. Poor Cece, married to a serial cheater. But the truth is, I knew. Maybe not about all of them, but I knew something was wrong, and I stayed anyway."

"Why?"

I toss the stone into the lake, watching the ripples spread across the surface. "Because leaving meant admitting I'd made a mistake. Because it meant disappointing my father, who performed our wedding ceremony and told everyone what a perfect match we were. Because it meant giving up the life I thought I wanted."

"What kind of life was that?"

"Safe," I say immediately. "Predictable. The kind where you know exactly what's expected of you at every moment." I glance at him sideways. "The opposite of this, I suppose."

"And how's that working out for you?"

I consider his question, watching a bird skim across the water's surface. "Well, this morning I publicly humiliated the mayor in a coffee shop, and now I'm sitting by a lake with a man whose motorcycle club probably has a file with the FBI. So I'd say it's going great."

Brayden throws his head back and laughs—a rich, genuine sound that echoes across the water. "FBI file? Jesus, what do you think we do, rob banks?"

"Don't you?" I ask, only half-joking.

"Not on Tuesdays," he says with that maddening, almost-smile. "We save the federal crimes for weekends."

I roll my eyes, but I'm fighting a smile of my own. "You're not going to tell me, are you?"

"Tell you what?"

"What your club actually does. The illegal parts."

He turns to face me fully, and suddenly the space between us feels much smaller. "You really want to know?"

There's something in his voice—a warning, maybe, or a test. Like he's daring me to ask for details about a world I'm not equipped to handle. The smart thing would be to laugh it off, change the subject, to keep things light.

Instead, I nod.

"We protect people," he says simply. "Sometimes that means bending rules. Sometimes it means breaking them completely."

"What kind of people?"

"The kind the system fails. Women running from abusive husbands who can't get protection from the cops. Kids aging out of foster care with nowhere to go.

People who get caught between the wrong elements and need muscle to even the odds."

I study his face, looking for signs that he's putting me on. But his expression is completely serious.

"Is that how you ended up one?" The question comes out before I can stop it. I didn't know much about him, outside of the town rumor mill and what Jillian had mentioned in passing when he came to stay with her. Back then, she'd asked for a lot of prayers for her nephew.

Something flickers across his face—pain, maybe, or just the memory of it. He's quiet for a long moment, staring out at the water like it holds answers he's not sure he wants to share.

"Something like that. My mom had a live-in boyfriend. Real piece of shit who liked to use his fists when he'd been drinking. Which was most nights."

My chest tightens. "Brayden—"

"One night he went too far," he continues, not looking at me. "Put her in the hospital. When she got out, she was too scared to press charges. Said he'd kill us both if she tried." He picks up his own stone, rolling it between his palms. "So I handled it myself."

"What did you do?"

He turns to look at me then, and there's something in his expression that makes my pulse skip. Something that reminds me exactly who I'm sitting with. "Let's just say he never laid a hand on anyone again."

I should be horrified. Should make some excuse and

ask him to take me back to town immediately. Instead, I find myself asking, "How old were you?"

"Fifteen."

Jesus. Fifteen years old and already taking justice into his own hands. "Is that when you got arrested?"

"First time, yeah. Not the last." He tosses the stone into the water with more force than necessary. "Spent a year in juvie. When I got out, she'd already moved on to a new guy. Told me I was too much trouble to keep around and dumped me on my aunt and her rich husband."

The casual way he says it—like being abandoned by your own mother is just another Tuesday—makes my heart ache for the boy he was. Fifteen and already carrying the weight of protecting someone who wouldn't even fight to keep him.

"I'm sorry," I say, and mean it.

He shrugs, but I catch the slight tension in his shoulders. "Ancient history. Point is, Jillian was the first person who didn't look at me like I was broken goods. She took me in like her own and gave me a real family." His mouth curves into a soft smile that transforms his entire face. "She never gave up on me."

"She's a good woman."

"The best." He stands suddenly, brushing dirt from his jeans. "She's also the reason I came back to help with the toy drive." He pauses, sighs, and then extends a hand down to help me up. "I'm glad she called us." He trails off like he's intentionally leaving out the rest of the sentence.

"Me too," I say, taking his hand. The touch sends a current through me that I try to ignore. His palm is warm and callused, his grip firm but gentle as he pulls me to my feet. I expect him to let go once I'm standing, but he doesn't—not right away. Our hands remain connected for a heartbeat longer than necessary, and when he finally releases me, I feel the absence like a physical thing.

"We should get back," he says, glancing at the sky. "I've got club business to handle, and your father is probably organizing a search party by now."

"Let them search." The words come out before I can stop them, surprising us both. "I mean—I don't care what they think. Not anymore."

He studies me, his head tilting slightly. "That's new for you, isn't it?"

"Very." I wrap my arms around myself against the sudden chill. "I spent my whole marriage caring what everyone else thought. It's exhausting."

He picks up my helmet from where it rests against the log. "You don't have to pretend anymore, Cece. Especially not with me."

As we walk back to his motorcycle, I'm struck by how comfortable this feels—being here with him, away from the prying eyes of San Salona. It's like stepping outside of my life and into a different version where I'm braver, less constrained.

"What's the club business?" I ask as he hands me the helmet.

"Nothing that'll make the evening news," he says,

helping me fasten the helmet again. His fingers brush my neck as he adjusts the strap, and I have to resist the urge to lean into the touch. "Just some business with another club passing through our territory. Routine stuff."

I want to ask what "routine stuff" means when it involves motorcycle clubs, but something in his tone tells me it's not really my business to know. Instead, I settle for, "Why do I feel like routine to you is like everyone else's headline on the six o'clock news?"

He pauses, his hands still on the helmet strap. "You worried about me, princess?"

The nickname makes my stomach flutter again, but this time I don't protest. "Maybe. Is that stupid?"

"Yeah," he says, but his voice is gentle. "It's stupid. And..." He trails off, shaking his head like he's arguing with himself.

"And what?"

"And kind of nice." He steps back, running a hand through his dark hair. "It's been a while since someone gave a shit whether I made it home in one piece."

My chest tightens at the admission. I want to tell him that's not true, that surely someone worries about him, but I realize I don't actually know anything about his life. Does he have someone waiting for him back in Carlsbad? A girlfriend who knows exactly what kind of business he handles for the club?

The thought bothers me more than it should.

"Come on," he says, swinging his leg over his bike before settling on the seat. "Wanna make a lap around

Main Street and watch all the old ladies clutch their pearls?"

I bite back a smile as the engine roars beneath him, the sound vibrating straight through me. I don't know why I say yes. Maybe because I don't want the moment to end, maybe because the thought of wrapping my arms around him feels recklessly tempting.

So I swing my leg over and slide onto the seat behind him, my heart already racing faster than the bike ever could.

CHAPTER 6

BRAYDEN

I'VE NEVER UNDERSTOOD men who celebrate with women they don't give a shit about. The music's pounding so hard it's making my teeth rattle, but that doesn't stop Domino from grinding against some chick dressed like a North Pole fantasy gone wrong. Red and white striped thigh-highs, a "dress" that barely covers her ass, and a Santa hat tilted at what I'm guessing is supposed to be a seductive angle.

The clubhouse is packed wall-to-wall with bodies. Our Carlsbad chapter knows how to throw a party, and tonight they've outdone themselves. Christmas lights strung across every surface, booze flowing like the second coming, and enough club girls to staff a small army of Mrs. Clauses—if Mrs. Claus wore crotchless panties and did body shots.

"Brother, you look like you're at a fucking funeral," Big says, materializing next to me with two shot glasses. He pushes one into my hand, amber liquid sloshing over the rim. "Drink up. It's a party for Christ's sake."

I down the whiskey in one swallow, letting it burn all the way to my stomach. "Just tired."

"Bullshit." He leans against the bar beside me, eyeing the room with satisfaction. "You've been in your head since we got back from that church gig. What's eating at you?"

"Nothing."

Everything.

My phone burns a hole in my pocket, screen dark with a message that hasn't come. It's been three days since I dropped Cece back at the church, watched her walk away with that glance over her shoulder that nearly made me turn off the bike and follow her inside.

"Jesus, you're even ignoring the sweet butts," Big continues, nodding toward Rabbit, who's hovering nearby with a bottle of Jack, waiting for permission to refill my glass. I motion him over, if only to shut Big up.

"I'm fine," I insist, letting Rabbit pour me another shot. "Just thinking about the run tomorrow."

Big snorts. "The run to San Salona? Again? That's the third time this week you've found an excuse to ride through that prissy little town."

I shoot him a look that would make most men back off. Big just grins wider, the asshole.

"Convenient how we suddenly have so much business in San Salona," he says, leaning closer. "Wouldn't have anything to do with a certain preacher's daughter, would it?"

"Fuck off."

"That's what I thought." He chuckles, clapping me on the shoulder hard enough to slosh my drink. "You know the rules, brother. Civilians are fine for fun, but—"

"I know the goddamn rules." I cut him off before he can finish the lecture I've heard a thousand times. No relationships that could compromise loyalty. Keep it simple, keep it contained, keep it temporary.

I down my second shot and slam the glass onto the bar, a decision I instantly regret when the bartender shoots me a dirty look. The problem isn't Big's words, it's that they're hitting too close to home.

"I'm not breaking any rules," I mutter, mostly to convince myself. "Just checking in on the charity situation."

"Right." Big's sarcasm could strip paint. "And I'm just drinking water tonight."

"You're not helping."

"Not trying to." He signals Rabbit for another round. "Look, brother, we all got our vices. Just be smart about yours."

I want to argue, but what's the point? I have been finding excuses to ride through San Salona. Yesterday I spent three hours at that shitty little coffee shop where I first saw her take on the mayor, nursing the worst latte I've ever tasted, pretending I was there for the WIFI while checking the door every time the bell jingled.

Pathetic doesn't begin to cover it.

"It's not like that," I say, the lie tasting worse than the cheap whiskey. "Just making sure the toy drive goes smoothly. My aunt would have my ass if it fell apart after all that effort."

Big gives me a look that says he's not buying what I'm selling, but he lets it drop when a blonde in a crop top that says *NAUGHTY* in glittery letters slides between us. She presses herself against me, all perfume and bare skin.

"Bray," she purrs, running a finger down my chest. "I've been looking for you all night."

I recognize her from last month's party, but her name escapes me. Jessica? Jennifer? Something with a J.

"Been right here," I say, gently extracting myself from her grip. Her face falls slightly, then brightens when Big wraps an arm around her waist.

"Don't mind him, sugar," he tells her. "Our VP's got his mind on...business tonight."

She pouts prettily. "All work and no play make Bray a dull boy."

"That's me. Dull as dishwater." I push away from the bar, ignoring Big's knowing smirk. "I'm gonna get some air."

The December night hits me like a slap when I step outside. Cold enough to make my lungs ache. I welcome it after the stuffy heat of the clubhouse.

Leaning against the wall, I fish a cigarette from my pocket, cupping my hand against the wind to light it.

The first drag burns, smoke curling in my lungs before I exhale it into the night. Above me, stars pierce the darkness like tiny holes in black velvet. Nothing like the view from that lake where I took Cece, but still beautiful in its own right. I'm halfway through my smoke when my phone buzzes. For a split second, hope flares in my chest—maybe it's her, maybe she finally decided to text me back. But when I check the screen, it's just Domino asking where I went.

I type back a quick response and shove the phone into my pocket, disappointed in myself for even caring. This is exactly the kind of shit I swore I wouldn't do—getting hung up on some woman who's nothing but complications wrapped in a pretty package.

But fuck if I can get her out of my head.

The way she felt pressed against my back on the bike, her arms wrapped around me like she trusted me completely. The sound of her laugh when I made some smart-ass comment.

I take another drag, letting the nicotine settle my nerves. Three days of radio silence shouldn't mean anything. She's probably busy sorting through all those toys we brought, getting ready for the distribution. Or dealing with the fallout from her very public confrontation with her ex-father-in-law.

Or maybe she's realized that riding off with a biker was a moment of temporary insanity, and now she's back to her senses.

The thought sits wrong in my gut, but it's probably for the best. Cece doesn't belong in my world any more than I belong in hers. She's all Sunday sermons and charity drives, while I am all the reasons people go to church and pray for forgiveness. Holy water and motor oil.

The door bangs open behind me, and I don't need to turn around to know it's Big. His heavy footsteps give him away before he even speaks.

"You're being a real buzzkill tonight, brother."

"Just needed some air." I flick ash into the wind, watching it scatter across the parking lot. "Party's not going anywhere."

"Neither are you, apparently." He leans against the wall beside me, breath visible in the cold air. "Wanna tell me what's really going on? Because this broody shit isn't like you."

I take another drag, buying myself time. Big's been my road captain for three years, and he knows me well enough to smell bullshit from a mile away. But admitting what's really eating at me would mean acknowledging something I'm not ready to face.

"Nothing's going on," I finally say. "Just thinking."

"About the girl?

It's not a question, and I don't bother denying it. "Maybe."

"Christ." He runs a hand over his shaved head. "Of all the women in three counties, you had to fixate on the one who screams complications."

"I'm not fixated."

"No? Then why haven't you touched a single woman in here tonight? Jessica was practically crawling into your lap, and you acted like she had the plague."

Because none of them are her. Because none of them have spring-colored eyes that see right through me, or a laugh that makes me want to listen for more. Because every woman in this clubhouse is just a distraction, and lately, I don't want to be distracted.

"Look," I say, grinding my cigarette under my boot, "it's nothing. I helped her out, we took a ride, end of story."

Big's eyebrow shoots up. "A ride?"

"Jesus, not like that." Though the image flashes through my mind before I can stop it—Cece's legs wrapped around me in a very different way, her hair tumbling down her back as she—

"You're doing it again," Big interrupts my thoughts. "That thousand-yard stare like you're seeing something the rest of us can't. Look, brother, if you want to fuck her, do it, but that girl wouldn't last a second in our world. Get her out of your system, Bray."

"I'm not trying to bring her into our world." The words come out sharper than I intended. "And I don't need to get her out of my system. There's nothing to get out."

Big gives me that look, the one that says he's been around long enough to see this story play out before. "Whatever you say, brother. Just remember, girls like that—they're fantasy material, not reality. She's probably already forgotten all about you. Now, you coming back inside?" Big asks, already moving toward the door.

"In a minute."

He nods and disappears back into the noise and chaos of the party. I pull out my phone again, thumb hovering over her name in my contacts. No messages, no missed calls.

Fuck it.

I tap out a quick text before I can talk myself out of it.

> Still waiting on that list of food items, princess.

Simple. Casual. Nothing that screams "I can't stop thinking about you." I hit send before I can second-guess myself, then immediately regret it. It's nearly midnight. She's probably asleep like a normal person, not hanging out at some club party surrounded by drunk bikers and women who think Santa lingerie is appropriate Christmas attire.

I'm about to pocket the phone when it buzzes in my hand. My heart does some stupid little skip as I see her name on the screen.

> Sorry I've been MIA. Been dealing with the fallout of my coffee shop showdown. You still in town?

I read it twice, trying not to feel like a goddamn teenager getting a text from his crush. It's just a message. Just words on a screen. But they hit different coming from her.

I'm in Carlsbad. Club party.

I send it before adding to it.

Could be in San Salona tomorrow. All you have to do is ask, princess, and I'll be there.

Three dots appear as she types, then stop, then start again. Like she's considering what to say. My chest tightens, waiting.

I could use the help. And maybe another ride after? If you're not busy with "club business."

I can practically hear the air quotes around those words, imagine the little quirk of her eyebrow when she says them. Fuck, I'm in trouble.

I stare at her message for a long moment, my thumb hovering over the keyboard. The smart thing would be to play it cool, maybe wait a few minutes before responding. But apparently my brain has checked out for the evening.

I will never be too busy to take a beautiful woman for a ride.

I hit send and immediately want to punch myself in the face. Way to sound desperate, asshole.

But her response comes back almost immediately.

How much have you had to drink?

Why?

Think I need to be under the influence
to call you beautiful, princess?

No.

I just...

Just what, princess?

Nevermind. Forget it.

There's nothing forgettable about you,
Cece. Tell me what you we're going
to say.

Nothing. Have a great time at your
party.

I pocket my phone and head back toward the club-house door, but the thought of going back to that noise and chaos makes my skin crawl. Instead, I walk to my bike, running my hand over the familiar leather seat.

The engine turns over with a satisfying growl, and I'm already backing out of my parking spot when Big appears in the doorway, shaking his head like he knows exactly where I'm headed.

He's not wrong.

The ride to San Salona takes just under an hour at

the speed I'm going, pushing the bike harder than I probably should on these back roads. But I need the cold air, need the focus that comes with handling a machine that could kill me if I make one wrong move.

By the time I reach the city limits, it's past 2 AM and the streets are empty except for the occasional cop car on patrol. I take a familiar turn down the winding driveway that leads to my aunt's place, the headlight of my bike cutting through the night in a sharp, narrow beam. The sprawling Victorian house sits quiet on the hill, no lights in the windows, but I'm not headed there. My destination is the smaller building tucked behind a row of oak trees at the edge of the property.

The guesthouse has been my refuge since I was sixteen. Even after I patched in with the Rejects, even after I became someone my aunt probably had every right to be afraid of, she's kept it ready. "Your home," she calls it, though I've never stayed more than a few nights at a time.

I kill the engine before I get too close, coasting the last hundred feet to avoid waking her. Stealing sleep from her is the last thing I'd do, not while her husband is still in the hospital. The garage door opens with a soft click from the remote I've kept on my keychain for years, and I ease the bike inside.

The familiar scent hits me the moment I step through the side door—cinnamon and pine. She keeps the place festive all year, but December is when she really leans in. The small Christmas tree in the corner is already lit, multicolored bulbs glowing gently in the dim room. She must have been out here earlier, hoping I'd show up.

I flip on a lamp and survey the space. Nothing's changed. I grab a beer from the fridge, popping the cap and taking a long pull while I wander through the familiar space. It's like stepping into a time capsule, everything exactly where I left it last time. My aunt's touch is everywhere, from the neatly folded throw blanket on the couch to the fresh towels in the bathroom. The woman's been taking care of me for fifteen years, even when I didn't deserve it.

I sink onto the couch, setting my beer on the coffee table. My phone feels heavy in my pocket, a constant reminder of the message I shouldn't have sent. What the hell am I doing? I should be back at the clubhouse, not sitting in my aunt's guest house, thinking about a woman who belongs to a world I left behind years ago.

But Cece's not like the rest of them. There's something about her–a fire that wasn't there when we were kids. Divorce has hardened her edges, given her a sharpness that catches the light differently. Makes me wonder what else it's changed about her.

I take another swig of beer, leaning my head back against the cushions. The clock on the wall reads 2:47 AM. In a few hours, my phone will buzz with her list of food items, and I'll have an excuse to see her again. The thought sends a current of anticipation through me that I haven't felt in years.

I should be sleeping, shutting this down before it ever starts. Instead, I find myself waiting for morning like a kid on Christmas, restless with the thought of seeing her again.

CHAPTER 7

CECE

I'VE ALWAYS THOUGHT the worst sin was envy, but this morning I'm redefining temptation as I pull into the church parking lot and spot him. Brayden Cole, leaning against his motorcycle, his thick dark hair slightly messy under a beanie. My stomach does a little flip that has nothing to do with the coffee I gulped down earlier and everything to do with the way his steel-gray eyes lock onto mine through my windshield.

Temptation, thy name is leather cut and bad decisions.

I take a deep breath before killing the engine, trying to calm the rapid flutter of my pulse.

"Morning, princess." His voice carries across the

parking lot as I step out of my car, the nickname making my cheeks warm despite the December chill.

"What are you doing here?"

"Figured I'd save you the trouble of sending me that grocery list. We can go get it together."

"Go get it together?" I repeat, sounding a bit dazed even to my own ears. "I haven't even made the list yet."

"Even better. We can figure it out while we shop." He pushes off his bike with that easy grace that seems unfair for someone his size. "Unless you've got other plans this morning."

I should say yes. I should tell him that I have a dozen church-related responsibilities to attend to, a meeting with my father about the toy distribution, maybe even a job interview to pretend to care about. But the truth is, I've spent the last three days hoping he'd message me again, jumping every time my phone buzzed.

"No other plans," I admit, tucking a strand of hair behind my ear. "But I'm pretty sure the only grocery store in town won't let you through the door. The Millers have been very clear about their 'no bikers' policy since that incident in '08."

"What incident?"

"Some guys from a passing club decided to redecorate their produce section with watermelons. It wasn't pretty."

His lips twitch. "Sounds artistic."

"The police report called it fruit-based vandalism."

"Creative cops in this town." He steps closer, and I

catch his scent again. How good he smells should be illegal. "Good thing I wasn't planning on Miller's. There's a warehouse club about twenty minutes outside town. Better prices, bulk quantities, and good selection."

"You planning to hitch a wagon to your bike?"

"Nah," he grins. "Think your dad will let you borrow it?" He jerks his head towards the church's passenger van.

I blink at him, processing what he just suggested. "You want me to ask my father if I can take the church van on a grocery run with a member of a motorcycle club?"

"When you put it like that, it sounds unreasonable."

"Because it is unreasonable." I cross my arms, trying to ignore how the morning light catches the blue flecks in his eyes. "My father barely tolerated you bringing the toys. If I ask to borrow church property to go shopping with you, he'll probably have me committed."

"Or he could see it as his daughter doing charitable work." Brayden's expression shifts to something more serious. "Look, we need to get food for nearly four hundred families. Your Honda's not gonna cut it, and my bike definitely won't. The van makes sense."

He's right, damn him. The practical part of my brain knows we need a bigger vehicle, but the part of me that's already caused enough scandal this week is sounding every alarm. Richard kept his promise and contacted the church executive board about Brayden's club donating to the toy drive. He conveniently omitted our run-in at the coffee shop, but the rumor mill handled that for him. My father was spitting nails after I got home from my ride with Brayden. The last time he lectured me that harshly was when I was five minutes late coming home from a high school party. Three days have passed, and he's still down to single word replies.

"Besides," he adds, that hint of a smile returning, "what's the worst that could happen?"

I stare at him. "Did you just ask me what's the worst that could happen? In my experience, that's usually when everything goes spectacularly wrong."

"You worried about being seen with me?"

The question catches me off guard with its directness. Am I worried about being seen with him? Yes. But not for the reasons he probably thinks.

"I'm worried about my father having a stroke."

"He'll survive. He's got the Lord on his side, right?" He runs a hand through his dark hair, messing it up further. "Sometimes doing the right thing means pissing off the wrong people."

The irony isn't lost on me that he's quoting something that sounds suspiciously close to sermon material. "Did you just give me a moral lesson?"

"Maybe I picked up a few things sitting in the back pew all those years."

Despite everything—the scandal, my father's disapproval, the voice in my head that sounds almost exactly like my mother warning me about boys of his caliber—I find myself nodding. "Fine. But you're the one explaining to my father why we need the van."

"Deal." He extends his hand as though we're finalizing a business agreement. When I take it, his palm is warm and rough against mine, sending that familiar jolt up my arm. "Where is he?"

"Probably in his office, preparing for this afternoon's emergency board meeting." I don't let go of his hand immediately, and neither does he. "The one where they'll discuss whether accepting donations from your club was appropriate."

"Sounds fun. Lead the way."

I drop his hand and start walking toward the church, hyperaware of him following behind me. The side door is unlocked, and the familiar smell of lemon polish and furniture wax hits me immediately. It's the scent of my childhood, of Sunday mornings and youth group meetings. I glance back at Brayden, suddenly aware of how out of place he looks here, his leather cut and heavy boots a stark contrast to the polished floors and framed Bible verses.

"This way," I murmur, leading him down the hallway toward my father's office. My heart thumps against my ribs with each step, the same way it did when I was sixteen and slipping in after curfew.

We're halfway there when Mrs. Whitaker emerges from the fellowship hall, a clipboard clutched to her chest. She stops dead when she spots us, her eyes going comically wide.

"Cecelia! What is—" Her gaze darts between Brayden and me, settling on his Heaven's Rejects patch with undisguised horror. "What is he doing here?"

"Good morning, Mrs. Whitaker," I say, summoning my most pleasant church-lady tone. "Mr. Cole is helping with the food box collection. We're on our way to speak with my father."

"I see." She clearly doesn't see at all. "Well, I was heading that way myself."

Of course she was. The woman has a sixth sense for drama—probably circling the building all morning, waiting for a chance to corner my father. She falls into step beside us, her sensible shoes clicking against the hardwood, each tap a tiny hammer of judgment. I can feel Brayden's amusement without even glancing at him.

"I was just telling Reverend Montgomery about the…concerns…some of the congregation has expressed," Mrs. Whitaker continues, her voice pitched to carry down the hall. "About recent events."

"Recent events such as feeding hungry children for Christmas?" I ask sweetly. "Truly shocking."

Brayden makes a sound that might be a suppressed laugh. Mrs. Whitaker's lips thin to a bloodless line.

"You know very well what I mean, Cecelia. The board is quite concerned about the church's reputation."

"More concerned about its reputation than its mission, apparently."

We reach my father's office door, which stands slightly ajar. I can see him at his desk, head bowed over paperwork, silver hair catching the morning light from the window. For a moment, I hesitate. Maybe this is a mistake. Maybe I should send Brayden away and handle this myself.

But then he steps forward, his shoulder brushing mine in a quiet show of support, and I find myself knocking on the doorframe.

"Dad? Do you have a minute?"

My father looks up, his expression shifting from concentration to surprise to something far more guarded when he spots Brayden. "Cecelia. Mrs. Whitaker." His gaze lands on Brayden's cut, disapproval radiating from him with the force of a furnace. "Brayden."

"Reverend," Brayden says with a casual nod, completely unfazed by my father's chilly reception. "Nice office. Very… biblical."

He's not wrong. Every available surface is covered with religious texts, framed scripture, or souvenirs from mission trips. The whole room feels more museum display than workspace—an exhibit devoted entirely to my father's faith.

"What can I do for you?" Dad asks, deliberately ignoring Brayden and focusing on me instead.

"We need to borrow the church van," I say, diving straight in before I lose my nerve. "For the food boxes. We're going to make a supply run."

"We?" He raises an eyebrow that could cut glass.

"Brayden has offered to help with the food collection," I explain, trying to sound as reasonable and church appropriate as possible. "Since the usual donations fell through, we need to purchase supplies in bulk.

My car isn't big enough, and his...transportation options are limited."

Mrs. Whitaker makes a small huffing sound beside me. "I must express my concern about using church property for this arrangement."

"It's not an arrangement," I say, perhaps a bit too sharply. "It's charity work. Which is kind of our whole thing, isn't it? 'Feed my sheep' and all that?"

My father looks pained, the vein on the side of his neck bulges as his exasperation grows.

"Cecelia, may I speak with you privately?"

"Actually, Reverend," Brayden interrupts, stepping forward with his hands clasped behind his back, posture straight and purposeful—as though he's reporting for duty. "This was my idea. Your daughter is simply trying to help feed families in need. If you have concerns about me using church property, I understand."

But my father surprises me. As he studies Brayden's face, something shifts in his expression. Not approval, exactly, but… consideration.

"Your aunt speaks highly of you."

"She's… generous with her praise," Brayden answers, choosing his words carefully.

"She mentioned you've been helping her with Harold's medical expenses. The bills from his surgery."

My chest tightens. I had no idea. Jillian never said a word about money, but that's her—she'd give away her last dollar before admitting she needed help.

"Family takes care of each other." Brayden lifts a

shoulder in a small shrug, as if it's no big deal, though the tension in his stance tells me this topic isn't easy for him. "She and Harold gave me a home when no one else would. Helping with the bills is the least I can do."

My father studies him for a long moment, his expression unreadable. Then he opens his desk drawer and pulls out a set of keys.

"The van needs gas," he says, tossing the keys to Brayden, who catches them with one hand. "And the passenger door sticks sometimes. You have to pull up while you open it."

Mrs. Whitaker makes a strangled sound beside me. "Reverend Montgomery, I must protest! The board will—"

"The board," my father interrupts, "can take up their concerns with me at the meeting this afternoon. In the meantime, there are families counting on us." He turns to Brayden. "I expect the van back by five. We have youth group tonight."

I'm too stunned to speak. My father, the man who lectured me for three days about the company I keep, is handing over church property to a leather-clad biker without so much as a background check.

"Yes, sir," Brayden says, pocketing the keys. "We'll have it back before then."

"And Cecelia," Dad adds, his gaze shifting to me, "remember who you're representing."

And there it is—the reminder that he's still pissed at me, and that I've backed him into a corner. Well, at least tonight at dinner, he'll speak more than one word to me. There's that to look forward to later.

"Like you'd ever let me forget, Dad," I manage.

Mrs. Whitaker looks like she's swallowed something sour. "I'll be documenting this conversation for the board meeting," she announces, clutching her clipboard tighter.

"You do that," Brayden says cheerfully. "Make sure you spell my name right. B-R-A-Y-D-E-N. One 'i,' no 'e' at the end."

I bite the inside of my cheek to keep from laughing. Mrs. Whitaker's face turns an impressive shade of purple.

"We should get going," I say quickly, before she can spontaneously combust. "Thank you, Dad."

He nods, already turning back to his paperwork in that way that signals the conversation is over. "Drive safely."

I follow Brayden out of the office, acutely aware of Mrs. Whitaker's disapproving stare burning between my shoulder blades with pinpoint precision. The hallway suddenly feels endless, every step echoing off the walls with the sharpness of gunfire in a cathedral.

"That went better than expected," Brayden says once we're out of earshot, his voice carrying that hint of amusement that seems to be his default setting.

"Better than expected?" I stare at him. "Mrs. Whitaker looked ready to start an exorcism, and my father just handed you the keys to church property after lecturing me for three days about my poor judgment."

"Yeah, but he handed me the keys." He dangles them from his finger, "That's what matters."

I shake my head, still processing what just happened.

"You going to stand there all day or....?"

"No, I'm coming," I say, still a bit dazed as I follow him down the hallway.

The bright morning sun hits my eyes as we step outside, and I squint against the glare. For a moment, I just stand there, watching Brayden stride toward the church van, moving with an ease that feels almost unreal in this setting. Seeing him here—his cut, his boots—against the pristine church grounds sends a strange jolt through me.

"You coming, princess?" he calls over his shoulder, already at the driver's side door.

"You're driving?" I ask, hurrying to catch up.

"Unless you want to." He holds the keys out, already knowing my decision.

"No, go ahead." I reach for the passenger door, remembering too late my father's warning. It sticks, exactly as Dad said it would. I tug, but it doesn't budge.

"Up and out," Brayden says, moving to my side. He reaches past me, his arm brushing mine as he grips the handle. "This way." He pulls up and out in one smooth motion, and the door swings open. The movement brings him close enough that warmth rolls off him, along with that familiar mix of leather and spice that always unsettles me in the worst—and best—ways.

"Thanks," I murmur, slipping into the seat before I lose my mind and do something reckless.

He closes the door with a quiet thud and walks back around to his side. I watch him through the windshield, noticing the steady confidence in each step, the certainty in the way he carries himself. It's a kind of self-assurance I've never possessed—not even when I thought I had my life sorted out.

The engine turns over with a rumble that vibrates through the van's worn seats. Brayden adjusts the rearview mirror before he shifts into reverse.

"So," he says as we pull out of the church parking lot, "warehouse club it is. You ever been to one of those places?"

"Once. With Ethan." The name slips out before I can stop it, and I immediately wish I could take it back. The last thing I want is to bring up my ex-husband while sitting in a church van with a man who makes my pulse race. "It was...overwhelming."

"Yeah, they're designed to make you buy shit you don't need in quantities that could feed a small army." He glances at me sideways. "Good thing we actually need to feed a small army."

I laugh despite myself. "Four hundred families definitely qualifies."

We drive in comfortable silence for a few minutes, the familiar streets of San Salona giving way to rural highway. I find myself stealing glances at Brayden as he drives.

His hands rest easily on the wheel, those same

hands that helped me with my helmet by the lake, that have probably done things I can't even imagine.

"You're staring," he says without looking at me, the corner of his mouth lifting in that almost-smile I'm starting to recognize.

Heat creeps up my neck. "Sorry."

"I didn't say stop."

That pulls a laugh from me. "Do you practice these lines, or do they just come naturally?"

"Both." Now he does glance at me, that half-smile playing at his lips.

I turn to look out the window, watching pine trees blur past. "You never told me what you did. After, I mean. When you left San Salona."

"You really want to know?"

"I wouldn't ask if I didn't."

He's quiet for a moment, deciding how much truth to give me. "Bounced around for a while. Construction work, bar security, whatever paid cash. Got into some trouble. Got out of it. Found the club when I was twenty-three."

"And that changed things?"

"Everything." The word carries weight—almost a prayer, almost a promise. "For the first time in my life, I belonged somewhere."

I nod, understanding more than he probably realizes. That hunger to belong, to find your place—I've felt it my whole life, even when surrounded by a community that claimed to embrace me.

"Your turn."

"What do you want to know exactly?"

"Who are you really, Cece Montgomery? The real you, not the woman you pretend to be."

I stare out the windshield, watching the white lines of the highway blur past. Who am I really?

"I don't know," I admit, the honesty surprising even me.

"Bullshit."

The blunt response makes me turn to look at him. "Excuse me?"

"I said bullshit." He keeps his eyes on the road, but I can see the intensity in his profile. "The woman who told off the mayor in a crowded coffee shop knows exactly who she is. She's just scared to let her out."

"I'm not scared—"

"Then why are you sitting there pretending you don't know who you are?" He glances at me briefly. "You want to know what I see when I look at you?"

My heart does something complicated in my chest. "What?"

"Fire. You've got this fire burning underneath all that politeness and propriety. It's what made you divorce your cheating husband when half the women in this town would have just looked the other way. It's what made you stand up to your ex-father-in-law. And it's what made you get on the back of my bike even though every rational part of your brain was screaming at you to run the opposite direction."

"You make it sound so simple."

"It is simple. You just make it complicated." He

takes the exit for the warehouse club, the van's turn signal clicking rhythmically. "When's the last time you did something just because you wanted to, without worrying about what everyone else would think?"

I start to open my mouth, but I snap it shut when I realize I don't have a good answer. Even sitting here with him, helping with the food boxes, I'm telling myself it's for charity, for the families. But the truth is, I wanted to see him again. I wanted to feel that spark of something real in a life that's felt like performance art for too long.

"Getting on your bike," I admit.

"How'd that feel?"

Like flying. Like drowning. Like coming alive for the first time in years.

"Terrifying," I say instead, because it's safer than the truth.

"Good terrifying or bad terrifying?"

I consider this as we pull into the massive parking lot of the warehouse store. Good terrifying, definitely. The kind that makes your blood sing and your skin tingle with anticipation. The kind that makes you wonder what other parts of yourself you've been keeping locked away.

"Good."

He parks in a spot near the back of the lot, away from the clusters of minivans and SUVs closer to the entrance.

"Good," he repeats. "Because I've been thinking about that ride a lot."

My breath catches. "Have you?"

"Yeah." He turns to face me, one arm draped over the back of his seat. "Been thinking about a lot of things, actually."

The space between us in the van's cab suddenly feels both too wide and not nearly wide enough. I'm hyper-aware of everything— the sound of my own heartbeat in my ears, the fact that we're sitting in a church van having a conversation that feels anything but appropriate.

"Brayden—"

"We should go in," he says abruptly, like he's cutting himself off before he says something he can't take back. "Figure out what we need."

I nod, though part of me wants to stay right here, suspended in this moment.

CHAPTER 8

CECE

THE CHURCH VAN door has always made that god-awful screeching sound—an unholy mix of nails on a chalkboard and a dying cat. But today, as I slide it open for the twentieth time, there's nothing but smooth, blessed silence.

"What kind of black magic did you work on this thing?" I ask, sliding the door back and forth with downright childish delight. "It's been screaming for as long as I can remember. Sunday School kids used to flinch whenever someone touched it."

Brayden grins, wiping his hands on a rag he pulled from his back pocket. "Just needed some silicone lubricant. That, and the track was bent." He says it casually, as though he didn't just fix in thirty minutes what entire generations of church maintenance committees couldn't manage.

"Well, the youth group will canonize you for this alone," I say, reaching for another box of canned goods. "You would not believe how many times that squeak exposed kids sneaking out during a lock-in."

"Speaking from experience, princess?" His eyebrow arches as he lifts two boxes effortlessly.

"I plead the fifth." I try to keep my face serious, but it's impossible. Something about him makes me want to laugh.

We've been unloading groceries for the better part of an hour, our rhythm so natural it's like we've been doing this for years instead of just a few hours. The warehouse club trip was a success beyond my wildest dreams. Between the little monetary donations we received and Brayden picking up the rest, our families won't go hungry.

"You know," I say, hefting a case of macaroni and cheese, "I think we might actually pull this off. Between the toys and now this food, we might save Christmas after all."

"Never doubted it. You're too stubborn to let the Kincaids win."

I laugh, feeling lighter than I have in weeks. "Stubborn? Me? I prefer determined."

"Same thing, different packaging." He reaches for the box in my arms, his fingers brushing mine. "Let me take that."

"I can handle it," I protest, but he's already lifting it from my grasp.

"I know you can. But you don't have to."

Something about those simple words hits me harder than they should. You don't have to. When was the last time someone offered to carry my burdens instead of adding to them?

Dad appears in the doorway of the fellowship hall, his expression a complicated mix of surprise and reluctant approval as he surveys the mountains of food we've managed to bring in. His gaze lingers on Brayden, who's arranging boxes of dry goods. "I see you've been busy."

"Very," I reply, trying not to sound defensive. "We got everything on the list and then some."

Dad steps further into the room, scanning the tables piled high with groceries with what might be genuine appreciation. "This is...impressive."

"Thank your daughter," Brayden says without looking up from the boxes he's organizing. "She's the one who knew exactly what the families would need."

Dad's eyebrows lift slightly at that, his attention shifting to me with a question I can't quite decipher. I straighten under his scrutiny, suddenly sixteen again and desperate to prove I'm responsible enough for the car keys.

"The van ran well?" Dad asks, changing the subject.

"Like a dream," I say. "Brayden even fixed the sliding door. No more screeching."

His brows rise. "You fixed it? We've had three different mechanics look at that door."

Brayden shrugs—half dismissive, half proud. "Sometimes you just need a fresh perspective on an old problem."

"Indeed." Dad straightens, "Well, I should let you finish up. The board meeting starts in an hour."

My stomach drops. I'd almost forgotten about the emergency meeting, the one where Mrs. Whitaker will undoubtedly present her detailed report on this morning's *concerning developments.*

"Dad," I start, but he holds up a hand.

"Don't worry about it, Cecelia. Some battles are worth fighting." He meets Brayden's gaze across the room. "Thank you. For all of this."

Brayden nods once, a gesture of acknowledgment between men. Then Dad's gone, leaving us alone with the echo of his footsteps.

"Think he'll survive the board meeting?" Brayden asks, breaking the silence.

"My father? He's tougher than he looks." I stack another box, trying to ignore the nagging feeling in the pit of my stomach.

"He'll be fine," Brayden says, reaching for the last box in the van. "Your dad seems like the kind of man who knows how to handle church politics."

We get lost in sorting through the boxes. It isn't until we're filling the final food box that the back door to the fellowship hall swings open. The temperature in the room seems to drop ten degrees as Richard Kincaid strides in, carrying himself with the certainty of a man who believes the entire building exists because of his family's "donations."

He probably thinks it does.

His eyes sweep the room, taking in the stacks of food boxes before locking onto Brayden. His face twists into pure disgust, his expression curdling as though he's just uncovered something foul on the bottom of his Italian leather shoes.

Brayden sets down the box he's holding with deliberate care, his movements controlled in a way that makes the hair on the back of my neck stand up. He moves to my side, putting himself between Richard and me. Every muscle in my body tenses as I watch him glide across the room. His lips are pressed into a thin line of disapproval, but strangely, he doesn't say a word. Not one snide comment, not one veiled threat. He simply walks past us before continuing toward the main hall where the board meeting will be held.

The silence is somehow worse than any confrontation.

Brayden's hand finds my elbow, his touch firm but gentle. "We're done here," he declares as he guides me toward the exit.

"What are you doing?" I argue, but I don't resist as he leads me through the back door and into the parking lot.

"Getting you out of here." His strides are long and purposeful, forcing me to jog to keep up.

"Brayden, wait." I tug against his hold, making him

pause. "My dad's meeting is about to start. I should be there to defend him—to defend us."

He turns to face me, his expression grave. "The last place you need to be right now is in that room with Kincaid."

"But my dad—"

"Can handle himself." His eyes soften slightly. "Remember when you asked about another ride?"

I hesitate, my heart thudding in my chest as I look back at the church where my father is about to face the board.

"Okay. Let's go."

Relief flashes across Brayden's face, so brief I almost miss it. He releases my elbow but stays close as we walk toward his bike.

"Shit," he mutters, giving me a once-over that makes heat bloom in my cheeks despite the chill in the air. "You'll freeze dressed like that."

I glance down at my thin sweater and jeans. I'd rushed out without my heavier coat, and the December wind slips straight through the fabric without the slightest resistance.

"I'm fine," I lie, even as a shiver betrays me.

Brayden gives me a look that says he's not buying it. "Hold on." He strides over to his bike and flips open one of his saddlebags, rummaging through it before pulling out a dark gray hoodie. "Here."

He holds it out to me, and I hesitate for just a moment before taking it. The fabric is soft and worn, clearly well-loved, and when I slip it over my head, I'm immediately enveloped in his scent.

The hoodie swallows me whole, sleeves covering my hands, the hem landing mid-thigh. Warmth settles around me, his scent woven into every inch of the fabric.

"Better?" he asks.

"Much." I push the sleeves up to free my hands, feeling oddly vulnerable and protected all at once, "Thanks."

Brayden nods, then reaches for the helmet hanging from his handlebar. "Come here," he says, gesturing me closer.

I step forward, and he gently places the helmet on my head, his fingers brushing my cheeks as he secures the strap. His touch is surprisingly tender, a stark contrast to the strength I know those hands possess.

"Too tight?" he asks, adjusting the strap beneath my chin.

"No, it's perfect." My voice sounds muffled inside the helmet, but I can't blame that for the breathlessness I hear in it.

He secures the strap under my chin. His eyes focused on the task but occasionally flicking up to meet mine. Something passes between us in those brief moments–a current of understanding, of want, that makes my skin prickle with awareness beneath his oversized hoodie.

"All set," he says, stepping back to admire his work. "Ready to go?"

I nod. He swings his leg over the bike and pats the seat behind him. I climb on less awkwardly this time, already more confident as I slide onto the seat behind him. Without hesitation, my arms encircle his waist, fingers locking together over the hard planes of his stomach. I press closer than strictly necessary, telling myself it's just for warmth.

The engine roars to life beneath us, vibrating through my entire body in a way that sends my heart racing. I lean into him as we pull out of the church parking lot, watching my father's house of worship grow smaller in the side mirror until it disappears completely around a bend.

We don't take the main roads this time. Instead, Brayden guides us through back streets. The town looks different from the back of his bike—more beautiful somehow, less suffocating.

I'm so lost in the sensation of the wind and the solid warmth of Brayden's back against my chest that I don't immediately register where we're headed until we turn down a familiar tree-lined drive. Jillian's house appears through the branches, its gingerbread trim and wrap-around porch exactly as I remember from childhood visits.

Brayden doesn't drive up to the main house, but to a small guest house on the back side of the property. He cuts the engine, and I reluctantly unwrap my arms from his waist as he dismounts, immediately missing his warmth.

"This is where you're staying?" I ask, pulling off the helmet and shaking out my hair.

"My aunt's kept this place ready for me since I was a teenager," he says, taking the helmet from my hands. "Said I'd always have somewhere to come back to, even when I was at my worst."

A loud rumbling sound interrupts the moment, and it takes me a second to realize it's coming from my stomach. Heat rushes to my face as Brayden raises an eyebrow, his lips quirking into that half-smile that makes my heart skip.

"When's the last time you ate something?" he asks, unlocking the door to the guest house.

I try to remember. Coffee this morning, but actual food? "Um..."

"That's what I thought." He holds the door open for me. "Come on. I'll make us something."

"You cook?"

The guest house is cozy and unexpectedly homey, with a small Christmas tree twinkling in the corner and throw pillows arranged neatly on a worn couch.

"Don't sound so shocked," he says, shutting the door behind us. "Been feeding myself for a long time."

"I'm not shocked," I lie, "Just...pleasantly surprised."

I hover awkwardly near the door, unsure if I should sit or stand. Being here in his space feels strangely intimate, like I've crossed some invisible boundary. My fingers fidget with the too-long sleeves of his hoodie.

"Make yourself comfortable," he says, opening the

refrigerator. "I'm not gonna bite." He pauses, glancing over his shoulder with that crooked half-smile. "Unless you ask nicely."

Heat rushes to my face as I settle onto one of the barstools at the kitchen counter. "Do those lines actually work on women?"

"You're still here, aren't you?"

"I'm here for the food," I retort.

Brayden laughs, the sound rich and genuine in a way that makes my chest tighten. "Whatever helps you sleep at night, princess."

"Well, I have some good news and some bad news. Which do you want first?"

"Bad," I say, watching him rummage through the nearly empty refrigerator.

"Bad news..." he confirms, closing the door with a sigh, "outside of beer and some soda, the fridge is empty." He turns toward the pantry and pulls open the door, scanning the shelves. "Good news..." he says, moving to the pantry, "I have spaghetti and store-bought pasta sauce. That okay?"

"Spaghetti sounds great," I reply, surprising myself with how comfortable this feels—sitting in his kitchen, wearing his hoodie, watching him cook for me. It's been so long since someone took care of me instead of the other way around. "Need any help?"

"Nope. Just sit there and look pretty." He pulls a pot from a cabinet and fills it with water, his movements efficient and practiced. "Though you're doing more than your fair share of that already."

The compliment catches me off guard, and I duck my head to hide my smile. "Do you actually have cooking skills, or should I be worried?"

"I can make a mean spaghetti, but with these ingredients, maybe temper your expectations down a bit. Next time, I'll grab some groceries and make you a proper meal."

"Next time? That implies you'll be around?" The question makes me pause. I know he has family here, but where does he call home? I never thought to ask. "Where is home exactly for you?"

"My club is based in Carlsbad, but figured I'd stick around a few days," he answers, turning on the burner with a quick twist of his wrist.

"Why?" I blurt out before I can stop the question from exiting my lips.

He pauses, his hand still on the burner knob, and I watch his shoulders tense slightly. For a moment, the only sound is the quiet hiss of gas igniting under the pot.

"Because I want to stay."

The simple honesty in his voice sends a flutter through my chest that I try desperately to ignore. "That's it?"

"That's it." He leans against the counter, crossing his arms over his chest in a way that makes the fabric of his T-shirt pull tight across his shoulders. "Sometimes things don't need to be complicated, Cece."

If only he knew.

If only it were that simple for me—just flip a switch, stop overthinking, stop caring so damn much. He says it as though the answer sits right in front of me, as natural as breathing. Meanwhile, I'm over here turning every feeling into a maze I can't escape.

"That's the understatement of the year," I mutter under my breath as he dumps the box of pasta into the boiling water.

"It really isn't princess. When you stop trying to make everyone else happy, and just focus on making yourself happy, complications just disappear."

Focus on myself.

Right. Like I've ever been good at that. Like my brain doesn't immediately spiral into what-ifs and worst-case scenarios and every possible way I could screw something up. And God, the way he says princess—he has no idea what that does to me. Or maybe he does. Maybe that's the problem.

The timer dings, and he drains the pasta before combining it with the sauce in a pan. The rich smell of tomatoes and herbs fills the small kitchen, making my stomach growl again.

Great. As if I wasn't already broadcasting enough of my problems, now my stomach has joined the conversation. Perfect.

He chuckles at the sound, shooting me a glance over his shoulder.

"Someone's hungry."

"Starving," I confess, not just talking about food.

And there it is—too honest, too quick. I can feel it hanging in the air between us, heavy and stupidly vulnerable. I wonder if he heard what I really meant. I wonder if he always does. I wonder if that's why he's looking at me like he knows exactly what kind of hunger I'm talking about.

God, CeCe, pull it together. It's pasta, not a confession booth.

He spoons the spaghetti onto two plates, the steam rising in delicate curls between us. Sliding one plate in front of me, he watches intently as I twirl the first bite onto my fork.

I close my eyes as the flavors hit my tongue, a small moan of appreciation escaping before I can stop it. "Oh my God, this is actually really good."

"Don't sound so surprised, but I can't take all the credit. The pasta sauce is from one of those fair-trade uppity grocery stores."

When I look up, he's watching me with an intensity that makes my skin tingle. I take another bite, suddenly aware of the way his attention lingers on my mouth.

The sauce is delicious—simple but rich, with just the right number of herbs. I haven't eaten anything this satisfying in days, though I'd rather die than admit it after my stupid comment.

"You've got something…" Brayden motions toward his own chin.

I swipe at my face with the back of my hand. "Did I get it?"

"No." He steps closer, rounding the counter with deliberate ease. "Here, let me."

Before I can protest, his thumb brushes against my chin, wiping away the sauce with a touch so gentle it steals my breath. But he doesn't pull back. Instead, his hand lingers, cupping my jaw as his gaze meets mine.

Time seems to suspend between us. I can count his heartbeats—or maybe they're mine—in the silence.

"Tell me to stop," he murmurs, thumb tracing the curve of my jaw. "If that's what you want."

But that's the problem—stopping is the last thing I want. Every nerve ending in my body is alive, hyperaware of his proximity, the heat radiating from him.

"I don't want you to stop," I admit, the words slipping out before I can think better of them.

Something flickers across his face—relief, desire, triumph—and then he's closing the distance, his mouth finding mine in a kiss that starts gentle but quickly turns hungry. His lips are softer than I expected. I gasp against him, and he takes advantage, deepening the kiss until I'm clutching his shoulders just to stay upright.

His hands slide into my hair, cradling the back of my head as he shifts my face toward him, granting him better access. I've been kissed before—plenty of times—but never in a way that leaves me feeling claimed, overwhelmed, undone.

When we finally separate, both of us are breathing hard. He rests his forehead against mine, his eyes still closed, as though he's savoring something he's ached for far too long.

Warmth unfurls in my belly, nerves lighting up as his breath meets mine. My lips are swollen, my pulse thrumming through me, reaching places it shouldn't. His hands are still tangled in my hair, but now his thumb grazes the edge of my jaw, a slow stroke that makes me shiver.

"I've wanted this since high school," he mutters. "You were the one I couldn't fucking touch."

The words rip through me. My fingers fist in his shirt, dragging him closer, desperate. When his mouth crashes back to mine, there's nothing gentle left, just fire and want and the raw promise of everything we've been denying. His tongue teases mine, his teeth catch my bottom lip, and I'm gasping into him, melting, burning, needing more.

By the time we break apart, my lungs are starving for air, but I don't care. I can still taste him, still feel the imprint of his body against mine, and all I want is to close the space again and lose myself in him completely.

I press my forehead to his chest, trying to steady my breathing. My whole body is buzzing, every inch of me alive from his touch, but the rush of it all collides with a heavy knot in my stomach. Too fast. Too soon.

He feels it—of course he does. His hands loosen in my hair, trailing downward until they fall away completely. He steps back, as though distance is the only thing holding him together.

"Damn it." He drags a hand down his face, his shoulders lifting and dropping in a rough attempt to shake off the last few seconds. "I shouldn't have done that. I'm sorry."

The words cut deeper than I expect, hollowing me

out. Sorry. Like the kiss we just shared was a mistake instead of the most alive I've felt in years.

I stare at him, thrown off balance, but he's turned slightly away now, fists flexing at his sides as if he's holding something in check.

"I want you," he finally grinds out, chest tight and restless, "but you just got out of hell. The last thing you need is me making it worse."

My throat tightens, caught between relief that he understands and a desperate ache that he's pulling away. Because if that kiss was any indication, worse might be exactly what I want.

CHAPTER 9

BRAYDEN

I'M the world's biggest asshole.

This thought has been on repeat in my skull all night, a bad country song looping endlessly while I stared at the guesthouse ceiling. Even now, as I pull into the hospital parking lot, it's still hammering at me. The sun has barely crawled above the horizon, but I've been awake for hours, replaying that kiss.

What the hell was I thinking? She just got out of a marriage with a serial cheater, and what do I do? I go after her the first chance I get, acting with all the restraint of a hormone-fueled teenager.

I kill the engine on my bike and sit there for a moment, letting the early morning chill settle into my bones. It feels deserved after the surge of heat that tore through me when her lips parted beneath mine and when her fingers gripped my shirt as though she needed something to hold on to.

"Fucking idiot," I mutter, pulling off my helmet.

Last night—after a kiss that nearly set the guest-house on fire inside my chest—I somehow found the strength to step back. To apologize. To finish feeding her spaghetti in awkward silence before driving her back to the church, where her father waited with a face that could've summoned a storm.

He hadn't said a word to me. Just nodded once, his eyes tracking Cece as she walked inside still wearing my hoodie.

She'd tried to give it back. I told her to keep it. Like some lovesick high school kid trying to hold onto a piece of her. I didn't tell her about the way my skin had burned where she touched me, or how I had to take the longest cold shower of my life after she left.

I shake my head, trying to clear it as I walk toward the hospital entrance. I'm not here for her. I'm here for my aunt.

The hospital's automatic doors slide open with a quiet hiss, releasing the distinctive smell of antiseptic. I've spent more time in places like this than I care to remember—waiting rooms while brothers got patched up after fights gone wrong, emergency rooms after road accidents, and once, a long night in a trauma center when I wasn't sure if I'd make it to morning.

"Visiting hours don't start until eight," the receptionist says without looking up as I approach the desk.

"I'm family," I reply, keeping my voice even despite the way her expression shifts when she finally looks at me, taking in the cut, the tattoos visible on my neck. "Jillian and Harold Miller. Room 342."

She hesitates, and I can practically see the debate flicker behind her composure—follow protocol or avoid confrontation with the scary biker.

"They're expecting me," I add, which isn't exactly a lie. My aunt is always expecting me, whether I show up or not.

"I'll need to see some ID."

I pull out my wallet and hand over my driver's license. She studies it longer than necessary, like she's memorizing my address or maybe just surprised I have legitimate ID.

"Thank you, Mr. Cole." She hands it back reluctantly. "Elevators are to your left."

I nod and head in that direction, ignoring the curious stares from the night shift nurses. I'm used to it —the sideways glances, the way people suddenly find something important to do when I walk by. My cut might as well be a force field for how effectively it keeps people at a distance.

The elevator ride to the third floor is mercifully empty. I lean against the wall, exhaling slowly as I try to get my head straight before seeing Aunt Jillian. She's got a sixth sense for when something's bothering me.

The doors slide open, and I follow the numbered signs down a quiet hallway. Most of the rooms are dark, patients still sleeping, but I can see light spilling from 342.

I knock softly before pushing the door open. "Morning."

Aunt Jillian looks up from her knitting, her face breaking into that sunrise smile that's been my one constant. She's sitting in the chair beside Uncle Harold's bed, her gray hair pulled back in its usual neat bun, a half-finished scarf draped across her lap.

"Brayden, what on earth are you doing here at this ungodly hour?" she asks, but her eyes are bright with pleasure. She sets her knitting aside and holds out her arms for a hug.

I cross the room and bend down, careful not to disturb the various tubes and wires connected to Uncle Harold as I embrace her. She smells like lavender and that fancy hand lotion she's been using since I can remember—the one she claims keeps her hands young despite decades of hard work.

"Just checking in," I say, straightening up to glance at Harold. He's sleeping peacefully, the steady beep of his heart monitor creating a soothing rhythm in the otherwise quiet room. "How's he doing?"

"Better. Doctor says we might be able to go home tomorrow if his numbers stay good." She pats the chair beside her. "Sit. You look like you haven't slept a wink."

I sink into the chair, not bothering to deny it. "Been busy."

"Mmhmm." She gives me that look—the one that says she can see right through my bullshit. "I heard you've been making quite the impression around town. Fixed the church van, brought in enough food to feed an army, and..." she pauses dramatically, "been spending time with Cecelia."

"It's not like that," I say automatically.

"Like you're interested in her," Aunt Jillian says with that irritating knowing smile she's perfected.

I shift uncomfortably in the hospital chair. "We're just working on the charity drive together."

"And riding motorcycles together. And having dinner together at my guesthouse."

I shoot her a look. "You spying on me now?"

"I have eyes and ears all over this town, Brayden. You know that." She reaches over to pat my hand, her touch gentle despite the arthritis that's starting to twist her fingers. "And I think it's wonderful."

"There's nothing wonderful about it," I mutter, dragging a hand through my hair. "She just got out of a bad marriage. The last thing she needs is someone making her life harder."

"Someone like you," Aunt Jillian repeats, brow lifting. "And what exactly is that supposed to mean?"

I gesture at myself—at the cut, the ink crawling up my arms, the whole rough-edged package. "Come on, Jillian. Look at me. You know."

"No," she says, setting her knitting aside, which is never a good sign. "I don't know. What I *do* see is a man who dropped everything to help run a toy drive for kids he doesn't even know. A man who's been taking care of his aging aunt and uncle without a single complaint. Riding a motorcycle and wearing a leather vest doesn't make you the villain, Brayden. You've had a soft spot for that girl since the day you set foot in this house. Don't throw away a second chance just because you're scared of what it means."

"That's not how I remember it," I say, keeping my voice low so I don't wake Harold.

"It's exactly how things turn out if you let them," Aunt Jillian replies, picking up her needles again. The quiet click-click fills the room, steady as her heartbeat. "And for what it's worth... Cecelia's been through more than you realize."

"Yeah, I know about her ex. Real piece of work."

"Not just him." She glances at Harold's sleeping form, then back at me. "That girl's been living her whole life trying to meet everyone else's expectations. First her father's, then Ethan's. She never got to figure out what she wanted."

Something in my chest tightens. "Sounds familiar."

"Thought it might." She gives me a knowing look. "Only difference is you ran away to find yourself. She did what was expected of her."

I lean back in the chair, letting her words sink in. "I didn't run away. I got kicked out."

"Semantics." She flicks her hand dismissively. "Point is, maybe what she needs isn't someone who fits neatly into that perfect little world she's been suffocating in. Maybe she needs someone who can show her there's life outside it."

"And you think that's me?"

Aunt Jillian's confidence in me is worse than any guilt trip she's ever laid on me. At least with guilt, I know how to push back. But this blind faith that I'm somehow what Cece needs? I don't know how to process that.

"You're giving me too much credit," I mutter, watching the steady rise and fall of Uncle Harold's chest. "I'm not some knight in shining armor."

"No, you're better," she says, those knowing eyes pinning me in place. "You're real. And that girl has had enough fairy tales to last a lifetime."

I scrub a hand over my face, feeling the stubble I didn't bother to shave this morning. "I kissed her," I admit, the words falling out before I can stop them. "Last night."

Aunt Jillian's knitting needles pause mid-stitch. "And?"

"And nothing. I apologized and took her home."

She stares at me like I've just told her I'm giving up motorcycles for competitive ballroom dancing. "You apologized? For kissing her?"

"Yeah," I shift uncomfortably. "It was too soon."

"Says who?"

"Says common sense. Says the fact that her life is complicated enough without adding me to the mix."

The needles start clicking again, faster now. "Did she kiss you back?"

"Yeah," I finally admit. "She did." I can still feel the way her fingers curled into my shirt, the soft gasp against my mouth.

"Well then." Her smile is triumphant, like she's just won an argument I didn't know we were having. "Maybe you should let her decide what's too soon for her, instead of making that choice yourself."

The heart monitor beeps steadily in the background as I consider her words. Uncle Harold stirs slightly in his sleep, mumbling something unintelligible before settling back into stillness.

"It's not that simple."

"Love rarely is." She sets her knitting aside and leans forward to take my hand in hers. Her skin is paper-thin now, blue veins visible beneath the surface, but her grip is still surprisingly strong. "But that doesn't mean it's not worth the trouble."

"Who said anything about love?"

"Nobody needed to, dear."

I'm saved from having to respond by a soft knock at the door. A nurse pokes her head in, her smile professional but her eyes wary when they land on me.

"Just checking vitals," she says, moving to Uncle Harold's bedside.

I stand up, grateful for the interruption. "I should get going anyway. Got some things to take care of."

She releases my hand with a sigh. "You're running away again."

"I'm not running," I protest, but the excuse sounds weak even to my ears. "I've got club business to handle."

"Mmm-hmm." She gives me that look again, the one that sees through my bullshit. "Well, before you go running off to your very important club business, you might want to know that the town tree lighting festival is tonight."

"And I care about that because…"

"It's Cece's favorite town holiday tradition. Just thought you'd like to know that."

"Since when do you keep track of Cece's favorite anything?" I ask, trying to sound casual.

"Oh, please. I've known that girl since she was in diapers. Her mother used to help me with the church bazaar before she passed. Cecelia loves Christmas more than anyone I know. That tree lighting is the one thing she never misses—not even the year she had mono in high school."

"Tree lighting," I repeat, as though I'm committing it to memory. I actually am, even though I'm pretending I don't care. "What time?"

Aunt Jillian's smile is so smug I want to roll my eyes. "Seven o'clock sharp in the town square. They do the countdown, light the big tree, then everyone sings carols and drinks hot chocolate. Very Norman Rockwell."

"Sounds miserable."

"For you, maybe. For *her*, it's magic." She picks up her knitting again, the needles clicking in a steady rhythm. "Though I suppose a tough biker such as yourself wouldn't be drawn to anything so wholesome."

I recognize the manipulation tactic for what it is. "I didn't say I wasn't interested."

"So you'll go?"

"I didn't say that either."

The nurse finishes checking Harold's vitals and writes something on his chart, then gives me a professional nod before leaving the room. I take that as my cue to go, leaning down to press a kiss to Aunt Jillian's soft cheek.

"Love you," I murmur against her skin, inhaling the familiar scent. "Tell the old man I said hey when he wakes up."

"I will." She pats my face with her weathered hand. "And Brayden? Sometimes the best Christmas gifts are the ones we don't think we deserve."

I give her a look at the not-so-subtle hint, but her words follow me out of the hospital room and into the elevator. Tree lighting. Seven o'clock. Town square. The information loops in my head as I stride across the parking lot to my bike.

I'm not going to that tree lighting. It's not my scene —too many people, too much cheer, too many memories of standing on the outside while the rest of the town celebrated without me. Besides, after last night, Cece probably needs space. Time to remember why getting involved with someone of my reputation is a terrible idea.

But as I swing my leg over my bike, I already know I'm full of shit. I'll end up at that damn tree lighting tonight, watching her from a distance the same way I did in high school, pretending I'm not hoping she'll look my way.

Some things never change.

CHAPTER 10

CECE

I HADN'T EVEN PLANNED on coming to the tree lighting tonight. After that kiss with Brayden yesterday, the one that's been replaying in my mind like a movie I can't stop watching, I'd planned to hide in my room with a bottle of wine and pretend the festival didn't exist. But Dad insisted, saying the church needed to "present a united front" after the board meeting drama.

So here I stand, freezing my ass off in the town square, wearing Brayden's hoodie under my coat because I couldn't bring myself to take it off. It still smells like him.

"Cece!" Mrs. Henderson waves frantically from the hot chocolate booth, her Santa hat tilted at a precarious angle. "Come help us serve! We're short-handed!"

Before I can stammer out an excuse, Mrs. Henderson thrusts a ladle into my hand and practically drags me behind the booth. Great. Now I'm stuck serving lukewarm cocoa to the gossip vultures. I'd been blissfully oblivious until this morning at Coastal Grounds. The moment I pushed through the door, twenty conversations crashed to a halt, leaving nothing but the hiss of the espresso machine and twenty pairs of eyes burning holes through my coat. Message received, San Salona. I'm the main course on your rumor menu this Christmas.

I pour cup after cup, my smile growing more strained with each "Merry Christmas" I force past my lips. The town square is packed, twinkling lights, holiday carols blast from the speakers, and even the fluttering of fake snow is shot into the air is doing nothing to improve my mood. I'm filling yet another cup when I see them.

My hand freezes mid-pour, hot chocolate spilling over the rim and onto my fingers. I barely register the burn.

Ethan stands by the massive Christmas tree, looking as though he stepped straight out of a J.Crew catalog in his camel coat and cashmere scarf. And draped on his arm, every bit the polished accessory, is Brittany—platinum hair cascading over shoulders that clearly aren't shivering in her too-thin coat. Why choose something warm when you can choose something attention-grabbing?

Brittany. My husband's former administrative

assistant. The woman who used to bring me coffee when I visited his office—while carrying on an affair with him the moment the place emptied out.

"Careful there, dear," Mrs. Henderson says, grabbing a napkin to blot up my spill. "You're wasting cocoa."

I can't look away as Ethan throws his head back, laughing at something Brittany said. The way his hand settles on the small of her back. The way she leans into him, sliding neatly into the role I once filled.

That used to be me.

"Cece? Are you listening? We need more marshmallows."

"Sorry," I mumble, passing the ladle to her. "I'll get them."

I duck under the table, grateful for the momentary escape, and pretend to search for marshmallows that are clearly visible in the plastic bin right in front of me. I need a minute to breathe, to steady my shaking hands, to swallow the lump of hurt that's suddenly blocking my throat.

It shouldn't matter. We're divorced. He moved on before we even signed the papers. I knew he was seeing her. But seeing them together—so public, so... happy—tears open a wound I thought had finally begun to heal.

"Found them," I announce with false brightness, emerging from under the table with the marshmallow bag. Mrs. Henderson gives me a look that's half concern, half curiosity.

"You alright, dear? You look like you've seen a ghost."

"I'm fine," I lie, the words automatic after months of practice. "Just cold."

I pour more hot chocolate, focusing intently on not spilling it this time. My fingers are sticky with the earlier spill, and I wipe them discreetly on a napkin. I can feel eyes on me, not just Mrs. Henderson's, but others too. Word has already spread that Ethan and his new girlfriend are here, and everyone wants to see the ex-wife's reaction.

San Salona's favorite spectator sport is watching other people's pain.

I'm so focused on appearing unbothered that I don't notice him approaching until Mrs. Henderson's breath catches audibly beside me.

"Oh my," she murmurs.

I look up, and my heart does something complicated in my chest when I spot Brayden striding through the crowd. He isn't trying to blend in—not that he could even if he tried. His cut is impossible to miss, a sharp presence in a sea of holiday cheer, and people practically leap aside as he makes a direct path toward the hot chocolate booth.

For me.

"Two hot chocolates," he says, his voice a steady rumble that somehow cuts through the Christmas music blaring from the nearby speakers. His gaze never shifts, and heat rises up my neck that has nothing to do with the steaming beverage I'm serving.

"Sure," I manage, grateful that my tone doesn't betray the riot in my chest. I fill two cups, my hands steadier than they have any right to be. "Marshmallows?"

"Definitely." The corner of his mouth quirks into that almost-smile that makes my stomach flip. "The more the better."

I pile marshmallows into his cups, acutely aware of Mrs. Henderson practically vibrating with gossip potential beside me. When I hand the drinks over, our fingers brush, and I swear I feel it all the way to my toes.

"Thanks, princess." The words are soft, meant only for me, and the nickname sends a shiver down my spine that has nothing to do with the December chill.

"You're welcome." I try for casual, but the words come out breathier than intended. "I didn't think this was your scene."

"It's not, but hey, life would be boring if you didn't try something new from time to time," he shrugs.

It's not lost on me that he ordered two cups. "Did you come here with Jillian?"

"Nope," he smirks.

A pit forms in my stomach. He ordered two cups, but if his aunt's not here, who is the second cup for? I'm about to ask who the other hot chocolate is for when he lifts one cup in a small toast.

"This one's for me," he says, taking a sip and leaving a tiny marshmallow mustache on his upper lip that makes him look surprisingly boyish. "And this one's for you. Figured you could use a break."

"I can't just leave," I whisper, though every cell in my body is screaming at me to do exactly that. "I'm supposed to be helping."

"Mrs. Henderson won't mind," he says confidently, loud enough for her to hear. "Will you, ma'am?"

Mrs. Henderson, who's been pretending not to eavesdrop, nearly jumps out of her sensible shoes at being addressed directly by a man in a motorcycle cut. "I...well..."

"See? She's fine with it." He holds the second cup out to me, challenging me to take it.

I hesitate for just a second before untying the volunteer apron. "I'll be back in a bit," I tell Mrs. Henderson, as I duck under the counter and join Brayden on the other side.

"No, you won't," he murmurs as he hands me the hot chocolate, his fingers brushing mine deliberately this time.

The warmth of the cup is nothing compared to the heat that flares in my chest at his touch. I take a sip to hide how my hands are shaking. The rich chocolate warmth slides down my throat, grounding me in this moment. With him.

"You planned this," I accuse, unable to stop the smile tugging at my lips.

"Guilty." He takes another sip, his gaze never leaving mine. "Heard it was your favorite Christmas thing."

"Jillian told you," I realize, feeling a rush of fondness for his meddling aunt.

"She might've mentioned it." He steps closer, his body shielding me from the curious stares around us. "She also mentioned you never miss it. Even had mono one year and still dragged yourself here."

"I can't believe she remembers that." I laugh, feeling the tension in my shoulders start to ease despite the crowded square and all the people watching. "I was sixteen and miserable, but I wasn't going to miss seeing that tree light up."

"Why is it so important to you?"

I take another sip, considering. "My mom loved Christmas. After she died, this was the one tradition my dad kept alive, exactly the way she did it. It's like...for these few minutes every year, she's still here."

Something shifts in Brayden's expression—a subtle softening that makes my heart flutter. "That's—"

"Well, well. If it isn't my ex-wife."

Ethan's voice cuts through the moment, sharp enough to freeze me in place. My entire body tightens as I turn slowly, my cup of hot chocolate suddenly heavy in my grasp. Brittany, his secretary, hovers at his side, her lips tilted in a practiced expression she must think passes for sympathy, though it lands closer to smugness.

His gaze flicks between Brayden and me, narrowing slightly when it lands on the Heaven's Rejects patch. "I see you've...moved on." The way he says it makes it sound like I've taken up with a serial killer. Though now that I think about it—nope. Not going there.

"Is there something you need?" I ask, deliberately ignoring his comment.

Brittany leans into him, her hand possessively clutching his arm. "We just wanted to say hello. Be friendly."

"Friendly," I repeat, the word tasting bitter on my tongue. "That's certainly a new approach for you two."

Ethan's polished smile falters for just a second. "No need to be nasty, Cece. It's Christmas, after all."

I feel Brayden shift beside me, his body angling slightly forward as if preparing to step between us. His presence feels solid at my back, steadying in a way I hadn't expected.

"Yeah, it *is* Christmas, which is why I'm trying to enjoy the festival. If you'll excuse us, I have better places to be."

Ethan's jaw tightens, and I can practically hear his veneers grinding. "I see that time apart hasn't fixed your attitude problem."

"Attitude problem?" I fire back. "My attitude wasn't the issue in our marriage, Ethan. Your inability to stay faithful was the issue. See exhibit A—" I gesture toward Brittany. "Or is she closer to Z by now? Have we moved on to numbers yet?"

Brittany gasps, her immaculately manicured hand flying to her mouth. The sound is so theatrical, I half expect a director to jump out from behind the Christmas tree and yell *cut.*

Ethan's face darkens, his carefully cultivated public image cracking right in front of me. "You know what? I felt bad for you. Thought maybe we could be civil. But clearly, you're still the same bitter, ungrateful—"

"Finish that sentence," Brayden cuts in, "I dare you."

The temperature seems to drop ten degrees as Brayden's massive frame shifts between Ethan and me. I can only see his back, but the sudden rigidity in his shoulders speaks volumes.

Ethan falters, the bravado draining from his face as he takes in Brayden's full height and build. "This doesn't concern you."

"See, that's where you're wrong," Brayden says, his tone conversational but with an undercurrent that raises the hair on my arms. "It became my concern the moment you opened your mouth."

People around us have gone quiet, the festive chatter dying as they tune in to the drama unfolding. From the corner of my eye, I can see Mrs. Henderson frantically waving to someone—probably my father.

"You have no idea who you're dealing with," Ethan hisses, trying to claw back some authority but ending up angrier lapdog than actual threat.

"Do I look concerned?" Brayden's voice drops to a deeper, harder register, and I see Ethan swallow.

"You should. My father—"

"Isn't here," Brayden finishes for him. "It's just you. And from where I'm standing, you're nothing but a spoiled little boy in daddy's expensive coat."

I step up beside Brayden, feeling strangely empowered by his presence. "It's not worth it," I tell him, though part of me would love nothing more than to see Ethan taken down a peg.

Brayden's eyes never leave Ethan's face, but I feel his body shift slightly closer to mine. "Your call, princess."

The nickname makes Ethan's face flush an ugly shade of red. "Princess? Is that what you're calling her? That's rich. You have no idea what you're getting yourself into. She's high maintenance, frigid, and—"

Brayden moves so fast I barely register it happening. One second he's beside me, the next he has Ethan by the collar of his expensive coat, lifting him slightly so he's on his tiptoes. Brittany shrieks and jumps back, her hot chocolate splashing onto the pavement.

Brayden growls, his face inches from Ethan's. "I told you to stop talking."

The crowd around us has gone completely silent, the Christmas music suddenly feeling jarring against the tension crackling in the air. I can see my father pushing his way through the crowd, his face a storm of concern and fury.

"Let him go," I say quietly, placing my hand on Brayden's arm. His muscles are rigid under my touch, coiled with restrained violence.

For a moment, I think Brayden won't listen. His grip tightens on Ethan's collar, and I catch the flicker of real fear crossing my ex-husband's face. Then, with visible effort, Brayden releases him, shoving him back so hard Ethan stumbles into Brittany.

"You're fucking crazy," Ethan gasps, straightening his coat with shaking hands. "Both of you."

"Care to test just how crazy I can be, asshole? Keep fucking insulting her, and you'll fucking find out."

"How dare you speak to me–"

Brayden snarls. "You have two choices, Ethan. Take your flavor of the week and leave or stay here and see what happens. Your choice."

Ethan opens his mouth like he's going to argue, but one look at Brayden's face changes his mind. He grabs Brittany's arm and pulls her away, muttering something about "calling my father" as they retreat through the parting crowd.

My father reaches us just as they disappear, his expression a mix of concern and disapproval. "Cecelia, what on earth. This is not the place for a scuffle. Have you no—"

"Not now, Dad," I cut him off, ignoring the hurt that flashes across Dad's face. My skin is buzzing with left-over adrenaline, and my heart's pounding so hard I can feel it in my ears.

Dad looks between Brayden and me, his mouth pressed into that thin line of disappointment I know all too well. "This isn't the place for...whatever this is."

"You're right," I agree, surprising him. "It's not."

I look at Brayden. He hasn't moved, still as stone beside me, but I can feel the tension rolling off him. His eyes catch mine—dark, feral, alive. I should fear that look. Instead, I feel it spark somewhere deep, where fear and want blur together.

"Let's get out of here," I say, the words coming out before I can second-guess them.

Brayden's expression shifts, surprise quickly replaced by that intensity that makes my knees weak. "You sure?"

"Cecelia," my father warns, stepping closer. "Think about what you're doing."

That's the thing—for once, I'm not thinking. I'm feeling. And right now, all I feel is the desperate need to be anywhere but here, with the entire town watching this drama unfold as though it's their own personal Hallmark movie gone wrong.

"I'll be fine, Dad," I tell him, even managing a smile.

"You're leaving with him?" Dad doesn't even hide his disapproval of the idea.

"Yes." Without a second thought, I turn to Brayden, reaching down to grab his hand. "Can we please go?"

Brayden nods once, his fingers curling around mine with a gentle pressure that grounds me. "My bike's around the corner."

Dad's face falls, that familiar disappointment etching deeper lines around his mouth. "The board meeting was difficult enough, Cecelia. This isn't helping matters."

For a moment, guilt tugs at me—the lifetime habit of trying to please him, to be the daughter he deserves. But then I feel Brayden's thumb brush across my knuckles, a silent reminder that I'm allowed to choose for myself.

"I'll see you at home later," I tell Dad, trying to soften the blow. "Save me some eggnog."

He doesn't answer—just stares with that wounded look as Brayden leads me through the parting crowd. The whispers start immediately, sharp and eager, but this time they don't make me flinch. Let them stare. Let them talk.

Tomorrow, the whole town will be buzzing about me walking away from the Christmas tree lighting on the arm of a biker...right after nearly throwing hands with her ex-husband.

Good.

Let them choke on the story.

I'm done living small just to keep everyone else comfortable.

"You okay?" Brayden asks as we reach the edge of the square, away from the worst of the crowd. He searches my face, and I realize he's genuinely concerned, not just asking to be polite.

"Yeah," I say, though I'm not sure if it's true. My heart is still racing, adrenaline coursing through my veins.

His fingers are still intertwined with mine, warm and solid and real. "If you want, I can take you home."

The thought of going back to my father's house, of sitting in tense silence waiting for the sermon he will preach to me about my poor decision making, makes my chest tighten. "I don't want to go home."

Brayden studies me for a long moment, his expression unreadable in the dim glow of the Christmas lights strung across the buildings. "Where do you want to go?"

"Anywhere," I tell him honestly. "Just...not here."

He nods, understanding without needing more explanation. That's the thing I'm learning about Brayden. He doesn't require the constant reassurances and justifications I've been trained to provide my entire life. He takes my hand and leads me to where his bike is parked just around the corner from the square. The massive machine gleams under the streetlights. Brayden pulls a helmet from his saddlebag and gently places it over my head, his fingers lingering as he fastens the strap under my chin before swinging his leg over the seat. I climb on behind him, wrapping my arms around his solid waist without hesitation this time. The engine roars to life between my thighs, sending vibrations through my entire body. I press myself against his back, seeking his warmth.

We pull away from the curb, leaving behind the twinkling lights and carolers, the hot chocolate and my father's disappointment. The cold wind stings my cheeks, but I don't care. For the first time in months, maybe years, I feel like I can breathe again.

CHAPTER 11

CECE

I'VE NEVER BEEN MUCH of a runner, but right now my legs are carrying me out of the town square with a determination I didn't know I had. Brayden's bike rumbles beneath us, devouring the asphalt as the festival fades behind. The wind lashes at my cheeks, leaving them stinging, but I don't care. All I register is the solid line of his back against my chest and the steady vibration of the engine beneath us.

"Hold tighter," Brayden calls over his shoulder, and I react instantly, wrapping my arms around him until there's no space left to close.

We take curves I've driven a hundred times, yet they feel transformed at this speed, on this machine, with him guiding us. Each bend pulls our bodies into the same motion, moving together as though this isn't our first ride but our hundredth. The ease of it should unsettle me, but instead it feels as though I've stepped into something I've needed for a long time without realizing it.

I don't ask where we're going. For once, I don't need a destination or a plan. Just being in motion—away from the stares, the whispers, and Ethan's self-satisfied expression—is enough.

When Brayden finally eases off the throttle, we roll into the overlook above town. During the day, tourists stop here to photograph San Salona tucked in its valley, every storefront and rooftop arranged so neatly it could be framed. At night, the view shifts into a spread of twinkling lights, the entire town glowing below us, transformed into something almost enchanted from this distance—far enough that none of its flaws can reach me.

I suck in a breath as Brayden kills the engine. The sudden silence feels deafening after the constant roar of the motorcycle. My arms are still wrapped around him, my fingers clutching the leather of his cut.

"You can let go now," he chuckles. "Or not. I'm good either way."

I reluctantly loosen my grip and slide off the bike, my legs wobbly beneath me. The adrenaline that carried me through the confrontation with Ethan is starting to fade, leaving me shaky in its wake. Brayden swings his leg over the bike with an easy grace that makes something flutter in my stomach.

He takes off his helmet, running a hand through his dark hair, "You okay?"

"I think so," I manage. "I just...I can't believe I did that."

"Did what? Stood up to that asshole?" Brayden steps closer, close enough that I can feel the heat radiating from his body in the cold night air. "He deserved worse."

"Not that." I shake my head, fumbling with my helmet strap. "Left. In front of everyone. With you."

His hands replace mine on the strap, gently undoing the buckle. "Regretting it already?"

"No," I say quickly. Too quickly. "That's the scary part. I don't regret it at all."

The helmet comes off, and the cold air slams into my face. I should be shivering at this height, yet Brayden's presence seems to blunt the worst of it. Or maybe the rush of adrenaline still hasn't settled.

"Come here," he says, leading me to the wooden guardrail that separates the overlook from the steep drop below. "Look at it."

San Salona glitters beneath us like fallen stars, the Christmas lights transforming the town into something beautiful and distant. From up here, you can't see the gossip and judgment, the narrow minds and narrower streets. Just light and possibility.

"It looks so small. So innocent."

"Hard to believe it's the same place down there that we just left," I murmur, wrapping my arms around myself against the chill.

"That's the thing about distance. It changes your perspective."

He shrugs out of his cut and drapes it over my shoulders before I can protest. The leather is still warm from his body, and that intoxicating scent of him envelops me.

"I can't take this," I protest, though I'm already sliding my arms through the arm holes.

"You're shivering," he points out. "And I run hot."

I run my fingers over the embroidered edges, feeling the worn leather beneath my fingertips.

"I know I am not that well versed in the whole biker culture, but are you supposed to just lend out your colors like this?" I ask, only half joking.

His mouth quirks up in that almost-smile that makes my heart stutter. "What they don't know won't hurt them."

I turn back to the view, trying to ignore how the leather seems to warm me from the inside out.

"So was she…?" he asks, trailing off.

"If you mean, was she the mistress that finally broke apart our marriage? Yup, that's her," I confirm. "I can't believe he brought her home for Christmas. He knew I was coming home."

"That's precisely why he did, sweetheart. To hurt you."

"You think?" I ask, though I know he's right. The realization stings more than the cold air whipping across the overlook. Ethan brought her here specifically to hurt me. To show everyone in town he'd upgraded from his boring ex-wife to the blonde bombshell who'd been waiting in the wings.

"I know," he sighs. "Men like that, they need to win. Need everyone to see them winning."

I let out a shaky laugh that clouds in the night air. "Well, it worked. Until you nearly lifted him off the ground by his cashmere scarf."

"Sorry about that," he smiles, though he doesn't sound sorry at all. "I should've controlled myself better."

"No. Don't apologize. It was..." I trail off, searching for the right word.

"Hot?" he supplies, that cocky smile playing at his lips.

"I was going to say satisfying."

"Liar," he teases, bumping his shoulder against mine. "But I'll take satisfying."

We stand in comfortable silence for a moment, watching the twinkling lights below. In the distance, I can make out the soft glow emanating from the town square, growing brighter by the second. The giant Christmas tree must be lit now, the culmination of the festival I just abandoned.

"Look," I mutter, pointing down at the sudden burst of light at the center of town. "They're lighting the tree."

Even from up here, I can see the massive pine transform from a dark silhouette into a towering beacon of multicolored lights. For twenty-five years, I've watched that tree light up from the ground, surrounded by familiar faces and hot chocolate. Now I'm seeing it from above, as if I've stepped outside my own life for a moment.

"First time you've missed it?"

"Yeah," I admit, surprised to find I'm not devastated. "But somehow, this view might be better."

He turns to look at me then, his eyes reflecting the distant lights of the town below. Something shifts between us. A current in the air that makes my breath catch. His gaze drops to my mouth, and I feel myself swaying toward him like he's gravity and I'm helpless against the pull.

"Brayden," I whisper, and it's both a question and an answer.

His hand comes up to cup my cheek, thumb brushing across my skin with a tenderness that makes my heart ache. "Tell me to stop," he murmurs, echoing his words from the night before.

This time, I have no desire to.

"Don't," I say, my voice barely audible over the wind. "Don't stop."

This time when his lips meet mine, there's no hesitation, no gentle introduction. He kisses me, pulling me closer until I'm pressed against the solid wall of his chest. I clutch at his shirt, suddenly grateful for the guardrail at my back because my knees have gone weak.

The kiss deepens, his tongue sliding against mine in a way that makes heat pool low in my belly. I gasp into his mouth, and he swallows the sound, his free hand settling at my waist, fingers digging into my hip through the layers of his cut and my coat.

When we finally break apart, we're both breathing hard, clouds of vapor mingling between us in the cold air. His forehead rests against mine, and I can feel the steady rhythm of his heart matching my own.

"I've been wanting to do that again since yesterday," he admits. "Haven't thought about much else."

"Me neither," I confess, surprising myself with my honesty.

His thumb traces my bottom lip, still sensitive from his kiss. "What are we doing, Cece?"

It's a loaded question—one I don't have an answer for. What are we doing? Crossing boundaries that shouldn't be crossed. But standing here with Brayden's taste still on my lips and his cut heavy on my shoulders, I can't bring myself to care.

"I don't know," I answer honestly. "But I don't want to stop."

"You sure about that, princess?" His voice dips. "Because if we cross that line… I'm not the kind of man who holds back."

A shiver rolls through me—heat, not cold. "Maybe I'm done with people tiptoeing around me," I say, breath catching. "Like I'm something fragile."

His hands find my waist, pulling me in until there's no space left between us. "You're a hell of a lot tougher than they give you credit for."

"Then prove it," I fire back. "Stop acting like I'll shatter."

For a heartbeat, he just looks at me, something unreadable flashing across his face. Then his mouth crashes back to mine. This kiss is all hunger and need, his hands claiming every inch they touch.

I try to get closer despite the layers between us. When his teeth graze my bottom lip, I gasp, and he takes advantage, deepening the kiss until I'm dizzy with want.

His hands slide down to my hips, lifting me easily until I'm sitting on the guardrail, the wooden edge digging into the backs of my thighs. The position puts us at eye level, and I wrap my legs around his waist instinctively, pulling him closer.

"Careful, princess," he warns against my lips. "We're playing with fire out here."

"I'm not afraid of getting burned," I whisper. And it's true. After the frost that defined my marriage, the heat rising between us feels almost redemptive.

His hands slip beneath his cut, then under my coat, and when his fingers find the spot where *his hoodie* has ridden up, they meet bare skin. Hot, rough, deliberate.

The first stroke up my waist nearly buckles my knees.

God—how can one touch hold so much? His fingers move with a care that makes me feel seen in a way I've never known.

I shiver, breath catching, but he knows damn well it isn't from the cold.

His gaze drops to the hoodie hanging off me, sleeves swallowing my hands, hem shifted by his touch. A look sweeps through his eyes—hungry, possessive.

"Fuck," he breathes, thumbs pressing harder into my hips. "You in my hoodie… you don't even know what that does to me."

Oh, I know. I can feel it in every place we're touching, every place we're not.

He leans in, his lips brushing a slow path along my jaw, each touch deliberate, as though he's memorizing the feel of my skin. His breath is hot, his voice even hotter.

"I should get you warm," he murmurs, though his hands are already beneath the edge of my hoodie, resting at my waist with a familiar certainty. "You're freezing."

"I'm warm," I whisper, tugging him closer by the front of his cut, dragging his mouth back to mine. *God, I need him. I need this.* "Don't stop."

He releases a sound that's half-groan, half-exhale, something unguarded that sends a spark racing through me. His grip tightens, drawing me fully against him, his breath rough against my throat as he tries—and fails—to steady himself.

If this is him holding back…I don't stand a chance when he really lets go.

He chuckles, the sound low and rough, rolling through me like a slow burn. It settles in my bones, in my stomach, in every place that already aches for him.

"As much as I'd love to forget the world right

here…" His thumb strokes my hip, lazy and possessive, and my breath catches. "You'll be shaking from the cold before I'm even close to being done admiring you."

His voice is pure gravel. That look in his eyes? It steals what little control I have left. Heat, want, and something that feels dangerously close to devotion.

He leans in just enough that his breath brushes my ear.

"When I fuck you for the first time," he murmurs, the words a promise and a threat all at once, "it's going to be somewhere warm. Somewhere I can put my hands everywhere I've been wanting to." His fingers tighten on my waist, dragging me closer. "Somewhere I don't have to rush. Somewhere I can take…my…time."

My knees nearly buckle, heat flashing through me so fast it's dizzying.

And God help me—I want that. All of it.

"The first time?" I ask softly.

His mouth curves, slow and certain. "First of many, baby."

The look in his eyes sends a shiver down my spine, half warning, half invitation. I swallow hard.

"Then take me somewhere warm," I whisper, my fingers brushing the line of his throat. "Take me back to your place."

His eyebrow arches. "Why not yours?"

I laugh, the sound carrying away on the night breeze. "My father's house? Are you insane? He'd have an exorcist waiting at the door."

"Fair point." His hands tighten on my waist, lifting me effortlessly off the guardrail and setting me on my feet. "My place it is."

CHAPTER 12

CECE

THE RIDE back to Jillian's property feels different than before. My body is pressed against his, my thighs squeezing his hips tighter than necessary, my hands wandering lower on his stomach than they need to be for safety. Every curve in the road is an excuse to hold him closer, to feel the hard planes of his body through his clothes.

By the time we pull up to the guesthouse, I'm practically vibrating with anticipation. Brayden cuts the engine. He swings his leg over the bike and helps me off, his hands lingering at my waist.

"Last chance to back out, princess," he reminds me as he removes my helmet.

I look up at him, feeling the weight of the moment

between us. This is a threshold I can't uncross. In my old life, this would be the moment I'd make the *responsible* choice—back away, thank him for the ride, and head home to my father's house where I'd lie awake all night wondering what could have been.

But I'm not that woman anymore.

"I'm not backing out. I want this. I want you."

He takes my hand, leading me toward the door. The anticipation building between us is almost unbearable as he fumbles with his keys. When the door finally swings open, we barely make it inside before his mouth is on mine again, hungry and demanding.

He kicks the door shut behind us, and I'm suddenly pressed against it, his body pinning me in place as his hands roam down my sides. His cut still hangs from my shoulders, heavy and warm, smelling of leather and him. I should take it off, but there's something thrilling about wearing it while he devours my mouth.

"You have no idea what you do to me," he growls against my lips. "Seeing you in my colors..."

I gasp as his calloused fingers trail fire across my ribs, inching higher. "Tell me," I demand, wanting to hear it.

"Makes me want to mark you as mine," he finishes, his voice a low rumble against my throat where his lips have started to trail hot, open-mouthed kisses. "Let everyone know you belong to me."

The possessiveness in his words should frighten me, but instead it sends liquid heat pooling between my thighs. I arch into him.

"Is that what this means?" I ask breathlessly as his teeth graze the sensitive spot where my neck meets my shoulder. "Wearing your colors?"

His hands slide higher, thumbs brushing the undersides of my breasts through my bra. "To anyone in my world? Yeah. It means you're claimed. Protected."

"And is that what you want?" I gasp as his fingers finally reach their destination, cupping me through the thin fabric. "To claim me?"

He pulls back just enough to look me in the eyes, his gaze burning with an intensity that steals my breath. "Since the moment I saw you in that coffee shop, tearing that asshole mayor a new one."

I laugh, the sound quickly transforming into a moan as his thumb brushes over my nipple. "That's what did it for you? Me making a scene?"

"You standing up for yourself," he corrects. "Not taking shit from anyone. Being the real you instead of who everyone expects you to be."

No one has ever wanted me for being myself. They've wanted me to be quieter, more obedient, more proper. But, Brayden, he sees me. The real me. The one hidden under all the layers. The woman who has been silently screaming inside of me, begging to be let out.

"Take me to your bed," I demand.

He doesn't need to be told twice. In one fluid motion, he lifts me, his hands cupping my thighs as my legs wrap around his waist. I cling to his shoulders, marveling at how easily he carries me through the darkened guesthouse. His mouth never leaves mine as he navigates the short hallway to the bedroom.

When he lowers me onto the bed, I expect urgency, the same hunger that's been building between us since that first ride on his motorcycle. Instead, he pulls back, standing at the edge of the bed looking down at me with an intensity that makes my skin flush.

"What?" I ask, suddenly self-conscious under his scrutiny.

"Just looking at you. Lying in my bed. Wearing my cut."

I glance down, realizing I'm still wrapped in his leather vest. The heavy patches gleam in the dim light filtering through the curtains—Heaven's Rejects in bold lettering. The mirror across the room shows my hair is wild from the wind and his hands, my cheeks flushed with desire, my lips swollen from his kisses. I barely recognize myself.

And I love it.

"Come here," I demand, reaching for him.

He shakes his head slowly, a smile spreading across his face. "Not yet, princess. First, I want to see you."

"You are seeing me," I point out.

"Not all of you." His hands go to the hem of his shirt, pulling it over his head in one fluid motion that makes my mouth go dry. His torso is a masterpiece of muscle and ink, tattoos spreading across his chest and down his arms in intricate patterns I want to trace with my tongue.

"Your turn," he says, and it's not a request.

I push his cut off my shoulders, letting it fall to the bed beside me. Then I reach for the hem of his hoodie pulling it over my head with far less grace than he managed. I'm suddenly grateful I wore my good bra today—black lace instead of the practical cotton I usually default to.

Brayden's eyes deepen as they move over my newly exposed skin. "Fuck," he breathes, the single word carrying so much awe it sends heat rushing through me.

"Look at you," he murmurs, his fingers tracing the edge of my bra where it meets my skin. "So fucking beautiful."

I've never felt beautiful with Ethan—pretty, maybe, when I was dressed up for his work functions. Attractive in the way a suitable accessory is attractive. But beautiful? Like this? Never.

"You don't have to say that," I whisper, my hands finding his shoulders, needing to touch him, to ground myself in the reality of this moment.

He looks up at me. "I don't say shit I don't mean, Cece."

His hands slide up my ribs, around to my back where he finds the clasp of my bra with practiced ease. He pauses, waiting for permission. I nod, unable to form words as anticipation tightens my chest.

The fabric falls away, and I resist the urge to cover myself. Ethan always made me self-conscious about my body—too curvy, not toned enough, never matching the women in the magazines he left around our bathroom.

But Brayden's gaze lands on me as though I'm something extraordinary.

"Christ," he breathes, his hands hovering just inches from my skin. When his calloused palms finally cup my breasts, I gasp at the contrast between rough skin and gentle touch. His thumbs brush over my nipples, a small moan escaping my lips.

"So responsive," he murmurs, leaning forward to replace one hand with his mouth. The hot, wet slide of his tongue sends a jolt through me, my fingers tangling in his hair to hold him closer.

My head falls back as he lavishes attention on my breasts, alternating between gentle kisses and hungry nips that have me squirming beneath him. I've never felt desire this sharp and insistent, overwhelming every rational thought until all that remains is emotion and urgency.

"Brayden," I gasp as his teeth graze a particularly sensitive spot. "Please."

He pulls back, looking up at me with a dark hunger. "Please what, princess? Tell me what you want."

"I want…" The sentence stumbles, old habits clamping down before I can finish it. Then I meet his eyes, see the way he centers his whole attention on me, and suddenly the truth doesn't feel so impossible to say. "I want to feel you. All of you."

A smile—not his usual half-smirk but something genuine and devastating—spreads across his face. "That can be arranged."

His hands move to the button of my jeans, flicking it

open with practiced ease. I lift my hips as he slides them down my legs, taking my underwear with them in one smooth motion. The cool air hits my bare legs, raising goosebumps across my skin.

"Beautiful," he says again, his eyes drinking me in as I lie before him, completely exposed. His hands run up my calves, over my knees, along my thighs, leaving trails of fire in their wake. When his fingers reach the apex of my thighs, I hold my breath, anticipation coiling tight in my belly.

His thumb brushes over me, and my hips buck involuntarily at the contact. A smug smile plays at his lips as he repeats the motion, more deliberately this time.

"So wet already. Is that all for me, princess?"

"Yes," I gasp as he applies more pressure. "Brayden, please."

"Please what?" he teases, his fingers tracing maddening circles that have me writhing beneath his touch. "Use your words, Cece. Tell me exactly what you want."

"Touch me," I manage.

"I am touching you," he points out, his wicked smile growing as his fingers continue their torturous path.

"More," I demand. "I need more."

His fingers slide inside me, and I gasp at the sudden intrusion, my back arching off the bed. His thumb continues its relentless circles as he works his fingers deeper, curling them in a way that makes stars explode behind my eyelids.

"Fuck, princess," he groans, his free hand gripping my thigh. "Your hungry cunt has a vice grip on my fingers. I can't wait to feel you wrapped around my cock."

I'm rambling now, half-formed words slipping out as the moment sweeps me under, everything in me tightening with a rising, breathless urgency I haven't felt in years. It's been so long since anyone has touched my heart, my needs, my longing with this kind of care —if anyone ever has. His focus is absolute, his attention so complete it feels as though nothing exists beyond the way he's trying to understand me, to read me, to give me space to feel everything I've been denying myself.

"Please," I beg.

"Not yet," he argues. "Not until I know you can take me, baby. You're too fucking tight, and I am not about to hurt you."

His thumb presses harder against my clit as his fingers work inside me, stretching and preparing me. My hips rise to meet his hand, desperate for more.

"I need to see you come," he growls, increasing his pace. "Need to feel you fall apart on my fingers before I take you properly."

The pressure builds with each thrust of his fingers, each circle of his thumb. I'm close—so close—teetering on the edge.

"That's it," he urges. "Let go for me, princess."

And I do. The release hits me hard, a rush that swallows my breath and scatters every coherent thought. His name tears out of me before I can stop it, my body reacting with a force that shakes me to my core. He stays with me through it, guiding me through every lingering tremor until I'm loose, breathless, and melted into the sheets.

When I finally manage to open my eyes, he's watching me with an intensity that sends my pulse skittering. Slowly—deliberately—he lifts his hand, the same one that undid me moments ago, and draws his fingers to his mouth. His eyes stay locked on mine as he does it, and the look he gives me… God. It sends heat curling low in my belly all over again, even though I'm still recovering from the last of those shattering tremors.

"I need you, Brayden." I reach for his belt, but he captures my hands, pressing them into the mattress.

"Patience, princess. We've got all night."

"I don't want patience," I argue, tugging my hands free to reach for him again. "I've been patient my whole life. I want you inside me."

"Then who am I to deny you?" He growls in agreement and pushes himself off me, moving to the bedside table. I watch him, admiring the play of muscles across his back as he yanks open the drawer. His movements suddenly still, and I hear him mutter something under his breath.

"What's wrong?" I prop myself up on my elbows.

"These condoms..." He holds up a small foil packet, examining it in the dim light. "Fuck. They expired when I was in high school." He tosses it back in the drawer with disgust.

My heart skips a beat, but not from disappointment.

The responsible part of me should be concerned, but something reckless has taken hold tonight.

"It's fine," I tell him, sitting up fully. "I'm on birth control. Have been for years." It was one of the few rebellions I'd managed against my father's expectations —a private decision he never knew about. "And I'm clean. Got tested after...after I found out about Ethan. Are you…"

"Clean," he freely admits. "Not that the idea of fucking you bare doesn't excite the shit out of me, but I'm going to ask again. You're good without a condom?"

"Yes," I answer as I slide forward on the bed. "More than okay."

I reach for his fly, my fingers working the button of his jeans. I'm done with hesitation, done with waiting. The metal gives way under my touch, and I drag the zipper down slowly, feeling his body tense as my knuckles brush against him through the denim.

"Jesus, Cece," he hisses, his hands fisting in the sheets beside my hips.

I look up at him through my lashes, enjoying the way his jaw clenches as I hook my fingers into his waistband. "You talk too much," I tell him, tugging his jeans down his hips. "Less talking, more action."

His laugh turns into a groan as my hand finds him through his boxers, stroking the hard length of him. He's...substantial. I now understand why he was stalling earlier. There is absolutely no way on this Earth that he will fit. Even with his very extensive prep work,

I'm starting to have doubts that this monster will not rip me in half.

Brayden notices. He steps in closer, crowding me until my back presses into the mattress again. One hand slides up my thigh, slow and sure, as if he's reminding me this was my idea and he's going to make damn sure I understand what I asked for.

"You look like you're about to say a prayer," he mutters. "Go on. Let's hear it."

I blink up at him, heart pounding. "What?"

He leans in, his lips brushing mine, just barely. "You want to get on your knees for something holy, don't you?" His hand curls around himself, and he strokes once, slow and dirty. "Then start praying, sweetheart. But not to your daddy's god. Pray to the man who is about to fuck you senseless."

My breath catches, heat flooding low in my belly. My thighs clench around him as he pushes them apart again with a quiet grunt. He drags the head of his cock along my soaked entrance, just enough to make my hips jerk. I'm already slick, already aching, but he doesn't push in. Not yet.

"Say it," he growls. "Say who you're begging for."

"Brayden." His name falls from my lips, breathless. Not nearly enough.

He slaps the head of his cock against my clit, just once.

"Not good enough."

I look at him, fire burning in my chest, my cheeks, my thighs. And I give him what he wants.

"I'm praying to you."

He smiles, and it's not kind. It's hunger. Triumph. Possession. "That's right. Say your prayers, Cece." Then he thrusts into me.

All the air leaves my lungs. My body stretches around him, shocked and greedy all at once. I cry out, legs instinctively locking around his hips, grounding myself as he buries himself to the hilt. He doesn't move. He waits, watching me take him.

"You feel that?" His hand wraps around my throat, not tight, just there. A promise. "That's your new religion."

I nod, mouth open, chest heaving, absolutely undone.

"Good girl," he says. Then he starts to move.

He starts to move, slow at first, just enough to let me feel the weight of him dragging against every nerve ending inside me. Each thrust is deliberate, grinding, his hips rolling with lethal control. Not fucking. Not yet. This is a claiming.

"You still praying?" he asks, lips brushing the edge of my jaw.

I can't speak. I nod, barely.

He pulls back and drives in harder. My breath punches out of me as if he knocked it from my lungs.

"Use your words, angel."

"Yes," I gasp. "I'm praying."

"To who?"

"You."

He groans like I just made him lose control. One

hand fists the sheets beside my head, the other tightens just slightly at my throat—not to choke, just to hold me there, to make me feel owned.

"That's right. Say it again."

I moan as he drives into me again, rougher this time, the sound of our bodies meeting loud in the quiet room. The preacher's daughter, legs spread, back arched, begging to be ruined by a man who doesn't play by rules. A man who would burn churches down before ever kneeling in one.

"You," I breathe. "I'm praying to you, Brayden. I want all of it."

His mouth crashes into mine. This kiss isn't tender. It's possessive, wet, and consuming, as if he wants to swallow every lie I was ever told about what love is supposed to look like.

"You've been waiting your whole life for this," he growls, dragging his teeth down my throat. "For someone to take what's theirs."

"Yes," I whimper, rocking up to meet him.

"For me to take what's mine."

He shifts, deeper now, angling his hips until he hits a spot that makes me cry out. He does it again. And again.

"That's it," he grits out, sweat starting to slick across his chest. "You feel that? This is where you break."

His fingers slide down between us, finding my clit without hesitation. He rubs tight, filthy circles in rhythm with his thrusts, eyes locked on mine, begging to see me fall apart.

"You come for me," he growls, rough and breathless. "Right here. Right now."

I try to hold on, but it's impossible. The pressure coils, white-hot and relentless, until it snaps all at once. I cry out his name, legs shaking, body clenching around him as the orgasm crashes over me.

He groans as I squeeze around him, his rhythm faltering.

"That's it, baby. You're mine now."

And when he follows me over the edge, spilling inside me with a growl torn from somewhere deep and primal, I swear I feel it everywhere. Not just inside, but under my skin, in my blood, in the places I thought were untouchable.

When it's over, he stays there, breathing hard against my neck, both of us tangled in heat and sweat and something neither of us dares name.

He presses a kiss just beneath my ear and whispers, "Amen."

His breath warms the hollow of my neck, slow and ragged, chest rising and falling against mine. He's still hard inside me, still holding me open around him, like he carved a place for himself inside of me, and now he refuses to leave.

I shift beneath him, sensitive and overstimulated, but craving more.

He feels it.

"Fuck," he growls, barely lifting his head. "You're still clenching around me."

I can't answer. My throat is raw from crying out his

name, and my body is still reeling. But I want it again. Deeper. Slower. Meaner. Whatever way he'll take me.

His hand finds my jaw, thumb dragging across my lower lip.

"You got one more in you?"

I nod, dazed. "Yeah."

"Thought so." He kisses me, slow this time, but no less intense. He tastes like sweat, and sin, and ownership.

Then he starts to move again.

The pace is different now. No urgency, no rush. Just long, deliberate thrusts that make me feel every inch of him, every inch of myself. I'm sore, stretched, and already unraveling all over again. And he doesn't let me hide from it.

"You feel that?" he murmurs. "That's me, inside every part of you."

I nod again, eyes fluttering.

"You're taking my cock so good, princess," he continues, breath thick and filthy. "Like you were made for it. Like you've been waiting for me."

"I have," I whisper.

A flicker crosses his face. That dark, disarming softness only men like him know how to wear. He leans in close, lips brushing my ear.

"Say it again."

"I've been waiting for you."

"Good girl," he rasps.

He thrusts harder, just once, and I cry out, nails digging into his arms. "Oh, God."

"You don't pray to him anymore. You pray to me now."

I moan, already close again. The rhythm of his hips becomes punishing, reverent. My name falls from his lips, a benediction wrapped in the grit of everything he isn't supposed to feel. He reaches between us again, fingers finding my clit, circling in time with his thrusts.

"You gonna fall apart for me again, baby?"

"Yes," I gasp.

"That's right," he growls. "Break for me."

And I do. Loud, feral, helpless. Another orgasm crashes through me harder than the first, stealing sound from my throat and thought from my head. I can feel him losing it too, his rhythm unraveling, his jaw tight, every muscle locked.

He thrusts one last time and holds himself there, deep inside, groaning my name like it's the only thing keeping him grounded.

When it's over, he collapses beside me, dragging me into his chest, still breathing hard.

The room is silent, save for the sound of our bodies cooling, the mess we made between us still warm.

He kisses the top of my head and mutters, "Guess I found something worth believing in."

CHAPTER 13

BRAYDEN

I WAKE to the unfamiliar weight of a woman's body pressed against mine. Not just any woman. *Her*.

For a moment, I lie completely still, convinced that if I move, she'll vanish. That last night was just another fucked up dream my brain cooked up to punish me.

But she's warm. Solid. Real. Her dark hair spills across my chest, catching the thin strips of morning light sneaking through the blinds. One of her legs is thrown over mine, her breathing slow and steady against my skin.

Cece. In my bed. Wearing nothing but the marks I left on her.

Jesus Christ.

I've had women. More than I probably deserve. But

waking up with her tucked against me, fitting there with an ease that unsettles me, feels like something entirely different—something I was never meant to cross into.

I should get up. Make coffee. Put some distance between us before she wakes and reality hits. Before she remembers who I am and starts regretting every moment of last night.

Instead, I pull her in closer. Her scent hits me, sweet and warm, tangled with sex and my own skin. She smells like mine.

Fuck.

She stirs against me with a soft little sound that curls straight down my spine. My body reacts immediately, pressing hard against her thigh. She feels it. I know she does.

Her lips curl into a smile against my chest before her eyes even open.

"Good morning," she murmurs. The sleepy rasp in her voice does dangerous things to me.

"Morning," I manage, trying to keep my voice neutral. Like I wake up with her every day. Like this isn't reshaping everything I thought I knew.

When she finally looks up at me, her eyes are clear. No regret. No panic. Just Cece—looking at me as though I matter.

"You're thinking too loud," she says, stretching against me with lazy confidence. The shift of her body sends warmth sliding across my skin, and I have to steel myself.

"Just wondering if you're having second thoughts," I admit, because there's no point in pretending otherwise.

She props herself up on one elbow, hair falling in a curtain around her face as she studies me. The sheet slips down, exposing the curve of her breast, marked with faint bruises from my mouth. Pride and a deep, unsettling satisfaction curls through me at the sight.

"Are you?" she asks.

I laugh, the sound harsh even to my own ears. "Fuck no."

Her smile is slow, satisfied. "Good." She leans down and presses her lips to mine, the ease of it making it feel as though this has always been ours. "Because I'm not either."

Relief hits me harder than it should. I slide my hand into her hair, holding her there for another kiss, deeper this time. She makes that little sound again, the one that makes me want to bury myself inside her all over again. My hand slides down her back, tracing the curve of her spine.

"I should probably warn you," she says, pulling back just enough to speak against my lips. "I'm not usually a morning person."

"Could've fooled me," I mutter, my hand finding the curve of her ass, squeezing hard enough to make her gasp.

She bites her lip, a flush spreading across her cheeks. "You're a bad influence."

"Baby, you have no idea." I roll us so she's beneath

me, her hair fanned out across my pillow like spilled gold. The sight of her there—sleep-warm and marked up, looking at me—it does something to my chest. Something I'm not ready to name.

I'm about to show her exactly how bad an influence I can be when her phone chimes from somewhere on the floor. She groans, dropping her head back against the pillow.

"Ignore it," I growl, dipping my head to taste the hollow of her throat.

"I can't." She squirms beneath me but makes no real effort to get away. "It could be my dad."

The mention of her father douses everything in an instant. Right. Her Preacher father. Whose daughter I thoroughly defiled last night. *Multiple* times.

I roll off her with a grunt, immediately missing her warmth. "Go ahead," I say, watching as she scrambles to find her phone in the tangle of clothes we left on the floor.

She hesitates, then slides out of bed. I peek at her from under my arm, watching as she moves naked across my bedroom, all soft curves and faint bruises. My marks. My claim. I've never been particularly possessive before, but something about seeing her wear the evidence of last night makes my blood run hot.

She digs through our discarded clothes, finding her phone in the pocket of her jeans. When she checks it, her whole body goes rigid.

"Shit," she mutters. "Shit, shit, shit."

I sit up. "What is it?"

"My dad," she says, her face going pale. "He's sent me five texts and called twice."

I sit up straighter, watching as she scrolls through her messages, her free hand coming up to cover her mouth.

"What does he want?" I ask, though I already know the answer. Daddy's little girl didn't come home last night. And I'm the reason why.

"He's worried sick. Says he waited up until midnight, then started calling hospitals." She looks up at me, panic replacing the soft contentment from moments ago. "He's threatening to call the police if I don't respond in the next thirty minutes."

"So call him," I say, trying to sound casual even as something tightens in my chest. This is how it starts—reality crashing in. Her remembering who she is, who I am, and all the reasons this was a mistake.

She nods, but doesn't dial. Instead, she stares at her phone as if it might bite her. "What do I even tell him?"

I swing my legs over the side of the bed, suddenly aware of my nakedness in a way I wasn't before. "Whatever you want. That you stayed with a friend. That you're fine. Or tell him the truth—that you spent the night getting fucked six ways to Sunday."

"Don't be an asshole."

"Just being realistic, princess." I stand, grabbing my boxers from the floor and stepping into them. "I'm just saying, you've got options."

The hurt in her eyes shifts to something more

complicated. Not anger, exactly, but enough to know that I am fucking this up already.

"Is that what you want me to do?" she asks. "Lie to him? Pretend this didn't happen?"

I scrub a hand over my face, suddenly feeling cornered. "I want you to do whatever makes this easier for you."

"That's not an answer, Brayden."

She's right, and we both know it. I'm dodging, because the truth is I don't know what I want her to do. Part of me—the part that's been keeping people at arm's length my whole life—wants her to lie. Keep me separate from her real life. The other part, the part I don't recognize, wants her to claim me.

"Look," I say, grabbing my jeans. "Call your dad. Tell him you're safe. The rest...we can figure out later."

She watches me for a long moment, then nods, her shoulders slumping slightly. She dials, pressing the phone to her ear while I try not to eavesdrop on her conversation.

"Dad? Yes, I'm fine. I'm so sorry I worried you." Her tone softens, slipping back into the polished composure she carried the first time I saw her in town. It's a mask settling into place.

But then something changes. Her spine lengthens, her shoulders lift with purpose, and a new steadiness sharpens her words.

"No, Dad." she says firmly. "I'm with Brayden."

I freeze in the middle of zipping up my jeans. Did she just...?

"Yes, I stayed with him last night."

Holy shit. I wasn't expecting that.

"No, Dad, I'm a grown woman." Her tone rises, edged with frustration. "I'm thirty-two years old. Who I spend my time with is my business."

I can hear the tinny murmur of her father on the other end, though not the words. Whatever he's saying makes Cece's jaw tighten.

"That's not fair and you know it." She paces a few steps, her free hand gesturing emphatically.

I lean against the wall, arms crossed, watching this unfold. I should probably give her privacy, but I can't make myself walk away. Not when she's defending me to her father.

"No, I will not pray for redemption. If you think I need prayers for spending the night with a man who has made me feel more in the last few days than in the last few years I spent married to Ethan, then maybe we need to have a different conversation about faith."

The fire in her is something to witness. She stands there with nothing but determination, gripping her phone as if it's a shield while she defends what happened between us. I should feel smug watching her take her holier-than-thou father down the few pegs he's earned, but part of me knows this surge of courage might be fleeting—a moment of boldness she may second-guess later.

"No, I won't be coming home right now." Her voice drops, hardening into something I haven't heard from her before. "I'll come by later today to talk. But right now, I'm hanging up."

She pulls the phone from her ear, her thumb hitting the end call button with more force than necessary. For a moment, she just stands there, staring at the dark screen, her chest rising and falling rapidly.

"Well," she says finally, not looking at me, "that went about as well as expected."

"You could have just lied to him, Cece."

She turns to face me, chin tilted up in defiance. "I could have," she shrugs. "But I was taught lying is a sin. I'm done hiding. Done letting other people decide who I should be." She runs a hand through her tangled hair, a gesture I'm starting to recognize as her gathering her thoughts. "I spent my entire marriage pretending to be someone I'm not. I won't do it again."

My throat feels tight. "Even if it costs you?"

"Fuck the costs."

My eyebrows shoot up at the curse coming from her perfect lips. I can't help the laugh that erupts from my chest, breaking the tension between us.

"Well, goddamn, princess. That's quite the dirty little mouth you suddenly got there."

Her eyes narrow, but there's a spark of playfulness dancing there that sends a pulse of heat through me.

"Maybe you've been a bad influence on me," she says, crossing her arms over her chest. The movement pushes her breasts together, and I force my gaze back to her face.

"Oh, I've definitely been a bad influence," I agree,

stepping closer to her. "And I plan on being an even worse one before I'm done with you."

She doesn't back away when I crowd her space. Instead, she tilts her chin up, defiant and beautiful in her nakedness.

"Is that a promise?"

"Baby, that's a guarantee." I reach out, tucking a strand of hair behind her ear, letting my fingers linger on her cheek. "You sure about this, though? About your dad?"

The playfulness dims slightly, replaced by something more serious. "Yeah," She leans into my touch. "I'm done living my life to someone else's standards."

"Even if it's me you're not hiding?"

She steps closer, completely unashamed of her nakedness. "The entire town already knows I rode off with you last night. It's not exactly a secret anymore, so there's no reason to start hiding now."

"Fuck," I breathe out, something expanding in my chest. Something volatile. Something that feels too much like hope. "You're something else, you know that?"

"Is that good or bad?" she asks, a hint of vulnerability slipping through her bravado.

"It's exactly what I wanted to hear," I tell her—and it's the truth. I draw her into my arms, her warmth settling against my chest. "Say it again."

"What part?" Her hands slide up my arms, leaving goosebumps in their wake.

"The part where you don't give a fuck what anyone thinks."

She grins up at me, wicked and beautiful. "I don't give a fuck what anyone thinks." The curse rolls off her tongue with the ease of someone who's been saying it her whole life, not just since I pulled her onto my bike.

"Christ, hearing you swear does things to me," I growl, my hands finding her hips, squeezing hard enough to make her gasp.

She knows exactly what she's doing, standing there naked and unashamed, full of fire. My fire.

I walk her backward until the backs of her thighs hit the edge of the bed. She lets me guide her, never breaking eye contact. That mouth of hers—defiant, dirty, irresistible—is parted slightly like she's waiting for what comes next.

"You know what else I want to hear from that mouth?" I ask.

She tilts her head, playing innocent. "What?"

I lean in close, letting her feel the heat of my breath against her ear. "I want to hear what you sound like when your dirty little mouth is put to work."

She shivers, just slightly, but doesn't flinch. Doesn't back down.

"On what?" she asks, soft and sharp at the same time.

I grip her jaw gently, tilting her face toward mine. "On me."

Her lips part, a flush creeping across her chest, and I

feel her pulse pick up beneath my fingers. She's breathing faster, but her gaze never drops. That's what makes her irresistible.

"You gonna kneel for me, Cece?" I murmur, letting one hand trail down her body, slow and deliberate. "Gonna show me just how unholy that mouth of yours can be?"

Her breath hitches. "Only if you ask nicely."

I let out a low, humorless chuckle, my thumb brushing the corner of her mouth. "There's nothing gentle about what I want from you right now."

She bites her lip, then sinks to her knees in front of me without another word.

Her knees hit the floor with a soft thud, and I swear I forget how to breathe. And fuck me, nothing in my life has ever looked more like worship.

I've seen women on their knees before, plenty of them, but never like this. Never with that look in their eyes.

She holds my gaze as her fingers find my zipper, tugging it down with deliberate slowness. I should help her, should hurry this along, but I'm transfixed by the sight of her kneeling before me like I'm worth the sin.

"You just gonna stare?" she asks.

"Maybe." I reach down, threading my fingers through her hair. "Maybe I enjoy seeing you this way."

She smiles, wicked and sweet all at once. "And here I thought you wanted my mouth busy with something other than talking."

"Oh, I do." I tighten my grip on her hair, just enough to make her gasp. "But don't rush. We've got time."

Her eyes flicker with something—surprise, maybe. Like she expected me to be all demand and no patience, she doesn't know yet that I could watch her for hours, tracing every freckle, every scar, every perfect imperfection of her.

She tugs my jeans down, along with my boxers, and I spring free, already hard enough to hurt. Yeah, she remembers what it felt like inside her.

"Go on," I murmur. "Show me what that mouth can do besides talk back."

She licks her lips, a nervous gesture that makes my cock twitch. Then she leans forward, gaze still locked on mine, and wraps her lips around the head.

Holy fucking Christ. I've never prayed a day in my life, but fuck, I may start now.

I hiss through my teeth, my hand tightening in her hair. Wet, hot suction envelops me, and it takes everything I have not to thrust forward, to take what I want. But I force myself to stay still, to let her set the pace.

She starts slow, tentative, almost as if she's relearning something forgotten. I wonder briefly if that dickhead ex-husband of hers ever let her do this, or if he was too concerned with propriety to let his wife get on her knees. The thought makes a deep, possessive pull stir inside me.

"That's it," I encourage, watching as she takes me deeper. "Just like that."

She makes a little humming sound, pleased with

herself, and the vibration sends a jolt straight to my core. I let my head fall back, a groan escaping my throat as she grows bolder, taking more of me, her tongue exploring with growing confidence.

"Fuck," I breathe, looking down to watch her. The sight nearly undoes me—her lips stretched around my cock. "Look at me."

Her eyes open, meeting mine. I cup her cheek with my free hand, feeling the movement of my cock inside her mouth. "That's it, baby. You're taking me so good."

She moans around me, and I feel her hand come up to grip my thigh, steadying herself as she takes me deeper. The other wraps around what she can't fit in her mouth, working me in rhythm with her lips.

"Jesus Christ," I hiss. "Where'd you learn to do that?"

She pulls back, just enough to speak, her lips shiny and swollen. "Maybe I'm a natural."

The sass, even now, makes me laugh—a strained, desperate sound. "Get back to work, princess."

She grins up at me, all wicked innocence, before taking me in again, deeper this time. Her tongue swirls around the head, teasing the sensitive spot underneath, and I feel my control slipping. My hips jerk forward involuntarily, pushing deeper into her mouth. She doesn't pull away—takes it, adjusts, even with tears streaking down her face.

"Fuck, I'm sorry," I mutter, trying to hold still.

She pulls back just enough to say, "Don't be," before

taking me again, deeper, her hand guiding my hip now. Encouraging.

Holy shit. She wants it. Wants me to let go.

I tighten my grip in her hair, testing. "You sure about this?"

Her answer is to relax her throat, taking me even deeper, and I swear I see stars. I start to move, careful at first, shallow thrusts that have her humming around me. When she doesn't pull back, I get bolder, setting a rhythm that has us both breathing hard.

"Look at you," I groan, watching her take me. "The preacher's daughter, on her knees for a man like me."

She moans her answer. She likes it. Likes the reminder of who she is, who I am, how wrong this should be. My perfect, filthy angel.

"You like that, don't you?" I growl. "Knowing what your daddy would say if he could see you now."

She moans around me, and I feel her free hand slip between her own legs. Fuck. She's touching herself while she sucks me off. The sight of her touching herself while I'm in her mouth is too much. I've never been a religious man, but watching Cece get herself off while taking my cock down her throat? That's a kind of worship I can get behind.

But as good as her mouth feels, as much as I want to finish right there between those now swollen lips, I want something else more. I want to send her back to her father's house with a reminder of exactly who she belongs to now. I want her walking through that sanctimonious house with my cum sliding down her thighs.

I pull back suddenly, yanking her up by her hair. Her eyes are glazed, lips swollen and wet. She looks confused, bereft.

"Brayden?" she questions.

"Get on the bed," I growl, already manhandling her up. "Hands and knees."

She scrambles onto the mattress, assuming the position without hesitation, looking back at me over her shoulder. Her ass is raised, presenting herself to me like an offering.

"Like this?" she asks, and there's a teasing note in her voice that makes me want to spank her.

So I do. My palm connects with her right cheek, the sharp crack echoing in the room. She gasps softly, her posture shifting in response.

"Exactly like that," I tell her. I position myself behind her, running my hands along the curves of her ass. She looks breathtaking in this moment—spine bending with confidence, hair cascading over her shoulders, daring me with nothing more than her gaze to ruin her.

"You ready for me, princess?" I ask, lining myself up against her entrance. She's already slick, already wanting.

"Yes," she breathes, pushing back against me. "Please, Brayden."

I push into her with one smooth thrust, bottoming out inside her. The tight heat of her nearly undoes me right there. She gasps, fingers clutching at the sheets as she adjusts to the sudden fullness.

"Fuck, you feel good," I groan, gripping her hips hard enough to leave marks.

I start moving, setting a punishing pace that has her moaning with each thrust. The sound of skin slapping against skin fills the room, mixed with her breathless cries and my own rough grunts. I reach up and thread my fingers through her hair, tugging just enough to tilt her head back. I need to see her—really *see* her.

The flushed cheeks.

The parted lips.

The unfiltered want in her eyes.

The sight of her like that—open, wrecked, meeting me with the same intensity I'm giving her—nearly undoes me.

"You like being fucked from behind like an animal by a man your daddy would call the devil himself?" I growl, driving deeper.

"Yes," she moans, the word broken and desperate. "God, yes."

I slam into her harder, watching her face contort with pleasure. There's something fucking beautiful about her coming undone on my cock, begging for more, taking everything I give her. Her skin is flushed pink, her lips parted, eyes half-closed in ecstasy.

"Touch yourself," I command. "I want to feel you come around me."

She obeys without hesitation, one hand snaking beneath her to find her clit. I feel the exact moment she touches herself—her walls clench around me, a broken moan escaping her throat. The feel of her pleasuring herself while I drive into her from behind is almost enough to push me over the edge.

But I hold back. I want to feel her come apart first.

"Take it," I growl, slapping her ass again, harder this time. "Take all of it."

She's close—I can feel her walls fluttering around me, her body shaking beneath my hands. I lean over her, one hand braced beside her head, the other snaking around to replace hers, my fingers finding her clit.

"Oh God," she gasps. "Brayden, I'm going to—"

"Do it," I demand, circling her clit faster, matching the rhythm of my thrusts. "Come for me. Let me feel it."

She shatters with a cry that sounds like salvation, her body clenching around me, milking me for all I'm worth. The sight of her coming undone beneath me, because of me, pushes me over the edge. I drive into her one last time, burying myself to the hilt as I empty inside her with a guttural groan.

For a moment, we stay frozen, both of us panting. Then her arms give out, and she collapses onto the mattress. I follow her down, careful not to crush her, my body still joined with hers.

"Holy shit," she breathes, her words muffled by the pillow.

I chuckle against her shoulder, pressing a kiss to the damp skin there. "Yeah."

I roll off her, careful not to hurt her as I collapse onto the mattress beside her. She turns her head to look at me, her cheek still pressed against the pillow, hair a tangled mess across her face. There's something so goddamn perfect about her like this, thoroughly fucked, glowing, mine.

"I don't think I can walk," she mumbles, a lazy smile spreading across her face.

"Good." I reach out, brushing her hair away from her face. "That was the plan."

She laughs, the sound soft and unguarded. "You're terrible."

"And yet, here you are."

"Here I am," she agrees, turning onto her side to face me properly. Her eyes search mine, suddenly serious.

For a long moment, neither of us speaks. The room feels smaller, quieter. The only sound is her breathing.

Her fingers drift along the edge of one of my tattoos, tracing the curve of ink as though she's trying to learn me through touch alone. "What happens now?" she whispers.

I could tell her the truth—that I don't know. That people in my world don't get to hold on to good things. That morning light has a way of burning down anything that feels right once the dark is gone.

But I can't make myself say any of it.

Instead, I catch her hand and press a kiss to her knuckles. "Now, you sleep. Let the world wait for once."

She studies me for another heartbeat, then nods, her lashes lowering as she settles back against me. Within moments, her breathing evens out, her body softening into mine.

I stay awake, staring at the cracked ceiling, her scent still lingering on my skin. The sun creeps through the blinds, painting stripes across the tangled sheets, across her shoulder, across me.

And for the first time in longer than I can remember, I don't feel the urge to run.

CHAPTER 14

CECE

THE WHOLE RIDE to my dad's house, I'm rehearsing what I'll say, but all the words evaporate the moment Brayden pulls up to the curb. Dad's probably watching from behind the curtains, counting my sins each second I spend pressed against Brayden's back.

"You sure you don't want me to come in?" Brayden asks as I swing my leg off his bike. "I don't mind facing the firing squad."

I hand him back his helmet, fighting the urge to run my fingers through my tangled hair. "And give my father an actual target? No thanks." I try for a smile, but it feels wobbly. "Let me handle him first. No sense in both of us getting crucified."

Brayden gives the house a once-over, his jaw tightening with a verdict he doesn't voice.

"If you need an escape, call," he murmurs. "I'll be here in five."

"I'll be fine." I rise on my toes to kiss him, quick but certain. "Can I come by tonight? I'll drive myself so you don't have to keep playing chauffeur."

He catches my hand before I can step away, his thumb tracing slow circles over my pulse. "And miss the excuse to keep you close?" A teasing curve lifts the corner of his mouth. "Not a chance."

The warmth of his gaze makes my knees weak, but I force myself to step back. "I'll text you when I'm free."

"I'll be waiting," he promises, revving his engine.

I stand on the sidewalk watching until his bike disappears around the corner. Only then do I turn to face my childhood home, squaring my shoulders like I'm walking into battle. Which, knowing my father, I am.

The front door feels heavier than it should as I push it open. The house smells the same as always—lemon polish and old books, with the faint undertone of coffee. Dad's Sunday sermons are spread across the dining table, pages of notes and highlighted Bible verses in his familiar scrawl.

"Dad?" I call out, hanging my purse on the hook by the door.

The silence stretches for a moment before I hear movement from his study. When he appears in the hallway, the disappointment on his face is exactly what I expected.

"Cecelia." Not Cece. Never Cece when he's upset. "I see you've decided to come home after all."

I resist the urge to fidget the way I used to when I came home past curfew. "I told you I would."

He studies my appearance—rumpled clothes, messy hair, the faint mark on my neck left by Brayden's mouth —as though he's cataloging every supposed wrong-doing etched on my skin. I've stood under this same scrutiny a hundred times before: after school dances, after my first date with Ethan, after news of my divorce spread through the congregation.

But this time, something in me refuses to fold under it.

"I was with Brayden, exactly as I said. And I'm not apologizing."

Dad's lips press into a thin line. "That man is dangerous, Cecelia. The people he associates with—"

"Are none of our business," I interrupt. The words feel foreign in my mouth. I've never cut him off before. "I'm a grown woman, Dad. I make my own choices."

"Choices have consequences." He gestures toward the living room. "We should sit."

I follow him, noticing how the house feels smaller now, as though I've outgrown the space without real-izing it. The floral couch—home to countless lectures over the years—greets me with an unsettling familiarity. Dad takes his usual armchair, the one that always positions him as though he's presiding over court rather than having a conversation.

"Your mother would be heartbroken to see you this way."

A familiar ache blooms in my chest at the mention of Mom. She's been gone for twelve years, yet Dad still wields her memory whenever he needs leverage.

"Mom would want me to be happy, Dad."

"Happy with a respectable man, Cecelia."

"I tried that, and look where it got me." I gesture to the room around us. "Things are different with Brayden."

Dad doesn't flinch. "Ethan made mistakes, but at least he came from a good family. At least he—"

"Cheated on me? Humiliated me?" My voice rises despite my attempt to stay steady. "Is that what you want for me? Another so-called respectable man who treats me like garbage once the doors are shut?"

"Marriage requires work and forgiveness."

"Not that kind of forgiveness," I say, the words sharp on my tongue. "And certainly not the kind of work where I pretend to be someone I'm not just to make him look good."

"And I suppose this...biker...lets you be yourself?"

The question catches me off guard. Does Brayden let me be myself? No. He demands it. Expects it.

"Yes," I say simply. "He does."

Dad sighs, rubbing his temples as though I'm the source of his migraine. "He's been trouble since he was sixteen. His father was a drunk, and his mother wasn't much better. The company he keeps—"

"I know who he is," I cut in again. "And I'm not asking for your permission or your blessing. I'm asking you to respect my choices."

Dad stares at me as if I've grown a second head. The Cecelia he raised never interrupted him, never pushed back. For a moment, something flickers in his eyes—not only disappointment, but confusion. Maybe even a trace of respect.

"I understand you're going through a phase," he says finally, his tone softening into the one he uses for wayward parishioners. "After what happened with Ethan, it's natural to rebel, to seek out someone completely different."

"This isn't rebellion, and it's not a phase. I'm not a little girl anymore, Dad. I'm a woman. A woman who is figuring out who I am when I'm not trying to please everyone else."

"By running straight into the arms of a man with a criminal record?" Dad's eyebrows rise. "Don't look surprised, Cecelia. Everyone in San Salona knows about the Heaven's Rejects. They're not exactly subtle with their...activities."

I bite the inside of my cheek. Dad would have done his research. He probably had the church secretary pull up every scrap of gossip about Brayden the moment I called this morning.

"I'm not blind to who he is," I tell him. "But I'm not

going to sit here and let you judge him based on rumors and ancient history."

Dad leans forward, elbows on his knees, hands clasped like he's about to deliver a particularly solemn sermon. "Two years ago, he was arrested for assault. Put a man in the hospital." His voice is calm but deliberate, each word a stone placed carefully in my path. "Did you know that?"

I swallow hard. Brayden hasn't told me everything about his past, but I'm not surprised by this revelation. "I know he has a history."

"A history of violence," Dad corrects. "The kind of man who solves problems with his fists isn't the kind who can build a stable future, Cecelia."

Something flares in me—defensiveness, loyalty, anger. "You don't know what happened. You don't know him."

"And you do? After what—a few days?" Dad's expression softens with pity, which somehow hurts more than his disappointment. "You've only just started to rebuild your life after Ethan. I don't want to see you tear it down again for someone who can't possibly give you what you deserve."

I laugh, the sound bitter even to my own ears. "What I deserve? What exactly do you think I deserve, Dad? Another man who looks good on paper? Someone who makes you proud when you introduce me at church functions? A man who tears me down until there's nothing left?"

"Someone who won't drag you into a world of

violence and lawlessness," he counters. "Someone with a future."

"Brayden has a future," I insist, though the truth hits me even as I say it—I don't actually know what that future looks like. We haven't talked about tomorrow, let alone next month or next year.

Dad must catch the uncertainty, because he goes straight for it. "What does he do for a living, Cecelia? Beyond whatever work those bikers do that keeps them in leather and on motorcycles?"

I open my mouth to answer and come up empty. We haven't discussed ordinary things—jobs, money, day-to-day responsibilities. I know he's with the Heaven's Rejects, but what that means in practical terms is still a mystery.

"That's what I thought," Dad says. "You're rushing into this because it feels exciting and different. Because he's the opposite of Ethan." He exhales, suddenly looking older than his sixty-two years. "You don't belong in his world, sweetheart. You're too good for that life."

"You don't get to decide that anymore." I stand up, needing to move, to put some distance between us. I pace in front of the fireplace where our family photos still line the mantel. My gaze catches on one—me at my wedding to Ethan, my father beaming beside us. I take it off the mantel and toss it into the fire. The glass shatters upon impact.

"What are you doing?"

"Burning the picture of a life I don't want anymore."

Dad's face turns to stone as he watches the flames lick at the edges of my wedding photo.

"You've lost your mind. This man has poisoned you against everything good in your life."

"No, Dad. Ethan did that all by himself." I stare into the fire, watching as the image melts into ash. "And you helped, pushing me to stay with him even when you knew what he was doing."

"I never knew—"

"Mrs. Calloway told you she saw him with Jessica Allen at the motel on Route 16. You told her to mind her business and pray for my marriage instead of spreading gossip."

Dad's mouth opens, then closes. For once, the great Reverend Montgomery is speechless.

"Did you think I wouldn't find out?" I continue, unable to stop now that the dam has broken. "This whole town is a fishbowl. Nothing stays secret for long."

"I was trying to protect you," he finally says. "Divorce is—"

"A sin? Is that what you were going to say?" I laugh, the sound hollow in the quiet room. "You know what else is a sin, Dad? Lying to your daughter. Pretending everything is fine when her husband is screwing any woman who doesn't have the good sense to shake him off."

"Language, Cecelia."

"Fuck my language!" The curse explodes from my lips.

Dad's face turns crimson. For a moment I think he might actually have a heart attack. Then he strides toward me, finger pointing at my chest.

"That's enough! I will not be spoken to this way in my own home!"

I turn on my heel and head for the stairs. I'm done with this conversation and done with his judgment. His footsteps follow me, heavy and determined.

"We are not finished discussing this, Cecelia!" he calls as I take the steps two at a time.

I push open the door to my childhood bedroom. Dad is right behind me, hovering in the doorway as I yank my suitcase from under the bed.

"What do you think you're doing?"

I snap the suitcase open on the bed. "What does it look like?" I pull open dresser drawers, grabbing hand-fuls of underwear, socks, and t-shirts, tossing them inside without bothering to fold anything. "I'm leaving."

"You can't just leave in the middle of a conversa-tion." He steps into the room, blocking my path to the closet.

I sidestep him. "Watch me."

I grab armfuls of clothes from the closet—jeans, blouses, dresses I'll probably never wear again—and dump them into the suitcase. I feel his eyes boring into my back, judging every movement as I frantically pack.

"Cecelia Montgomery, you stop this nonsense right now." His voice thunders through the small bedroom as he steps closer.

I ignore him, moving to my desk where I snatch my laptop, shoving it into its case before tossing it into the suitcase. Next comes my phone charger, yanked from the wall with enough force that the plug bends slightly.

"What exactly do you think you're doing?"

"I'm leaving, Dad."

"And going where? To him? To that criminal's bed?"

I zip the suitcase with enough force that it nearly breaks. "Yes."

"I forbid it." He steps between me and the door, drawing himself up to his full height.

The word "forbid" hits me like a slap. I'm transported back to a hundred different moments—Dad forbidding me to go to prom with Tyler Jenkins because his parents were divorced, forbidding me to apply to colleges more than two hours away, forbidding me to wear a bridesmaid's dress in my cousin's wedding because the neckline was immodest.

"Frankly, Dad, I don't need your god damn permission."

His face contorts with shock at my defiance. He physically recoils, taking a step back as if I struck him.

"What will the congregation think?" he sputters, his hand clutching at his collar. "Have you considered that at all?"

I laugh, the sound bitter and sharp even to my own

ears. "I guess I'm becoming the next example of immorality in your sermon, huh, Dad? Another cautionary tale about the wages of sin?"

His face pales. I've never called him out so directly on how he uses other people's mistakes to fuel his Sunday messages.

"That's not fair," he says, but there's a flicker of guilt that tells me I've hit the mark.

"Isn't it? How many sermons have you preached about fallen women? About the importance of appearances? About honoring thy father?" I hoist my suitcase off the bed. "I bet you've already drafted the one about me."

"This isn't about my sermons. This is about your safety—your soul."

"No, it's about your reputation." I push past him.

Dad follows me down the hallway, his footsteps heavy behind me. "You're making a terrible mistake, Cecelia. That man will ruin your life."

I spin around at the top of the stairs, nearly losing my balance with the weight of my suitcase. "Maybe I need to destroy who I was to become who I'm meant to be."

He opens his mouth to argue, but the words falter. For the first time, I think he actually sees me—not the obedient daughter he crafted, but someone far beyond his reach now.

The silence stretches between us, thick as the years I spent trying to make him proud.

"I'll pray for you."

I take a breath, steady and sure. "You should probably save your prayers, Dad. I've already found something else to believe in."

His face falls. I don't wait for his answer. I just walk
out of my family home for what may be the last time.

CHAPTER 15

CECE

I DRIVE STRAIGHT to Brayden's, my foot heavy on the gas pedal, as though I'm trying to outrun my father's prayers. The memory of his face—shock shifting into disappointment—stays with me, a snapshot of the exact moment I finally broke free.

My hands shake on the steering wheel. I've never spoken to my father that way. Never cursed at him. Never walked out. The adrenaline that carried me through our confrontation is already fading, leaving me hollow and jittery at the same time. I crank the radio up, loud enough to drown out the voice in my head that sounds far too much like Dad's. The one insisting I'm about to make the mistake of my life.

Maybe I am. Maybe tomorrow I'll wake up and regret everything.

But right now, as I pull onto the dusty road leading to Jillian's property, all I feel is a wild, terrifying freedom. Like I've jumped from a plane and haven't hit the ground yet.

I park beside Brayden's bike and sit for a moment, staring at the modest guesthouse where everything shifted. My reflection in the rearview mirror startles me —flushed cheeks, bright eyes, hair mussed from running my hands through it on the drive. I barely recognize myself. The obedient preacher's daughter is gone, replaced by someone unpolished and real.

Before I can talk myself out of it, I grab my suitcase from the passenger seat and head for his door. Three sharp knocks, and then I wait—my heart pounding against my ribs as though it's trying to break free.

The door swings open, and there he is—Brayden, still toweling off from a recent shower, bare shoulders damp, jeans slung on in a hurry. His gaze moves from my suitcase to my face, surprise flickering through his eyes, though not enough to hide the sense that he'd already guessed this moment was coming.

"That was fast," he says, leaning against the doorframe. His gaze drops to my suitcase. "I'm guessing it didn't go well."

"You could say that." My voice catches, and I clear my throat. "I told my father to go to hell. Not in those exact words, but close enough."

A slow smile spreads across his face. "Wish I could've seen that."

"No, you don't. It wasn't pretty." I shift my weight, suddenly unsure. We've shared a bed, shared our bodies, but this feels more intimate somehow. More permanent. "I need a place to stay. Just until I figure things out."

He steps back, opening the door wider. "Come in, princess."

I walk past him into the small living room, the reality of what I've done finally hitting me full force. My legs feel weak, and I set down my suitcase before I drop it.

"I burned my wedding photo," I say, the words tumbling out before I can stop them. "In the fireplace. Right in front of him."

Brayden's eyebrows shoot up. "Holy shit."

"Yeah." I laugh, but it comes out shaky. "I think I might have traumatized him."

Brayden crosses the room in two strides and pulls me against his chest. The solid warmth of him steadies me, his heartbeat a grounding rhythm under my ear. His arms wrap around me, and I let myself collapse into his strength, just for a moment.

"You okay?"

"I don't know." I pull back just enough to look up at him. "I've never done anything like that before."

His hand comes up to cup my face, thumb brushing across my cheekbone. "Burning wedding photos? Or telling your old man to fuck off?"

"Both." I lean into his touch. "All of it. Running away. Coming here." I gesture to my suitcase. "Showing up on your doorstep like some cliché romance novel."

"If this were a romance novel, it'd be raining," he says, mouth curving in amusement. "And you'd be wearing something far more dramatic than…" His gaze drifts down my body, taking in my faded jeans and plain T-shirt. "Still, you pull it off."

I laugh, and this time it feels more genuine. The knot in my chest loosens a fraction.

"So," he says, tucking a strand of hair behind my ear. "You need a place to crash."

It's not a question, but I nod anyway. "Just until I figure things out. I can pay rent, or—"

"Stop." He presses his thumb gently against my lips. "You're not paying me shit. This place is barely mine anyway. Besides, my aunt would kick my ass if I turned you away."

"I don't want to impose." The words sound ridiculous even as they leave my mouth.

Brayden's expression shifts, sharpening as he studies me. "You think I mind having you in my space? In my bed?" His hand moves to the back of my neck. "Trust me, princess, that's the opposite of a problem."

The way he's looking at me makes my skin flush hot. Even after everything we've done together, the raw hunger in his stare still catches me off guard.

"I just—" I swallow hard. "I don't want you to feel trapped. Like you have to take care of me."

He laughs, a low rumble that I feel more than hear.

"Nobody's ever accused me of being a caretaker before." His thumb traces my jawline. "But you're welcome to stay as long as you want."

The casual way he offers his space should scare me. This is moving too fast, too intense. But I don't care. I need this—need him—right now, when everything else in my life feels like it's burning down around me.

I don't know what comes over me, but something inside me snaps. Whatever it is, I launch myself at him.

My hands grab his face, pulling him down to me as I crush my mouth against his. It's not gentle. It's not sweet. It's desperate and hungry and wild. I can tell I've caught him off guard by the way he stumbles back a step, but his arms wrap around me instantly, lifting me off my feet.

"Whoa," he breathes against my lips, but I don't let him finish.

I wrap my legs around his waist, clinging to him like he's the only solid thing in a world and I'm spinning out of control. My fingers tangle in his hair, tugging harder than I mean to. He groans into my mouth, the sound vibrating through me.

"I need you," I gasp between frantic kisses. "Right now."

He doesn't question it. Doesn't try to slow me down or tell me I should take a breath. He just carries me to the kitchen counter, my body still wrapped around him, my mouth still devouring his. He sets me on the cold counter with a thud, his hands already working up the hem of my shirt. I press into him, desperate for the contact, for the distraction, for anything that will pull my mind away from what I've just done.

"You sure about this?" he asks, voice ragged as his mouth trails down my neck.

"Strip me, please. I need to feel your hands on my skin," I pant, yanking at his belt.

His expression shifts. Without hesitation, he pulls my shirt over my head and tosses it aside. The sudden chill against my skin sends goosebumps racing across me.

"Fuck, princess," he mutters, his voice low, hungry. His fingers work quickly, undoing the clasp of my bra.

"Don't be gentle," I tell him. "I don't need gentle right now."

Something flickers across his face—not surprise, but something deeper. Recognition. He knows what this is. Knows what I'm asking without having to say more.

"Then I won't be," he says, voice rough from restraint.

Before I can draw another breath, he drops to his knees in front of me. My words falter. His hands grip my thighs with quiet command. He looks up, gaze steady, a wicked curve on his mouth that sends a fresh flush of heat through me.

"Hold onto something," he warns.

I barely have time to grip the edge of the counter before he yanks my jeans and underwear down in one rough motion. The cold surface against my bare skin makes me gasp, but that sound is nothing compared to the moan that tears from my throat when his mouth finds me.

There's no teasing, no gentle exploration. He devours me, his tongue hot and relentless against my most sensitive flesh. I arch my back, one hand flying to his hair, gripping the dark strands between my fingers.

"Oh God," I breathe, my head falling back as his tongue circles my clit in tight, knowing patterns.

He growls against me, the vibration jolting up my spine. His hands grip my thighs harder, keeping me open, exposed to his hungry mouth. I can feel his stubble scraping against my inner thighs, the slight burn only heightening every sensation.

"Brayden," I pant, not sure what I'm begging for.

He responds by sliding two fingers inside me, curling them in a way that makes my vision blur. The pleasure is almost unbearable as his mouth claims me completely. My thighs tremble against his shoulders, and I'm gasping for air like I've forgotten how to breathe. Every stroke of his tongue, every curl of his fingers inside me—it's pushing me toward something I desperately need.

"Don't stop," I beg, my voice hardly recognizable. "Please don't stop."

He looks up at me without breaking rhythm as his mouth works me over. The sight of him between my legs is almost enough to send me over the edge.

"Don't fucking come yet," he says against my flesh.

The command sends a sharp thrill through me, a counter to the desperate need building between my thighs. I want to disobey just to see what he'd do. To know how he'd punish me for defying him.

"Please," I whimper instead, my fingers tightening in his hair.

He growls against me, the vibration making me shudder. "Not yet. I want you desperate first."

His fingers slow inside me, dragging against my walls with deliberate pressure while his tongue makes lazy circles that drive me insane. He's building me up only to keep me on the edge, and the frustration is exquisite.

"Brayden," I moan, trying to pull him closer with my thighs.

He chuckles darkly, the sound reverberating against my core. "Patience, princess." His free hand comes up to press against my stomach, holding me in place as I try to rock against his mouth. "You wanted it rough? Then you take what I give you, when I give it."

A shiver runs through me, sweat collecting on my skin even in the cool air. Every nerve ending is on fire, my body strung so tight I might shatter at any moment. I need release like I need air, but he keeps me suspended in this sweet agony.

"Look at me," he demands, pausing his assault on my senses.

I force my eyes open, gazing down at him between my thighs. His eyes are dark with hunger, his lips glistening with my arousal. The sight of him looking up at me makes me dizzy with need.

"Beg for it," he says, the words a low rumble that vibrates through me. "I want to hear you beg for me to let you come."

In my old life, I would have been mortified. The proper preacher's daughter doesn't beg for pleasure—she doesn't even admit to wanting it. But I left that woman behind in my father's house.

"Please," I breathe, the sound breaking as need overtakes me. "Please let me come, Brayden. I need it. I need you."

He holds my gaze for one more torturous moment, then his mouth is on me again, relentless now. His fingers curl inside me, finding that perfect spot while his tongue flicks over my clit with devastating precision. The pleasure builds so fast it's almost painful, a white-hot surge that crashes through me with brutal force.

I come with a scream, my body convulsing around his fingers, against his mouth. He doesn't let up until I'm gasping for mercy, my hands pushing weakly at his shoulders.

Before I can catch my breath, he rises to his feet, finishing unbuckling his belt with a quick swipe of his hand. His jeans hit the floor, and he's on me in an instant, lifting me off the counter and spinning me around, bending me over. I barely have time to brace myself before he's pushing inside me with one powerful thrust.

"Fuck," he groans, his hands gripping my hips hard enough to bruise. "You're so wet for me."

I cry out, my oversensitive body struggling to adjust to his size. The stretch burns in the most delicious way, pleasure and pain blending until I can't tell where one ends and the other begins.

"You wanted it rough," he growls, pulling back only to slam into me again. "Tell me, princess—is this what you've been craving? To forget everything but how I feel inside you?"

"Yes," I gasp, my cheek pressed against the cool counter, hands scrambling for purchase. "God, yes."

He sets a punishing pace, each thrust driving the air from my lungs. The sound of skin slapping against skin fills the kitchen, punctuated by my desperate moans and his guttural groans. One of his hands slides up my back, then tangles in my hair, drawing me against him.

"Look at you. Bent over my kitchen counter, taking my cock like you were made for it."

I should be ashamed—of what I'm doing, of how much I love his filthy mouth—but all I feel is liberated.

"What would Daddy think of his little girl now?" he rasps, his fingers digging into my hip. "Moaning for a Heaven's Reject, begging for my cock."

The mention of my father should kill the mood, but instead it fuels something rebellious inside me. I push back against Brayden's thrusts, taking him deeper.

"I don't care," I pant. "I don't care what he thinks anymore."

Brayden growls his approval, "That's my girl."

My girl. The possessiveness in his words makes me clench around him, drawing a harsh curse from his lips. He responds by driving into me harder, the edge of the counter digging into my hips with each powerful thrust. The slight pain only enhances the pleasure building inside me again, impossibly soon after my first orgasm.

"You gonna come for me again?" he asks, his rhythm never faltering. "Gonna come all over my cock like my good girl?"

"Yes," I gasp. "I'm close."

His fingers find my oversensitive clit. The touch is almost too much, making me cry out and attempt to squirm away, but he holds me firmly in place.

"No running. You take what I give you."

His fingers work me mercilessly as he pounds into me. The intensity is overwhelming. My head spins as pleasure builds in my core again, my body trembling with each relentless thrust. Just when I think I can't take any more, Brayden suddenly pulls out completely, leaving me empty and aching.

"Get up," he orders.

Before I can respond, he turns me around and lifts me into his arms. My legs instinctively wrap around his waist as he carries me to the living room, his mouth never leaving mine, devouring me with hungry kisses that steal what little breath I have left.

He drops onto the couch, still holding me so that I'm straddling his lap, his cock pressing insistently against my core. His hands grip my hips, guiding me to position myself over him.

"Take what you need," he growls. "Show me how bad you want it."

I sink down onto him in one fluid motion, crying out as he fills me from this new angle. The sensation is overwhelming. He's deeper than before, hitting places inside me I didn't know existed.

"That's it," he encourages as I begin to move, lifting myself up before sliding back down his length. "Ride me, princess."

I brace my hands on his broad shoulders, finding my rhythm. Slow at first, savoring the delicious stretch of him inside me, then faster as need takes over. His hands roam my body—cupping my breasts before one hand inches up around my throat.

The gentle pressure of his hand at my throat makes me gasp, my eyes locking with his as he holds me there. My hips stutter in their rhythm, the unexpected sensation sending shivers down my spine.

"You like that?"

"Yes," I breathe, surprised by how much I mean it. "God, yes."

His fingers flex slightly, just enough to make me feel owned, possessed. The vulnerability of it should terrify me, but instead, it's freeing. In his hands, I don't have to be in control. Don't have to make the right choices or be the good girl. I just have to feel.

"Keep moving," he commands, his other hand gripping my hip hard enough to bruise. "Don't stop until I tell you."

I obey, riding him with renewed vigor, my body slick with sweat as I chase my release. He holds me captive with his gaze as surely as his hand at my throat. I've never felt so exposed, so seen. He's stripping away every defense I've ever built until there's nothing left but honest need.

"That's it," he encourages as my pace quickens, my movements becoming erratic as I near the edge. "Let go for me, baby. Show me what you look like when you fall apart."

The tension inside me builds to a breaking point, my thighs trembling as I slam down on him one last time. His hand tightens slightly around my throat, and that's all it takes to send me careening over the edge.

"Brayden!" I cry out as the orgasm rips through me, more powerful than the first. My body clamps down around him, each rush of feeling hitting harder than the last.

His grip on my throat loosens as he thrusts up into me, meeting my movements with his own desperate rhythm. I can feel him getting closer—his breathing ragged, muscles tensing beneath my hands.

"Fuck," he growls.

I collapse against his chest, boneless and spent, but he's not finished. In one fluid motion, he flips us so I'm beneath him on the couch. He hooks one arm under my knee, opening me wider as he drives into me.

"I'm going to fill you up," he promises. "Mark you from the inside out."

"Yes," I whimper, too sensitive for another orgasm but still craving the feeling of him losing control. "Please."

His rhythm falters, becomes erratic. His fingers dig into my thigh as he buries himself deep inside me one last time, his whole body going rigid. The sound that tears from his throat is otherworldly. He collapses on top of me, his weight pressing me into the couch as we both struggle to catch our breath. His face is buried in my neck, his stubble scraping against my sensitive skin as he plants lazy, open-mouthed kisses along my collarbone. I can feel him still pulsing inside me, aftershocks of his release making both our bodies twitch.

"Jesus Christ," he mutters against my skin. "Are you trying to kill me?"

I laugh breathlessly, my fingers trailing up his sweat-slicked back. "If I was, what a way to go."

He lifts his head, looking down at me with those storm-gray eyes. There's something in them I can't quite read—a softness that seems at odds with the man who just bent me over his kitchen counter.

"You okay?" he asks, brushing a strand of hair from my face.

The tenderness of the gesture nearly undoes me. After everything—my father, the fight, the desperate sex—this simple touch threatens to break my fragile composure.

"I think so," I whisper, not trusting my voice with anything louder. "Just...processing."

He nods, understanding without needing me to explain. Carefully, he pulls out of me, both of us wincing at the sensitivity. Then he gathers me against his chest, shifting us so we're lying side by side on the narrow couch, my back pressed to his front.

His arms encircle me, one hand splayed protectively across my stomach, the other cradling my head. The silence stretches between us, comfortable yet fragile, like a bubble I'm afraid to burst.

But there's a question burning in my throat. One I can't swallow down anymore. Maybe it's the vulnerability of being naked in his arms, or the emotional whiplash of the past twenty-four hours, but I suddenly need to know where we stand.

"Is this just sex for you?" I ask quietly. I feel his body tense slightly behind me, and I rush to add, "Not that I mind if it is. I just...I should probably know what this is."

His breathing changes and becomes more deliberate. For several heartbeats, he says nothing, and I fight the urge to fill the silence with nervous babble.

"If this was just sex, I wouldn't have let you bring your suitcase inside."

My heart does a strange little flip in my chest. "What does that mean?"

He sighs, his breath warm against my neck. "It means I don't know what the fuck this is, but it's not just sex." His arm tightens around my waist, pulling me closer. "I don't let women stay over, Cece. I definitely don't let them move in."

I turn toward him, searching his face. A shielded look has taken hold there, a quiet caution that hints he's deciding what pieces of himself to show me.

"I've never been good with words," he admits, his thumb absently stroking my hip. "And I'm not gonna promise shit I can't deliver. But..." He pauses, his jaw tightening. "This feels different. You feel different."

I hold my breath.

"I'm not looking to complicate your life more than it already is," he continues. "But I am a selfish bastard who can't bring himself to let you walk away either."

I swallow hard, his words settling into my chest. Different. I feel different with him too.

"My father said things about you," I whisper, my fingers tracing the edge of a tattoo on his chest. "About your past."

His body tenses slightly beneath my touch, but he doesn't pull away. "I figured he would."

"He mentioned an arrest. For assault." I force myself to look up, meeting his gaze. "Said you put someone in the hospital."

Brayden's jaw tightens, but he doesn't look away. "That's true. Guy was roughing up his girlfriend outside a bar. Wouldn't stop when I told him to. So I made him stop." His voice is calm, unapologetic. "Broke his jaw and three ribs."

I should be shocked. Horrified. But instead, I nod slowly. "Would you do it again?"

"In a heartbeat." His stare is steady, unwavering. "I don't regret it. Never will."

I absorb this, trying to reconcile the violence with the man whose arms are cradling me so carefully. "What else should I know?"

A humorless smile tugs at his lips. "You asking for my rap sheet, princess?"

"That depends," I say, tracing a pattern on his chest. "Are there a lot of pages to go through?"

He chuckles, but there's no humor in it. "More than you'd think, less than your dad probably implied."

I push myself up on one elbow to look at him properly. His expression is guarded, but not shut down. It carries the sense of a man offering me an exit if I want it —one last chance to step back before I wade deeper into his world.

"I don't need your entire history," I tell him. "Just the important pieces. What I should know if I'm going to be here."

He studies me for a long moment, trying to decide whether I'm steady enough to hear what he's kept buried. At last, he exhales—a slow, resigned breath.

"I've done time. Twice. Once when I was nineteen—possession with intent to distribute. Did fourteen months in county. Second time was for the assault I just told you about. Got six months but served four."

My stomach tightens, but I force myself to nod. "Drugs?"

"Not anymore." His answer is immediate, firm.

"Haven't touched that shit in years. The club doesn't deal either. Not since Big took over as president."

I absorb this information, trying to reconcile it with the man holding me. "What about now? What do you do?"

"Officially?" His lips quirk up. "I'm a mechanic. Co-own the garage with Domino."

"And unofficially?"

"Even with my colors on your back, princess, there's only so much I can tell you about the club's business."

His reluctance makes me wonder what exactly the Heaven's Rejects do that he can't talk about. A hundred possibilities run through my mind.

"Can you at least tell me if it's...legal?"

"Some of it is. Some of it exists in gray areas."

"Gray areas," I repeat.

"Look," he says, shifting to face me more directly. "The club protects its own. We handle problems that the law can't or won't. Sometimes that means operating outside the lines." His hand finds mine, thumb tracing circles on my palm. "But I'm not going to lie to you. We're not choirboys."

I almost laugh at the understatement. "I figured that much out on my own."

"Does it scare you?" he asks, studying my face with an intensity that makes me shiver.

"A little," I admit, because there's no point in pretending. "But I'm more scared of going back to being who I was before."

He nods slowly, as though he understands every

part of what I'm not saying. "Sometimes the devil you don't know is still the safer option."

"Are you calling yourself the devil?" I smile, trying to lighten the mood.

His answering smile is sharp enough to cut, "Your devil."

"Can you show me?"

"Show you what?" His fingers pause their lazy exploration of my skin.

"Your world." I sit up straighter, pulling the throw blanket from the back of the couch to wrap around myself. "The club. The parts of your life you can share."

His expression shifts, wariness replacing the relaxed intimacy of moments before. "Why?"

"Because it's part of who you are." I reach out to trace the outline of the raven tattooed on his shoulder. "I don't want to be kept in some separate box, away from everything that matters to you."

"The club isn't a tourist attraction, princess. It's not something you visit like a petting zoo."

"I'm not asking to pet anything. I'm asking to understand the man I'm..." I hesitate, not sure how to finish that sentence. Sleeping with? Living with? Falling for?

Brayden watches me struggle, clearly entertained by every second I spend trying to articulate my feelings for him. Bastard. "The man... you're what?"

"The man I'm choosing," I finally say, because it's the truest thing I can offer right now.

Brayden studies me for a long time, unreadable, as though he's weighing whether I truly mean every word.

The silence stretches until I start to think he's going to shut the whole idea down.

Then he nods once—slow, deliberate. "I need to check in at the clubhouse anyway. Might be a good change of scenery for you."

A flicker of warmth stirs in my chest. "So you'll take me?"

He exhales through his nose, the sound carrying a hint of resignation. "Yeah. I'll take you."

Some part of me already knows I've just agreed to far more than a ride.

CHAPTER 16

BRAYDEN

I REALIZE I've made a terrible fucking mistake the second we roll into the clubhouse lot.

The parking area is already packed with bikes and cars—way too many for a regular Thursday night. Bass thumps through the walls loud enough that I can feel it vibrating in my chest even outside. A couple of hang-arounds are smoking by the entrance, shirtless, despite the chill in the air, red plastic cups in their hands. One of them wolf-whistles as I cut the engine.

Fuck. Me. Running.

I feel Cece's hands tighten around my waist as she takes in the scene. The neon sign above the door casts an eerie red glow across her face when she pulls off her helmet.

"Is it always this...lively?" she asks, her voice careful. Too careful.

"No," I mutter, helping her off the bike. "It's not."

I shouldn't have agreed to this. Not tonight. Not when she's still on edge from the blowout with her father. Not when we haven't even defined whatever the hell this thing between us is. I planned to introduce her to the club slowly. Maybe bring her by during the day when it's just the brothers hanging around, playing pool, talking shit. Not during what sounds like a full-blown rave.

"We can turn around," I offer, already knowing what her answer will be. I've learned enough about her to recognize the mile-long stubborn streak she has.

Cece straightens her spine and squares her shoulders. I recognize that look by now. She is about to walk straight into hell and dare the devil to blink first.

"No," she says, sliding her hand into mine. "I want to see."

I inhale deeply, trying to ignore the warning bells clanging in my head. "Alright. But we stick together. And if I say it's time to go, we go. No questions."

She nods, clearly trying to project confidence, but her grip on my hand tightens as we approach the entrance. The hang-arounds straighten when they spot me, their attention shifting from my face to Cece with undisguised interest.

"Bray," one of them nods, his gaze lingering on Cece a beat too long. "Didn't expect to see you tonight."

"Wasn't planning on it," I reply, moving slightly to block his view of her. "Big inside?"

"Yeah, man. Everybody is." He grins, revealing a missing tooth. "Surprise party for Domino. His old lady set it up."

Fuck. A surprise party. That explains the crowd and the noise. Domino's girlfriend, Tasha, has been planning this for weeks, and I completely forgot about it in the Cece-induced fog I've been living in.

"Come on," I mutter, steering Cece toward the door. We push through, and the clubhouse slams into us—a full-force hurricane of bad decisions waiting to happen. Smoke hangs thick in the air, booze spills across every surface, and the music pounds hard enough to rattle my teeth.

None of that is what stops me cold.

It's the naked women. Everywhere.

At least three stripper poles have been set up around the main room, each occupied by a woman in various stages of undress, their bodies glistening under colored lights. Between the poles, topless waitresses weave through the crowd carrying trays of shots, their breasts bouncing with each step. In one corner, a girl wearing nothing but a G-string is giving some prospect a lap dance while his brothers cheer him on.

This isn't just a party. It's a fucking strip club on steroids.

I feel Cece freeze beside me, her hand going rigid in mine. When I glance down, her face is drained of color, her expression wide with shock as she takes in the scene.

"Shit," I mutter, already pulling her back toward the door. "We're leaving."

But before we can make our escape, Big's voice booms over the music.

"Bray! You made it, brother!"

The club president barrels toward us, arms outstretched, clearly three sheets to the wind. His massive frame parts the crowd, and there's no slipping out unnoticed now.

"—and you brought company!" Big's grin stretches across his bearded face as he zeroes in on Cece.

I instinctively pull her closer to my side, my arm wrapping around her waist. "Just stopping by for a minute," I say over the thumping bass. "Didn't realize Domino's party was tonight."

Big laughs, the sound booming even over the music. "Surprise, motherfucker!" He throws his arms wide, sloshing beer from his bottle. "And who's this pretty little thing?"

I can feel Cece's body tensing under my arm, but her face remains composed when she extends her hand. "I'm Cece."

Big's eyebrows shoot up as he engulfs her hand in his massive paw. "The preacher's daughter?" He turns to me with renewed interest, a knowing glint in his eye. "You here to save our souls the way your daddy tries to, sugar?"

"That's more my father's specialty," Cece replies

smoothly. "But if you're hunting for redemption, I can give you his number."

Big throws his head back and roars, the sound booming through the room as he smacks his thigh in approval. A few people glance over, curious about the commotion.

"I'm telling you, Bray—this one's a keeper!" He jabs a thick finger toward Cece. "She's got fire in her belly."

I feel her relax slightly beside me, but I know better than to let my guard down. Big can flip from jovial to threatening in the space of a heartbeat, especially when he's been drinking.

"We're just passing through," I say, trying to steer us toward the bar where it's marginally quieter. "Thought I'd show Cece around, but we picked a bad night."

"Nonsense!" Big booms, throwing a heavy arm around my shoulders and nearly knocking me off balance. "No better night to see what we're all about. The family is all here!"

Some family. I glance around at the chaos. Wrecker doing body shots off a blonde's stomach while Skelly cheers him on, Hammer getting a very public lap dance in the corner, and at least three prospects I don't recognize passed out on various tables.

"Come on," Big insists, already dragging us deeper into the madness. "You need to make the introductions."

I shoot Cece an apologetic look, but she surprises me with a small nod.

I can already tell she's putting on a brave face, and

I'm not sure if I should be impressed by her guts or terrified by what she's about to witness. Either way, my protective instincts are in overdrive as Big hauls us toward a group of my brothers near the makeshift bar.

"Listen up, assholes!" Big bellows. "Bray brought his woman!"

Fuck. This is exactly what I'd been afraid of—and what some twisted part of me knew would happen.

The second Cece steps inside, the whole clubhouse shifts. Heads snap up, eyes rake over her like slow, hungry hands. Fresh meat. Exactly what they see. Exactly what I didn't want.

Brothers nudge each other, heat sparking in their stares, and it makes my pulse slam—rage and desire tangling until I can't tell them apart.

She has no clue what she does to a room. What she does to *me.* I step closer, claiming space at her side, every instinct roaring the same thing.

Look all you want. She walked in with me.

"We can still leave," I whisper in her ear.

Her fingernails dig into my forearm as she plasters on a smile that doesn't come close to reaching her expression. "I'm fine," she whispers. "Really."

She's lying through her teeth, though I can't help respecting the nerve it takes. Most women would've been gone already. A small part of me almost wishes she'd done the same.

Wrecker detaches himself from the blonde and saunters over, giving Cece a once-over that makes my fists twitch. He's my brother, but right now, the possessive beast inside me doesn't care.

"Well, well," he drawls, swiping tequila from his beard. "What do we have here?" His gaze sweeps over her with the enthusiasm of a drunk man spotting the last slice of pizza.

I step in front of her, my jaw clenched tight enough to crack teeth. "This is Cece. She's with me."

The weight of those last three words doesn't miss. His eyebrows lift, and he backs off a step, hands raised in mock surrender.

"Just being friendly," he says, flashing the shit-eating grin that always makes me want to rearrange his face. "Welcome to the family fun house, darlin'. We don't get many ladies like you in here."

"I gathered that," Cece replies, her attention flicking briefly to a topless waitress passing by with a tray of tequila shots.

Big claps his hands together, oblivious to the tension. "Get the lady a drink! What's your poison, honey?"

Cece hesitates, and I can practically see her calculating how to navigate this minefield. "Just a beer, please."

"A beer?" Big looks offended. "This is a party, not a church picnic!"

"Beer's fine," I interject, shooting him a look that says *back off*. To my surprise, he does, waving at the bartender to bring one over.

I scan the room, looking for the safest corner to steer

Cece, but we're immediately surrounded by three more brothers. Domino, the birthday boy himself, pushes through the crowd with a crown made of beer cans perched crookedly on his head.

"Holy shit, you actually showed up!" He wraps me in a bear hug. When he pulls back, his bloodshot eyes land on Cece. "And you brought the preacher's daughter? Man, I thought Skelly was bullshitting about that."

I feel Cece stiffen beside me. "Word travels fast."

"Sweetheart, nothing travels faster than club gossip," Domino grins, offering her a mock bow that nearly sends his beer can crown tumbling. "Especially when it's about our resident brooding bastard here finally getting himself a woman."

I clench my jaw so hard my teeth might crack. "She's not a sideshow, Dom."

"Course not," he agrees, suddenly serious despite his drunken state. He looks directly at Cece. "Any woman who can get this grumpy fuck to smile is welcome in my clubhouse."

A cold beer appears in Cece's hand, delivered by a topless waitress who gives me a wink before sauntering off. I watch Cece closely as she takes a long pull from the bottle, her throat working as she swallows, doing her best to hide whatever discomfort she's feeling.

There's fire in her expression—determination, laced with something else. Maybe curiosity. Maybe rebellion. Either way, she's holding her own better than I expected, which both impresses and terrifies me.

"Who do we have here?" a female voice cuts

through the noise, and I turn to see Tasha, Domino's girlfriend, pushing her way toward us. Unlike the half-naked women circling the room, she's fully dressed in jeans and a tight tank top, her dark hair pulled into a severe ponytail. She turns to me, one perfectly shaped eyebrow raised. "You couldn't have brought her on a regular night, Bray? Had to throw her straight into the shark tank?"

"Wasn't planning on coming at all," I mutter, grateful for Tasha's intervention. She might be a ball-buster, but she's got a protective streak a mile wide when it comes to outsiders. "Didn't realize it was party night."

"Well, since you're here..." Tasha links her arm through Cece's, smoothly extracting her from my side. "Let me show you around. I need a break from the boys."

Before I can object, Tasha is already pulling Cece away from me, disappearing into the crowd. My first instinct is to follow, but Dom claps a heavy hand on my shoulder, anchoring me in place.

"Relax, brother," he says, his words slurring slightly. "Tasha will take care of her. Besides, you look like you need this more than me." He shoves a shot of whiskey into my hand.

I down it without thinking, the burn doing nothing to loosen the knot in my stomach. Watching Cece disappear into this chaos feels as though I'm sending a lamb straight into a wolf den. Not because she's helpless—far from it—but this place is built to overpower anyone who isn't used to it. Hell, even I feel unsteady tonight, and I've been coming to this clubhouse for years.

"So," Big says, leaning in close enough that I can smell the bourbon on his breath. "I can see you didn't take my advice. She the reason you've been missing the last few days?"

"Didn't realize I needed your permission to have a life," I growl, snatching another shot from a passing tray. The liquor burns down my throat, doing nothing to calm the anxiety churning in my gut as I scan the room for Cece.

Big laughs, but there's no humor in it. "When that life involves bringing civilians into our world? Yeah, brother, you do."

"She's here now, isn't she?" I fire back at him. "Nowhere in our charter does it say you get to vet the people patches fuck, Big."

Big's eyes narrow, his jovial demeanor evaporates. "This isn't just about who you're sticking your dick in, Brayden. This is about loyalty. About priorities."

"My loyalty to the club has never been in question," I snap. "Not once in ten fucking years."

"Until now." Big's voice drops, meant for my ears only. "You've been MIA for days. Missing runs. Skipping church. All for what? A piece of pussy that'll run screaming once she sees what we really are?"

I take a step forward, closing the distance between us until we're nearly chest to chest. "Watch your fucking mouth."

Big doesn't back down—he never does—but something shifts in his expression. Surprise, maybe. I've never challenged him this directly before.

"Interesting," he says, studying me as though I'm some new species he's just uncovered. "I've watched you drop men without blinking, but mention your little church mouse and suddenly you're ready to square off with your own president."

"She's not what you think."

"No?" Big's eyebrows climb. "Then what is she? Because from where I'm standing, she's a distraction. The kind that gets brothers killed. The kind that has a man picturing fences and Sunday dinners while he forgets who he really is."

I clench my fists at my sides, fighting the urge to knock that knowing smirk off his face. "You don't know shit about her."

"I know her type." He takes a swig of his beer. "Good girls slumming it with bad men, thinking they can save us. Fix us."

"She's nothing of the sort," I argue, unable to blunt the edge in my voice. "She's not trying to fix me. She's trying to claw her way out of the life she was trapped in."

Big's eyebrows shoot up, genuine surprise replacing the earlier condescension. "Out of what?"

"Out of a world where she's only ever been what everyone else needed her to be. They kept her boxed in. She's finally breaking free."

"And you're the crowbar she grabbed."

"Maybe we're both prying our way out of something." I scan the crowd again, my unease growing every time I fail to spot her. "Where the hell did Tasha take her?"

"Ladies' room, most likely," Dom slurs, waving a hand toward the back hallway. "Tasha always scoops up the newcomers before the scene gets too much. She's good at that."

I toss back another shot, the burn sharpening my focus. My attention keeps snagging on the hallway where they vanished. Every second Cece is out of sight tightens something in my chest.

Yeah. That's enough waiting. She's been gone too long.

"I'll be right back," I tell Big and Dom. I slip past them in the direction I last spotted Cece. I push through the crowd, ignoring the brothers calling my name and the half-naked women trying to catch my eye. The music pounds in my skull, the smoke and sweat and booze making everything feel unreal. All I can think about is Cece—what she's seeing, what she's thinking. Whether she's already regretting ever getting involved with me.

The hallway leading to the bathrooms is dark, the bass vibrating through the walls. I spot Hammer pinning some girl against the wall, his hand up her skirt, her leg hooked around his waist. He doesn't even notice me passing by.

The women's bathroom door is closed. I hesitate, my hand hovering over it when I hear her voice coming from down the hallway. I follow the sound, rounding another corner where the hallway opens into a small lounge area. Cece's sitting on a worn leather couch with Tasha beside her, their heads bent close together in conversation. Relief floods through me, followed immediately by wariness when I notice they both go silent the moment they spot me.

"Um...hi?" Cece says, a nervous smile playing at her lips when she sees me standing there.

Tasha rolls her eyes dramatically. "Seriously, Bray?"

"What?" I shrug.

"You might be worse than Dom. She was gone for ten minutes from your sight."

Twelve, but I definitely wasn't counting. Not at all.

"See. Cave men, the entire club of them," Tasha chuckles.

"What else have you told her?"

"That you couldn't have picked a worse time to bring her to the clubhouse for the first time."

"Didn't realize it was Domino's party," I admit, leaning against the doorframe.

"Clearly," Tasha snorts. She turns back to Cece. "I was just telling your girl here that we're not usually quite so..." she pauses, searching for the right word, "...excessive. I mean, don't get me wrong, the boys are always animals, but the strippers are special occasion only."

I watch Cece's face carefully, trying to gauge how much damage control I need to do. To my surprise, she doesn't look horrified. Uncomfortable, yes, but she's not checking for escape routes.

"I'm fine, really," Cece insists, though her knuckles

are white around her beer bottle. "It's just...a lot to take in at once."

"That's one way of putting it," Tasha laughs. "My first club party? I made it twenty minutes before locking myself in the bathroom and crying until Dom took me home."

"But you didn't let it scare you off," I say.

"What can I say? I love the bastard. Speaking of which, I should get back to the birthday boy," Tasha says, standing up and smoothing her jeans. "You two good here?"

"We're fine," I answer before Cece can speak. "Thanks for the rescue mission."

Tasha winks at Cece. "Us old ladies have to stick together. Come find me if you need another break from the testosterone."

I watch Tasha saunter back down the hallway. When we're alone, Cece looks up at me with those big green eyes, uncertainty written all over her face. "I'm sorry if I embarrassed you," she says quietly.

"Embarrassed me?" I push off the doorframe and move to sit beside her. "Why the fuck would you think that?"

She shrugs, picking at the label on her beer bottle. "This is your world, and I'm clearly not...part of it. I stick out like a preacher at a porn convention."

I can't help the laugh that escapes me. "You're worried about embarrassing me? In this fucking place?"

"Well, yeah." She gestures vaguely toward the hallway where the sounds of the party booms. "I'm clearly not the type of woman your friends expected you to bring around."

I reach for her hand, relieved when she doesn't pull away. "Trust me, princess, if anyone should be embarrassed, it's me. I shouldn't have brought you here tonight."

"Because you're ashamed of me?"

"Christ, no." I tug her closer until our thighs touch on the worn leather couch. "Because I wanted to ease you into this world, not throw you into the deep end."

She smiles a little at that, her fingers relaxing in mine. "I'm tougher than I look, you know."

"I know exactly how tough you are." I brush my thumb across her knuckles. "That's not the point."

"Then what is the point?"

I exhale slowly, trying to organize my thoughts. The shots I downed aren't helping with clarity. "The point is that this—" I gesture toward the party "—isn't who we are all the time. It's not who I am. Normally, when shit gets wild like this, I make an appearance, drink a beer, and head out."

"You're telling me, in complete seriousness, you have never participated in a club party? With all those naked girls out there begging for your attention."

"I won't lie to you and say that I am a Boy Scout. I spent my fair share of nights with club girls in the early days. But that shit gets old fast."

"So what changed?"

"I did." I run a hand through my hair, struggling to articulate something I've never had to explain before.

"Look, when you first patch in, everything's a fucking rush. The brotherhood, the parties, the women who throw themselves at you just because of what you're wearing on your back. It's easy to get caught up in it."

"But you didn't."

"No, I did. For a while. Then you realize most of those women don't give a shit about you. They either want a property patch or just want to fuck around."

"What's a property patch?" Cece asks, her head tilting slightly. Her fingers trace the beer label, picking at the corner where the condensation has loosened the paper.

I run my hand through my hair, wondering how to explain this particular aspect of club life without making her run screaming.

"It signals commitment. A brother chooses a woman, she gets a property patch, and the club recognizes her as someone they safeguard. Nobody crosses that line."

"Property? Like...ownership?"

"It's not as medieval as it sounds," I explain. "It's about protection more than possession. Means if anyone fucks with property of one of our patched members, they answer to the whole club, not just her man."

"And the women...they're okay with this?"

I shrug. "The ones who stick around are. Club life isn't for everyone. Most women who get patches know exactly what they're signing up for."

"Tasha has one?"

"Yeah. She wears it proudly. As does Skelly's girlfriend, Mirna."

Cece is quiet for a moment, absorbing this. I can practically see her mind processing what this means.

"So if we..." she trails off, her cheeks flushing slightly. She looks down at our joined hands, her thumb tracing circles on my palm. "If we became...whatever we're becoming. Would you expect me to wear one of those patches?"

I answer matter-of-factly. "Yes."

Her lips part, surprise flickering across her face at my blunt answer. For a second, I'm sure I've pushed too hard, too fast. But then something shifts—a curious heat replacing the initial shock.

"That's...presumptuous."

"It's honest," I counter, leaning closer. "If you're with me—*really* with me—then yeah, I want you marked. But we're nowhere near that conversation yet, princess."

She studies me, her gaze steady and intent, as though she's searching for something beneath the surface. "Would I get any say in it?"

"In wearing my patch? That's entirely your choice. But if you're asking if I'd let another man touch what's mine—" I let the sentence hang, unfinished but clear.

A small smile curves at the corner of her mouth. "You're very territorial for someone who claims we're nowhere near that conversation."

"I know what I want," I say simply. "Always have."

She doesn't look away. I can tell she's turning the words over, weighing what they mean—for her, for us.

Before she can respond, the door bangs open, shattering our bubble of quiet.

"There you are, you antisocial motherfucker!" Dom's slurred voice blasts through the small room as he stumbles in, wearing what appears to be a second beer-can crown stacked on top of the first. "Been looking everywhere for you two!"

I suppress a groan. "We're having a private conversation."

Dom waves that off as though it holds zero relevance. "Forget that! It's my birthday! You can talk later." He sways a little, grinning at Cece. "You don't mind if I borrow him, do you? The boys are setting up the shot table, and we need our resident champion."

Cece glances between us, clearly trying to decide how to handle this circus of a man.

"We were actually thinking about heading out," I tell Dom, not trying to hide my irritation.

"What? No!" Dom presses a hand to his chest, wounded to his core. "Come on, brother. One round. For my birthday." Then he turns those pleading eyes on Cece. "Tell him he has to stay. Just for a little while."

The last thing I want is for her to feel pressured into sticking around this madhouse longer than she wants. But instead of looking uncomfortable, she seems to be considering it.

"It's up to you," I say, my tone making it clear I'm

perfectly fine with leaving. "We can go whenever you want."

She bites her lower lip, glancing from me to Dom's ridiculous beer can crown, then back again. "Maybe we could stay a little longer?" she says, surprising me. "I mean, it *is* his birthday."

Dom punches the air triumphantly. "See? She gets it! Birthday rules!"

I narrow my gaze at her. "You sure? This isn't exactly the quiet introduction to club life I had in mind."

She shrugs, a glint of challenge playing across her face. "I think I can handle it. Besides, I'm curious about this *shot table* champion title."

"Fuck yeah!" Dom cheers, nearly toppling over in his enthusiasm. "She's a keeper, Bray!"

I'm still hesitating, not entirely convinced this is a good idea. "I've had a few drinks already," I admit, not wanting to risk riding back impaired with her on the back of my bike. "If we stay, we might need to crash here tonight."

To my surprise, this doesn't seem to faze her. "If you want to stay, it's fine. Really."

"One round," I tell Dom, pointing a warning finger at him. "Then we reassess."

"Fair enough!" Dom throws his arm around my shoulders, nearly knocking us both off balance as he steers us toward the door. "Come on, preacher's daughter! Let me introduce you to the fine art of competitive drinking!"

I shoot Cece an apologetic look, but she just smiles and follows us back into the chaos.

CHAPTER 17

CECE

I'M TIPTOEING BEHIND BRAYDEN, the floor beneath my bare feet cold enough to make me wince. My head is pounding with the special kind of regret that only comes from tequila shots and bad decisions, and I'm desperately trying not to make eye contact with the half-naked woman passed out on the pool table.

"Almost there," Brayden whispers, his massive hand wrapped around mine as he guides me through the wreckage of last night's party. Empty bottles, discarded clothing, and at least three unconscious bodies are scattered across the clubhouse floor, casualties of their own terrible decisions.

"Did I really challenge Big to a drinking contest?" I

whisper, flashes of the night hitting me in a disjointed reel of chaos.

Brayden's shoulders shake with quiet laughter. "You did. And you held your own until the fifth round."

"Oh God." I press a hand to my temple, where a construction crew appears to be operating heavy machinery. "No wonder I feel as though I've been run over."

"Shh," he warns as we approach a snoring prospect sprawled in the hallway. Brayden steps over him with ease, then turns to guide me around the obstacle. I tug on Brayden's hand, forcing him to stop.

"Remind me why we're sneaking out," I whisper. "It's morning. We could just walk out the front door."

Brayden looks back at me, amusement tugging at his mouth. "Trust me, princess. I'm sparing you from the chorus of vomiting that's about to kick off once these degenerates wake up. And the hangover complaints? Absolute torture."

I wince at the mental image. "Fair point."

"Besides," he adds, "after the way you danced on that table last night, you might want a head start before anyone remembers."

"I did what?" My stomach drops so fast I'm surprised it doesn't crash through the floor. "Please tell me you're joking."

His grin widens, and I can't tell if he's messing with me or not. "Come on, lightweight. Let's get you home before the walking dead rise."

We finally reach the front door, and Brayden eases it

open. The morning sunlight hits me like a physical assault, and I groan, shielding my eyes.

"Oh god, turn it off," I mutter, which earns me another low chuckle from Brayden.

"Not sure I have that ability, but I can try."

Brayden keeps a steady arm around my waist as we cross the gravel lot. The stones attack my bare feet with zero mercy, and it suddenly occurs to me—in true walk-of-shame fashion—that my shoes have vanished into the void.

"Um, Brayden? My shoes..."

"In my hand," he says, holding up my sandals that I hadn't even noticed him carrying. "You insisted they were 'torture devices designed by the patriarchy' around midnight."

"Oh God," I groan, mortification heating my cheeks. "Please tell me I didn't actually dance on a table."

His silence is answer enough.

"Kill me now," I mutter, pressing my palms against my face. The movement makes my head spin, and I stumble slightly.

"Easy there," Brayden says, tightening his grip on my waist. "Let's get you home and into bed."

The thought of climbing onto his motorcycle makes my stomach turn. The vibration, the noise, the motion—every part of it feels destined to end in spectacular embarrassment.

"I don't think I can handle your bike right now," I admit, swallowing against the nausea climbing up my throat. "My head feels ready to burst."

Brayden studies my face, then nods. "I figured as much. Don't worry, I've got us covered."

He guides me toward a beat-up black truck parked at the edge of the lot.

"Whose is this?" I ask as he opens the passenger door for me.

"Hammer's. He loaned me the keys last night when he saw how wasted you were getting." Brayden helps me into the seat with surprising gentleness.

The fact that these intimidating bikers were looking out for me, planning for my inevitable hangover, does something warm to my chest, or maybe that's just the tequila still burning through my system.

"That was...surprisingly thoughtful," I manage as Brayden shuts my door and circles around to the driver's side.

"Club takes care of its own," he says simply as he slides behind the wheel.

Its own. The phrase settles over me like a blanket. Is that what I am now? One of them? The thought should terrify me, but in my current state, it just feels oddly comforting.

"What about your bike?"

"One of the prospects will bring it down later when he comes after Hammer's truck."

Brayden turns the key and the truck rumbles to life. Even that gentle vibration is enough to make my stomach perform an uncomfortable flip. I close my eyes and lean my head against the cool window glass.

"I've never been this hungover in my life," I

mumble. "I don't even remember how many shots I had."

"Seven," Brayden says, pulling out of the parking lot. "Plus, whatever Tasha kept slipping you when I wasn't looking."

"She was trying to get me drunk?"

He chuckles. "Not maliciously. She said something about you needing to loosen the church girl shackles."

"Well, mission accomplished," I groan. "I think I've loosened them right into the next county."

The truck hits a pothole and I moan dramatically, clutching my stomach. "Please tell me I didn't embarrass myself too badly."

Brayden reaches over and places his warm hand on my thigh. The touch is comforting, grounding.

"You were fine. Actually, you impressed a lot of people."

I crack one eye open to look at him skeptically. "By dancing on a table?"

"By holding your own. Most of the guys' old ladies won't even set foot in parties like that, much less end up in the middle of everything."

"I'm not sure 'jump' is the right word. More 'dragged'—courtesy of Tasha and Dom. I'm honestly shocked I still have any dignity left," I admit, glancing down at my clothes. At least I'm still fully dressed, which feels like a small miracle after what I witnessed in that clubhouse.

"I wouldn't have let anything happen to you,

princess. And for the record… it was good seeing you cut loose."

"It certainly doesn't feel nice right now," I fire back.

Brayden's lips quirk into that half-smile that somehow makes my stomach flutter despite the nausea. "Lie down," he says, patting his thigh. "Bench seat's big enough. Best cure for a hangover is to sleep it off anyway."

I hesitate for just a second before the pounding in my head convinces me. "If I throw up on you, remember this was your idea," I warn, unbuckling my seatbelt.

"I've survived worse," he chuckles as I awkwardly maneuver myself down, resting my head on his muscular thigh.

His hand comes to rest on my hair, fingers gently stroking through the tangled strands. It feels impossibly good.

"This is nice," I murmur, my eyelids already growing heavy. The steady rumble of the truck's engine, the warmth of his body, the rhythmic motion of his fingers in my hair.

"Sleep, princess," he says softly. "I've got you."

Those words follow me down into darkness.

I don't know how long I've been asleep when I wake with a start, disoriented by the unfamiliar softness beneath me. This isn't the truck.

I'm in Brayden's bed.

As I blink into the dim light filtering through unfamiliar curtains. My mouth tastes like something died in it, and my head still pounds, but the violent nausea seems to have passed.

"Welcome back to the land of the living," Brayden's voice rumbles from somewhere nearby.

I turn my head carefully, wincing as the movement sends a fresh wave of pain through my temples. He's sitting in a chair by the bed, shirtless, a mug of something steaming in his hands. His hair is damp from a shower, and he's watching me with an amused expression that makes me want to crawl under the covers and die.

"How long was I out?"

"About four hours." He sets his mug down and leans forward, elbows on his knees. "How's the head?"

"Still attached, unfortunately." I push myself up to sitting position and realize I'm wearing one of his t-shirts instead of my clothes from last night. "Did you change me?"

"You insisted on it when I carried you in from the truck."

I groan, covering my face with my hands. "I don't remember that part."

"Not surprised. You were pretty far gone." He reaches for something on the nightstand. "Water and painkillers," he explains, holding out two white pills and a glass of water. "Best I can offer until we can get some real food in you."

I take them gratefully, swallowing them down with several large gulps of water. I hadn't realized how desperately thirsty I was until the cool liquid hits my parched throat.

"Thank you," I manage, my voice still rough from sleep and too many tequila shots. "I'm sorry for being such a mess."

Brayden shakes his head, that half-smile playing at his lips. "You don't need to apologize. Everyone's entitled to let loose sometimes. You hungry? I can make you something."

My stomach lurches at the mere mention of food. "God no," I mumble, pressing a hand against my queasy middle. "The thought of eating anything right now might actually kill me."

He nods, understanding without judgment. Then, instead of heading to the kitchen, he moves toward the bed, lifting the covers.

"Scoot over," he says softly.

I shift to make room, and he slides in beside me, the mattress dipping under his weight. With gentle hands, he guides me onto his chest, one arm wrapping securely around me. His skin is warm against my cheek, his heartbeat steady beneath my ear.

"Better?" he asks.

"Much," I whisper, relaxing against him. His chest hair tickles my cheek.

Brayden reaches for the remote on the nightstand and clicks on the flat screen mounted to the wall opposite the bed. The TV flickers to life, and he starts scrolling through channels, then suddenly stops.

"Christmas Vacation. Haven't seen this in years."

"You like Christmas movies?"

"Don't be so shocked."

"I didn't expect you to be the kind of guy who enjoys watching Chevy Chase fall off a ladder," I say, trying to adjust my position without jostling my throbbing head.

"There are a lot of things about me you don't know yet, princess." His fingers trace lazy patterns on my arm. "Besides, everyone likes watching Chevy Chase fall off a ladder. It's practically an American tradition."

I snuggle closer, breathing in his scent. The combination is oddly comforting.

"I used to watch this with my mom every Christmas," I admit quietly. "She'd make hot chocolate with these tiny peppermint marshmallows she could only find at this one store in Carlsbad. We'd wait until Dad was at a church meeting and make a whole night of it."

Brayden's hand pauses momentarily in its gentle stroking. "You don't talk about her much."

"It's still hard sometimes." I focus on the TV, where Clark Griswold is struggling with Christmas lights. "She was the buffer between my father and me. After she died, everything got...stricter."

"How old were you?"

"Twenty. Breast cancer. It was quick—diagnosed in February, gone by October." I swallow against the familiar ache that rises whenever I talk about her. "My dad threw himself into the church."

"And you threw yourself into your marriage."

"It seemed like the sensible thing to do at the time. I

thought maybe if I did that one thing right, it would fill the hole she left."

Brayden's fingers resume their gentle patterns on my skin. "Did it?"

"Not even close." I close my eyes, the movie forgotten. "It just made a different kind of emptiness. One I didn't recognize until it was too late."

"That's all in the past now, princess. You can be whoever, whatever you want to be. Maybe steer away from table dancing, though."

I smack his arm hard. "Not funny."

"It's a little funny."

"Hush," I tell him, pressing a finger to his lips. "It's getting to my favorite part."

On screen, Aunt Bethany stands with her hands folded, ready to say grace over the family's Christmas dinner. I find myself mouthing the words along with her as she launches into the Pledge of Allegiance instead of a prayer.

Brayden's chest rumbles with silent laughter beneath my cheek, but he doesn't interrupt. His fingers resume their gentle stroking through my hair, each touch somehow easing the persistent throbbing in my temples.

I smile against his skin as the Griswold family awkwardly joins in Aunt Bethany's misguided patriotism. There's something deeply comforting about this scene—the family's chaotic love for each other despite all their dysfunction. Maybe that's why I've always loved this movie. It reminds me that families come in all shapes and sizes, messy and imperfect, but still bound together.

"My mom would laugh so hard at this part," I mutter, not really expecting a response. "She had this ridiculous snorting laugh that used to embarrass me as a teenager, but now…I'd give anything to hear it again."

Brayden's hand pauses momentarily in my hair before continuing its soothing rhythm. He doesn't offer platitudes or try to fix my grief. He just holds me a little tighter. And somehow, that's exactly what I need.

We finish the movie in silence. It's not until the credits begin to roll, soft music filling the quiet room, that I notice his hand has finally stilled.

When I glance up, his head is tilted back slightly, breathing slow and even. He's fallen asleep.

A small smile tugs at my lips. "She would've liked you," I whisper to the quiet room.

The screen fades to black, and before I can think too much about it, my own eyes drift shut, the steady rhythm of his heartbeat pulling me under.

CHAPTER 18

CECE

THE SUNSHINE STREAMING through the diner window feels like it's personally attacking my brain from the lingering hangover headache, but the smell of melting cheese is slowly bringing me back to life. I'm hunched over what might be the greasiest pizza in San Salona, and it's exactly what my body needs.

"I can't believe this place is still here," I say, tearing off another slice. "I thought for sure they'd have gone under by now."

Brayden smirks across the red vinyl booth. "Tony's pizza has survived three recessions and a health inspector with a vendetta. Pretty sure it'll outlast us all."

I look around Tony's Pizzeria, taking in the chipped

Formica and the ancient jukebox in the corner still committed to its five-song Bon Jovi playlist. The walls are covered with faded team photos and yellowing clippings, all frozen in time. Walking in feels as though I've stepped straight back into high school.

"God, I haven't been here since senior year," I muse, dabbing at a string of cheese dangling from my chin. "Remember when this was the only place anyone ever wanted to hang out?"

"Not much else to do in this town," Brayden says, reaching for his soda. "Unless you count getting drunk at Miller's Pond or making out behind the bleachers."

"I wouldn't know anything about that." I catch the knowing gleam he doesn't bother to hide. "What, you think I spent my Friday nights behind the bleachers?"

"I think every teenager in this town spent at least one night behind those bleachers."

"I'll have you know I was a very well-behaved teenager."

"Bullshit," he says, grinning. "Nobody's that good."

I take another bite of pizza to avoid answering, though I can't help the smile tugging at my lips. The truth is, I wasn't nearly as rebellious as some of the other kids, but I had my moments. Little things my father never knew about. Sneaking out after curfew. A stolen beer with Emma behind the community center. Fun in small doses. Nowhere near the chaos my friends chased.

"Fine," I concede. "Maybe I wasn't completely innocent. But compared to you, I was practically a saint."

Brayden leans back, one arm stretched across the back of the booth. The motion pulls his T-shirt snug across his chest, and I catch a glimpse of ink curling out from under his sleeve.

"If you still want to live some of those teenage dreams," he says, voice low, "I can make that happen, princess."

The look he gives me sends heat blooming in my cheeks. There's something about Brayden's casual promises of sin, delivered in that gravel-drenched tone, that makes my pulse skip.

"You're terrible."

"And yet, here you are."

His gaze holds mine across the table, and for a moment, I forget we're in a public place. I forget everything except the memory of his hands on my skin.

The bell above the door jingles and the spell shatters. I glance over and immediately regret it. Ethan walks in with Britney on his arm. Her hand tucked into the crook of his elbow like she always belonged there.

"Shit," I mutter, ducking my head.

Brayden's posture shifts instantly. His shoulders tense as he watches my ex make his way across the restaurant.

"Want to leave?" he asks, already half-rising.

"No," I say, surprised by the steel in my own voice. "I'm not running from him anymore."

Brayden settles back, but the easygoing calm from earlier is gone.

I try to focus on my pizza, silently praying Ethan

won't notice us. But of course, the universe can't resist irony. He moves toward our booth, all smugness and smiles.

"Still slumming it, Cece?"

Brayden's jaw locks.

"Funny," I reply, voice steady. "I was just thinking the same thing about you."

Ethan's smile is razor-thin. "I see you've fully committed to your little rebellion." His gaze flicks dismissively over Brayden before snapping back to me. "Your father is beside himself, you know. The whole congregation is praying for your return to sanity."

I take a deliberate bite of my pizza, chewing slowly before answering. "How thoughtful. And here I was worried no one would notice I'm having the time of my life."

Britney shifts uncomfortably beside him, her bleached-blonde hair falling in perfect curls around her surgically enhanced features. She tugs at Ethan's arm. "Baby, our table's ready."

Ethan ignores her, leaning down until his hands are flat on our table. "This won't last, Cece. You know that, right? Whatever thrill you're getting from this—" he flicks his gaze toward Brayden, "—criminal will ruin you."

I feel Brayden's energy shift beside me. "The only thing that will be ruined is your fucking face, when I rearrange it with my fist, asshole."

Ethan's eyes narrow, but he doesn't move. "Go

ahead. I'm sure assault charges would look great on top of your already impressive record."

"Ethan, stop," I hiss. "Just go to your table."

Britney tugs harder at his arm. "Please, baby. People are staring."

They are. The few other customers in Tony's are watching our table with undisguised interest. In a town this small, public confrontations are better than television.

Ethan straightens, adjusting his collar with a flick of his wrist. "You'll come to your senses eventually, Cece. And when you do, don't expect anyone to welcome you back with open arms. You've made your choice."

"Best decision I ever made."

He gives me one last contemptuous look before allowing Britney to lead him to a table near the back.

"Let's get out of here," Brayden growls, his eyes fixed on Ethan's retreating back as if he could set it on fire through sheer will.

I nod, the pizza in front of me suddenly as appealing as cardboard. "I've lost my appetite anyway."

Brayden catches Tony's eye and makes the universal *check, please* gesture. The owner nods, already pulling out his receipt pad.

"I need to use the bathroom first," I say, sliding out of the booth. "Meet you outside?"

"I'll pay the tab." He nods, though I can tell he hates the idea of letting me out of his sight while Ethan's still in the room. "Make it quick."

I weave through the tables, heading toward the hallway marked *Restrooms*, and feel the weight of Ethan's stare as I pass. I keep my chin up, refusing to let him see me flinch.

The women's bathroom is empty, thankfully. I lock myself in a stall and lean against the door, drawing slow breaths to steady the jittery feeling beneath my skin. The confrontation rattled me more than I want to admit.

Ethan still has that effect. This subtle, insidious way of making me feel small. I hate it.

At the sink, I splash cold water on my face and study my reflection in the smudged mirror. My cheeks are flushed—not with shame this time, but with anger. My gaze burns a little too bright.

Progress, I guess.

I take my time washing my hands. I don't want to rush out. I don't want Ethan to think he chased me off. Because I'm done running. Done letting him think he holds any power over me.

The door swings open just as I'm reaching for a paper towel. I freeze, my wet hands dripping onto the floor as Ethan slips inside, closing the door behind him with a soft click.

"What the hell are you doing?" I back up against the sink.

"We need to talk," Ethan says, his voice softer now, reasonable. It's the tone he used to use when he wanted to convince me I was overreacting. "Alone, without your pet criminal breathing down my neck."

"Get out, Ethan." I try to move toward the door, but he steps sideways, blocking my path.

"Two minutes," he says, holding up his fingers. "That's all I'm asking."

"I have nothing to say to you." My heart pounds against my ribs.

Ethan moves closer, his cologne wrapping around me like a noose. "I'm worried about you, Cece. Everyone is."

"Worried?" I laugh, but it sounds brittle even to my own ears. "That's rich coming from the man who spent our entire marriage making me miserable."

"Making you miserable?" Ethan's face contorts with disbelief. "I gave you everything, Cece. A beautiful home, financial security, social standing. What more could you possibly have wanted?"

"I don't know, maybe a husband who didn't screw every available woman in town?"

He steps closer, backing me against the sink. "You want to know why I strayed? Why I had to look elsewhere?" His eyes harden as he looks me up and down. "You were frigid. A goddamn ice queen in our bedroom."

The shock lands hard, stealing my breath. "Excuse me?"

"You heard me." He leans in, voice dropping to a cruel whisper. "You think I wanted to cheat? I didn't. But one can only take so many nights of putting their dick in a cold fish before giving up. All those nights you'd lie there, stiff as a board, waiting for it to be over." He shakes his head with mock sympathy. "No wonder I had to find my pleasure elsewhere."

Hot shame floods my cheeks, followed immediately by **white-hot anger** so intense my vision blurs at the edges.

"Brayden would disagree with you." I spit back.

Ethan's face transforms instantly, tightening with the kind of fury I remember all too well. His hand shoots out, clamping around my wrist hard enough to make me wince.

"You little slut," he hisses, leaning in so close I can feel his breath on my face. "You're fucking him?"

I try to wrench my arm away. "Let go of me."

"Did it feel good to debase yourself? To let that piece of garbage touch you?" His grip tightens. "Did you think about me while he was inside you?"

"Not even once," I say as I grit my teeth. "And he's twice the man you'll ever be."

Something unsettling flickers across Ethan's face. For a moment, I think he might actually hit me. Instead, he drags me closer, his face inches from mine

"You think he actually cares?" he spits. "Men like that don't care about anything but what's between a woman's legs."

"Like *you* cared so much?" I try to pull away, but his grip tightens. "Let me go, Ethan. Now."

"Or what?" His mouth twists into a cruel smile. "You'll call your biker boyfriend? Have him beat me up? You are my fucking wife, and I will do with you what I wish."

I shove at his chest with both hands. "Stop it! I'm not your wife anymore!"

His expression turns sharper as he grabs my other wrist, pinning both arms to the sink.

"Come on, Cece. Don't pretend you don't miss me sometimes."

"We could try again," he murmurs, leaning closer, crowding me back against the cold porcelain. "I'd take you back. I know what you need."

Revulsion ripples through my spine. "Don't touch me."

I twist my head away, but he follows the movement, his lips scraping too close to my ear. His free hand drifts lower, hovering at my hip, lingering there with ugly intent.

"You remember how it was," he says softly. "You used to like it when you couldn't fight me."

My stomach churns. "Ethan, stop."

He laughs under his breath, low and eager, the sound of a man who thinks he has already won. His fingers tighten on my hip, pressing me harder into the sink, and the look in his eyes shifts into something cold and hungry—something that tells me exactly what he came in here planning to do.

My pulse spikes with panic.

"Let me go," I whisper, voice breaking.

He smiles, slow and cruel. "Why would I? We still have unfinished business."

His body traps mine against the porcelain, his eyes

taking on a hunger that has nothing to do with affection.

"Ethan, stop," I rasp.

He doesn't. He leans in, closing that last inch of space, lips brushing my cheek as he tries to force my head toward him—

The bathroom door suddenly explodes inward with a deafening crack.

Brayden storms through, his massive frame blocking out everything behind him, fury radiating from every line of his body. His eyes snap to Ethan's hand beside my face, and a charged quiet settles over us, the kind that heralds trouble.

"Get your fucking hands off her." His voice is deadly quiet, scarier than if he'd been shouting.

Ethan drops my wrists immediately and takes a step back. "This is a private conversation between me and my wife."

"Ex-wife," I correct, rubbing my wrists where his fingers have left red marks.

Brayden's gaze drops to the marks on my skin, and something shifts in his expression. The controlled fury fractures into something fierce and undeniable. In two strides, he's across the bathroom, grabbing Ethan by the throat and slamming him against the wall hard enough to crack the cheap tile.

The crack of Ethan's head hitting the wall echoes in the small bathroom. I gasp, frozen in place as Brayden's massive forearm presses against Ethan's throat, lifting him until his feet barely touch the ground.

"Touch her again, and you'll learn exactly how many bones are in the human hand." Brayden's voice drops, every word edged in warning. His grip tightens. "Those fingers that just marked her skin? I'll take my time with each one. And when I'm done, the only prayer you'll remember is the one begging me to stop."

Ethan's face is turning a deep, mottled purple. He claws at Brayden's arm, choking, panicked.

I should be horrified. Should be pleading for him to stop. But there's a vicious part of me that wants to watch Ethan struggle just a little longer.

"Brayden," I manage finally, voice soft but steady. "Not here."

He doesn't spare me a glance. His entire focus remains on Ethan, his restraint pulled taut and ready to break.

"He hurt you," Brayden growls.

"I know." I step closer, placing my hand on his tensed shoulder. "But I don't want you arrested for murder in a bathroom. He's not worth it."

For a terrifying moment, I think he won't listen. Then, with visible restraint, he eases the pressure just enough for Ethan to drag in a wheezing breath.

"You're insane," Ethan gasps, still pinned to the wall. "I'll have you arrested for assault."

"You'll have me arrested?" Brayden laughs. "I just walked in on you trying to sexually assault your ex-wife in a fucking women's restroom, motherfucker."

"Go ahead," Ethan wheezes, his face still flushed with anger and lack of oxygen. "You think anyone in this town will believe your word over mine? A convicted felon versus a respected businessman?"

Brayden's grip tightens again, and I can see the muscles in his forearm flexing with restraint. "I bet there are cameras out in that hallway that show you following her into the bathroom. Why would a 'respected businessman' need to be in a women's restroom?"

"She came onto me," Ethan spits, his gaze darting to me. "Tell him, Cece. Tell him how you've been texting me, begging me to meet you."

"What?" I nearly choke on my disbelief. "You're delusional."

"Show me your phone," Brayden demands, his free hand already extending toward me. "Now."

I fumble in my pocket, pulling out my cell and unlocking it before handing it to him. "Look at whatever you want. He's lying."

Brayden keeps Ethan pinned with one arm while scrolling through my messages with the other. His jaw clenches as he finds nothing.

"You're pathetic," he tells Ethan, tossing my phone back to me. "A fucking liar on top of everything else."

"She—she must've deleted them," Ethan stammers, thrashing weakly in Brayden's grip.

Brayden doesn't even blink.

He slams Ethan into the wall so hard the drywall cracks. "Enough."

Ethan gasps, but Brayden leans closer. "Here's what's going to happen. You're going to walk out of here, back to your little Barbie doll slut, and you're going to erase Cece from your brain. If I find out you've been within fifty feet of her, I will make sure the pieces of your body will never be fucking found."

Ethan's gaze flicks between us, calculation slowly replacing fear. "You can't threaten me."

"It's not a threat," Brayden says flatly. "It's a promise. One I have no problem keeping, asshole."

The look on Ethan's face shifts from defiance to something I rarely seen in him—genuine fear. His focus darts around the small bathroom, searching for an exit, but Brayden's massive frame leaves no way out.

"You're fucking crazy," Ethan snarls, trying to put on a brave front, but the tremor in his voice betrays him.

With one final shove, Brayden slams him back against the wall before stepping away.

Ethan slumps forward, gasping, one hand rubbing at the angry red marks on his throat.

"Get out," Brayden says. His voice is quiet now, dangerous. "Now."

Ethan straightens his collar, trying to salvage what little dignity he has left. When he finally looks at me, his expression is stripped of charm or mockery—just cold, festering hate.

"This isn't over, Cece."

"It's been over for a long time."

Ethan pushes past Brayden, careful not to touch him, and stumbles toward the door. He pauses in the doorway, looking back at us.

"You two deserve each other," he spits, then he's gone, the broken door swinging behind him.

As soon as he disappears, my knees suddenly buckle. The adrenaline that kept me standing during the confrontation drains away all at once, leaving me shaking. Brayden is at my side instantly, his arm around my waist, the only thing keeping me upright.

"I've got you," he murmurs, guiding me to sit on the closed toilet lid. "Breathe, Cece. Just breathe."

I try to do what he says, but my lungs feel restricted, every breath too shallow. My hands won't still, and the red marks on my wrists seem to beat along with my frantic pulse.

"He grabbed me," I whisper, staring at the angry welts. "He actually put his hands on me."

Brayden kneels in front of me, gently taking my hands in his. His thumbs brush over the marks on my wrists, touch feather-light despite the **anger** still simmering just beneath the surface.

"I should've killed him."

"No." I shake my head, suddenly desperate to make him understand. "That's what he wants. He wants you to snap so he can use it against me."

Brayden's jaw tightens, but he nods. "Smart bastard."

"Not smart enough to know I'd never go back to him." I swallow hard, fighting the nausea crawling up my throat. "The things he said…"

"Were lies," Brayden finishes, his fingers still circling

my wrists in slow, calming motions. "Every word out of that fucker's mouth was a lie."

I nod, but I can't quite bring myself to look at him. Ethan's voice still echoes in my head—cruel, cutting. The words settle like barbs beneath my skin. What if there was truth in them? What if I really had been...

"Hey." Brayden's voice cuts through my spiral. He tilts my chin up, coaxing me to meet his gaze. "Whatever he said before I got in here—whatever's putting that look on your face—it's bullshit. You know that, right?"

I try to nod, but tears spill instead. "He said I was frigid. That I was the reason he cheated. Because I was...inadequate."

The muscle in Brayden's jaw twitches. Fury pours off him, but he doesn't move to leave. Doesn't explode. Instead, he takes a slow, controlled breath and cups my face with surprising tenderness.

"Listen to me. His kind ruins you and then tells you to apologize for it."

"But what if—"

"No." His thumb sweeps away a tear I didn't even feel fall. "Do not carry his blame. Every bit of this is on him."

"I need to get you out of here," Brayden says, helping me to my feet. "Can you walk?"

I nod, even though my legs are unsteady, soft under me. "I'm okay." It isn't true, but I need the words to hold.

He wraps an arm around my waist as we move

toward the door. I keep my head down, not wanting to see the stares that are surely waiting for us in the restaurant. The last thing I need is to become even more of a spectacle for the town gossips.

We step through the doorway and nearly collide with an elderly woman standing right outside. Her silver hair is pulled into a tight bun, and her faded blue eyes widen at the sight of us emerging from the women's restroom together.

"Mrs. Holloway," I manage, recognizing my father's long-time church secretary. Of all the people to witness this moment.

Her gaze travels from my face to my wrists, then to the splintered bathroom door hanging off its hinges. Something shifts in her expression—not the judgment I expect, but something softer, almost knowing.

"Are you alright, dear?" she asks.

"She's fine," Brayden answers as he maneuvers past her, ignoring the question. Instead of going up front, Brayden leads me further down the hallway until we come to a service entrance door. He shoves it open, stepping out first before reaching back for me.

"Stay here," he orders before disappearing around the corner towards the front of the restaurant. I hear the rumble of his motorcycle from the alley, and a few seconds later, he comes around the corner.

Brayden holds out his helmet, jaw tight. "Get on."

My hands keep shaking as I take it. The air hits me with a clarity that feels wrong, as if nothing should look untouched after what almost happened. I fasten the strap and climb on behind him, fighting to pull in a deep breath.

The engine rumbles beneath us as he pulls away from the alley. My chest tightens, a mix of anger, shame, and relief twisting together until I can't tell them apart.

I press my forehead against his back, eyes stinging, and let the motion of the bike pull me somewhere—anywhere—else.

CHAPTER 19

BRAYDEN

EVERY MILE on the road isn't enough to outrun the fury burning through my veins. I can still feel Ethan's throat beneath my forearm, the give of his windpipe, how fucking close I came to crushing it completely. Three more seconds of pressure, and the world would've had one less piece of shit in it.

I shouldn't have let her stop me.

The wind whips around us as I push the bike faster feeling Cece's arms tighten around my waist. Her body trembles against my back, whether from the cold or the aftershock, I can't tell. Probably both. The red marks on her wrists flash in my mind with every blink—perfect impressions of that motherfucker's fingers marking what's mine.

What's mine. The thought hammers through me with each heartbeat. She's mine to protect, mine to keep safe, and I fucking failed.

I pull off the main road, cutting down a side street that leads to Jillian's property. Cece doesn't question where we're going, just holds on tighter as we take the curves too fast. I need to get her somewhere safe—somewhere I can make sure she's okay, somewhere I can finally let this anger out before it burns me alive from the inside.

When we reach the guesthouse, I kill the engine but don't move immediately. I need a moment to get myself under control. To push down the urge to get back on this bike, track Ethan down, and finish what confrontation I started.

I feel Cece's hands slide around to my chest, her touch light but steadying. She seems to sense I'm hanging by a thread.

"Brayden," she murmurs, her voice soft against my ear. "Let's go inside."

I nod, not trusting myself to speak. My hands are still shaking with adrenaline as I dismount the bike and help her down. She winces when she pulls off the helmet, and that small flash of pain sends another surge of fury through me. I want to punch a wall—anything to drown out the image of what I'd do if Ethan were in front of me right now.

I unlock the door and guide her inside, my hand resting protectively at the small of her back. Once we're in, she stands in the middle of the living room, looking lost, arms wrapped around herself as though she's trying to keep everything from unraveling.

"Do you want some water?" I ask, desperate for something normal to do—anything that doesn't involve imagining all the ways I could make Ethan pay.

She shakes her head. "I just need…" The words fade, unfinished.

I move toward her carefully. When I reach her, I take her hands in mine and turn them over, examining her wrists. The marks have deepened, faint red bands that'll bloom into bruises by morning. I brush over them with my thumbs, keeping my touch as gentle as I can manage.

I'm going to kill him. Plain and fucking simple. It isn't a question of *if*—it's *when*.

The thought is so sharp, so vivid, it nearly slips past my lips. I choke it back, but the taste of violence lingers on my tongue, cold and metallic.

"I need to clean these. Sit down."

She obeys without argument, sinking onto the couch while I head to the bathroom for the first aid kit. My hands are still shaking when I return, but I force them steady as I kneel in front of her.

"This might sting," I warn, dampening a cotton pad with antiseptic. There are small crescent marks where his fingernails dug into her skin. I dab at them gently, watching her face for any sign of pain.

"I'm sorry," she whispers, and something inside me snaps.

"Don't you dare apologize. Not for this. Not for him."

"I should have—"

"No." I look up from her wrists and meet her gaze. "He followed you into that bathroom. He put his hands on you. There's nothing you should or shouldn't have done."

She bites her lower lip, blinking hard as tears threaten—but refuse—to fall. I've never wanted to hurt someone as badly as I want to hurt Ethan in this moment. The need for violence sits in my chest like a living thing, coiled and ready to strike.

The cotton pad tears in my hand. I force myself to breathe, to keep my grip gentle on her wrists, even as frustration pulses through me.

"I should've killed him," I mutter, the words slipping out before I can stop them.

She shakes her head, a single tear finally trailing down her cheek. "And then what? You'd be in prison, and he'd still win."

"He'd be dead. Sounds like a win to me."

"Brayden." She cups my face in both hands, firm but tender, anchoring me. "I don't need you to kill for me. I need you *here*. With me."

I close my eyes and lean into her touch. Her hands are soft, warm—a lifeline. I want to believe her. Want to let it go. But the image of Ethan's hands on her plays again behind my lids, relentless and vivid.

"He was going to hurt you," I say hoarsely. "And he would've done worse if I hadn't shown up."

"But you *did* show up." Her thumbs move in slow strokes along my cheekbones. Only then do I notice how tightly my jaw is clenched, the ache settling into bone.

"You protected me."

"Not enough. Not soon enough."

I open my eyes to find her watching me, steady and shining with unshed tears. Silent proof that she's still here, still shaken, still strong.

"If I'd been there a minute later—"

"But you weren't."

I pull away from her touch, standing up so abruptly that she flinches. The movement sends another spike of fury through me. She shouldn't be flinching. Not around me. Never around me.

"I need a minute," I mutter, striding into the kitchen. I brace both hands on the counter, fighting to breathe through the red haze tightening my vision. My heart slams against my ribs, each beat sending another rush of fury through my system.

I hear her soft footsteps behind me but don't turn. I can't. Not with my hands still shaking. Not with the storm in my head refusing to settle.

"Brayden," she says quietly. "Talk to me."

"You don't want to know what's in my head right now."

"I do." Her hand lands between my shoulder blades, barely a touch, but enough to ground me for half a second.

"I'm thinking about finding him." The words scrape out of me before I can stop them.

"Cornering him somewhere no one can interfere. Making sure he finally understands fear. Making sure he pays for what he did to you."

The confession hangs there—raw, unfiltered, dangerous—and once it's out, there's no pulling it back.

She doesn't pull away. Doesn't look at me with disgust or fear. Her hand stays steady against my back.

"And then what?" she asks softly.

"Then I'd make him apologize to you. Make him crawl on his knees and beg for forgiveness before I finish him."

"You don't mean that."

I turn to face her, meeting her eyes so she can see exactly how serious I am. "I do mean it. Every fucking word."

She studies my face, her expression unreadable. Then she reaches for my hand, the one clenched in a white-knuckled fist on the counter. Her fingers slide over mine, gentle but insistent, until I let her pry them open.

Her touch is too gentle for the monster I'm becoming. I want to pull away, to keep her at a distance from everything boiling inside me, but I'm too fucking selfish. I need her hand in mine, need her touch.

"I wish I could tell you I don't mean it. That I'm just angry and saying shit I don't mean. But I can't lie to you, Cece. Not about this."

She intertwines her fingers with mine, and I watch her smaller hand vanish in my grasp. The contrast hits hard—her soft skin against my rough palm, her healing wrist beside my scarred knuckles. Everything about her feels too good, too untouched by the world I come from.

"I understand wanting to hurt him," she says quietly. "Believe me, I do. But revenge isn't worth losing yourself over."

I laugh, the sound rough even to my own ears. "Losing myself? Princess, this *is* me. The violence, the fury. It isn't some extra part I can switch off. It's woven into who I am."

"No." She shakes her head and steps closer, her warmth brushing against me. "That isn't the whole of you. I've seen the rest, even if you can't."

I want to believe her. God, I want to. But the anger still beats under my skin, a relentless second rhythm demanding release. She thinks she sees something in me worth saving—something I'm not convinced exists.

"You're wrong." Her closeness is doing something to me, making it harder to hold onto the fury. "You don't know what I'm capable of."

"I know exactly what you're capable of." Her hand reaches up to touch my face again, and I fight the urge to lean into it like some touch-starved animal. "I saw you stop today when every instinct was telling you not to. That took more strength than giving in ever would."

I close my eyes, unable to face her. The faith she has in me cuts deeper than any condemnation.

"Don't put me on some fucking pedestal, Cece. I'm not a good man."

"I'm not asking you to be good," she whispers, her thumb stroking gently along my cheek. "I'm just asking you to be *here.* With me. Not out there hunting him down."

When I finally look at her, she's watching me with a quiet intensity that steals the breath from my lungs.

No fear. No judgment.

Just love—or something dangerously close to it.

"I can't promise I won't hurt him if I see him again," I admit. "I can't promise that."

"I know." She nods, still not pulling away. "But right now, I need you more than I need you to avenge me."

The need for violence doesn't disappear—it's still there, simmering under my skin—but it recedes just enough for me to breathe again.

"What do you need?" I ask. "Tell me what you need from me right now."

She steps closer, eliminating what little space remains between us. "Just hold me," she whispers. "Just make me feel safe."

I wrap my arms around her, careful not to squeeze too tight despite the urge to crush her against my chest. She melts into me, her body softening as she presses her face into my shirt. I can feel her tears soaking through the fabric, her shoulders shaking with silent sobs she's been holding back since we left the restaurant.

"I've got you," I murmur into her hair. "You're safe now."

We stand like that in the kitchen, her crying quietly against my chest. Part of me is still back in that bathroom, finishing what I started with Ethan. The other part is here, holding the only thing that matters, trying to be what she needs instead of the monster I know I am.

"I'm sorry," she says again, her voice muffled against my shirt.

"Don't," I warn her, my hand stilling in her hair. "You don't have to apologize to me."

"No, I need to say it," she insists, pulling back just enough to look at me, her face streaked with tears. "I'm sorry I let him get to me. I'm sorry I let him make me doubt myself."

I brush a strand of hair from her face, tucking it gently behind her ear.

"He's spent years getting inside your head. That kind of damage doesn't disappear overnight."

"I hate that he still has that power."

"Then take it back."

I cup her face in my hands, my thumbs gently sweeping away the tears on her cheeks. "Every time you choose what *you* want, you take some of that power back."

She leans into my touch, letting her eyes close for just a moment. When they open again, something has shifted—still hurting, yes, but steadier. There's steel under the softness now.

"I want you. I want this life I'm building. With you."

The simple declaration hits me with unexpected

force. I've spent my life being wanted for what I could do—damage I could inflict, protection I could offer, needs I could satisfy. But being wanted for who I am? That's a different kind of shock.

"You sure about that?" I ask, giving her one last chance to walk away from the storm that is me. "Because I'm still the same man who nearly put your ex-husband through a bathroom wall twenty minutes ago."

"I know exactly who you are," she says, rising onto her toes. "And I'm still choosing you."

Her lips meet mine—soft, insistent, tasting faintly of tears. I freeze for a heartbeat, stunned by her courage, her certainty. Then I'm kissing her back, my hands framing her face with a care I didn't know I had, holding her as though she's something rare and fragile.

Which she isn't. She's proven that today and every day since I've known her.

She pulls back just enough to whisper against my lips, "Take me to bed."

Those four words cut through the last of my rage, replacing it with a different kind of heat altogether. I search her face, looking for any sign of hesitation or fear.

"Are you sure that's what you need right now?"

She nods, her fingers twisting in the fabric of my shirt. "Do you always question a woman wanting you to take her to bed, or is that reserved just for me?"

"Only for you, princess,"

The smile that curves her lips is small but genuine.

"Is that so bad?" she asks, her fingers anchored in my shirt as though the touch itself is what's keeping me beside her.

"No," I admit, reaching down to brush a strand of hair from her face. "But I need to know this isn't just about forgetting what happened. About using me to erase him."

Her expression flashes—anger, maybe, or pure determination. "This isn't about him. It's about *us*. About what I want."

And *fuck*, I believe her. There's no hesitation, no fear, just that same stubborn fire that's been pulling me toward her since the beginning. I could drown in it and die happy.

"What you want," I echo, my thumb brushing along the curve of her lower lip. "Tell me, Cece. Say it."

She doesn't blink, doesn't falter. "I want you to take me to bed and make me forget everything except your name."

That's all it takes.

In one smooth motion, I scoop her up. Her legs wrap around my waist like she was made to fit there. Her lips find the side of my neck, trailing fire along my skin, and it takes every shred of control not to lose myself right there.

I ease her down gently, my hands unsteady for reasons I can't quite name as I hover above her.

"You sure about this?" I ask one last time, giving her an out that part of me prays she won't take.

She answers by pulling me down to her, her mouth

finding mine with a hunger that matches the storm raging inside me. Her kiss tastes like salvation and sin all at once—sweet and desperate and consuming. I lose myself in it, in her, letting her pull me under until the anger that's been burning through me transforms into something else entirely.

My hands find the hem of her shirt, sliding beneath to feel the warm skin of her stomach. She leans into my touch, a soft gasp escaping her lips when my fingers trace the underside of her breast. I want to worship every inch of her, to erase any memory of that bastard's hands with my own.

"Please," she whispers against my mouth, and that one word undoes me.

I tug her shirt over her head, revealing the simple cotton bra beneath. Nothing fancy, nothing meant to seduce, and somehow that makes it all the more perfect. This isn't a show. It's just us, raw and real in this moment.

"Beautiful," I murmur, trailing kisses along her collarbone. "So fucking beautiful."

She shivers beneath me, her hands fumbling with the buttons on my shirt. I help her peel it off and toss it aside. When she touches me, her fingers tracing the outline of the raven on my shoulder.

"Brayden," she whispers, and my name on her lips is like a fucking prayer.

I reach behind her, unhooking her bra. As it falls away, I take in the sight of her—skin flushed pink, nipples hardening under my gaze, eyes bright with want and something deeper. The marks on her wrists stand out against her pale skin, and I feel that rage threatening to resurface.

I push it down, focusing on her instead. On this. On us.

"What do you need?" I ask again, needing to hear it.

Her hand slides up my chest to cup my face, thumb stroking over my stubbled jaw. "You," she says simply. "Just you."

I lean down to capture her mouth again, slower this time, savoring the taste of her. My hand cups her breast, thumb brushing over her nipple. I trail kisses down her neck, across her collarbone, taking my time as if we have all the hours in the world.

When I take her nipple into my mouth, her fingers tangle in my hair, holding me to her. The soft sounds she makes drive me wild, each gasp and sigh like music. I move to her other breast, giving it the same attention while my hand slides down her stomach to the waistband of her jeans. Her hips lift slightly, an invitation I can't resist.

I unbutton her jeans, dragging the zipper down slowly. She's trembling beneath me, but not from fear. I know that tremor, recognize it from every time I touch her—it's anticipation, desire, need.

"Lift up," I murmur against her skin, and she raises her hips so I can slide her jeans down her legs. I follow the denim with my mouth, pressing kisses to her thigh, her knee, her calf as each inch of skin is revealed. By the time I toss her jeans aside, she's breathing hard, her chest rising and falling in a rhythm that matches my own pounding heart.

I look up at her from between her legs, taking in the sight of her. Her hair is spread across my pillow, her lips swollen from my kisses, her eyes dark with want. She's never looked more beautiful than she does right now, vulnerable and strong all at once.

I press a kiss to her inner thigh. Then I move higher, trailing my lips along the sensitive skin until I reach the edge. I press my lips to her heated skin, brushing against the cotton covering her center. She whimpers, hips rising to meet my mouth. I can smell her arousal, feel the dampness seeping through the thin fabric. My cock strains against my jeans, begging for attention, but this isn't about me right now. This is about her—about making her feel good, about reclaiming what's mine, about erasing any trace of him from her body and mind.

I hook my fingers in the waistband of her panties, dragging them slowly down her legs until she's completely bare before me. Her thighs tremble as I push them apart, exposing her to my hungry gaze.

"Brayden," she whispers, a note of vulnerability in her voice that makes my chest ache. "I need you."

I press a kiss to her inner thigh, then higher, until I'm breathing hot against her core. "You have me, princess. All of me."

When I finally taste her, she arches off the bed with a gasp that turns into a moan. I take my time, savoring her like she's the last meal I'll ever have. My tongue traces slow circles around her clit, teasing but never quite giving her what she needs. Her fingers clutch at the sheets, at my hair, at anything she can reach as I work her into a frenzy.

"Please," she begs. "I need more."

I slide one finger inside her, groaning at how wet she is for me. She's already soaked, her body responding to my touch in a way that makes my dick throb painfully against my jeans. I add a second finger, curling them to hit that spot inside her that makes her cry out my name.

"That's it," I encourage. "Let me hear you, princess."

I work her with my fingers while my tongue circles her clit, building her up slowly. Her thighs begin to tremble, her breathing coming in short, desperate gasps. I can feel her getting close, her walls tightening around my fingers.

"Brayden," she moans. "I'm going to—"

"Not yet," I growl against her flesh, pulling back just enough to deny her release. "Not until I'm inside you."

She whimpers in frustration, her face flushed as she looks down at me. The sight of her—desperate, on the edge—nearly makes me lose what little control I have left. I rise to my knees, unbuckling my belt with hands that aren't quite steady. She watches every movement, her breathing quickening as I unzip my jeans and push them down along with my boxers.

My cock springs free, already hard enough to hurt. She reaches for me, but I catch her wrists gently, mindful of the marks there.

"Let me," I say, positioning myself between her

thighs. I line myself up against her entrance, the head of my cock sliding through her wetness. She gasps, her hips lifting toward me, seeking more.

"Look at me," I demand, needing to see her when I enter her.

She obeys, her gaze locking with mine as I push forward slowly, inch by agonizing inch. The heat of her surrounds me, so tight and perfect I grit my teeth to keep from losing control. Her mouth falls open in a silent gasp as I fill her completely.

"Fuck," I groan, stilling once I'm buried to the hilt. "You feel so good, princess."

Her hands come up to grip my shoulders, nails digging into my skin. "Please move," she whispers, voice strained. "I need you to move."

I pull back slowly before thrusting forward again, searching her features for any sign of discomfort. There's only pleasure there, her expression hungry but vulnerable as she holds my stare. I set a rhythm that's deep but measured, each stroke deliberate, wanting to make this last.

"You're mine. Say it, Cece. Tell me you're mine."

Her eyes lock with mine. "I'm yours," she gasps, her body shivering violently beneath me. "Only yours."

The words hit with brutal force, stopping my breath. Something fierce and overwhelming surges through me, rising so fast it steals my control. I slam into her harder, possessed by a savage need to brand her from the inside out, to obliterate any memory of him that might still linger in her body's memory.

"That's it," I snarl, my voice barely human as I watch her face contort with pleasure. "Take. All. Of. Me." Each word punctuated with a punishing thrust.

Her legs vise around my waist, nails raking bloody trails down my back. I wrench her hips up with one hand, the new angle making her scream as I hammer against that spot that makes her clench like a fist around me. The pressure of her squeezing my cock is excruciating, magnificent. My vision blurs at the edges.

"Brayden," she chokes out, her voice breaking. "I can't—I'm going to—"

"Look at me," I command. "Don't you fucking look away. I want to see you shatter."

Her pupils blow wide, drowning in black. There's nothing else in her eyes but me. Not him. Not her past. Just us, fused together in this brutal communion.

I reach between us, thumb pressing hard against her swollen clit. "Now," I growl against her mouth. "Come for me. Only me."

She fractures beneath me, my name ripped from her throat as her body seizes around my cock with violent, pulsing contractions. Her nails break skin as she clings to me, her spine arching so severely I fear it might snap. The sight of her—face contorted in primal ecstasy, eyes wild yet still locked on mine—carves itself into my soul. Her inner muscles clamp down with bruising force, dragging me toward the abyss.

We sink into the quiet that follows, breath still unsteady, bodies pressed close enough that I can feel the thundering rhythm of both our hearts. The world narrows to shared warmth, shared air, and the wild rush still echoing through us. I'm crushing her but can't find the strength to move until her fingers dig into my shoulder blades. I roll us, keeping her locked against me, unwilling to break our connection.

"You still with me?" I rasp, voice shredded, fingers tangling in her hair to tilt her face up.

Her eyes meet mine, glazed yet burning with something that makes my chest constrict. "Never left," she whispers.

In her gaze, I see no walls, no doubts—just Cece looking at me like I'm her salvation instead of her ruin. Like she'd burn down paradise just to stand in my hell.

CHAPTER 20

CECE

MY PHONE VIBRATES against the nightstand, dragging me out of the deepest sleep I've had in years. The room is still dark, morning only a faint suggestion beyond the curtains. I groan and fumble for my phone, trying not to wake Brayden.

The screen blazes to life, momentarily blinding me. Multiple texts from Maya.

> HELLO? Are you alive?

> Cece, it's been two weeks. TWO WEEKS.

If you don't answer in the next hour, I'm calling the police to report you missing. Not kidding.

Or your dad. Which would be worse?

I smile despite the early hour. Maya has always had a flair for the dramatic that makes even my recent life choices seem tame by comparison.

I shift carefully, propping myself up on one elbow to type a response, when Brayden's arm tightens around my waist, pulling me back against the solid warmth of his chest. He mumbles something incoherent into my hair, still deep in sleep.

I pause, struck by the sight of him. His lashes rest against his cheeks, his breathing slow and even. The tattoo on his shoulder peeks out from beneath the sheet, the raven's wing stretching toward his collarbone.

Before doubt can catch up to me, I switch to the camera and take a quiet photo. Brayden asleep in our bed. The image feels stolen, a tiny piece of peace that belongs only to us. I turn back to Maya's texts, typing quietly.

Not dead. Just busy. Small town, big drama. Will call you soon.

I hit send and set the phone back down. His eyes flutter open, those steel-gray irises finding mine immediately. Even half-asleep, his gaze is intense enough to make my breath catch.

"Morning," I whisper.

"Who's texting you at—" he squints at the clock "—five-thirty in the fucking morning?"

"Just Maya. My best friend from Boulder. She thinks I've been kidnapped or something."

He grunts, pulling me closer until my back is flush against his chest, his morning hardness pressing against me in a way that sends a delicious shiver down my spine. "Tell her you have been. Stockholm syndrome's kicking in nicely."

I laugh softly, turning in his arms to face him. "Is that what this is?"

His hand slides down my back, cupping my ass and pulling me tighter against him. "Call it whatever you want, princess. Just don't leave this bed yet."

"Are you holding me hostage?"

He smirks, pretending to consider the question. "Can you be a hostage if you came to this bed willingly?"

"I prefer the term *willing captive*," I say, running my fingers along his stubbled jaw.

His smile is slow and devious as he rolls me onto my back in one fluid motion. He settles between my thighs, deliciously heavy as he braces himself on his forearms.

"Willing, huh?" His voice is rough with sleep, a hint of teasing slipping in. "And how willing would that be?"

I press against him, enjoying the small hiss of breath he takes when I press against his hardness. "Very."

He lowers his head, lips hovering just above mine. "Show me."

I slide my hands up his arms, feeling the corded muscles tense beneath my touch. Just as I'm about to pull him down to me, my phone vibrates again, the buzz against the nightstand impossibly loud in the quiet room.

Brayden groans, dropping his forehead to my shoulder. "Your friend has shit timing."

I reach over, fumbling for my phone without dislodging him. Three more texts from Maya.

> Busy? BUSY? That's what you're giving me after two weeks of radio silence?

> What kind of drama? The good kind or the 'I'm hiding a body' kind?

> And WHO are you busy WITH? Details. NOW.

"She's persistent," I mutter, dropping the phone back onto the nightstand. "She's not going to stop until I call her."

Brayden makes a low, growling sound in the back of his throat. "Tell her you'll call later." His mouth finds my neck, teeth grazing lightly over my pulse point in a way that makes coherent thought nearly impossible.

"She'll just keep texting," I manage to say, tilting my head to give him better access. "Maya doesn't understand the concept of boundaries."

"Turn it off," he suggests, his hand sliding up my bare thigh.

The phone buzzes again, more insistent than before.

I sigh, pushing gently at his chest. "Five minutes. Just give me five minutes to call her and then I'm all yours."

He pulls back just enough to look down at me. "Three minutes."

"Five," I counter, trying not to smile at his impatience.

"Four," he offers, dipping his head to nip at my earlobe. "And I get to touch you while you talk."

A shiver runs through me at the thought. "That's not fair."

"Never claimed to play fair, princess." His hand inches higher on my thigh, teasing. "Clock's ticking."

I grab the phone before I can change my mind, quickly hitting Maya's contact. She answers on the first ring.

"Holy shit, you are alive! I was this close to filing a missing persons report."

"I'm fine," I tell her, trying to ignore Brayden's hand as it inches higher on my thigh. "I just got caught up with...things," I say, biting my lip as Brayden's hand slides even higher, his fingers now tracing the edge of my underwear.

"What kind of things? Or should I say who?" Maya's tone turns sly. "You're breathing weird. Do you have someone there with you right now?"

I try to shoot Brayden a warning look, but he just

smirks as his fingers slip beneath the fabric. I barely stifle a gasp.

"I, um—yes, I'm not alone," I manage, the words strained as his thumb circles dangerously close to where I'm already embarrassingly wet. "Can I call you back later?"

"Oh my God!" Maya shrieks, loud enough that I have to pull the phone away from my ear. "Cecelia Marie Montgomery. Who is with you?"

Brayden's eyebrow arches, clearly able to hear her through the phone. His fingers pause their torment, but the knowing smile on his face tells me I'm not off the hook yet.

"A friend," I answer. Brayden must take offense to that label because he goes from slow torture to fully cupping me in a split second. The sudden change makes me gasp.

"What was that?"

"Nothing," I lie.

"It doesn't sound like nothing. He can hear me, right?." Brayden slips a finger inside of me, and the answer I want to say disappears.

"I'll take that as a yes…hey, guy who is distracting my best friend," Maya calls out. "Thank you for finally getting my best friend laid! It was long overdue!"

"Maya!" I hiss, mortification washing over me.

Brayden laughs. "You're welcome."

"Oh shit. Girl…that voice. No wonder you fell into bed with him. Say something else."

"Maybe another time, I really need to, um, go. Can I call you back later?"

"Definitely call me back," Maya chirps. "With details. Lots and lots of details. I want to know everything about Mr. Sexy Voice."

I stare at the ceiling, torn between laughing and dying from embarrassment. "Goodbye, Maya," I say firmly, and end the call before she can protest further.

I drop the phone onto the nightstand and cover my face with my hands. "I'm so sorry about that."

Brayden's fingers are still teasing me, making it hard to concentrate. "I like her already," he murmurs, his mouth finding my neck again. "Anyone who wants you to get laid is good in my book."

"Oh my God," I groan, but it turns into something else entirely when he slides another finger inside me. "That's...not fair."

"I warned you," he reminds me, his breath hot against my skin. "Four minutes. And you went over."

My hips rise to meet his touch of their own accord. "You're terrible."

"That's not what your body is saying," he whispers, his thumb circling my clit in a way that makes my toes curl. "It's saying I'm pretty fucking fantastic."

I can't argue with that. My body is already wound tight, every nerve ending singing under his expert touch. The embarrassment of Maya's call fades, replaced by the burning need he always manages to ignite in me.

"Brayden," I gasp.

His name slips out of me, a prayer shaped by need and devotion. I reach for more words, but they dissolve as his fingers work their magic, drawing me closer to the edge with each deliberate stroke.

"You like that?" he asks.

"Yes," I breathe. "Don't stop."

His mouth finds mine, swallowing my gasp as he increases the pace of his fingers. I clutch at his shoulders, nails digging into skin, anchoring myself as pleasure builds inside me. The room fills with the sound of my ragged breathing and his occasional murmurs of encouragement.

"That's it," he whispers against my lips. "Let go for me, princess."

The heat coils tighter, a spring wound to breaking point. When he curls his fingers just so, hitting that perfect spot inside me while his thumb circles my clit, I shatter. My release crashes through me, my body shivering under his touch as his name slips from my lips again.

Before I can catch my breath, he's shifting above me, settling between my thighs. The blunt head of his cock presses against my entrance, teasing but not entering.

"Please," I whimper, desperate for him to fill me completely. I'm still sensitive from my orgasm, but I need him inside me, need to feel that perfect stretch and fullness that only he can give me.

He watches me with those stormy eyes, his jaw clenched with restraint. "Say my name again."

"Brayden," I breathe, lifting my hips to try to take him in.

"Again," he growls, pushing just the tip inside me, enough to make me gasp but not enough to satisfy.

"Brayden, please," I moan, my hands sliding down to grip his hips, trying to pull him deeper.

With one powerful thrust, he buries himself inside me to the hilt. I cry out as he stretches me. He stills for a moment, letting me adjust to his size.

"Fuck, you feel good," he murmurs, beginning to move in slow, deep strokes that make my toes curl. "You're so fucking wet, princess. You're dripping for my cock."

I wrap my legs around his waist, drawing him deeper with each thrust. His pace increases, the drag of him against my oversensitive flesh. I'm already climbing toward another peak.

"Brayden," I gasp. "Oh god, Brayden."

"When you pray, princess, you pray to me. Not to God. Not to the devil. Me."

The blasphemy should horrify me, but instead it makes something molten pool in my belly. I've spent my whole life praying to a God who never answered, but Brayden—he answers every plea with his body, his touch, and his possessive words.

"Say it," he demands, slowing his thrusts to an agonizing pace. "Who do you pray to?"

"You," I gasp, my fingers digging into his shoulders. "Only you."

The confession tears from my throat. His eyes flash with something primal, and he rewards me by picking up his pace, driving into me with renewed purpose.

"That's right," he growls, his hand sliding down to grip my hip, angling me even better. "I'm the only one who can make you feel like this. The only one who knows what you need."

He's right. No one has ever read my reactions the way he does, known exactly how to touch, how to move inside me. Ethan never made me feel even a fraction of what Brayden does.

"I'm close," I whimper, my body tightening around him. "Please don't stop."

"Never," he promises, his rhythm never faltering.

My attention is all on him. His pupils are blown wide, just a thin ring of steel-gray around the black, and there's something primal and possessive there that makes my heart stutter. I couldn't look away if I tried.

"Only you," I whisper, the words tumbling out before I can stop them. "It's only ever been you."

He growls, a sound so deep I feel it vibrate through my core, and his thrusts become more urgent, more desperate. I'm climbing higher, my body tightening around him as pressure builds between my legs. His hand slides between us, finding that sensitive bundle of nerves, and the dual sensation of him filling me completely while his fingers work their magic is too much.

My vision blurs at the edges as I shatter around him.

I'm vaguely aware of crying out his name and my nails digging into his back hard enough to leave marks.

"Fuck, Cece," he groans, his rhythm faltering as my body pulses around him. With one final, powerful thrust, he buries himself deep inside me and finds his own release, his body going rigid above mine.

For several heartbeats, we stay frozen, both panting, slick with sweat. Then he lowers himself carefully, rolling to the side and pulling me against his chest. His heart hammers beneath my ear, gradually slowing.

I lay there in the stillness, listening to his heartbeat slow, feeling his fingers trace lazy patterns on my skin. The morning light is beginning to filter through the curtains, casting the room in a soft golden glow that makes everything feel dreamlike. My body is deliciously sore, pleasantly exhausted in a way that only comes from being thoroughly loved.

Loved.

The word echoes in my mind, impossible to ignore. Is that what this is? This overwhelming feeling that's been growing inside me since the moment I showed up at his door with my suitcase?

"What's going on in that head of yours? You're thinking so loud I can practically hear it."

I hesitate, suddenly terrified. We've shared our bodies, our space, our darkest moments—but this feels like jumping off a cliff without knowing how deep the water is below.

"I..." The words stick in my throat. I swallow hard,

gathering my courage. "I think I'm falling in love with you."

His body goes completely still beneath me. Even his breathing seems to stop for a heartbeat. I keep my face pressed against his chest, too afraid to look up and see his reaction.

"I know it's probably too soon," I rush on, the words tumbling out now that I've started. "And I'm not expecting you to say it back or even feel the same way." I rush to fill the silence, my heart hammering against my ribs. "It's just...I've never felt this way before. Not with Ethan, not with anyone. And it terrifies me because everything about us has happened so fast, but it also feels more real than anything I've ever experienced and I—"

"Stop," Brayden orders. His hand comes up to cup my chin, tilting my face until I'm forced to look at him.

My stomach drops. This is it. This is where he tells me I'm moving too fast, expecting too much. That this thing between us is just physical, just convenient while I figure out my life. I brace myself for rejection, already planning my retreat to the bathroom where I can cry in private.

But then his thumb brushes across my cheek, so tenderly it steals my breath.

"You think you're the only one falling?" he asks quietly. "I don't let people this close. Not to my life. Not to my space. Not to me."

I blink, trying to process his words. "You're not...freaked out?"

A small smile tugs at the corner of his mouth. "I'm fucking terrified," he admits. "But not because I don't feel the same way."

Hope blooms in my chest, fragile but insistent. "How do you feel?"

He exhales slowly, his fingers tracing the curve of my jaw. "It feels as though you've turned my whole fucking world upside down," he says finally. "Nothing made sense until you crashed into my life."

My heart stutters in my chest. "That doesn't sound like a bad thing."

"It's not, but it's not simple either. I'm not good at this shit, Cece. Relationships. Feelings. I've spent most of my life avoiding both."

"I'm not exactly an expert either," I remind him. "My only serious relationship ended in divorce and public humiliation."

His thumb traces my lower lip, sending tiny shivers down my spine. "We're a fucking mess, aren't we?"

I can't help but laugh at that. "Complete disaster."

"But we're a disaster together," he says, his tone dropping to that gravelly register that makes my insides melt. "And I wouldn't change a damn thing about how we got here."

I reach up to touch his face, tracing the stubble along his jaw. "Even the part where I showed up at your door unannounced with all my baggage?"

"Especially that part." He turns his head and presses a kiss to my palm. "Best fucking surprise I've ever gotten."

The tenderness in his touch clashes so sharply with his rough exterior that it makes my throat tighten. This man—who can silence half the town with a single glance—handles me as though I'm something precious to him.

A sharp knock at the door shatters the moment between us.

"What the—" Brayden sits up, every muscle tightening. It's barely six in the morning. No one should be at our door.

"Expecting someone?" I murmur, pulling the sheet up to cover myself.

Brayden shakes his head, already sliding out of bed. "Stay here." His tone shifts completely—tenderness gone, replaced by a hard, cautious edge.

I watch as he pulls on his boxers, muscles rippling across his back with each movement. The raven tattoo seems to come alive as he rolls his shoulders, preparing for whatever—or whoever—is on the other side of that door.

The knock comes again, more insistent this time—three sharp raps that echo through the small guesthouse like gunshots.

"Coming," Brayden calls. He glances back at me, his expression unreadable. "Stay in bed."

I nod, though every instinct tells me to follow him. Something feels wrong. The timing, the early hour. It can't be good news.

Brayden disappears down the hallway, and I strain to catch what happens next. The front door creaks open, and then—silence. A heavy, terrible silence that stretches for one heartbeat, then two.

"Where is my daughter?"

My blood turns to ice. That sound—deep, commanding, edged with fire and brimstone.

Shit. My dad.

CHAPTER 21

CECE

NOTHING—AND I mean *nothing*—sends a person into instant cardiac arrest quite like their father showing up at their biker boyfriend's door at 6 AM on a Sunday. Every life choice I've ever made flashes before my eyes in rapid-fire montage, and none of them look good.

I launch myself out of Brayden's bed so fast I nearly face-plant. I grab the nearest clothing—which happens to be his T-shirt—and yank it over my head while hopping around trying to find my underwear. My heart is doing its best impression of a trapped bird inside my chest, and honestly? Same. I, too, would like to fling myself out a window right now.

"I know she's here." My father's voice booms

through the apartment, that sermon-projecting thunder he uses to scare teenagers straight. "Her car is outside."

"With all due respect, Reverend Montgomery," Brayden replies, sounding infuriatingly calm for a man currently half-naked and arguing with a preacher, "it doesn't matter if she's here or not."

"She's my daughter."

"She's a grown woman."

I rake my fingers through my hair, instantly regretting it when they snag in a knot the size of a small woodland creature. Fantastic. I look *exactly* like what he's terrified to find: his daughter who spent the night doing activities that require strategic hydration and lower back stretches.

"I want to see her. Now." His tone sharpens as footsteps close in on the bedroom door. It swings open just as I step toward it. My father's expression hardens, and a flicker of pure disdain crosses his face. "It's true. You're staying here with him."

"Clearly, Dad."

My father's gaze drops to my wrists, and his expression shifts from disapproval to something far more severe. His eyes widen as he takes in the purple-blue marks circling my skin, grim and unmistakable.

"What has he done to you?" he demands, stepping closer with his Bible clutched in one hand like a weapon.

"Dad, it's not—"

"Don't defend him," my father snaps, his face flushing with rage as he turns to Brayden. "You put your hands on my daughter? Is this how you treat women?"

Brayden's entire body goes rigid.

"I would never hurt her," he says, each word precise and deadly quiet.

"Then explain those," my father says, pointing at my wrists, his finger shaking with indignation. "Did you think I wouldn't notice? You've harmed her."

I step between them, my heart pounding so hard I can feel it in my throat. "Brayden didn't do this," I say, holding up my wrists. "This wasn't him."

My father scoffs, his disbelief palpable. "Do you expect me to believe you did this to yourself?"

"Do you really think so little of me, Dad, that I would be willing to stay with someone who abuses me? That I am so desperate for a man to love me that I would tolerate him putting his hands on me? To hurt me?"

My father's face changes, the anger momentarily giving way to confusion. He wasn't expecting that response.

"Then who?" he demands, his gaze darting between Brayden and me. "Who did this to you?"

I take a deep breath, squaring my shoulders. "Ethan. He cornered me in the bathroom at Tony's yesterday."

The color drains from my father's face. "Ethan?"

"Yes, Dad. Your precious ex-son-in-law. He followed me into the women's bathroom. He grabbed me. Threatened me."

My father's grip on his Bible tightens. He looks

momentarily lost, the righteous fury giving way to something more complicated.

"Had Brayden not been there to stop him, I would have far more to worry about than a few bruises."

For a long moment, my father is silent, his face an unmoving mask of shock. His eyes move between my bruised wrists and my face, as though he's struggling to reconcile two utterly different realities.

"That's… impossible," he finally says, but there's no conviction behind the words. "Ethan wouldn't—"

"Wouldn't what, Dad? Wouldn't hurt me? Wouldn't try to intimidate me?" The words spill out before I can stop them, years of frustration finally breaking loose. "Or is it just that you don't want to believe it because then you'd have to admit you were wrong about him? About everything?"

Brayden steps closer, his hand finding the small of my back, A silent show of support that steadies me more than he could know. My father catches the movement, his expression tightening.

"I need to speak with my daughter," he says to Brayden, his tone cold. "Alone."

"Not happening," Brayden replies, calm enough to be unsettling. "Not in my home."

My father's face flushes a deep, furious red. "I'm her father!"

"And this is my house," Brayden snaps. "She's not going anywhere with you unless she wants to."

They lock eyes, neither willing to back down, two forces measuring each other in charged silence. The air tightens, electric and volatile, and suddenly I'm acutely aware I'm standing in the middle of a minefield—one wrong step and everything could detonate.

"Dad," I say, keeping my tone as even as I can, "I'll talk to you. But I'm not leaving. Brayden stays."

My father's jaw clenches so tight I can practically hear his teeth grinding. He's not used to having his authority challenged, especially not by me.

"Fine," he says at last, though every syllable makes it clear he means the opposite. He gestures stiffly toward the living room. "Shall we at least sit down and talk as civilized people?"

I nod, mostly because I desperately need this confrontation to happen *somewhere other than the bedroom I just slept in with a biker*. Standing here in nothing but Brayden's T-shirt and my underwear, hair a disaster from sleep and sex, is not exactly the footing I'd choose for facing down my father.

"You can take a seat on the couch," he adds, already turning away.

I watch him leave, shoulders rigid, judgment radiating off him with every step. Brayden's gaze tracks him until he disappears around the corner, then shifts to me. He doesn't speak—he doesn't need to. His eyes ask the question plainly: *You holding up?*

I nod, though "okay" feels ambitious. I'm upright. I'm breathing. That's about the extent of it.

"I…need clothes," I whisper, suddenly aware of just how exposed I am. Vulnerability slips in under my skin, cold and unwelcome.

Brayden closes the bedroom door with quiet finality, shielding us from whatever storm waits on the other side. "You don't owe him anything. If you want him gone, say the word."

"I know."

I move to the dresser where Brayden had stashed my things, pulling out jeans and a bra. He watches, silent, while I dress.

He grabs a pair of jeans for himself, not bothering with a shirt. It's intentional, I realize—the tattoos on full display. A quiet rebellion. A not-so-subtle message to the man in our living room.

"Just say it," he says, stepping behind me as I twist my hair into a ponytail. His hands find my shoulders, warm and grounding. "No explanation needed. I'll take care of it."

I lean back into him, letting his strength bleed into my bones. "I have to do this."

"Your call, princess." He presses a kiss to the crown of my head. "But you're not doing it alone."

We walk into the living room together. His hand stays at the small of my back—a quiet claim, a protective promise. My father stands by the window, framed in cold daylight. He turns as we enter.

His eyes hit Brayden's bare chest, then slide to our bodies—too close, too connected for his comfort. His jaw tightens. That familiar look of disapproval tightens his mouth into a straight, bloodless line.

But I don't flinch. Not this time.

"I see you've made yourself quite at home," he says to me.

"I have," I reply. "Would you like some coffee, Dad? We were just about to make some."

The ordinary question lands with a thud. My father's eyebrows rise, the barest shift, revealing his incredulity—as though he's stunned I'd bother with politeness in a place he's already condemned as a den of iniquity.

"No, thank you," he says stiffly. "I'm not here for coffee."

"Then why did you come?" I ask, sinking onto the couch. Brayden sits beside me, close enough that our thighs touch. A small gesture of solidarity that doesn't go unnoticed by my father.

"Mrs. Holloway called me yesterday evening," he says, remaining standing. "She said she saw you at Tony's. Said you looked...distressed." His eyes flick to my wrists again. "She mentioned marks. And him." He nods to Brayden.

"So you thought barging into his home at an ungodly hour was the best way to approach me about it?"

"I thought—"

"No, Dad, you assumed."

"Yes," he forcibly admits. "When she said you were hurt, I was sick with worry."

"Before this goes any further, I want to make something abundantly clear, Reverend. The last person you need to worry about hurting your daughter is me. I would rather carve out my own heart than ever lay a hand on her or cause her pain," Brayden interjects.

My father's face shifts at Brayden's words, surprise briefly overtaking his anger. He clearly wasn't expecting such a direct declaration, especially not from the tattooed biker he's already decided is the villain in this story.

"Pretty words," my father says after a moment, "but actions speak louder."

"Like showing up unannounced at someone's home to make accusations?" I can't keep the edge from my tone. "Or did you mean Ethan's actions? Because those spoke pretty loudly too."

Dad's jaw clenches, his gaze flicking between my face and my wrists. The conflict is plain. The urge to protect his daughter fighting against the possibility that he might've been wrong about Ethan.

"I need to understand what happened," he finally says, his words softer now. "Mrs. Holloway said you looked frightened. That this man—" he gestures at Brayden "—was dragging you out the back door."

"He wasn't dragging me anywhere," I correct him. "He was getting me away from Ethan before things got worse."

"And what exactly happened with Ethan?" my father asks, his tone tight, carefully measured.

"Ethan saw us at Tony's together. He came to our table and tried to pick a fight. When he didn't get what he wanted…" I take a deep breath, feeling Brayden's thigh press reassuringly against mine. "He took matters into his own hands while Brayden was paying our bill. He followed me to the bathroom. He cornered me, grabbed my wrists, and was trying to force himself on me when Brayden walked in."

My father's face turns ashen. "Force himself on you?" he repeats. "You're saying Ethan tried to..."

He can't even say the word. The mighty Reverend Thomas Montgomery, who's preached against every sin imaginable from his pulpit, can't bring himself to name what almost happened to his own daughter.

"Yes," I say firmly. "And if Brayden hadn't shown up when he did—"

"He would have...assaulted you," my father finishes.

"Yes," I affirm. "He would have raped me in that bathroom to prove a point. "

"What point?"

"I'm not sure you want to hear this part, Dad. It's enough that Brayden wants to kill him. I don't need you to forsake the sixth commandment, too."

"You let him go?"

"Yes, but only because Cece asked me to let him go," Brayden admits. "Part of me hopes she changes her mind."

The blunt honesty makes my father flinch, but I'm grateful for it. No more lies, no more pretending. This is who we are now.

"Dad, you need to understand something," I say, leaning forward. "Ethan isn't who you think he is. He never was. The perfect Christian husband was always an act."

"An act?" My father shakes his head like he's trying to dislodge my words. "Cece, I've known that boy since he was sixteen years old. He's been nothing but—"

"A liar," I cut in. "A manipulator. You need to take him off the pedestal you still have him on, Dad." I peer over at Brayden as he reaches out, taking my hand in my lap, reassuring me.

My father's eyes track Brayden's hand over mine, his expression shifting. I can see him wrestling with what I've just told him, the foundations of his beliefs starting to give way.

"What exactly are you saying, Cece?" he finally asks, strain tightening his words. "That Ethan… deceived us all? That the man who sat in my study every Sunday for years, who led our youth group, who prayed with me over dinner…was some kind of monster?"

"I'm saying he showed you what you wanted to see," I reply, the truth bitter on my tongue. "He knew exactly how to play the part in public. But behind closed doors? He was cruel. Controlling. And when I finally stopped being the obedient wife he wanted, he made sure I paid for it."

My father sinks slowly onto the armchair across from us, looking suddenly older than his sixty-seven years. The Bible he's been clutching slips from his grasp onto the coffee table.

"Dad?" I say softly, watching him seem to collapse in on himself.

Before he can answer, the unmistakable sound of sirens cuts through the morning air. Brayden's head snaps up, his whole body tensing as he moves to the window.

"What the hell?" he mutters, pushing the curtain aside.

"What is it?" I ask, my pulse spiking.

"Two police cruisers just pulled up," Brayden says, his tone hardening. He turns toward my father, accusation written all over his face. "You called the cops on me?"

My stomach drops. "Dad, tell me you didn't."

My father looks genuinely confused, his eyes widening as he shakes his head. "I didn't call anyone. I swear it."

"Then why are there two Sheriff's deputies getting out of their cars right now?" Brayden snaps, his entire body drawn taut, readiness radiating off him as he gears up for a fight.

I move to the window beside him and peer out. Sure enough, Sheriff Miller and one of his deputies are walking up the path to the guesthouse, their hands resting on their holsters.

"Dad, if you didn't call them, who did?" I ask, panic rising in my throat.

"I don't know," he insists, and for once, I believe him. The confusion on his face seems genuine.

A heavy knock sounds at the door. Brayden and I exchange glances.

"Let me handle this," Brayden says, moving toward the door.

My father stands up, his expression shifting from confusion to concern. "Maybe I should—"

"No," Brayden cuts him off. "This is my house."

I follow close behind Brayden, my heart hammering against my ribs. Something feels wrong. Very wrong.

Brayden pulls open the door, his broad shoulders blocking most of my view. "Sheriff, what can I do for you?"

"Mr. Cole," Sheriff Miller's gravelly voice carries through the doorway. "We need to speak with Cecelia Montgomery. We've been told she's staying with you."

I step out from behind Brayden, trying to keep my face neutral despite the panic clawing at my throat. "I'm here, Sheriff. What's this about?"

The sheriff's weathered face is unreadable as his eyes move from Brayden to me, then past us. "Ms. Montgomery, we've got a situation."

Footsteps behind us. My stomach sinks before I even turn. "What kind of situation requires you to come to speak to my daughter, Jim?"

Sheriff Miller's jaw tics. He's uncomfortable, and that's somehow worse. "We received a report this morning," he says, glancing at me, then away. "From Ethan Kincaid."

Ice floods my veins. "A report about what?"

His gaze hardens, locking onto mine. "Mr. Kincaid has filed charges against you. Assault and battery. He claims you attacked him at Tony's."

"What?" My voice breaks around the word. My knees almost give out, but Brayden's arm is there, solid around my waist.

"This is bullshit," Brayden growls. "She didn't touch him. He's the one who—"

"I'm going to have to ask you to step back, Mr. Cole," Sheriff Miller interrupts, hand drifting toward his holster in a gesture that's more habit than threat.

My father steps forward. "Jim, there must be a mistake. My daughter would never—"

"Dad," I snap, sharper than intended. "Stop."

Brayden's voice cuts in, steel in every syllable. "Let's see the warrant."

The deputy steps forward, pulling a folded document from his jacket. Brayden snatches it from his hand, scanning quickly. His shoulders stiffen with every line. His fingers curl tight around the paper.

"That fucking son of a bitch," he mutters.

"Watch your mouth, son," the Sheriff says, but the reprimand is hollow, almost reflexive. His eyes drift to my wrists. I see the flicker of doubt there.

"Ms. Montgomery," he says quietly. "I need you to come with us."

"She's not going anywhere," Brayden snaps, stepping halfway in front of me again. "Not until we call a lawyer."

"She has that right," the Sheriff concedes with a nod. "But the arrest still has to happen."

My mind spins. *Assault?* Ethan cornered me. He left

these bruises. He was the one— *He did this. And now he's flipping the story.*

"Jim," my father says again, this time with more force. "Look at her. Look at her wrists. You're really going to tell me those marks were made in self-defense?"

The Sheriff hesitates. I see it. See the part of him that hates this—knows it smells wrong.

"I see them," he says finally. "And it'll be documented. But I've got a warrant signed by a judge. I don't have a choice."

Brayden's hand finds mine, steadying me. His voice drops, edged with quiet danger. "This is Mayor Kincaid pulling strings," Brayden says, a growl simmering beneath the words. "Using his influence to protect his precious son."

Sheriff Miller's jaw tightens. "I'm just doing my job, Mr. Cole. Now, Ms. Montgomery, as much as it pains me to say this, I have to place you under arrest."

"You can't be serious," I say, disbelief making my words shake. "Ethan is the one who should be arrested. He assaulted me!"

Sheriff Miller's expression stays professionally neutral, though a flicker of something crosses his face—discomfort, maybe even sympathy. It doesn't change anything.

"Ms. Montgomery, please turn around and place your hands behind your back."

"Jim, for God's sake," my father protests, stepping

forward. "You've known Cece her entire life. You really believe she would assault anyone?"

"What I believe doesn't matter right now, Reverend," Sheriff Miller says, tone steady but not unkind. "I have a sworn statement and a warrant."

I feel Brayden's body tensing beside me. His arm tightens around my waist, and for a terrifying moment, I think he might actually try to stop the sheriff physically. The thought of him getting arrested too sends a jolt of panic through me.

"Brayden," I whisper, placing my hand on his chest. "Don't."

The cuffs click shut, biting into my already bruised wrists. I flinch, but I don't make a sound.

Brayden does.

It isn't a word, not even a growl—just a harsh, guttural sound torn from his chest. His fists clench at his sides, jaw so tight I can almost hear his teeth grind. One more step, just one, and I know he'll cross a line neither of us can undo.

"Brayden," I whisper, because I need him to look at me, *not* at the deputy. "Please."

His eyes snap to mine. The rage is still there—boiling, volcanic—but he locks it down with visible effort. For me.

"I'll fix this," Brayden declares. "I don't care how many strings I have to pull or bridges I have to burn— I'll get you out."

"I know." My voice is steadier than my hands. "That's why I need you out here."

The sheriff mutters something procedural, but it blurs into nothing. All I see is Brayden—braced, furious, struggling to keep himself from snapping the cuffs off me and tearing the walls down.

As they turn me toward the door, I finally glance at my father.

He stands there stiffly. His mouth is tight, eyes full of conflict—believing me, but paralyzed by the weight of who he is. He says nothing. Not a word. Not even my name.

The silence from him hits harder than the handcuffs.

Brayden notices.

His head turns, slow and cold, voice dropping into something dangerous enough to still the whole room. "Hell of a thing," he says, eyes locked on my father. "Watching a man of God stand there and do nothing while his daughter is dragged out in her worst moment."

My father's jaw trembles, but he doesn't speak.

Brayden steps closer, fury simmering just under the surface. "You talk about saving souls, preaching love and protection—but when she needs you?" He shakes his head, disgust cutting sharp. "You choose to be silent."

The words hang there, heavy with judgment. And my father still has no answer.

When he stays silent, Brayden shifts his focus back to the sheriff, anger sharpening every line of his body.

"If she doesn't press charges for what that bastard

did in that bathroom, then I damn well will. And if I find out you had any part in covering this up—"

"Enough." Sheriff Miller's voice snaps through the room, authority finally settling into place. "Everyone stand down."

The door swings open. Sunlight floods in, harsh and unforgiving, illuminating the quiet street beyond. Morning in this town has an eerie stillness—too calm for what's unfolding.

The walk to the patrol car stretches out before me, a distance that feels impossibly long.

Brayden follows, every step a silent promise.

I don't look away until the door closes behind me and the engine starts. And even then, I can feel his eyes burning holes in the back of the cruiser, willing me to feel how hard he's coming for me.

CHAPTER 22

BRAYDEN

I'VE NEVER FELT A STRONGER URGE to break something than I do right now, watching Reverend Montgomery pace the police station's dingy waiting area. He stalks back and forth in tight lines, shiny leather shoes clicking against the scuffed linoleum, the only marker of the endless minutes we've been stuck in this hellhole while Cece sits in a holding cell.

"Could you please sit down?" I finally growl, the words dragging out of my throat, rough and sharp. "You're making me fucking dizzy."

The Reverend halts mid-stride, his Bible clutched to his chest, held high as though it's armor. The look he sends me could strip the paint off the walls.

"Watch your language, young man. This is a house of the law."

I snort. "More of a house of bullshit, if you ask me."

His face reddens, that particular shade I'm starting to recognize far too well. "This attitude isn't helping my daughter," he says, each word tight enough to snap.

"And your pacing isn't doing a damn thing either," I shoot back. "At least I'm not the one who spent years defending the bastard who put her in there."

The words hit him hard. His shoulders lock up, tension rolling through him. For a moment, I honestly think he might hurl that Bible at my skull. Instead, he swallows whatever sermon he's choking on.

I drop into one of the uncomfortable plastic chairs lining the wall. Every muscle in my body aches from holding too much anger with nowhere to put it. I check my watch for what has to be the hundredth time. The church's lawyer should've been here an hour ago.

"Where the hell is your attorney?" I mutter, running a hand through my hair.

The Reverend glances at the station clock, his own impatience finally showing through his righteous facade. "Harold is very reliable. He's never been late for church business."

"This isn't church business," I remind him. "This is your daughter being railroaded by your golden boy ex-son-in-law."

He sits down heavily in the chair across from me, looking suddenly older than his years. "Harold has handled the church's legal matters for twenty years. He knows what he's doing."

"And how many criminal cases has he handled?" I ask, already knowing the answer. "Tax exemptions and property disputes aren't the same as assault charges."

Before he can respond, my phone buzzes in my pocket. I check the caller ID and feel a surge of relief.

"It's my aunt," I tell him, standing up to take the call.

Jillian's voice comes through clear and pissed off. "I just heard what happened. That little shit Ethan is dead meat."

"Get in line," I growl, walking a few paces away from the Reverend. "Have you talked to Joe?"

"He's on his way. As am I."

"Good," I say, running a hand over my face. "We need Joe. This church lawyer sounds like he handles bake sales and property easements, not criminal defense."

"Damn right. That Kincaid boy's father has half the town in his pocket. But we've got connections of our own."

"How fast can Joe get here?" I check my watch again. Cece's been in holding for almost three hours.

"He was in court when I called, but he said he'd be there as fast as he could. And Brayden?"

"Yeah?"

"Don't do anything stupid before he gets there." Her tone makes it clear she knows exactly what I'm thinking. "I mean it. You getting arrested won't help Cece."

"I'm not making any promises," I mutter, watching as another deputy walks past, deliberately avoiding eye contact. "These assholes know exactly what they're doing."

"That's why we need to be smarter than them. Joe will handle it."

I end the call and turn back to find the Reverend staring at me, his expression unreadable.

"Who is Joe?" he asks.

"Joseph Mendez. Best criminal defense attorney in three counties." I tuck my phone away. "Your church lawyer handles paperwork and tax exemptions. Mendez handles real fights."

"We can't afford—"

"I'm paying," I cut him off.

"I don't need your charity," the Reverend recoils. Pride clearly getting the better of him. Pride he's going to have to shove down because it's not going to help his daughter's situation.

"It's not charity," I snap, my patience hanging by a thread. "It's for Cece, not you."

We stare at each other across the dingy waiting room, two men who couldn't be more different yet somehow find ourselves on the same side of this mess. The fluorescent lights flicker overhead, casting harsh shadows across his face that make him look haggard and worn.

"My daughter is all I have left. Her mother would never have allowed this to happen."

Something in his tone catches me off guard—

genuine grief, maybe even regret. For a second, I see past the judgmental preacher to the father beneath. A father who, despite his many flaws, loves his daughter in his own fucked-up way.

"Then let's get her out of here. Your lawyer isn't showing. Mine will be here soon. Swallow your pride and let me help."

Before he can answer, the station door swings open with a bang. A man in an expensive suit strides in, his silver hair slicked back, his smile as fake as the Rolex on his wrist. Fucking Richard Kincaid.

My fists twitch at my sides. Every instinct in me wants to drive Kincaid into the nearest wall.

But I stay still. Not yet.

This is not the alley behind a bar. This is the sheriff's station with witnesses, and a man who performs best when he has an audience. He wants me to lose control. He wants a scene he can twist.

I force my voice calm. Cold. "You talk about the law as if it belongs to you. Your son assaulted her, and now you are trying to bury it."

Kincaid's expression shifts for a heartbeat. A small crack in the smug mask he hides behind. It seals up again almost instantly.

"Harsh accusations," he murmurs, chin lifted. "Reputations in this town are fragile. She has already damaged hers."

The words hit me harder than any punch. She is in a cell behind those doors, alone, and he is still trying to paint her as the problem.

My teeth grind. "Her reputation means nothing to me. The truth does. Your son pinned her in that bathroom. Grabbed her. Humiliated her. She is not the one who should be sitting in a cell right now."

The room goes still. Deputies who pretended to ignore us are openly watching now.

Kincaid's jaw tightens. "You have made powerful enemies. I hope you understand that."

My vision heats. "I do. I understand exactly what kind of man you are. And you should remember something, Richard. I have toppled men far more powerful than you. You and your boy will answer for what happened."

He adjusts his cufflinks, stiff and deliberate, as if this is a board meeting instead of a threat spoken in front of half the sheriff's staff.

"Do not count on rescuing her today," he says, already turning away. "Cells have a way of swallowing girls her age. Men such as you, though...you vanish into places like this without anyone blinking."

I release a slow breath and stare down the hallway leading to her cell. My hands are still unsteady—not from fear, but from holding myself back. She's back there, depending on me, and I will not fail her. I swear on every oath I've ever broken that I'll get her out. Richard Kincaid doesn't get the final word. Not today. Not ever again.

"Careful, Mr. Cole. Threatening an elected official is a serious offense. One more to add to your impressive record, perhaps?" His smile is all teeth, no warmth.

"Though I suppose compared to your other crimes, it would barely register."

The front desk deputy shifts nervously, his hand still hovering near his weapon. I force myself to take a step back, even though every muscle in my body screams to lunge forward and wipe that smug look off Kincaid's face.

"My son has filed a legitimate complaint," Kincaid continues, smoothing his tie. "The evidence speaks for itself."

"Evidence?" I laugh, the sound harsh even to my own ears. "You mean the marks on her wrists that your precious son left when he cornered her in a bathroom?"

"These are serious allegations, Mr. Cole. If you have evidence of such an assault, I suggest you file a report." His tone suggests he knows exactly how that would go in a department that answers to him. "Now if you'll excuse me, I need to speak to the Sheriff."

I feel a red haze descending over my vision. I've only felt this kind of rage a handful of times in my life, and it's never ended well for whoever was on the receiving end. The deputy's hand is still on his weapon, but I'm beyond caring. All I can see is Kincaid's smug face, and all I can think about is Cece sitting in a cell because of this man's son.

"You son of a bitch," I snarl, stepping forward again despite the deputy's warning posture. "You know exactly what your boy did."

The Reverend's hand lands on my arm, his grip

surprisingly strong for a man his age. "Brayden, don't. This is what he wants."

I shrug him off, but the momentary interruption is enough to clear my head slightly. Kincaid is watching me with the calculated patience of a man who's spent decades manipulating situations to his advantage. He wants me to lose control. Wants me to give him an excuse.

"Listen to the good Reverend, Mr. Cole," Kincaid says, his voice dripping with false concern. "Violence is never the answer. Isn't that right, Thomas?"

The Reverend's face is a mask of barely controlled fury, but he manages a stiff nod. "Richard, I'm asking you as someone who's known you for thirty years. Drop these charges. You know Cecelia didn't do this."

Kincaid sighs, spreading his hands in a gesture of helplessness. "The justice system must run its course. I can't interfere with due process simply because we've known each other for years."

"Due process?" I bark out a laugh. "Is that what you call this railroading?"

The station door swings open again, and a balding man in an ill-fitting suit hurries inside, clutching a worn leather briefcase to his chest. He's breathing hard—clearly sprinted from the parking lot.

"Reverend Montgomery," he wheezes, pushing his crooked glasses up his nose. "Terribly sorry I'm late. Traffic from Millerville was a nightmare."

This has to be Harold, the church's lawyer—the one

who files bake sale permits and mediates disputes over who gets the good folding tables. Wonderful.

"I came as soon as I got your message," he continues. "This is highly unusual. Cecelia has always been such a good girl."

Kincaid's smile spreads, all polished teeth and concealed malice. "Mr. Pemberton, always a pleasure. I believe we last saw each other at the church fundraiser?"

Harold's complexion drains a shade, his gaze darting between Kincaid and the Reverend as though he's stumbled into a battlefield without armor.

"You'll be representing Ms. Montgomery?" Kincaid asks, his voice oozing courtesy that feels anything but.

Harold swallows and grips his briefcase tighter. "Yes, well, that's why I'm here. To assist the Reverend's daughter in this…misunderstanding."

A snort escapes me before I can stop it. This man? This trembling, overworked paper-pusher? He looks ready to faint if someone so much as raises an eyebrow. The way he's visibly caving under Kincaid's stare tells me exactly how this would play out: badly.

"Harold," the Reverend says, "perhaps we should discuss our strategy in private."

"Excellent idea," Kincaid interjects smoothly. "Sheriff Miller is expecting me." He turns to leave, then pauses, glancing back at me with cold calculation. "Mr. Cole, a word of advice—your presence here isn't helping Ms. Montgomery's situation. People might get the wrong impression about the company she keeps."

"The wrong impression? Like the one where your son is anything but a predatory piece of shit?"

Kincaid's smile freezes. "Slander is a serious offense."

"It's not slander if it's true," I spit back.

Kincaid's smirk cuts me deeper than any knife could as he turns away, disappearing down the hallway toward Sheriff Miller's office. I watch him go, imagining all the ways I could wipe that self-satisfied look off his face. None of them would help Cece right now.

I turn my attention back to the Reverend and his lawyer, who's already pulling papers from his briefcase with trembling hands.

"Now, as I understand it," Harold says, adjusting his glasses nervously, "we're dealing with a simple assault charge. I primarily handle church matters, but I did take a criminal law course back in '82, so I'm confident we can—"

"A course in '82?" I interrupt, unable to hide my disbelief. "Are you fucking kidding me?"

Harold blinks at me like I've just spoken in tongues. "I assure you, Mr.—"

"Cole. Brayden Cole."

"Yes, Mr. Cole. I assure you that while criminal defense isn't my specialty, I've handled minor disputes for church members many times over the years."

"Minor disputes?" I lean forward, watching him shrink back. "This isn't a parking ticket or a noise complaint. This is Ethan Kincaid and his father using their influence to frame Cece for something she didn't do."

Harold's face pales further, sweat beading along his receding hairline. "Well, I'm sure once we explain the situation, the charges will be dropped."

The words die on Harold's lips as his gaze shifts to something behind me. I turn to see my aunt striding through the station door with Joe Mendez right behind her. My aunt's face is set in that determined expression I've seen a thousand times—the one that means someone's about to get their ass handed to them. Joe looks every inch the high-powered attorney in his tailored charcoal suit, carrying a sleek leather briefcase that probably cost more than Harold's entire outfit.

"Thank Christ," I mutter, relief washing through me.

Harold's mouth opens and shuts in rapid succession, useless and soundless, while Joe closes in.

She gives me a quick hug before turning to the Reverend with a curt nod. "Thomas."

The Reverend looks between Joe and my aunt, confusion evident on his face. "What are you doing here?"

"Same as you," she replies. "Making sure Cece gets proper representation."

I step forward, placing my hand on Harold's shoulder. "Harold, I appreciate you coming down on such short notice, but we won't be needing your services after all."

Harold looks almost relieved as he clutches his briefcase tighter. "Well, I...that is...if the Reverend agrees..."

"The Reverend doesn't have a say in this. You can leave. Joe has it from here."

Harold doesn't even hesitate. He practically melts with relief, shoving papers back into his briefcase.

"Yes, well, if that's settled then..." he mumbles, already backing toward the exit. "I'll just...I have a property easement to review anyway. Good luck, Reverend." And with that, he's gone, the door swinging shut behind him with a soft click.

The Reverend stares at the empty space where his attorney stood seconds ago, his mouth slightly open. "Harold?" he calls weakly, but the man is already halfway across the parking lot, moving faster than I would have thought possible for someone so out of shape.

"Well, that was easy," I mutter, turning back to Joe. "Guess he wasn't too invested in his criminal law comeback tour."

The Reverend's face flushes an alarming shade of red as his gaze shifts from the door to Joe. "Now wait just a minute. I can't afford—"

"I already told you," I cut him off, "I'm paying. And before you start with the pride bullshit again, this isn't about you. It's about getting Cece out of that cell as fast as possible."

Joe steps forward, extending his hand to the Reverend. "Joseph Mendez, Reverend Montgomery. I've handled several cases against families such as the Kincaids. I know exactly how they operate."

The Reverend hesitates, staring at Joe's hand as though it might strike him.

Joe lets it fall and shifts his attention to me. "All right. I'm going to check in and get back to where they're holding her. With any luck, I can have this wrapped up before dinner."

He heads for the front desk, speaking to the sergeant in a voice so calm it borders on soothing. The sergeant barely glances up as he pushes a clipboard across the counter. Joe signs, nods once, and disappears through the door at the back. The lock clicks into place behind him, sealing him into whatever bureaucratic labyrinth exists beyond that wall.

I stay where I am, elbows on my knees, eyes fixed on the scuffed tile. Reverend Montgomery sits beside me, hands clasped tight, lips moving in quiet prayer that never seems to end. The clock above the desk ticks on, each second pounding through the waiting room with unnerving precision.

The waiting is the worst part. The whole world feels suspended, caught in a breath it refuses to release.

CHAPTER 23

CECE

THERE ARE EXACTLY twenty-seven ceiling tiles in this interrogation room. I've counted them four times, tracing the water stains that spread across the corners in rusty blooms. Detective Simmons thinks his silence will wear me down, but silence is just another weapon in a man's arsenal. I've lived through far worse than a sterile room with a flickering fluorescent light.

"Ms. Montgomery," he tries again, tapping his pen against his notepad with measured impatience. "We can do this all day if necessary."

I shift in the unforgiving metal chair, the handcuff on my right wrist clinking against the table ring they've locked it to. The bruises from Ethan's fingers sit beneath the cold steel, faint but undeniable.

"I've already told you I'm waiting for my lawyer."

Same answer I've given for two hours, but he keeps circling back, relentless and hungry for a crack he can exploit.

"And as I've told you, answering a few simple questions now could clear this whole thing up. Don't you want to go home, Ms. Montgomery?"

Home.

The word hangs in the air, dangled in front of me with all the subtlety of bait on a hook.

I'm not biting.

"Home is where my lawyer is, and I'm not saying another word until he gets here."

Detective Simmons sighs dramatically. "You know," he says, leaning back in his chair, "your father is out there, worried sick about you."

I almost laugh at that. Dad might be worried, but not for the reasons Simmons thinks.

"Is that supposed to make me talk? Bringing my father into this?"

Simmons shrugs, a casual gesture that doesn't match the predatory look in his eyes. "Just thought you should know. He and that biker boyfriend of yours have been waiting for hours. Strange bedfellows, those two."

The mention of Brayden sends a jolt through me that I hope doesn't show on my face. I picture him pacing the waiting room, barely containing his rage, my father clutching his Bible nearby. The image would be almost comical if I weren't sitting here in handcuffs.

"Detective," I say, meeting his gaze directly, "I

understand you have a job to do. But so does my lawyer, and until he gets here, this conversation is over."

Simmons leans forward, his chair creaking as he rests his elbows on the table. "You know what's interesting, Ms. Montgomery? Your ex-husband has a very different version of events. According to him, you've been harassing him for weeks. Calling, texting, showing up places where he'd be." He flips through his notes. "Says you couldn't accept that he'd moved on."

I keep my expression neutral, though my pulse quickens. Ethan's always been good at crafting narratives that paint him as the victim. It's what made him such an effective liar for all those years.

"No comment."

"He claims you followed him into the men's room at Tony's—not the other way around—and when he rejected your advances, you became violent." Simmons watches me closely, looking for any reaction. "Says your boyfriend then assaulted him when he tried to defend himself."

My fingers twitch against the cold metal table. "That's quite a story. Does it come with dragons and unicorns too?"

Simmons doesn't appreciate my sarcasm. His friendly facade slips for a moment, revealing the frustration underneath. "Ms. Montgomery, I'm trying to help you here. Mayor Kincaid is pushing hard for charges."

"That should be proof enough of my innocence."

Simmons ignores my comment, flipping through his notes again. "What I find interesting is that no one at Tony's remembers seeing Mr. Kincaid follow you into any bathroom. In fact, the waitress says she saw you heading toward the restrooms right after Mr. Kincaid excused himself from his table."

My stomach tightens. Of course Ethan would have thought this through, planned every detail to make me look guilty. He's had years of practice manipulating narratives to his advantage.

"Are we really still doing this, Detective? I've made it clear I'm not speaking without my lawyer."

The door opens, and I nearly sag with relief when a man in an immaculate charcoal suit steps inside. He looks every inch the attorney who charges more per hour than most people make in a day. Thank God. It's not Harold.

Because Harold—sweet, trembling, bake-sale-permit Harold—would've walked into this interrogation room, taken one look at the handcuffs, and immediately fainted onto the floor. Best-case scenario, he'd try to defend me using a church brochure and a prayer. Worst case, he'd accidentally confess *for me* out of sheer nerves.

This man, though? He looks ready to dismantle the entire police department with nothing but a briefcase and a well-timed eyebrow raise.

"This interview is over," he announces, placing his leather briefcase on the table with a decisive thud.

Detective Simmons's face tightens, his mouth

forming a thin line as he glares at my lawyer. "And you are?"

"Joseph Mendez, Ms. Montgomery's attorney." He doesn't offer his hand, just stands there radiating expensive confidence. "I'll need a moment alone with my client."

"We were in the middle of—"

"You were in the middle of questioning my client after she repeatedly invoked her right to counsel," Joe cuts him off smoothly. "Which means anything she might have said would be inadmissible anyway. So let's not waste any more time."

I keep my expression neutral, but inside I'm practically singing. Joe Mendez carries the exact energy of a man who turns small-town detectives into cautionary tales before his first cup of coffee.

Simmons rises slowly, gathering his notes. "Ten minutes," he says, as though granting us a royal favor.

"We'll take as long as necessary," Joe replies, setting his briefcase on the table and snapping it open with surgical precision. "And those cuffs come off. Now."

"She's being held on assault charges—"

"Alleged assault charges," Joe interrupts, his tone making it clear how ridiculous he finds this. "Unless you believe my 135-pound client is going to overpower both of us and escape through the ventilation system, there's no security justification for restraints."

I bite the inside of my cheek to keep from smiling as Simmons weighs his options. After a moment of silent standoff, he frees my wrists before trudging out the door. I rub my wrists where the handcuffs have left angry red marks on top of Ethan's bruises. The relief of having competent representation washes over me as Joe pulls out a chair and sits across from me.

"Ms. Montgomery," he says, his voice lower and warmer than the professional tone he used with Simmons. "I'm Joseph Mendez. Brayden asked me to represent you."

"Thank you." I clear my throat. "How bad is it?"

Joe arranges several documents on the table, his movements deliberate and calm. "Let's start with the facts. Ethan Kincaid has filed a complaint claiming you assaulted him in the men's restroom at Tony's Pizzeria yesterday afternoon. According to his statement, you've been harassing him for weeks and became violent when he rejected your advances."

"That's complete bullshit," I say, anger finally breaking through my careful composure.

"I believe you, Ms. Montgomery," Joe says simply, and the quiet confidence in those two words nearly makes me cry with relief.

"So what happens now?"

"Now we fight back," Joe says, pulling out a legal pad. "I need you to tell me exactly what happened, every detail." I take a deep breath, gathering my thoughts. Explaining what happened means reliving it, but Joe's calm presence makes it easier somehow.

"Ethan and his girlfriend walked into Tony's when Brayden and I were there eating. We tried to ignore them, but Ethan came over to our table and started making comments." I trace a water stain on the table with my finger. "When I went to the bathroom—the women's bathroom—Ethan followed me in. He grabbed me by the wrists and started saying...things."

"What kind of things?" Joe asks, his pen poised above his legal pad.

"That I was frigid. That's why he cheated. That I'm only with Brayden to get back at him." The words taste bitter in my mouth. "When I tried to leave, he got more aggressive. That's when Brayden found us."

Joe nods, writing quickly. "And the bruises on your wrists?"

I hold them up, the marks still vivid against my skin. "Ethan did this when he grabbed me. He was squeezing harder and harder while he talked."

"And at no point did you enter the men's room?"

"God, no. He followed me into the women's bathroom." I shake my head, disgust rising in my throat. "He's flipped everything around and made himself the victim."

"Classic DARVO," Joe mutters, writing something down. "Deny, Attack, Reverse Victim and Offender." He looks up at me. "It's a common manipulation tactic used by abusers. They twist the narrative to make themselves appear to be the victim while casting the actual victim as the perpetrator."

"That's Ethan in a nutshell," I say, feeling a bitter laugh bubble up in my throat. "He's had years of practice."

"Mayor Kincaid's influence complicates things," Joe

continues, his pen moving across the page. "But power doesn't make them untouchable. It just means we need to be smarter."

A knock at the door interrupts us, and Detective Simmons pokes his head in. "Time's up."

Joe doesn't even glance up from his notes. "We'll need another twenty minutes, Detective."

"Sheriff wants to process her," Simmons says, his tone suggesting this isn't negotiable.

Joe finally looks up, his expression mild but his eyes sharp. "Process her for what, exactly? You haven't formally charged her yet."

"Assault and battery. It's in the warrant."

"A warrant based on the uncorroborated statement of an ex-husband with an obvious motive to lie." Joe closes his notebook with deliberate slowness. "Detective, let me be clear. If you proceed with formal charges against my client without substantial corroborating evidence, I will file a civil rights lawsuit so fast it'll make your head spin."

Simmons' face reddens.

"I'd advise you to think very carefully about your next move, Detective," Joe continues. "My client has visible defensive injuries that contradict Mr. Kincaid's version of events. We have a legitimate claim of self-defense against an alleged sexual assault."

I watch Simmons' Adam's apple bob as he swallows. The mention of sexual assault has clearly thrown him off-script. This wasn't part of Ethan's carefully crafted narrative.

"That's a serious allegation," he says finally.

"Yes, it is," Joe agrees. "One that should have been investigated before you slapped handcuffs on the victim."

Simmons shifts his weight, suddenly looking uncomfortable. "We're just following procedure based on the complaint filed."

"A complaint filed by the son of the man who signs your department's budget," Joe points out. "Quite a coincidence."

The detective's eyes narrow. "Are you implying something, counselor?"

"I'm stating facts. You can draw your own implications." Joe stands, gathering his papers. "Now, unless you're formally charging my client—in which case we'll be requesting an immediate bail hearing—I believe we're free to go."

I hold my breath, watching the internal struggle play out across Simmons' face. He nods towards my bruised wrists, then back to Joe's impassive expression.

"We'll need to discuss this with the Sheriff," Simmons finally says, his authority crumbling under Joe's steady gaze.

"By all means," Joe replies, gesturing toward the door. "Lead the way."

I stand on shaky legs, trying not to show how relieved I am. Joe places a steadying hand on my elbow as we follow Simmons down the hallway toward the Sheriff's office. My heart pounds against my ribs with each step, hope and anxiety warring in my chest.

The station is busier now than when I was brought in, deputies moving between desks with coffee cups and file folders. A few glance our way, their expressions ranging from curiosity to discomfort.

Sheriff Miller looks up from his desk as we enter, his weathered face giving away nothing. Mayor Kincaid sits across from him, and the sight of him makes my stomach clench. He rises slowly, straightening his expensive tie with manicured fingers.

"Well, well," he says. "Ms. Montgomery. I was just discussing your situation with the Sheriff."

"I bet you were," I mutter, earning a warning squeeze on my elbow from Joe.

"Mayor Kincaid," Joe says smoothly, extending his hand. "Joseph Mendez, Ms. Montgomery's attorney. I wasn't aware you had an official role in the justice system."

Kincaid's face tightens as he takes Joe's hand, his grip visibly firm as if trying to establish dominance through a handshake. "I'm simply here as a concerned citizen, Mr. Mendez. When a violent assault occurs in our community, it's my duty to ensure justice is served."

"Violent assault?" I can't help the bitter laugh that escapes me. "That's rich coming from the father of the man who did this." I hold up my wrists, the bruises now darkening to an ugly purple-blue.

Sheriff Miller clears his throat, looking distinctly uncomfortable. "Perhaps we should discuss this privately."

"I think that's an excellent idea," Joe says smoothly. "Though I'm curious why the mayor needs to be present for a law enforcement matter. Unless, of course, this isn't about law enforcement at all."

Kincaid's politician smile slips for just a second. "I'll leave you to it, Sheriff. I trust you'll handle this...appropriately." The threat in his words isn't even thinly veiled. It's spelled out in flashing neon lights.

As Kincaid brushes past us, he pauses beside me. "Such a shame, Cecelia," he murmurs, just loud enough for me to hear. "Your father must be so disappointed."

I bite my tongue until I taste copper, forcing myself not to respond. Joe's hand on my elbow tightens, silently warning me not to take the bait.

Once the door closes behind him, Sheriff Miller gestures to the chairs in front of his desk. "Please, sit down."

Joe and I take our seats, and I notice how the sheriff avoids looking directly at my bruised wrists. Guilt, maybe? Or just discomfort at being caught in the middle of Kincaid's political machinations?

"Sheriff," Joe begins, "my client should never have been arrested in the first place. The evidence clearly contradicts Mr. Kincaid's statement."

Sheriff Miller leans back in his chair, the leather creaking beneath him. "The evidence I have is a sworn statement from Ethan Kincaid claiming he was assaulted."

"And the evidence I have," Joe counters, gesturing to my wrists, "is physical proof that Ms. Montgomery was the one being assaulted. Not to mention potential witnesses at Tony's who can testify to Mr. Kincaid's aggressive behavior prior to the incident."

"Those marks could have happened during the struggle."

"With all due respect, Sheriff, those are fingerprint bruises," Joe retorts. "Look at the pattern—four distinct marks where fingers gripped, and a thumb print on the opposite side. These aren't random injuries from a struggle. They're consistent with someone forcibly restraining her wrists."

I watch the sheriff's face as he processes this, seeing the conflict playing out behind his eyes. He's known me since I was a child, watched me grow up singing in my father's church choir. Now he has to decide if he believes I'm the kind of woman who would follow her ex-husband into a bathroom to assault him.

"There's something else you should consider," Joe continues when the sheriff doesn't immediately respond. "My client is prepared to file sexual assault charges against Ethan Kincaid."

The sheriff's eyebrows shoot up. "Sexual assault?" Sheriff Miller rubs his hand over his face, suddenly looking tired. "This complicates things."

I barely hold back a bitter laugh. "Complicates things? A man with a history of emotional abuse cornered me in a bathroom and left bruises on me. What's complicated about that?"

"Cece," Joe warns softly.

I take a deep breath, trying to rein in my anger.

Getting emotional won't help my case, even if it's completely justified.

Sheriff Miller opens a folder on his desk, flipping through several pages before looking up at us again. "The problem is, we have conflicting stories and no witnesses to what actually happened in that bathroom."

"Except Brayden," I point out. "He saw Ethan with his hands on me."

"Mr. Cole has a...complicated relationship with our department," the sheriff says diplomatically. "His testimony might be viewed as biased, given your relationship."

"So my word means nothing because I'm dating Brayden?" The injustice of it burns in my throat. "What about these?" I thrust my wrists forward again. "Do these mean nothing too?"

The sheriff shifts uncomfortably. "Those injuries are concerning, Ms. Montgomery. I'm not dismissing them."

"Then why am I the one sitting here in handcuffs while Ethan walks free?"

Joe places a calming hand on my arm. "What my client means, Sheriff, is that there seems to be a double standard at play. Mr. Kincaid's statement was taken at face value, while hers is being dismissed without proper investigation. We're asking for the courtesy of due process."

Sheriff Miller studies us for a long moment, then sighs heavily. "I'm going to level with you both. This situation is...politically delicate."

"You mean because of Mayor Kincaid," I say flatly.

The sheriff doesn't deny it. "The mayor is an influential man in this town."

"And that trumps justice?" I can't keep the bitterness from my voice.

"No," Sheriff Miller says, surprising me with his firmness. "It doesn't. But it does mean we need to be thorough. Careful." He closes the folder and leans forward, clasping his hands on the desk. "Here's what I'm prepared to do. I'll release you on your own recognizance while we investigate both claims—yours and Mr. Kincaid's."

Joe straightens beside me. "And the charges?"

"Pending," the sheriff says. "Not dropped, but not formally filed either. We'll take statements from potential witnesses at Tony's, review any security footage if it exists, and have a medical professional document Ms. Montgomery's injuries."

It's not a complete victory, but it's something. I feel a knot of tension loosen slightly in my chest.

"And what about Ethan?" I ask. "Will you be investigating my claims against him with the same...thoroughness?"

Sheriff Miller meets my gaze directly for the first time since I entered his office. "Yes, Ms. Montgomery. Your claims will be investigated with equal thoroughness."

Something in his tone makes me believe him, despite everything. There's a weariness in his eyes that speaks of a man caught between duty and politics.

"Thank you," I say, the words feeling inadequate but necessary.

Joe stands, extending his hand to the sheriff. "We appreciate your fairness, Sheriff Miller. I trust you'll expedite my client's release paperwork?"

The sheriff nods, rising from his chair. "Detective Simmons will handle it. You should be out of here within the hour."

An hour. After everything that's happened, sixty more minutes in this place feels like an eternity, but it's better than spending the night in a cell.

"One more thing," Sheriff Miller adds, his hand on the doorknob. "I'd advise both you and Mr. Cole to stay away from Ethan Kincaid while this investigation is ongoing. Any contact could complicate matters."

"Believe me," I say, "the last person I want to see is Ethan."

The sheriff gives me a look that's almost sympathetic before opening the door. "Detective Simmons will be with you shortly to process your release."

Once we're alone again, I slump back in my chair, the adrenaline that's been keeping me upright suddenly draining away. My wrists throb, a constant reminder of how close it all came to going wrong.

The clock on the wall ticks louder than it should. Every second stretches. I stare at the door, waiting for it to open.

CHAPTER 24

CECE

BEING QUESTIONED IS its own special kind of hell. After giving my statement to the sheriff, I had hoped that would be the end of it. But, here I sit on the couch in the guesthouse living room, a mug of tea growing cold between my palms as Joe, my father, and Brayden all stare at me.

"Let me get this straight," Joe says, his pen hovering above his legal pad. "Ethan followed you into the women's restroom at Tony's, cornered you against the sink, and then proceeded to verbally and physically intimidate you?"

"Yes." I hold up my wrists where Ethan's fingerprints are still branded into my skin, now a sickening blend of purple and yellow. "He grabbed me here when I tried to leave."

Brayden paces behind the couch as I recount the story again.

"And what exactly did he say to you?" Joe asks.

I swallow, glancing at my father who sits rigidly in the armchair across from me. "He made comments about our marriage. Intimate details. He implied that our marriage failed because I did not please him."

I take a deep breath and force myself to look directly at Joe rather than my father. "When Ethan realized I was...intimate with Brayden, he became enraged. He called me a slut, demanded to know if I'd thought about him while Brayden and I were intimate..." I trail off, my cheeks burning. "When I tried to leave, he grabbed me harder. He pushed me against the wall and said—" my voice catches, "that I should let him remind me what a real man feels like."

The sound of Brayden's fist hitting the wall makes me jump. My father's face has gone completely white.

"He was trying to force himself on me," I finish quietly. "If Brayden hadn't come in when he did..."

My father rises abruptly. His face is a mask of shock and a hard, unforgiving sternness I've rarely seen directed at anyone but the most egregious sinners in his congregation. Joe continues writing, his pen scratching against the paper, the only sound in the room besides my father's labored breaths.

"And what did you do to him specifically, Brayden?"

"I slammed him against the wall," Brayden answers, "Had my arm across his throat. Told him if he ever touched her again, I'd break every bone in his hands."

My father's eyes widen, but I notice he doesn't condemn the violence. Not this time.

"Did you strike him?" Joe asks, his pen poised above the paper.

"No," Brayden says. "Just held him there until Cece asked me to let him go."

Joe nods, jotting something down. "That distinction matters. Restraint versus assault changes the entire legal picture."

The room goes quiet again.

My father hasn't spoken in several minutes. He sits stiffly, hands twisting around one another, his Bible untouched beside him. His eyes haven't lifted from the table, as if the grain in the wood might offer an answer he's spent years avoiding.

Then he turns toward me.

Tears track down his cheeks, slow and heavy. In my entire life, I've only seen my father cry twice: at my mother's funeral, and when he gave me away to Ethan.

"This…" His voice catches, the word breaking in half. "All this time… I did not see it."

My breath stalls. I've imagined this moment for years, the moment he finally acknowledged the truth, but now that it's here, I don't know how to breathe around it.

"Dad—"

He lifts a hand to stop me. "No. Let me speak."

Joe glances up but stays silent, sensing the shift.

My father inhales sharply, his shoulders tightening under the weight of words he never imagined he'd have to say. "I should have seen it. A father is supposed to protect his daughter. I preached that. I believed it. And yet, under my own roof, in my own family, I let a predator slip a ring onto your finger."

The confession hangs in the room like a fragile glass, one wrong move away from shattering.

Reverend Montgomery—unshakeable, righteous, immovable—finally cracking under the truth he'd refused to see.

"It wasn't your fault," I say softly, though the words scrape on their way out. "Ethan hid who he was. He fooled a lot of people."

My father closes his eyes. Slowly shakes his head.

"No. I fooled myself." His voice deepens with grief and something close to self-loathing. "I chose to believe him. I chose the easier story. I chose the man who quoted scripture and shook my hand in public… instead of the daughter who was crying out for help in ways I never bothered to understand."

My throat burns.

He looks at me then—really looks—and the pain in his eyes is staggering. "I encouraged you to marry him," he says, the truth ripping out of him. "I placed you in the hands of a man who hurt you. I did that. And I have to live with it."

And for the first time, he is no longer my preacher. No longer the man who told me what God wanted. Just a broken father finally realizing the depth of the damage his blindness caused.

Brayden stops pacing, his eyes locked on my father. I can feel the grudging respect building between them —two men who can barely stand each other finding common ground in their hatred of Ethan.

"What matters now," Joe says, his voice steady but edged with urgency, "is strengthening what we already have. The sheriff's office took the initial photos, but that isn't enough. We need documentation from someone outside the mayor's reach. Cece, I want a second medical evaluation. A full set of photographs and an examiner's report from a professional who isn't tied to Kincaid. That will give us evidence no one can tamper with."

I nod, though the thought of more strangers examining me, documenting my humiliation, makes me want to crawl out of my skin. "When?"

"Today, if possible. I know a doctor who can see you this afternoon." Joe turns to my father.

"I can make that happen," Brayden agrees. "Whatever we need to do, we'll do it."

"What can I do?" my father interjects. "Give me something. Anything."

"You mentioned that one of your congregants came to you about what happened yesterday. I will need to speak to her. I will also get in contact with the restaurant owner and any of his staff who were working. Maybe we'll be lucky, and he'll have security cameras."

"The Kincaids have their fingers in everything," I

say quietly, setting my untouched tea on the coffee table. "Even if there was footage, it's probably long gone by now."

"We won't know until we try," Joe replies. "And regardless, witness testimony will be crucial. People saw you both at the restaurant. They saw Ethan approach your table."

My father straightens his shoulders as he takes his seat again. "Mrs. Holloway will speak the truth. She's been my secretary for thirty years. Her loyalty is to the church, not to the Kincaids."

"Dad, no offense, but the church isn't exactly neutral territory when it comes to me versus Ethan." The words come out more bitter than I intended, but I can't take them back now.

His face falls slightly. "The past is behind us now."

Is it, though? I want to believe him, but trust is hard to rebuild. I open my mouth to say more but stop myself. This isn't the time to unpack years of resentment and hurt.

"Joe," I say instead, turning to face him directly, "you need to understand something. This isn't just about what happened in that bathroom." I lean forward. "This is personal for the Kincaids. I didn't lay a finger on Ethan other than defending myself. This is them punishing me for divorcing Ethan and for publicly embarrassing them."

Joe's pen pauses over his legal pad. "Punishment for the divorce?"

"Exactly." I run a hand through my hair, frustration

building in my chest. "I thought hurting the church by pulling their funding for the Church fundraiser was going to be the most damage. But they aren't going to back off. Not now, not ever."

Brayden's hand comes to rest on my shoulder. "They're powerful, but they're not untouchable."

"Exactly," Joe agrees, tapping his pen against his pad. "The Kincaids are used to getting their way, which makes them arrogant. Arrogant people make mistakes."

"What kind of mistakes?" my father asks, leaning forward in his chair.

"They overreach. They get sloppy." Joe looks at me with renewed purpose. "This false accusation against you? That's an overreach. They're counting on their influence to overcome facts. But facts are stubborn things, and we have them on our side."

I want to believe him, but fear tightens around my heart, squeezing until it's hard to breathe. "What if it's not enough? What if they've already poisoned the well? This is a small town, and people talk."

"Then we'll speak louder," my father says, surprising me with the force behind his words. "From the pulpit if we have to."

I stare at him, momentarily stunned. The thought of my father standing in front of the congregation and defending me against Ethan feels unreal—a glimpse of a world where the past five years unfolded differently, where he chose me over appearances.

"You'd do that?"

My father looks wounded by my doubt. "You're my

daughter, Cecelia. The only family I have left. I will not tolerate the Kincaids hurting you, me, or my church any longer. This ends now."

"Dad," I start. "I appreciate that, but I don't want to drag the church into this mess."

"The church is already involved," he says firmly. "When they attacked you, they attacked me. When they withdrew their funding to punish you, they punished the children who benefit from our charity drive."

Brayden's hand tightens on my shoulder, a silent show of support that steadies me more than he knows.

"Thomas is right," Joe says, surprising me with his use of my father's first name. "The Kincaids have made this bigger than a personal vendetta. They've weaponized their influence against both you and the church. That gives us more leverage, not less. We just have to prove it, and that is going to take some time."

"So what do we do in the meantime, Joe? Sitting and waiting is not one of my strong suits," Brayden asks.

Joe taps his pen against his legal pad, considering Brayden's question. "You keep on living your life, and we don't give them any ammunition to use against us."

"That's the lawyer answer. I'm asking what we actually do while these assholes are out there painting Cece as some kind of psycho ex-wife."

"We stay smart," Joe replies. "The Kincaids want you to react, to do something rash that would justify their narrative. Don't give them that satisfaction."

I twist my hands in my lap, the dull throb in my wrists a constant reminder of what happened. "Maybe we should just leave town for a while. Let things cool down."

"No." The word comes from both Brayden and my father simultaneously, overlapping in rare agreement.

"Running looks like guilt," my father says, his jaw set in that stubborn way I know too well.

"And it gives those bastards exactly what they want," Brayden adds, his hand squeezing my shoulder gently. "You gone, me gone, problem solved for them."

I sigh, leaning back against the couch. "So we just pretend everything is okay?"

"Precisely," Joe answers. "You need to be seen in public. Preferably still taking care of your duties at the church. We need to continue the narrative that you aren't capable of the accusations."

I stare at Joe, his words dropping into my mind one after another, heavy and unavoidable. Public appearances. Maintaining the narrative. It all feels like another performance, another role I'm supposed to step into. And God, I'm exhausted. I'm so tired of pretending, of shaping myself to fit what everyone else needs me to be.

"And what happens if Ethan shows up to taunt me? What if he corners me again? I can't exactly ignore him if he's in my face."

Joe sets his pen down deliberately, his expression calm but serious. "If Ethan approaches you, you walk away. You don't engage, you don't respond, you simply remove yourself from the situation."

"And if I can't?" The memory of being trapped against that bathroom wall makes my skin crawl.

"You won't be alone," Brayden says immediately.

Joe holds up a hand. "Actually, that's not the best approach. Brayden, you need to keep your distance from Ethan. Any confrontation between you two plays right into their narrative."

Brayden opens his mouth to argue, but Joe continues before he can speak.

"I'm filing for a protective order as soon as I leave here," he says, his tone leaving no room for debate. "Given the evidence of physical harm," he gestures to my wrists, "we have solid grounds for approval."

"And if they grant it?" my father asks.

"Then Ethan legally can't come within a specified distance of Cece. If he violates that order, it will only add more evidence to our case."

Joe stands, sliding his legal pad into his briefcase with practiced efficiency. "I'll text you the details for your medical examination once I've made the arrangements. Should be later today if my contact is available."

"Thank you," I say, feeling a strange mix of relief and anxiety at the thought of documenting my injuries. More evidence means a stronger case, but it also means more people examining the marks Ethan left on me, more explaining, more reliving what happened.

Joe hands me a business card, a heavy-cream stock embossed with his name and contact information. "Put this in your phone immediately," he says, his tone gentle but insistent. "If Ethan approaches you or tries to contact you in any way, call the police first, then call me. Day or night."

I take the card, nodding as I slip it into my pocket. "I will."

My father rises, extending his hand to Joe. He shakes my father's hand, then Brayden's, before turning back to me. "We're going to get through this, Ms. Montgomery. You have my word."

As the door clicks shut behind Joe, an awkward silence fills the living room. My father shifts uncomfortably in his chair, his fingers drumming against his Bible as he stares at the closed door. When he finally turns back to me, his face is drawn with more emotion than I've seen from him in years.

"Cecelia, I need to apologize—"

"Don't," I cut him off, raising my hand. "Not right now, Dad. Please."

His mouth snaps shut, surprise flashing across his features.

"I appreciate what you're trying to do," I continue. "But I can't handle one more emotional conversation today. I just...I can't."

Brayden moves to sit beside me on the couch, his thigh pressing against mine in silent support. My father tracks the movement, but for once, he doesn't flinch or scowl at our closeness.

"I understand. Perhaps another time."

"Another time," I agree, relief washing through me. I'm not ready for whatever heart-to-heart he's prepared to offer—not when I can still feel the ghost of Ethan's fingers around my wrists, not when my emotions are this raw and exposed.

My father clears his throat, shifting gears with practiced ease. "Maybe we can have dinner when you're ready. All three of us."

"I'd enjoy that."

The idea of my father and Brayden sitting at the same table still feels surreal, but a small smile edges onto my face. Awkward? Definitely. But the fact that my father is even willing makes something warm unfurl in my chest.

"Well," Brayden mutters, rubbing the back of his neck, "breaking bread with a preacher wasn't on my bingo card, but… sure. I can behave for a meal." His hand settles over mine, warm and steady. "You're worth the effort."

My father stands, tucking his Bible under his arm. "I should go. I'll speak with Mrs. Holloway first thing. She's usually at the church office by seven, organizing the weekly bulletin." He straightens his shoulders, determination hardening his features. "And then I'm calling an emergency meeting with the community outreach committee. We need to discuss the Kincaids' past donations and what this means for our charity work."

"Dad, you don't have to—"

"I do, Cecelia. Perhaps revisiting their financial history with the church will help our case. Show a pattern of behavior." He hesitates, then adds, "Money often reveals a person's true character."

I nod, too exhausted to argue. "Thank you."

He moves toward the door but pauses with his hand on the knob. For a moment, it seems he might say something more, but instead he simply nods. "I'll call you tomorrow."

I let out a breath I didn't even realize I'd been holding as the door clicks shut behind him. The room instantly feels lighter, as if some invisible weight has lifted with his departure. And beneath that relief is something stranger—seeing him actually stand up for me instead of pushing back feels unreal in a way I'm still trying to process.

Beside me, Brayden exhales hard, his entire body loosening at once, tension spilling out of him after being wound tight for far too long.

"Jesus fucking Christ," he mutters, dropping his head back against the couch. His hand finds mine, fingers gently tracing the bruises on my wrist. "Seeing you in those handcuffs..."

I turn to look at him—really see him—for the first time since this nightmare began. The shadows beneath his eyes tell me he hasn't slept.

"It wasn't exactly a high point for me either," I say, trying for humor that collapses the moment it leaves my mouth.

Brayden's expression tightens as his thumb glides gently over my skin, his features shifting into a storm of barely restrained emotion.

"I'm going to kill him. Not today. Not tomorrow. But someday, when all this legal shit is over, when no one's watching anymore...I'm going to make him pay for putting his hands on you."

I feel a twisted sense of comfort in his promise—in knowing someone would go that far to protect me. I've never had that before.

"Brayden." I shift my hand until it closes around his. "We can't let our heads go there. Joe's right. We beat them by outthinking them, not by reacting."

He lifts my wrist to his lips, pressing a gentle kiss against the bruises. "Being smart doesn't mean letting him get away with it," he murmurs against my skin. "It just means being patient.

I should argue, should tell him that revenge isn't worth the cost. But the truth is, part of me wants Ethan to suffer too. Wants him to feel even a fraction of the fear and humiliation he's inflicted on me. What does that say about who I've become?

"I'm so tired," I admit. "Tired of fighting him. Tired of being afraid."

Brayden pulls me against his chest, and I go without hesitation, sinking into his warmth. His arms feel like the only safe place left in the world. I press my face to him, breathing in the familiar mix of leather and soap. The steady rhythm of his heartbeat beneath my ear quiets everything inside me—the doubts, the fear, the relentless what-ifs.

"Come on," Brayden murmurs into my hair. "You need to rest before your appointment."

I let him guide me toward the bedroom, too worn down to resist. My limbs feel heavy, every step an effort. The adrenaline that kept me standing through the interrogation, through Joe's strategy session, through my father's unexpected support... it's gone now, leaving me drained and aching in every way that matters.

Brayden pulls back the covers and helps me sit on the edge of the bed. When he kneels to remove my shoes, the tenderness of the gesture makes my throat tight. This man, who radiates danger and violence to the rest of the world, treats me with a gentleness that still catches me off guard.

"I can undress myself," I protest weakly, even as he's already sliding my socks off.

"I know you can, but you don't have to."

I surrender, because I don't have the strength to do anything else. Because, for once, it feels good to let someone take care of me.

Brayden helps me settle against the pillows, pulling the blanket up around me. The soft rustle of fabric and the faint trace of his cologne wrap around me, another layer of comfort I didn't realize I needed. He sits on the edge of the bed for a moment, brushing a loose strand of hair from my forehead.

"Try to sleep," he says quietly.

Something in his voice loosens the final knot in my chest. I reach out, my fingers resting lightly on his wrist. "Stay."

He hesitates for only a heartbeat before kicking off his boots and sliding in beside me. His arm curves around my waist, steady and warm, drawing me close until my back settles against his chest. Heat radiates from him, easing the chill that has lived under my skin for days.

For the first time in what feels like forever, the silence isn't suffocating. It's gentle, filled with the rhythm of his breathing and the calm, steady pulse beneath my palm where our hands rest together.

My eyes grow heavy, thoughts blurring into a haze. Somewhere in the space between waking and sleep, I feel his lips brush the crown of my head.

"You're safe now," he murmurs.

And I believe him.

The last thing I'm aware of is the slow rise and fall of his chest beneath me, the sound of his heartbeat lulling me under until the darkness takes me, safe in his arms.

CHAPTER 25

BRAYDEN

I CAN'T DECIDE what pisses me off more—watching some stranger document the bruises on Cece's wrists, or folding my six-foot-two frame into her toy-sized Honda. Both make me want to put my fist through something. Preferably, Ethan Kincaid's face.

"You're quiet," Cece says as we pull into the church parking lot. "What's going on in that head of yours?"

"Nothing good," I admit, shifting my knees away from the dashboard for the hundredth time. The temperature dropped overnight, too cold for my bike, which means I'm crammed into this tin can on wheels. My knees practically touch my chin, and my shoulders are so hunched I'll need a chiropractor by noon.

She reaches over, her fingers brushing my forearm.

Even that light touch sends electricity up my spine. "Yesterday was rough."

"Rough doesn't begin to cover it." The memory of watching her wrists being photographed, measured, documented—each bruise a testament to what that piece of shit did to her—makes my blood boil all over again. The doctor had been professional, but I'd wanted to tear the examination room apart with my bare hands.

I take a deep breath, trying to push down the rage that's been simmering just below the surface since Tony's. "But Joe's right. The more evidence we have, the better chance we have to get this thrown out."

"And we need to be seen," Cece says, her fingers tightening on the steering wheel as she parks the car.

I can tell she doesn't want to be here. Hell, I don't want to be here either. But Joe was clear. We can't hide away like we're ashamed or guilty.

"I know you'd rather be anywhere else right now," I tell her, reaching over to squeeze her hand. "But remember what Joe said. We need to keep living our lives normally."

She nods, but her eyes are fixed on the church entrance, her shoulders tense. "What if Ethan shows up?"

"Then I'll handle it."

"Brayden..."

"Legally," I add quickly. "I'll handle it legally. They granted your protective order, remember? He can't come within a hundred yards of you without violating it, princess." I scan the parking lot, relief washing through me when I spot several familiar vehicles. Domino and Big's trucks. "Seems like we have some visitors."

"Wait, what?" Cece's eyebrows shoot up as she follows my gaze. "Your club brothers? Here? At the church?"

"Apparently." I'm just as surprised as she is. I hadn't called anyone, hadn't asked for backup. But here they are.

"Come on," I say, unfolding myself from her car with a groan. "Let's see what they're up to before your father tries to perform an exorcism or something."

We walk toward the church entrance, my hand resting protectively at the small of her back. The moment we step inside, I hear them before I see them. Big's booming laugh echoes through the fellowship hall, followed by Skelly's distinctive cackle.

"You guys here for the monthly exorcism?" I call out.

Four heads turn my way, and Domino's face breaks into a grin. He's wearing his cut over a hoodie, looking like he just walked off a biker magazine cover rather than standing in a church fellowship hall. Big and Skelly are to our left setting up several long tables. Wrecker walks out with a large box in his hands. A Santa hat on his head peaking over the top of the box. "Ho Ho Ho, asshole," he calls out.

"You're in a church, dumbass. Watch your language."

"I can't say asshole, but you can call me a dumbass. Rude."

"It's not swearing if it's your legal name."

Wrecker starts to shoot me the bird just as a few of the church ladies shuffle in from the side entrance. He reels it in fast before one of them catches him desecrating the house of the lord with his vulgarity.

Cece and I walk over towards Big, who meets us halfway. "Nice to see you again, heathen."

"Heathen?" Cece blinks at Big, confusion flickering across her face. "When did you call me that?"

Big chuckles, his massive frame making him look comically out of place among the church's modest decor. "At the party a few nights ago. After your third tequila shot, you said your daddy would have a heart attack if he knew you were hanging with the 'heathens' as he calls us."

"I don't remember that," she says, her cheeks flushing pink.

"That's because you were three sheets to the wind, darlin'," Skelly calls over, grinning as he unfolds another table. "Started singing some church hymn, but with dirty lyrics. It was impressive."

She turns to me. "Please tell me I didn't."

I shrug. "I plead the fifth of tequila, princess."

She smacks me hard in the arm. "You should have told me."

"And miss seeing your reaction? Well worth the bodily harm."

"What are you all doing here anyway?" I ask,

looking around at my brothers scattered throughout the church hall.

Big scratches his beard. "Your aunt called me, said your girl here ran into some trouble. Figured we'd come help with the distribution to make sure her ex stays well away from her."

I stare at Big for a second, my brain stuck on one bizarre detail. How in the hell did my aunt have Big's number? It's not as if the club keeps a phone tree printed off somewhere. My aunt is full of surprises, but this connection makes zero sense. I've been careful to keep my club life and family life separate. And yet somehow my aunt is calling up the club president like they're old friends?

"Wait. Since when does my aunt have your number?"

Big's laugh rumbles through the church hall, drawing curious glances from a couple of older ladies setting up a refreshment table. "Since about three years ago, she needed some help with a project."

"You're kidding me." Why did she go to him, and not to me? "None of this makes any sense."

"Nope. We text sometimes." He pulls out his phone, scrolling through messages. "She sends me recipes. I send her pictures of the food I make with them."

I run my hand through my hair, trying to wrap my head around this. My aunt has been secret buddies with my MC president for years. The woman operates on a level of quiet influence I clearly never gave her enough credit for—moves in the dark, pulls strings, and somehow no one ever sees it coming. A stealth ninja disguised as a churchgoing, cookie-baking aunt.

"Unbelievable," I mutter.

Cece squeezes my arm, clearly enjoying my bewilderment. "I think it's sweet."

"Sweet isn't exactly the word I'd use," I mutter, still trying to wrap my head around my aunt's secret friendship with Big.

Big claps his hands together, the sound echoing through the fellowship hall. "Alright, Cece. You're running this show. What do you need us to do? Put us to work."

Cece straightens her shoulders, and I can see her shift into organizer mode. The confidence looks good on her, a welcome change from the tension that's been shadowing her face since the arrest.

"Okay, so the system works like this," she explains, gesturing around the room, "the church ladies will check in the families at the front table. They've got a list of everyone who pre-registered. Once they're checked in," Cece continues, "they'll come through here where we have the toys arranged by age group. Each child gets three toys and a book. After that, they move to the grocery section where they can get a holiday meal box and some pantry staples."

"Where do you want us stationed?" Domino asks, walking over to join us.

"You guys would be great for helping with the toy section," Cece says. "Some of the families have multiple children, and they might need help carrying everything."

"We can handle that."

"That would be wonderful," Cece says, her smile brightening. I watch her take charge, directing everyone with a confidence that makes my chest tighten. This is her element—organizing, helping, making sure no one gets left behind. It's one of the many things I love about her.

Suddenly, Cece freezes mid-sentence, her face draining of color. "Oh no. I completely forgot about Santa."

"What about Santa?" I ask.

"The mayor always plays Santa," she mutters. "He hands out candy canes and takes photos with the kids. I can't believe I didn't think of this until now."

My jaw clenches so hard I'm surprised my teeth don't crack. "That's not happening. Not this year."

"But the kids—" she starts, worry creasing her forehead.

Before either of us can say another word, Wrecker comes barreling across the fellowship hall, nearly knocking over a stack of gift bags in his enthusiasm.

"Did someone say Santa?" he asks, grinning like he's just won the lottery. "I couldn't help but overhear you're in need of a Santa."

"You?" she says, eyeing Wrecker with a mix of disbelief and amusement. "Playing Santa for a bunch of church kids?" Considering the first time she met him, he was taking body shots off a stripper at our club-house, I can understand her hesitation.

Wrecker's grin widens, "I know I'm not exactly what these church folks expect for their Santa. But I can be jolly as fuck—I mean, jolly as holly." He corrects himself with a quick glance toward the church ladies. "And I promise not to scare the little ones."

I watch Cece consider this unexpected offer, her teeth worrying at her bottom lip. The idea of Wrecker playing Santa for a bunch of kids should be laughable. But there's also something weirdly perfect about it.

"The costume might not fit," she says, but I can tell she's warming to the idea.

"I'll make it work," Wrecker insists. "Come on, Cece. You need a Santa, and I need to spread some Christmas cheer. It's a win-win. I'll beg if I have to, sweetheart. Please, pretty please," Wrecker adds, clasping his hands together like he's actually praying in this church. "I've always wanted to be Santa. It's been my lifelong dream."

I stifle a laugh at the sight of this tattooed biker begging to play Santa Claus. "Since when?"

"Since right this second when I realized it was an option." He tugs at the Santa hat on his head, adjusting it to a jaunty angle. "Come on, I'm already halfway there with the hat."

Cece looks up at me, uncertainty written across her face. I can practically see the wheels turning in her head —weighing the disaster of having no Santa against the potential disaster of Wrecker in the role.

"He's actually good with kids," I tell her quietly. "His sister has three little ones. They adore him."

She blinks, surprise flickering across her features. "Really?"

I nod. "He's their favorite uncle. Takes them to the zoo, builds them blanket forts, the whole nine yards."

Wrecker beams at my endorsement. "I can do the 'ho ho ho' and everything. Watch!" He takes a deep breath and lets out a booming "HO HO HO!" that echoes through the fellowship hall, making several church ladies jump and clutch their pearls.

"Maybe dial it back about twenty percent," I suggest.

Cece laughs—a genuine laugh that lights up her face. "The church's costume is in the back. Come on. I'll show you where it is."

I watch Cece lead Wrecker toward the back room, the Santa hat bobbing with each excited step he takes. He's practically bouncing, talking a mile a minute about how he's going to "crush this Santa gig" and asking if there's a specific way to say "ho ho ho" that won't offend the church crowd. I can't help but smile at his enthusiasm, though I only let them go because I know Wrecker will keep her safe.

The moment they disappear around the corner, I turn to Big, my smile fading.

"Did my aunt really call you?" I keep my voice low, glancing around to make sure none of the church ladies are within earshot.

Big's massive shoulders rise and fall in a shrug. "She did. But so did Joe."

"Joe? Our lawyer Joe?" That catches me off guard. "Since when does he have your number?"

"Since he's done some work for the club in the past." Big scratches his beard, eyes tracking the room with the constant vigilance I've come to expect from him. "Helped us out of a few tight spots. Man knows how to navigate the system."

"So you're telling me, my aunt, my lawyer, and my club president are all in cahoots behind my back?" I ask, not sure if I should be pissed or impressed.

Big chuckles. "Not exactly behind your back. More... bolstering your efforts. Your aunt was worried about Cece. Said that Kincaid prick might try something after the restraining order went through." His voice drops even lower. "Joe filled us in on the rest. Figured we could be useful, so here we are. Just enough of a presence to make a point without turning it into a spectacle. Four bikers helping with a church charity? That's a heartwarming news clip. Twenty bikers? That's intimidation—and not the kind your father's congregation would appreciate."

I nod, gratitude pushing up through the anger that's been welded to my ribs these past few days. "Thanks, man. I owe you."

"You don't owe a damn thing." Big claps a hand on my shoulder, steady and solid. "She's yours. That makes her family."

In all my years with the MC, I've never brought a

woman into the fold this way. Never had anyone who mattered enough to bind my club life to my personal life. I haven't even given her a property patch yet, and they're already stepping up to protect her.

The realization hits deep, stirring something fierce and proud in my chest.

Damn, it feels good to be a Heaven's Reject.

"So what's the plan?"

"Domino's on the door," Big answers, nodding to the club and their positions. "Skelly's floating, keeping an eye on all entrances. I'm staying wherever she is, and you..." He gives me a meaningful look. "You just try not to murder anyone in a house of God."

"Tall order," I mutter, but I appreciate the thought they've put into this. "What about Wrecker?"

"Santa's job is to see everything," Big taps his temple with one thick finger. "He can see who comes in, who's watching too closely. Plus, who would fuck with Santa?"

I snort at the image of Wrecker in a Santa suit beating the shit out of Ethan. Talk about Christmas miracles.

"Mayor's not gonna appreciate us being here," I say, watching more volunteers trickle in. "Ethan won't either."

"That's the idea," Big replies. "But remember— we're here as model citizens helping with a charity event. Pure community service. Anyone who complains ends up looking like an asshole."

The sound of Cece's laughter pulls my attention.

She's walking back with Wrecker, who is now fully suited up as Santa. The beard's crooked, the hat's sliding off, and the entire outfit looks two sizes too small—pant legs hovering above his boots, coat buttons fighting for their lives against his shoulders. But the grin on his face radiates genuine joy, and damned if it isn't exactly the kind of ridiculous brightness today needed.

"How do I look?" Wrecker asks, spinning with his arms out. "Jolly enough?"

"You look as though Santa hit a growth spurt," I say, and Cece laughs again.

That sound hits me right in the chest, warm and grounding in a way I wasn't prepared for.

"We'll make it work," she says, adjusting his fake beard. "The kids won't care if the pants are a little short."

Wrecker strikes a pose, hands on his hips. "Santa doesn't skip leg day. That's my official story."

Big walks over, eyeing the costume with amusement. "Maybe stuff a pillow in there. You're looking a little lean for the big man."

"Already on it," Wrecker says, patting his midsection. "Got two throw pillows from the pastor's office. Don't worry, I'll put them back."

Cece's eyes widen. "You took pillows from my father's office?"

"Borrowed," Wrecker corrects with a wink. "It's for the children, sweetheart. I'm sure Jesus would approve."

Before Cece can respond, the doors to the fellowship hall swing open, and I turn to see Reverend Montgomery striding in with purpose. He stops dead in his tracks when he spots Wrecker in the too-small Santa suit, his expression cycling through shock, confusion, and something that might be reluctant amusement. "What in heaven's name..." he begins, approaching our little group with measured steps.

"Dad!" Cece hurries over to him, clearly trying to head off any potential conflict. "I was just coming to find you. We had a slight...adjustment to our Santa situation."

The Reverend studies Wrecker—his tattooed neck peeking out above the Santa collar, his boots showing beneath the too-short pants. "I can see that." He turns his attention to Wrecker, who's standing there with his beard slightly askew, looking like the world's most dangerous mall Santa.

"And you are?"

"They call me Wrecker," he says, then catches himself. "I mean, I'm...Robert. Robert Wreckman." I nearly choke trying to suppress my laugh. Wrecker's never used his real name in the five years I've known him.

"Robert has volunteered to be our Santa."

"The costume is a bit...snug," he observes dryly.

"Santa's been hitting the gym," Wrecker says without missing a beat. "Mrs. Claus says I've been letting myself go."

A startled laugh escapes the Reverend, quickly

covered by a cough. "Well, Mr...Wreckman, was it? I think you'll do just fine as our fill-in Saint Nicholas."

Before anyone can respond, the kitchen doors burst open and a flurry of church ladies spill into the room, all talking at once and waving clipboards.

"Families are arriving!" one announces. "Everyone to your places, please!"

The room explodes into motion. Volunteers hurry to the craft tables, kids dart between legs, and Wrecker adjusts his Santa beard with a resigned sigh. Cece turns, lighting up as she surveys the chaos, and for a moment, everything else fades away.

She looks happy. Genuinely happy.

And I can't stop watching her.

Whatever it takes, I'll make sure she keeps that light in her eyes. I'll make sure she stays safe.

Even if it means standing guard in a church full of tinsel and sugar cookies.

CHAPTER 26

CECE

I'M STILL RIDING the Christmas miracle high as we pull out of the church parking lot, my cheeks actually hurting from smiling so much. Today was everything I'd hoped for and more. Over four hundred families will have food on their tables and presents under their trees because of what we did.

"I still can't believe Wrecker managed to keep it G-rated the entire time," I say, glancing over at Brayden, who is somehow folded into my passenger seat in a way no human his size should logically manage. "I was convinced he'd slip up the moment that kid asked about the reindeer."

Brayden chuckles, a low rumble filling the car. "Wrecker may look tough enough to chew through steel, but he's a marshmallow when it comes to kids. You should've seen him last year at his niece's ballet recital. Front row, bouquet of flowers, tearing up during the bow."

"I would pay good money to see that," I say, turning onto Main Street. The Christmas lights strung across the lampposts cast everything in a warm glow, making even our small town look magical. "Seriously though, I don't know how to thank you and the guys. Without you all stepping up, we would've had to cancel the whole distribution."

"Don't mention it, princess." Brayden shifts in his seat, trying to find a position that doesn't make him look like a human origami project. "The guys were happy to help."

I feel warmth spreading through my chest that has nothing to do with my car's temperamental heater. A month ago, I was drowning in divorce papers and humiliation. Now I'm driving home from a successful charity event with a man who rallied his intimidating biker brothers to save Christmas. Life is weird sometimes.

"Still," I insist, "I want to do something to thank them. Maybe dinner at the guesthouse?"

"You really want to feed those animals? Skelly alone eats enough for three grown men." Brayden's hand finds my thigh, his thumb tracing lazy circles that make it hard to focus on the road. "But if you're serious, they'd love it. Just don't tell them I called them animals."

"Your secret's safe with me." I cover his hand with mine, enjoying the contrast of his rough skin against my palm. "Can you text Big and invite him over? We'll have to stop by the grocery store on the way back."

"Hold up." Brayden's entire body tenses beside me, his hand suddenly gripping my thigh. "Do you recognize that car behind us?"

I glance in the rearview mirror, my pulse instantly accelerating as I spot the sleek black Mercedes following too closely behind us. The tinted windows make it impossible to see who's driving, but I don't need to see the driver's face to know exactly who it is.

"Ethan," I breathe, my fingers tightening around the steering wheel. "It's his dad's car."

"Don't stop," Brayden demands. "Keep driving."

"He's not supposed to be anywhere near me. The protective order—"

"Exactly. Which is why we're calling it in. We need to call from your phone so they can trace it. Where is it?"

"My purse."

Brayden reaches for it, but I jerk the car, slamming him into the passenger side door.

"He's trying to pass us," I say, panic rising in my throat.

"Don't slow down. Don't stop. If he gets in front of us, he might try to block the road."

I press harder on the accelerator, but my little Honda is no match for a Mercedes. Ethan's car pulls alongside us, engine growling as he accelerates.

"He's trying to run us off the road," I gasp as the Mercedes swerves toward us. He veers closer, metal nearly kissing metal. My heart pounds so hard I can barely hear anything else. Ethan's face appears in the window again, mouthing something I can't understand. Brayden finally fishes my phone out of my purse, punches 9-1-1, then puts it on speaker.

"911, what is your emergency?"

"We're on Main Street heading toward Oakwood Drive," I say. "My ex-husband, Ethan Kincaid, is following us. He's violating a protective order and trying to run us off the road."

The Mercedes suddenly accelerates, cutting in front of us so sharply I have to slam on the brakes. My seatbelt locks, digging into my chest as the car fishtails slightly.

"Shit," Brayden hisses. "He's stopping."

Sure enough, the black car screeches to a halt directly in front of us, blocking the road. I brake hard, my little Honda skidding to a stop just inches from Ethan's bumper. My heart hammers against my ribs as I watch Ethan throw his car door open and step out onto the street.

"Stay in the car," Brayden commands, already reaching for his door handle.

"No!" I grab his arm. "That's what he wants. If you touch him, you'll be the one arrested."

The dispatcher's voice crackles through my phone. "Ma'am, are you still there?"

"Yes, he's blocked the road and gotten out of his car. Please hurry."

Ethan stalks toward us, his styled hair and expensive coat a stark contrast to the fury twisting his features. He looks unhinged in a way I've never seen before. This isn't the polished, calculating man he shows the world. This is the version he kept tucked behind forced smiles and gentle tones—the one who surfaced only when doors were closed and no one else could hear.

His eyes dart, wild and unfocused, and there's a sharp edge to his movements that sends a chill straight through me. This isn't rational Ethan. This is the side of him built on control and entitlement, the one that always simmered beneath the surface, waiting for the moment someone dared to challenge him. This is something far more dangerous.

"You need to get officers here now. I can't promise I won't break his fucking neck if he tries to touch her." Ethan reaches my door. He pounds his fist against my window so hard I'm surprised the glass doesn't shatter.

"Get out of the car, Cece! We need to talk!"

I press the lock button, making sure all doors are secured. My hands are shaking so badly I can barely hold the phone. "I'm not getting out!" I shout back, though I'm not sure he can hear me through the glass. My heart is a frantic drum in my chest, adrenaline making my limbs feel weightless and useless all at once.

"Ma'am. What is the man doing?"

Ethan's face contorts with fury, and he slams his

palm against my window again. "Open the goddamn door, Cece! You're embarrassing yourself with this restraining order bullshit!"

"He's trying to force me out of my car," I tell the dispatcher, my voice shaky.

"Units are enroute," the dispatcher assures me. "Stay inside your vehicle and keep the doors locked."

"No shit," I mumble back to her.

Ethan's attention shifts to Brayden, his gaze narrows to slits. "You think you can just take what's mine?" he shouts, his words slightly muffled through the glass. "You think this is over? It's not over until I say it's over!"

Brayden's jaw clenches so tight I can hear his teeth grinding. His hand grips the door handle.

"Don't," I plead, grabbing his arm. "That's exactly what he wants."

"I'm not going to sit here while he threatens you," Brayden growls, but he doesn't open the door. Not yet.

Ethan circles around to Brayden's side, pounding on his window now. "Get out of that car and face me like a man!" Ethan screams, his face contorted with rage as he slams his fist against Brayden's window. "Or are you only tough when you're jumping people in bathrooms?"

I can feel Brayden's muscles tensing under my grip, his entire body vibrating with barely contained violence. The expression on his face scares me, not because I fear him, but because I know what he's capable of doing to protect me.

"Brayden, please," I whisper, tightening my grip on his arm. "The police are coming. He'll be arrested for violating the order."

Ethan circles back to my side, his face inches from the glass.

"You really think you can hide behind a piece of paper?" He laughs, the sound manic and chilling. "My father owns this town, Cece. Owns the police. Owns the judges. You think your little restraining order means anything?"

I try to keep my face neutral despite the fear clawing up my throat. The dispatcher's voice in my ear asks for updates, but I can barely form coherent sentences with Ethan's face pressed against my window.

"He's—he's still here," I manage. "He's intoxicated."

"Get off the phone," Ethan snarls, slamming his palm against my window again. The glass vibrates dangerously under the impact. "You think calling the police is going to help you? They work for my father!"

My breath stutters, my pulse hammering as Ethan's rage intensifies, rising around us with terrifying speed.

"Please hurry," I yell into the phone.

Ethan suddenly stops pounding on my window, his expression shifting from rage to something calculated and cold. The change is more terrifying than his anger. Without a word, he turns and strides back to his car.

"He's going back to his vehicle," I tell the dispatcher, relief washing through me. Maybe he's giving up. Maybe he realized how badly he's screwed himself by violating the order.

But my relief evaporates instantly when I see what happens next.

He goes to his car, pulling out the tire iron, and Brayden knows exactly what he plans to do with it. He's had enough. He's out of the car before I can stop him.

"Brayden, no!" I scream, lunging across the console, but my fingers only brush the back of his jacket as he slams the door shut behind him.

"Stay in the car!" Brayden shouts back, already squaring off against Ethan in the middle of the street.

Ethan brandishes the tire iron, clearly having waited for this moment, a sick grin stretching across his face as he advances on Brayden. The streetlights cast long shadows across the pavement, turning the scene into a waking nightmare.

"Finally," Ethan taunts. "The delinquent comes out to play."

Brayden doesn't move. He stands in the middle of the street, broad and unshakable, his shadow cutting through the headlights.

"Put it down, Ethan."

Ethan's grin twists. "You think you can steal my wife and get away with it? You think you can play the hero?"

"I didn't steal her," Brayden growls. "You lost her by sticking your tiny little prick into anything that wouldn't shake you off."

Ethan lets out a rough, humorless laugh—and charges.

The tire iron comes down fast. Brayden blocks the first hit with his forearm, the sound a dull, heavy crack that makes me flinch. The second blow glances off his shoulder, hard enough to spin him sideways. Brayden recovers and drives a fist into Ethan's ribs, the impact echoing through the still night.

They crash into the hood of my car. Metal dents, glass trembles, the impact reverberates through me. I can hear the dispatcher shouting on the phone, but her words are distant, drowned out by the chaos outside.

"Brayden!" I scream, fumbling with my seat belt.

He glances toward me—just a heartbeat of distraction—and Ethan swings. The tire iron connects with Brayden's jaw. The sound it makes—thick and final—tears a gasp from my throat. Blood splatters across the hood, bright and shocking under the streetlight.

Brayden stumbles but doesn't go down. He lunges forward, driving Ethan backward until his spine cracks against the hood of the car. Metal dents under the impact. Ethan tries to twist away, but Brayden's grip clamps tighter.

They wrestle across the slick surface, boots scraping, fists flying. Ethan's heel slips, and Brayden uses the moment. He pivots, shoving Ethan sideways off the hood and dragging him toward the passenger side.

Brayden seizes the front of Ethan's jacket and slams him into the door so hard the entire frame shudders. The passenger-side window explodes outward, glass raining onto the pavement in a glittering cascade.

Ethan swings wild, a desperate, poorly aimed punch

that catches Brayden in the ribs. Brayden grunts, barely reacting, then cocks his fist and delivers a strike to Ethan's jaw that drops him to the ground

"Stay down!" Brayden roars.

But Ethan does not listens. He wipes at the blood running from his nose, his grin twisted and manic. "You'll never have her," he spits, charging again.

Brayden meets him head-on. They hit the pavement hard, rolling, fighting for control. The tire iron scrapes across the asphalt as they grapple, each strike heavier, more desperate. The sound of flesh hitting flesh is sickening.

I can't breathe. I can't just sit there and watch him die for me. I throw open the door and stumble out, still holding the phone in my shaking hand. "The police are almost here!" I shout, my voice breaking. "Please, stop!"

Brayden blocks another hit, but Ethan rams his shoulder into him, sending them both crashing into the gravel at the edge of the road. Brayden's breathing is harsh, ragged. Ethan grabs a handful of dirt and throws it in his face, then tackles him again, slamming his fists down. Brayden takes the hits, twisting, grappling, trying to get control.

"Brayden!" I cry, taking off toward them.

He pushes himself up, blood running from his mouth, eyes dark and unfocused. He's hurt—badly hurt —but still fighting. Ethan lunges again, shouting, his face smeared with blood and rage. Brayden drives his elbow into Ethan's stomach, forcing a guttural cry from him. The tire iron drops to the pavement with a sharp clang.

They're both on their knees now, exhausted, breathing hard, the cold night air steaming around them.

"Don't even think about touching my woman," Brayden snarls.

Ethan shoves him away, spitting blood. "She's mine!"

"No!" I shout, my throat raw as I sprint toward them. "I'm not!"

Ethan whirls on me, and before I can react, his hand shoots out and clamps around my arm.

"Ethan—no!" I struggle, twisting, clawing at his wrist, but his grip is unyielding.

"You think you can humiliate me?" he hisses against my ear. "You think you can hide behind him? You're mine, Cece. You've always been mine."

"Let me go!" I kick, shove, and dig my nails into his skin, but he yanks me closer, dragging me toward his car. "We're going home," he growls. "You're done ruining my life."

"Brayden!" I scream.

He forces himself up, staggering toward us, blood pouring from his jaw and side, his breath coming in short, painful bursts.

Then—sirens.

The wail splits through the night, growing louder, closer. Blue and red light wash over the street as Sheriff

Miller's cruiser skids to a stop, gravel spraying across the pavement.

"Let her go, Ethan!" the sheriff's voice booms, sharp and commanding.

Ethan freezes, breathing hard.

"Now!"

For a moment, it's silent. Even the air holds its breath.

Then Ethan's hand trembles. The fight drains out of him as the flashing lights paint his face. Deputies rush forward, shouting, tackling him before he can take another step.

I barely notice. I'm focused on Brayden.

He's down on one knee, blood dripping from his chin, one arm wrapped around his ribs. He looks pale, barely upright.

"Brayden," I whisper, stumbling toward him. My knees hit the cold pavement beside him as I cup his face in my hands. "Oh my God—Brayden."

He tries to smile, but it comes out as a wince. "I'm fine. Just a scratch."

"Don't lie to me!" His blood is warm against my palms. "You need help."

He glances up at me, "Hey," he murmurs, rough and unsteady. "Don't cry, princess. I'm right here."

The word shatters me. A sob escapes as I press my forehead to his, my tears mixing with the blood on his skin. "You scared me," I breathe. "You can't ever do that again."

He exhales shakily, his hand finding mine. "Don't plan to."

Sheriff Miller cuts through the chaos. "EMS is on the way," he says, his tone gentler now. "He's gonna be okay, Cece."

I nod, though his words barely register. All I can do is hold Brayden's hand and whisper his name, again and again, as the flashing lights wash over us.

Deputies shout orders in the background, Ethan's protests rising and fading as they push him into the back of the cruiser. But the only thing that matters is the slow, steady rhythm of Brayden's breathing.

I don't let go until the paramedics arrive. Even then, I stay close, my fingers still laced with his, refusing to be separated.

The night smells like blood and asphalt and winter. The world feels broken and whole at the same time.

And as Brayden squeezes my hand, whispering, "Told you I've got you, princess," I realize—he does.

He always has.

CHAPTER 27

CECE

HOSPITALS ARE FILLED with two things: people who are dying, and people who are terrified someone they love might be. I fall into the second category, watching the ER doctor probe at Brayden's jaw with latex-covered fingers.

"Can you open your mouth wider for me?" The doctor's voice is clinically detached, treating Brayden's split lip and the ugly purple swelling along his jawline as if they're nothing more than an interesting puzzle to solve.

Brayden tries to comply, wincing as the movement stretches his busted lip. Fresh blood wells up from the crack, and I fight the urge to slap the doctor's hands away. He's been poking at Brayden's injuries for ten minutes now, each prod making my stomach clench tighter.

"You're lucky," the doctor announces, stepping back to make notes on his tablet. "No fracture to the mandible, but you've got significant contusions and soft tissue damage. That tire iron could have shattered your jaw if it had hit just a bit harder."

I swallow hard at the word "shattered," the image of Ethan swinging that metal bar at Brayden's face replaying in my mind for the hundredth time. Two inches to the left, and we might be in a trauma center instead of the ER.

"What about his ribs?" I ask. "He could barely breathe in the ambulance."

"X-rays show bruised ribs, not broken," the doctor says, scrolling through something on his tablet. "He is going to be in significant pain for a while, but there is no internal bleeding or organ damage."

He pauses, then adds, "We are concerned about a concussion. His responses were slow when he came in, so we will need to monitor him closely for the next several hours."

Relief floods through me so intensely I grip the edge of the exam table to stay upright. Bruised, not broken. He's going to be okay.

"So he can go home?" I ask, already calculating how I'm going to get him comfortable in the guesthouse.

The doctor looks up from his tablet with a frown. "I'd like to keep him overnight for observation. Head injuries can be tricky, and given the force of impact—"

"No." Brayden's voice is rough but firm, the single syllable brooking no argument. "I'm not staying."

"Mr. Cole, I strongly recommend—"

"I said no." Brayden shifts, grimacing as he puts weight on his elbow to sit up straighter. "Just give me whatever paperwork I need to sign."

I place my hand on his shoulder, feeling the tension radiating through him. "Brayden, maybe you should listen to—"

"I'm not spending the night in this place," he cuts me off, his voice harsh. His eyes meet mine, a silent plea in them that I understand all too well. Hospitals mean vulnerability, helplessness. For Brayden, that's worse than physical pain.

The doctor sighs, clearly used to difficult patients. "Then you'll need to sign an AMA form—Against Medical Advice. And someone will need to monitor you for the next twenty-four hours for signs of concussion or internal bleeding."

"I'll watch him," I say immediately. "I won't leave his side."

Brayden's hand finds mine, squeezing gently despite his battered knuckles. The gesture makes my heart ache more than any of his visible injuries.

"Fine." The doctor taps something on his tablet with more force than necessary. "I'll have the nurse bring the paperwork and discharge instructions. You'll need to fill these prescriptions immediately." He scribbles on a prescription pad and hands me the sheet. "Pain management, antibiotics for that facial laceration, and anti-inflammatories."

When the doctor leaves, I step between Brayden's knees, careful not to touch his injured ribs. "Are you sure checking yourself out is a good idea?"

"I hate hospitals," he says simply, his good hand coming up to rest at my waist. "Nothing good ever happens in them."

I think of my mother's final days—the antiseptic smell, the harsh fluorescent lights seared into my memory, a permanent scar I still carry. "I know," I whisper, resting my forehead gently against his. "We'll get you out of here soon."

He leans into my touch, breathing carefully so he doesn't jostle his ribs. The vulnerability in his eyes makes something deep in my chest twist.

"How bad do I look?" he asks. "Tell me the truth."

I pull back just enough to take him in. His lip is split, a thin line of red at the corner. The swelling along his jaw is getting worse by the minute, and the butterfly bandage on his forehead is barely holding the cut from Ethan's first swing.

"You look rough," I admit, attempting a shaky smile. "Really rough."

His thumb moves in slow circles on my hip, a touch meant to reassure *me* even though he's the one in a hospital gown, bruised and stitched together.

"And you?" he asks softly. "Are you holding up?"

It's so very him—to worry about me when he's the one who took the blows. "I'm okay," I say, though my voice betrays a tremor. "Ethan never got the chance to hurt me."

I swallow hard. "Because of you."

Brayden's expression hardens at Ethan's name. "Where is that piece of shit now?"

"Jail," I confirm. "Violation of the protective order, aggravated assault with a weapon, attempted kidnapping, operating under the influence—the list goes on. Sheriff Miller said they're holding him without bail until his arraignment."

"Good." The single word burns with Brayden's fury, even through his pain-strained voice. "Hope they throw away the fucking key."

A nurse appears with a clipboard of discharge papers, her expression professionally neutral despite Brayden's colorful language. "Mr. Cole, I need your signature on these forms acknowledging that you're leaving against medical advice."

While Brayden scrawls his name across the dotted lines, I step aside to text Jillian with an update. My hands are still shaking slightly, adrenaline not fully faded from my system.

"All done," the nurse says, tucking the clipboard under her arm. "I'll get your discharge instructions and prescriptions ready. There's a twenty-four-hour pharmacy three blocks from here if you want to fill these tonight."

"Thank you," I tell her, grateful for her matter-of-fact efficiency.

Once she leaves, Brayden attempts to slide off the

exam table, his face going alarmingly pale with the effort. I rush forward, slipping my arm around his waist to steady him.

"Easy," I murmur.

I'm reaching out to grab him when the exam room door swings open. Big and Wrecker burst in. Their faces shift from worry to determination when they see Brayden struggling.

"Whoa there, brother," Big says, moving with surprising speed for a man his size. He reaches Brayden just as his knees start to buckle, catching him with one massive arm. "We got you."

"I'm fine," Brayden protests. The stubborn idiot would rather collapse than admit he needs help.

"Sure you are," Wrecker says, positioning himself on Brayden's other side. "And I'm the real Santa Claus."

I step back, relief washing over me as they take Brayden between them. Even injured, Brayden is too proud to fully surrender, but he doesn't fight as they steady him.

"How'd you know we were here?" Brayden asks, his breathing labored.

"Jillian called," Big explains, carefully adjusting his grip to avoid Brayden's injured ribs. "Said you'd gotten yourself beat to hell playing hero."

"Wasn't playing," Brayden mutters, wincing as they help him sit back on the edge of the exam table.

"Where are my clothes?"

"In evidence," I offer. "Sheriff Miller's orders."

"Guess you're riding home with your ass out," Big jokes.

"Do you think they can loan him something to wear home?"

"Christ," Wrecker says, running a hand over his face. "Your girl's right. We can't have you flashing your junk all over town." He turns to me with a grin that doesn't quite hide his concern. "No offense, Cece, but I think that view should be exclusive."

"I'll run to the gift shop," Big announces, already heading for the door. "They might have some sweatpants or something."

Left alone with Wrecker and Brayden, I let myself sink into the plastic chair in the corner. The adrenaline is finally wearing off. I wrap my arms around myself, trying to stop the trembling that's started deep in my bones.

"Hey," Brayden says softly, his eyes finding mine across the room. "Come here."

I hesitate, afraid of hurting him worse than he already is.

"Princess," he murmurs, and the gentle command pulls me to my feet. I cross the room and carefully position myself between his knees again, my hands hovering uncertainly over his battered body.

"I don't want to hurt you," I whisper.

"You won't." His good hand reaches for mine, tugging me closer. "I'm tougher than I look."

Wrecker snorts. "You look like hamburger meat right now, brother."

"I can still kick your ass," Brayden grumbles, though the grimace that follows kills any illusion of menace.

I want to laugh, but the reality of how close I came to losing him crashes over me again. My throat tightens as I take in his battered face. The bruising has spread, deepening into ugly purples and blues along his jaw.

"I'd pay money to see you try," Wrecker says, though a flicker of worry betrays him. "You can barely stand upright."

The door swings open as Big returns, holding a gray sweatshirt and black sweatpants. "Best I could scavenge," he says, tossing them onto the exam table. "Enjoy strolling around with 'Pinewood General Hospital' stamped across your ass."

"Better than nothing," Brayden mutters, giving the clothes a look that suggests they personally insulted him.

"Need help getting dressed?" I ask softly.

He shakes his head—then immediately winces. "I've got it."

"Sure you do," Big says, rolling his eyes. "Just the same way you 'had' Ethan Kincaid. And we all witnessed how that worked out."

"He's in jail, isn't he?" Brayden growls. "I had to make sure that he fucked up enough so the charges would stick."

"Yeah, fucked up is the right word to explain why you are in a hospital gown and he's behind bars." Wrecker points out. "Call it a draw."

I bite my lip, torn between wanting to help and respecting Brayden's wishes.

"I can handle it," Brayden insists, though the way his jaw tightens when he tries to sit up straighter tells a different story.

I exchange a glance with Big, who gives me an almost imperceptible nod. "Guys, can you give us a minute?" I ask.

Wrecker raises his eyebrows, but Big is already heading for the door. "We'll be right outside," he says, dragging Wrecker with him. "Holler if you need us."

When the door closes behind them, I turn back to Brayden. His face is pale beneath the bruising, a sheen of sweat on his forehead betraying how much pain he's really in.

"You don't have to pretend with me," I say softly. "Not after everything we've been through."

He closes his eyes briefly, some of the tension leaving his shoulders. "I hate feeling weak," he admits. "Especially in front of you."

"You're the strongest person I know," I tell him, carefully taking his hand. "Letting me help you doesn't change that."

A ghost of a smile crosses his battered face. "You're not going to let this go, are you?"

"Not a chance. So pick your poison. I help you, or I go grab Wrecker. Your choice."

"Definitely you," he says, the ghost of a smile pulling at his split lip. "At least you'll appreciate the view."

I can't help but laugh, even though my face is still damp with tears. "That's the only reason I offered."

I carefully untie the hospital gown, letting it fall away from his shoulders. The bruising on his torso steals my breath—angry purple blooms spread across his ribs, stark against his tattooed skin. I trace my fingers just above the worst of it, not quite touching.

"Jesus, Brayden," I whisper.

"Looks worse than it feels," he lies, watching my face.

"Bullshit." I grab the sweatshirt first, bunching it up to make the neck hole wider. "Arms up—slowly."

He obeys, grimacing as he raises his arms just enough for me to slide the soft fabric over his head. I guide each arm through the sleeves with gentle movements, trying not to jostle his injured ribs.

"Almost done," I murmur, tugging the sweatshirt down over his torso. The hospital logo stretches across his broad chest, making him look bizarrely like a hospital employee. "Now for the hard part."

I grab the sweatpants, kneeling to help him thread his feet through. His hand rests on my shoulder for balance, fingers gripping slightly as he lifts each foot.

"I much prefer when you're kneeling with my cock in your mouth, princess."

I smile despite everything, letting out a shaky laugh. "Glad to see your sense of humor survived the beating."

"Only thing that got me through it," he says, wincing as I carefully pull the sweatpants up his legs.

"Stand up just a little," I coax, supporting his weight as he rises enough for me to pull the pants over his hips. His body radiates heat against mine, and I catch a whiff of antiseptic mixed with his familiar scent. "There. Now you won't be mooning the entire hospital on our way out."

"Shame," he murmurs, his good hand finding my face. His thumb brushes across my cheek, wiping away tears I didn't even realize were falling. "Hey. I'm okay, princess. Really."

"You could have died," I whisper, the words catching in my throat. "If that tire iron had hit you just a little differently—"

"But it didn't." His eyes hold mine, intense despite the pain clouding them. "I'm right here. A little banged up but still breathing."

I lean into his touch, careful not to put pressure on any of the places that still look painful. "Promise me you won't do something that reckless again."

"Can't make that promise," he murmurs. "Not when it involves keeping you safe."

Before I can argue, the nurse returns with a wheelchair and a folder of paperwork. "Your chariot awaits, Mr. Cole," she says, brisk and efficient.

Brayden starts to protest, but I put a hand on his shoulder.

"Don't even think about it," I warn. "Hospital policy. You're getting wheeled out the doors whether you approve or not."

He mutters something under his breath—"bullshit"

is definitely in there—but he lowers himself into the wheelchair without further fight. Every movement is slow, deliberate, his jaw tightened against the flare of pain. Watching him push through it twists something inside me.

The nurse hands me the folder. "Pain medication every four to six hours as needed. Antibiotics twice a day with food. The discharge instructions list symptoms you shouldn't ignore—worsening pain, fever, dizziness. If anything concerns you, bring him right back."

"I will," I say, tucking the folder into my purse.

Big and Wrecker are waiting in the hallway, arms folded across their chests, standing guard in that unspoken way the club has mastered. They fall in step beside us as the nurse wheels Brayden toward the exit. Outside, Wrecker's truck idles at the curb with Domino behind the wheel. Big swings the passenger door open without a word.

"Heard you needed a ride."

"Thank God," I say, relief washing through me at the sight of the truck. Getting Brayden home just got a whole lot easier. "I was wondering how we were going to manage with my little car."

The nurse helps Big and Wrecker transfer Brayden from the wheelchair to the passenger seat, each movement drawing a sharp intake of breath from him despite his attempts to hide his pain. My heart clenches watching them settle him into the truck.

"I'll ride in back with him," I say, climbing in behind

the passenger seat. I want to be close enough to touch him, to reassure myself with each mile that he's still here, still breathing.

Domino gives me a nod in the rearview mirror. "Jillian's waiting at the guesthouse. Said she's got everything ready."

"Thanks for coming," I tell them, my voice catching. "All of you."

"Family," Big says simply, climbing into the backseat beside me. It's a tight fit with his massive frame, but I'm grateful for his solid presence. "That's what we do."

As Domino pulls away from the hospital entrance, I lean forward, my hand finding Brayden's shoulder. His fingers immediately reach up to cover mine, squeezing gently despite his battered knuckles. The simple touch steadies me more than he could know.

"Pharmacy first," I remind Domino. "We need to fill his prescriptions."

"We'll wait in the car," Domino says, pulling into a spot near the pharmacy entrance. "You get what he needs."

I slip out of the truck, hurrying inside to hand over the prescriptions. The pharmacist barely glances at the paperwork, weariness softening her gaze as recognition flickers when I give Brayden's name.

Twenty minutes and nearly two hundred dollars later, I'm back in the truck with a white paper bag full of pill bottles. Brayden's eyes are closed, his breathing shallow, but his hand reaches for mine when I slide into the seat beside him.

"Got everything?" he murmurs, without opening them.

"Everything the doctor ordered," I confirm, squeezing his fingers gently. "We'll get you home and doped up in no time."

The ride to the guesthouse is mercifully short. Brayden grits his teeth with each bump in the road, his face growing paler by the minute. By the time we pull into the driveway, he's sweating despite the cold, his jaw clenched so tight I can see a muscle ticking in his cheek.

Jillian is waiting on the porch, her face tight with worry as Domino and Big help ease Brayden from the truck. To my surprise, my father stands beside her.

Jillian rushes forward as they bring Brayden up the steps, her hands fluttering anxiously around him without actually touching. "Oh my God, look at you," she gasps. "Those Kincaids have gone too far this time."

My father steps aside to let them pass. The guesthouse has been transformed in our absence. The living room couch is piled with extra pillows and blankets. A tray of water and glasses sits on the coffee table, and I can smell chicken soup simmering from the kitchen. Jillian has been busy.

"Bedroom," I direct, pointing down the hallway. "He needs to lie down."

Big and Domino carefully maneuver Brayden through the narrow hallway, each step drawing a hiss of pain from him despite his efforts to remain stoic. My heart aches watching him struggle, his face ashen beneath the bruises.

"Easy does it," Big murmurs as they lower Brayden onto the bed.

I set the pharmacy bag on the side table. I fumble through the bag, searching for the pain medication while Jillian fusses with the pillows, trying to make Brayden as comfortable as possible. His face is tight with pain, jaw clenched as he settles against the mattress.

"Water," I say, and my father—to my surprise—is already there with a glass from the nightstand. Our fingers brush as he hands it to me, a fleeting moment of connection that catches me off guard.

"Thanks, Dad."

I help Brayden take the pills, supporting his head as he swallows. He grimaces, whether from the pain or the bitterness of the medication, I can't tell.

"Better?" I ask softly.

"Ask me in twenty minutes when these kick in," he mutters. His gaze shifts past me to my father, standing awkwardly at the foot of the bed. "Didn't expect to see you here, Reverend."

My father shifts uncomfortably. "I wanted to...that is, I needed to see that you were alright."

The surprise on Brayden's face mirrors my own. Before either of us can respond, the front door opens again, and I hear Joe's voice in the living room.

"Where is he?" Joe calls out.

"Back here," Big answers.

Joe appears in the doorway, his suit impeccable despite the late hour. The briefcase in his hand tells me this isn't just a social call. His sharp gaze sweeps over the scene, taking in Brayden's battered face, the pill bottles on the nightstand, and the small crowd gathered around the bed.

"Everyone out," Joe announces, his tone leaving no room for argument. "Except Cece. I need to speak with them both."

There's a moment of hesitation before Jillian starts herding everyone toward the door. "Come on, let's give them some privacy. I've got soup in the kitchen."

My father lingers, his expression meeting mine with a question I can't quite decipher. I give him a small nod, reassuring him that I'm okay. He returns it and follows the others, closing the bedroom door quietly behind him.

Joe waits until their footsteps fade before setting his briefcase on the foot of the bed and clicking it open. "I came as soon as I heard. Sheriff Miller called me directly."

"How bad is it?" Brayden asks, his voice strained as he tries to shift into a more upright position. I quickly adjust the pillows behind him, my hand lingering on his shoulder.

"For Ethan? Very bad." Joe's expression is grim but satisfied. "Multiple felony charges, including aggravated assault with a deadly weapon, violation of a protective order, attempted kidnapping, and driving under the influence. His blood alcohol was nearly twice the legal limit."

"No chance of his father bailing him out?" I ask, relief and disbelief warring inside me.

"Not this time," Joe says, pulling out several documents from his briefcase. "Mayor Kincaid may have influence, but the sheriff has dashcam footage of the end of the attack. Even Richard Kincaid can't make this disappear."

"Good," Brayden mutters, wincing as he tries to adjust his position again. I place my hand gently on his shoulder, silently urging him to stay still. The bruises on his face look even worse in the soft bedroom light, stark against his pale skin.

"There's more," Joe continues, his expression serious. "The DA is considering adding attempted murder to the charges. The use of a tire iron shows deliberate intent to cause serious harm."

"What about Brayden? He was defending himself— defending me."

Joe nods, shuffling through his papers. "The sheriff's report clearly indicates self-defense. You won't face any charges," he says directly to Brayden. "In fact, your actions may have saved Cece from serious harm."

Brayden's hand finds mine.

"Ethan had handcuffs, chloroform, and ropes in the truck of his car."

My blood freezes in my veins. "What?"

"The trunk search was conducted after his arrest," Joe continues. "Sheriff Miller believes Ethan was planning to abduct you, possibly take you across state lines."

The room reels around me. Chloroform. Ropes. The images slam into me—everything that might have happened if Brayden hadn't arrived, if the police hadn't intervened. My knees give way, dropping me onto the edge of the bed beside him, all strength draining from my limbs.

"Jesus Christ," Brayden whispers, his fingers tightening around mine. Even through his pain, I can feel the protective rage radiating from him. "That son of a bitch was going to—"

"He didn't get the chance."

Joe sets the papers down on the bed, his expression grim. "The evidence suggests this was premeditated. The restraining order pushed him over the edge, but he'd been planning something like this for a while."

"How do you know?" I ask, struggling to breathe normally.

"The receipt for the chloroform was two days prior to the attack at the pizzeria," Joe recalls.

My stomach lurches. I press my hand against my mouth, fighting the wave of nausea.

"Which brings me to your charges, Ms. Montgomery. In light of the circumstances, the charges against you have been dropped."

"Good riddance," I mutter, still processing the horror of what Ethan had planned.

"The prosecutor is pushing for denial of bail at the arraignment," Joe continues, organizing his papers.

"With this evidence, I don't see how any judge could grant it. Not even with Kincaid's influence."

"So he's staying in jail?" I need to hear it confirmed, need to know that Ethan won't be walking free anytime soon.

Joe nods. "For the foreseeable future. The charges alone carry potential sentences of fifteen to twenty years. If they add attempted murder, we're looking at much more."

I let out a shaky breath, relief washing through me. Brayden's hand tightens around mine, his thumb tracing small circles against my skin despite his obvious pain.

"What about the mayor?" Brayden asks. "He's not going to take this lying down."

"Richard Kincaid is already attempting damage control," Joe admits. "He's called an emergency press conference for tomorrow morning. My sources tell me he'll be announcing a leave of absence to support his family during this difficult time."

"Damage control," I repeat, bitterness coating the words. "That's all it ever is with him. His son tried to kidnap me, and he's worried about his public image."

"Politics," Joe says simply. "I have a feeling he will be resigning in the coming weeks."

"Resigning," I echo, trying to wrap my head around everything Joe has just told us. It feels surreal, like we've entered an alternate universe where the Kincaids finally face the consequences of their actions. "I never thought I'd see the day."

"Richard Kincaid is many things," Joe says, closing his briefcase with a definitive snap, "but stupid isn't one of them. He knows when to cut his losses."

I glance at Brayden, whose eyes have grown heavy as the pain medication starts to take effect. The bruising along his jaw looks even more pronounced against his paling skin, but the lines of tension are softening. My heart squeezes at the sight of him, battered and broken because of me.

"I should let you rest," Joe says, noticing Brayden's drooping eyelids. "The arraignment is scheduled for Monday morning. Neither of you needs to be there, but I'll keep you updated."

"Thank you," I say, rising to walk him to the door. My legs feel strangely disconnected, as though they're moving on instinct rather than direction. Shock, probably. The full weight of what Ethan had planned still hasn't settled in.

Joe pauses at the bedroom doorway. "One more thing," he says quietly. "The sheriff mentioned that your father was quite...vocal at the station. Apparently, he gave Mayor Kincaid quite the dressing down when he showed up to try to handle things."

"My father?" I blink, trying to process this new information. "He confronted Mayor Kincaid?"

Joe nods, a hint of admiration crossing his face. "According to Sheriff Miller, the Reverend quoted scripture while informing Richard exactly where he could expect to spend eternity after enabling his son's behavior. Quite colorful for a man of the cloth."

I can't help the small laugh that escapes me, despite everything. The image of my father unleashing biblical fury on Richard Kincaid is both shocking and strangely satisfying. Maybe people really can change.

"Call me if anything changes or if you need anything at all."

I walk Joe to the living room where everyone is gathered in awkward silence. My father stands when we enter, his face lined with concern.

"How is he?" he asks quietly.

"The medication's kicking in," I reply. "He'll sleep soon."

Joe shakes hands with Big and nods to the others before letting himself out. The click of the door seems unnaturally loud in the tense silence that follows.

Jillian breaks it first, rising from her perch on the armchair. "I'll get some soup for you both," she says, patting my arm as she passes. "He'll need something in his stomach with those pills."

I turn to my father, suddenly exhausted beyond words.

"I'm okay, Dad," I say, wrapping my arms around myself. "Just...processing everything." I glance toward the hallway, suddenly desperate to be back with Brayden. "I need to check on him."

"Go," my father says, surprising me with his understanding. "We can talk tomorrow."

I nod, unable to find more words.

Jillian appears from the kitchen with a tray holding two bowls of soup and some crackers. "Take this."

"Thank you," I murmur, accepting the tray. My arms feel leaden, my body moving on autopilot.

"We'll stay in the living room," Big says, his deep voice oddly comforting. "Nobody's getting past us tonight."

The implicit promise in his words steadies me. I manage a small smile before heading back to the bedroom, balancing the tray carefully.

Brayden's eyes are closed when I enter, but his hand reaches out for mine as I set the tray on the nightstand. "Thought you left me," he mumbles, the words slightly slurred from the medication.

"Never," I answer, carefully, perching on the edge of the bed. "Just getting you some soup. Jillian's orders."

His gaze flickers open, unfocused and heavy-lidded. "Not hungry."

"You need to eat something with those pills," I insist, dipping the spoon into the steaming broth. "Just a few bites."

He grimaces but doesn't argue as I hold the spoon to his lips. The simple act of watching him struggle to swallow breaks something inside me.

"Why are you crying?" he asks, his fingers brushing weakly against my cheek.

I hadn't realized I was. "Because I hate seeing you hurt," I admit, wiping at the tears with the back of my hand. "And because I can't stop thinking about what could have happened."

"But it didn't. We're both here. We're okay."

I nod, not trusting myself to speak as I offer another

spoonful of soup. He takes it obediently, wincing as the movement pulls at his split lip.

When he finishes, I set the bowl aside and smooth the blanket over his chest. "You need to get some sleep," I say softly.

"I'm fine," he mutters, eyes half-open.

"No," I counter, brushing my hand along his arm. "You're exhausted. Close your eyes."

His lashes lower a fraction, a faint smirk tugging at the corner of his mouth. "Bossy woman."

"Someone has to keep you in line," I whisper, brushing a stray lock of hair from his forehead.

His lips twitch in a tired smile. "Good luck with that, princess."

The nickname hits me with a quiet thud in my chest. Gentle. Familiar. Safe in a way nothing else has been today.

The tears come again, but they don't burn this time. They feel clean, as if something inside me is finally letting go.

I lean in and press my lips softly to his bruised jaw. "You don't get to scare me again," I whisper.

His hand lifts weakly, fingertips skimming my wrist. "Then come here."

"Brayden—"

"I'm not arguing," he says, eyes barely open but still locked on mine. "The only way I'm getting any sleep tonight is if I know you're right next to me."

My breath hitches. "You should be resting, not... whatever you're thinking."

He gives a quiet, rough laugh. "Sweetheart, I'm too beat to think about anything except this bed. But I sleep easier with you beside me." His gaze drops to my mouth, then back to my eyes. "You calm me down."

Heat flutters through my chest. "You're a menace."

"Maybe." His fingers brush the hem of my shirt, feather-light. Not pulling. Just inviting. "But you're safe in my arms. And knowing you're here is the only thing letting me close my eyes."

The world outside fades to a distant ache.

The fear.

The noise.

All of it can wait.

I slip onto the edge of the bed beside him, letting his arm settle around me. His breathing steadies almost immediately, warm against my neck.

And for the first time in twenty-four hours, the tightness in my chest finally loosens. I close my eyes, letting that sound wash over me, and for the first time in what feels like forever, peace isn't something fragile or temporary.

It feels real.

And it's ours.

CHAPTER 28

BRAYDEN

I'M PRETTY sure Jesus didn't get his ass kicked by a tire iron before his first Christmas, but here I am, limping up the church steps, a battered, budget-version messiah. Every breath sends a stab through my ribs, and the bruises on my face have settled into a sickly yellow-green pattern that makes me look diseased. Merry fucking Christmas to me.

"You're scowling again," Cece whispers, her arm threaded through mine as we approach the entrance. She's in a red dress that fits her so damn well it should be illegal, her hair falling in soft waves around her shoulders. Even with my face still resembling abstract art, I'm the luckiest bastard here just having her beside me.

"I'm not scowling. This is just my face now, courtesy of your ex."

She flinches, and regret hits me hard. "Sorry, princess. Shitty joke."

"It's okay." Her fingers tighten on my arm. "I'm just glad you're here. And walking. And not, you know, in a ditch somewhere."

"Takes more than a spoiled rich boy with daddy issues to put me down." I tug at the collar of my shirt, which feels more restrictive with every step. It's the closest thing to church-appropriate clothing I own— hastily bought yesterday when Cece reminded me about her father's Christmas Eve service. Black button-down, dark jeans. This is the peak of my formal wardrobe.

A tie, though? No chance. Even love has its limits.

"Are you sure you're up for this?" Cece asks for the third time since we left the guesthouse. "We can still turn around. Dad would understand."

"And miss my chance to see Wrecker play Joseph in the nativity? Not a chance." The mental image of my tattooed brother in a biblical costume has been the only thing getting me through this whole church service idea. "Besides, your father invited me personally. Pretty sure that's one of the signs of the apocalypse."

She laughs, and the sound washes over me—steady, warm, easing something tight inside my chest. A week after Ethan's attack and her laughter comes easier now. The shadows that once lived behind her eyes are finally thinning, replaced by something calmer. Something close to peace. It suits her more than anything she's ever worn.

"Dad's been full of surprises lately," she admits as we reach the church doors.

"Do you mean him stopping by every day to check on me, treating me as if I somehow ended up on his pastoral roster?" I ask, still half-convinced I hallucinated it. The reverend had shown up daily, awkward as hell, Bible tucked under his arm, making stiff commentary about the weather. The whole thing had been painful in more ways than my ribs, but I can't deny I respect the effort. "Or the church ladies bringing us meals every day?"

Inside, the church is packed to capacity, every pew filled with families in their Christmas best. There's even a tree near the altar, decked in gold and white ornaments, and enough twinkling lights to make me squint. The air smells of pine, candle wax, and something spicy —cinnamon, maybe.

"Cecelia!" Mrs. Holloway calls, "We saved you seats!"

Cece waves back, tugging me gently toward the front of the church. I hesitate, feeling exposed. Being up front means the entire congregation can stare at my bruised face and judge the tattooed biker who is corrupting their preacher's daughter.

"Front row?" I mutter. "Seriously?"

"Dad wants us up front," she whispers. "It's a big deal, Brayden."

The significance isn't lost on me. This is the

Reverend's way of publicly declaring his support for Cece, for us. It's a statement to his entire congregation. I can't fuck this up.

"Fine," I sigh, straightening my shoulders despite the protest from my ribs. "But if someone tries to make me sing, I'm out."

The Reverend steps up to the pulpit, adjusting his glasses as the murmurs settle into expectant silence. His eyes sweep the congregation with the authority of a man who has spent his entire life commanding a room without raising his voice. But when his gaze lands on Cece and me again, I swear something gentler flickers there—quick, but real.

He clears his throat, the microphone crackling softly. "Welcome, everyone, to our Christmas Eve service."

A few pews back, I hear Mrs. Whitaker inhale sharply, as if preparing to take offense at anything that comes out of his mouth.

Cece squeezes my hand once. My ribs scream, but the warmth in my chest drowns it out.

"Tonight, before we get to our normal festivities," the Reverend continues, "I want to talk about the unexpected ways grace finds us."

A ripple of whispered interpretation moves through the sanctuary. Because this is a small town, and everyone here knows exactly who he's talking about. Hell, even the nativity figurines probably know.

He goes on, voice steady, eyes locked on the back wall but clearly aimed at every gossip in the room.

"Sometimes grace shows up in forms we don't antici-pate. Sometimes it looks...different from what we pictured. And sometimes we must learn that the measure of a man is not where he came from, but what he chooses to stand for."

Cece's breath catches beside me, her shoulders going tight, her eyes shining. I can feel her trying not to look at me, because if she does, she'll cry.

"We are called," her father continues, "to see people as they are now, not as they used to be. And to recog-nize courage when we witness it—especially when it protects the vulnerable."

A beat of silence follows.

Jesus Christ, I think. *I'm being sermonically endorsed.* This has to be the highest honor a preacher has ever given a biker without involving an attempted baptism or a pitchfork. Then the Reverend looks at me directly. Not a glare. Not disapproval. Something closer to grati-tude. And for the first damn time in my life, I don't look away.

Cece's fingers tremble in mine. Her thumb brushes over the back of my hand and that one small touch hits harder than Ethan's tire iron ever could.

I lean close enough that only she can hear me. "Guess your dad just gave me the church-approved stamp," I murmur.

Cece bites her bottom lip to hide a smile. "Don't get cocky," she whispers back. "It's still church. You're only half a miracle."

I grin, ribs aching, heart steady. If this is what a Christmas miracle feels like?

Yeah. I'll take it.

The Reverend clears his throat softly, letting the weight of his words settle over the room. "And with hearts open to that kind of grace, let us prepare ourselves in song."

The choir begins singing some hymn about angels, their voices rising in harmony that actually sounds pretty decent for a small-town church. I glance at Cece and find her mouthing the words, her face soft in the glow of the candles. Something tightens in my chest that has nothing to do with my injured ribs.

"You okay?" she whispers, catching me staring.

"Better than okay," I murmur back, squeezing her hand.

The final notes float through the sanctuary, fragile and bright, settling over the congregation like fresh snowfall. As the choir takes their seats, the Reverend steps forward again, hands resting lightly on the pulpit.

"For many of us," he begins, his gaze sweeping the room before landing—unmistakably—on our pew, "this season is a reminder that light finds us in the moments we expect it least. I find myself reflecting on the true meaning of grace," he begins, his gaze sweeping over the congregation. "We often speak of God's grace as something freely given, unearned, and undeserved. But how many of us truly understand what it means to extend that same grace to others?"

I shift uncomfortably, wondering if this is where he

subtly calls me out as the church's resident sinner. Mrs. Holloway leans forward slightly beside Cece, nodding emphatically.

"Recent events in our community have forced me to examine my own understanding of grace," the Reverend continues, his attention settling briefly on me. "When my daughter was falsely accused, when violence touched our lives, I witnessed something remarkable. I saw grace extended from the most unexpected places."

My throat goes tight, the kind of tight that sneaks up on you and hits harder than any punch. I shift in the pew, the wood groaning under me as I try—unsuccessfully—to ease the sharp stab in my ribs. Doesn't matter. Every word coming out of the Reverend's mouth hurts more.

"A group of men—men I had judged harshly, men I had deemed unworthy of God's love—showed my family more Christian charity than many who sit in these pews every Sunday."

The sanctuary reacts instantly. Whispers surge through the room, rustling through the congregation like wind whipping through tall grass—soft but impossible to ignore. Some folks look curious. Others look scandalized. One woman clutches her pearls with such force I'm shocked they don't snap and rain onto the floor.

But I don't look at them. I look at him. Because I've heard a lot of sermons in my life—most against my will —but never one aimed straight at me.

The Reverend continues, voice gaining strength with every word.

"They gave their time. Their labor. Their hearts. Not for recognition or praise…but because someone in need asked for help. And they showed up."

Another wave of murmurs. Another shift of shoulders.

But I hardly notice. My chest aches in a way that has nothing to do with cracked ribs. Because for the first time, I think he sees us—sees me—not as a threat or a mistake, but as something that might actually belong beside his daughter.

"These men, with their leather vests and tattoos, embodied the very spirit of Christmas that we celebrate tonight. They fed the hungry, clothed the poor, and brought joy to children. They protected the vulnerable when others would not. And one man in particular—" his gaze finds mine directly now "—was willing to lay down his life for someone he loves."

I resist the urge to look around, to check if there's some other battered hero sitting behind me that he might be referencing instead.

"That, my friends, is the true meaning of Christmas. Not the presents under the tree or the lights on our houses, but the willingness to see past our differences, to recognize the divine spark in those we least expect."

A weight settles in my chest that has nothing to do with my injuries. I've been called a lot of things in my life—most of them not fit for church walls—but never an example of the true meaning of Christmas. It's enough to make me wonder if I hit my head harder than I thought.

"Greater love hath no man than this," the Reverend continues, "that a man lay down his life for his friends. John 15:13.

Cece's fingers tremble slightly against mine. When I glance at her, tears shimmer in her gaze, catching the candlelight and turning into tiny diamonds. I squeeze her hand, suddenly aware of every pair of eyes in this church. A strange vulnerability spreads through my chest, as if the Reverend has reached in and peeled back my skin, revealing all the messy, complicated parts of me I usually keep hidden.

"As we prepare our hearts to celebrate the birth of our Savior, let us remember that Christ came not for the perfect, but for the broken. He came for the outcasts, the sinners, the people society deemed unworthy." His gaze sweeps across the congregation, lingering on a few faces that suddenly look uncomfortable. "And He calls us to do the same."

I shift again, wincing as my ribs protest. Mrs. Holloway leans forward, dabbing at her eyes with an embroidered handkerchief.

I stare at the wooden cross hanging behind the pulpit, trying to process everything that's happening. A month ago, I was just another Heaven's Reject, doing club business and keeping to myself. Now I'm sitting in a church on Christmas Eve while a preacher uses me as some kind of sermon illustration.

The Reverend's voice softens as he continues.

"Tonight, as we celebrate the greatest gift ever given, I ask you to look around this sanctuary. Look at the faces of your neighbors—some familiar, some new. Each one created in God's image. Each one worthy of grace."

His gaze meets mine again, and there's something there I've never seen before—respect. Not just tolerance or reluctant acceptance, but genuine respect. It hits me harder than Ethan's tire iron ever could.

"Let us pray," the Reverend says, bowing his head.

I lower my head, not because I suddenly believe, but because I respect what this means to Cece. Her father is extending an olive branch in the most public way possible. The least I can do is meet him halfway.

When I look up again, the children are filing in for the nativity scene. I spot Wrecker immediately, towering over the other shepherds in his costume. He catches my eye and gives me a subtle nod.

"Remind me why he volunteered for this again?" Cece leans over and whispers into my ear.

"At least, he asked to be a shepherd, and not baby Jesus. Though I have to admit, I'm a little sad baby Jesus' penis didn't pop back up again."

Cece lets out a small snort, her body shaking with suppressed laughter. She starts to elbow me in the ribs, but stops mid-motion, her eyes widening in horror as she remembers my injuries. Her hand freezes, hovering inches from my side.

"Oh my God, I'm sorry," she whispers, mortification replacing her amusement. "I wasn't thinking."

I catch her hand before she can pull it away

completely, pressing it gently against my side. "It's fine, princess. I'm not made of glass."

But the truth is, I'm grateful for her restraint. My ribs are still tender enough that even a playful jab would've had me seeing stars. Not that I'd ever admit that to her. She's been treating me like I'm breakable for days, and while the pampering has its perks, I miss her fire.

"Still," she murmurs, her fingers now carefully tracing the outline of my ribs through my shirt, "I should be more careful."

"If you want to make it up to me," I whisper, leaning closer so only she can hear, "I've got some ideas that don't involve my ribs at all."

Her cheeks flush pink, and she gives me a look that promises both punishment and reward later. Mrs. Holloway clears her throat loudly beside us, reminding me that we're still sitting in the front row of a church during Christmas Eve service. Right. Probably shouldn't be having unholy thoughts right now.

I force myself to focus on the nativity scene, trying to ignore the heat of Cece's fingers still resting lightly against my side. The touch is innocent enough, but my body doesn't seem to care that we're in a church surrounded by people who probably still think I'm one motorcycle ride away from eternal damnation.

The children playing the Three Wise Men stumble forward, clearly nervous as they present their gifts to Mary and plastic baby Jesus. One kid trips on his over-sized robe and nearly faceplants into the manger.

Wrecker reaches out with surprising grace, steadying the boy before disaster strikes. The kid looks up at him with wide eyes, probably wondering how a man with neck tattoos ended up in the Christmas pageant.

"He's good with them," Cece whispers, nodding toward Wrecker.

"Always has been," I murmur back. "Kids don't care about the tattoos or the cut. They just see someone who listens to them."

The pageant continues with all the awkward charm of children trying their best not to forget their lines. Mary looks terrified, Joseph keeps picking his nose when he thinks no one's watching, and one of the sheep has decided to sit down and refuses to get back up. It's chaotic and sweet and strangely perfect.

When the final carol begins, everyone stands. I rise more carefully this time, my body reminding me with sharp twinges that I'm still healing. The congregation lifts small candles, their flames creating a sea of light that transforms the sanctuary. Cece holds our candle, careful to keep the flame away from me. The soft glow illuminates her face, making her skin look like it's lit from within. She's never been more beautiful than she is right now, singing some ancient hymn about silent nights and heavenly peace.

The final note hangs in the air, soft and fragile, before fading into silence.

Cece leans against me, her head resting on my shoulder, the candle still flickering between us. Around us, the church glows with warmth and quiet joy.

For the first time in a long while, everything feels still.

I look at her, at the peace on her face, and know this is what we fought for.

Our own kind of Christmas miracle.

EPILOGUE

CECE - 1 YEAR LATER

IT'S weird how a town can feel so different and yet exactly the same. As Brayden's bike rumbles down Main Street, I find myself searching for changes in San Salona like I'm on some kind of scavenger hunt. The Christmas lights are strung in the same lazy patterns across storefronts. Tony's Pizza still has that flickering neon sign. Even the courthouse steps where I once stood in handcuffs look unchanged, just dusted with a light coating of fake snow because San Salona never gets the real thing.

But I'm different. The woman who left here a year ago is gone.

I tighten my grip around Brayden's waist as he slows at a stoplight, his body against mine still sending shivers through me even after all this time. His hand covers mine briefly, a silent question checking if I'm okay. I squeeze back, letting him know I am. Mostly.

Coming back to San Salona for Christmas wasn't my idea. I was content to spend the holiday in our cozy apartment above Petal & Thorn, my new flower shop in Carlsbad. But my father's invitation—more of a plea, really—was something I couldn't ignore. Not after everything that's happened.

"You doing alright back there, princess?" Brayden calls over his shoulder as we pass the "Welcome to San Salona" sign.

"I'm good," I call back, leaning closer to his leather-clad back. "Just strange being back."

The town feels smaller somehow, like I've outgrown it. A year can change so much. I've built a life 90 miles away that feels more authentic than all the years I lived in this town.

We cruise past the newly renovated town hall, where a "Happy Holidays" banner flaps in the December breeze. No sign of the Kincaid name anywhere. After Ethan's conviction, his father's resignation was swift and silent. Twenty-five years behind bars for attempted kidnapping, assault with a deadly weapon, and a laundry list of other charges that made my stomach turn during the trial. I still remember the hollow look in Ethan's eyes when the verdict came down, like he couldn't believe his family name hadn't saved him.

Nobody has seen Richard Kincaid since he cleaned

out his office and disappeared. Rumor has it he moved to Arizona or maybe Florida—somewhere he could reinvent himself without the stain of his son's crimes following him.

San Salona has moved on without the Kincaids, though. That much is clear as we pass the newly elected Mayor Ortiz's campaign signs still taped to light posts. The town didn't implode without its royal family, despite what everyone feared. Life just...continued.

Brayden guides his bike toward my father's church, the familiar white steeple rising above the tree line. My stomach tightens with each block we get closer. I've only seen my father twice since we moved to Carlsbad —both times he came to visit us. This will be my first time back in his church since the Christmas Eve service last year, when he surprised everyone by practically canonizing Brayden from the pulpit.

Brayden pulls into the church parking lot, the bike's engine echoing against the empty space before he cuts it off. I slide off the back, removing my helmet and shaking out my hair while looking around.

"That's weird," I say, scanning the deserted lot. "Dad said he'd be here waiting for us."

Brayden props the bike on its stand and gets off, stretching his long frame after the ride. "Maybe he's inside already?"

I approach the main doors and tug on the handle. Locked. I try the other door with the same result. Through the glass, I can see the empty foyer, no lights on except for the safety fixtures.

"That's...strange." I pull my phone from my pocket, an uneasy feeling creeping up my spine. I haven't been gone so long that I've forgotten my father's obsession with punctuality. The Reverend Thomas Montgomery is never late, especially not when he's expecting company.

I dial his number, but it goes straight to voicemail. I switch to texting instead.

> Dad, we're at the church but it's locked. Where are you?

Brayden comes to stand beside me, his arm sliding around my waist. "Everything okay?"

"I don't know. He's not answering his phone."

We wait in the chilly December air for a few minutes before my phone finally buzzes.

> Mrs. Holloway was taken to the hospital. I'll be there as soon as I can.

I read the message again, concern trickling through me. Mrs. Holloway has been my father's right hand at the church for as long as I can remember. She's well into her seventies now, and the thought of her in the hospital sends a pang through my chest.

My phone buzzes again with another text from my father:

> Use the side entrance code: 1225. Make yourselves comfortable. I shouldn't be more than an hour.

"Everything okay?" Brayden asks, peering over my shoulder at the message.

"Mrs. Holloway's in the hospital. Dad's there with her." I show him the text. "He says we should let ourselves in through the side door."

Brayden nods, already lifting our bags from the bike's storage compartment. "Lead the way, princess."

We circle around to the side entrance, our boots crunching on the gravel path. The familiar keypad greets me, and I can't help but smile at the code. 1225— December 25th. My father's security measures have always been more sentimental than secure.

The lock clicks, and I push the door open into the darkened hallway that leads past my father's office to the fellowship hall. The church smells exactly as I remember—old hymnals, lemon polish, and the lingering scent of coffee from the perpetually brewing pot in the kitchen.

"Home sweet home," I murmur, flicking on lights as we move through the corridor.

"But it looks so different," I say, stopping in my tracks as we reach the hallway that opens into the sanctuary. I flick on the lights, illuminating the space that's both familiar and foreign. "When did all this happen?"

Where there was once a simple wooden pulpit and a piano, there's now a sleek stage with a drum kit and several microphone stands. Professional lighting rigs hang from the ceiling, and mounted screens flank either side of the altar area.

"Looks like your dad finally dragged the church into the 21st century," Brayden remarks.

"This is..." I walk further into the sanctuary, running my fingers along the edge of what appears to be a brand-new keyboard. "Dad fought for this for years. Richard Kincaid always insisted the church remain traditional. No amplification beyond the basic microphone system, no drums, definitely no screens."

"Guess your dad finally got his way." Brayden fiddles with one of the switches, causing a light to flicker above the stage.

I walk down the center aisle, toward the alter. The podium sits in the center with the band's setup flanking him on both sides. Christmas trees line the stage, brightly lit with a rainbow of colors.

I'm still taking in all the changes when I feel strong arms circle my waist from behind. Brayden's chest presses against my back, his warmth seeping through my riding jacket as his chin comes to rest on my shoulder.

"Not very often that we have an entire church to ourselves, princess," he murmurs.

His lips brush against my neck, and I catch his meaning immediately. The thought should scandalize me—this is my father's church, for heaven's sake—but instead, a delicious heat unfurls in my belly. A year with Brayden has certainly changed me in ways my former self wouldn't recognize.

"Are you suggesting what I think you're suggesting?" I ask, leaning back into him as his hands slip beneath the hem of my jacket.

"Just saying we've got at least an hour before your dad gets back," he whispers, his fingers tracing circles on my hip bones. "Seems like a shame to waste it."

I should say no. I should remind him that this is a church, that my father could return early, that this is absolutely crossing a line. Instead, I turn in his arms and press a quick kiss to his lips.

"Come with me," I say, taking his hand and leading him toward the back of the sanctuary where a narrow staircase winds up to the balcony.

"Where are we going?" he asks, though the slight curve of his mouth makes it clear he isn't all that concerned about the destination.

The stairs creak beneath our weight as we ascend to the balcony where the choir usually sits during special services. Up here, we're hidden from view of the main entrance, tucked away in our own private sanctuary within the sanctuary. The balcony is decorated with garlands and twinkling lights, casting a soft, intimate glow over the space.

"My father would have a heart attack if he knew what I was thinking right now," I whisper, turning to face Brayden. His eyes sharpen with unmistakable intent, the gray deepening as he closes the distance between us.

"Then maybe we shouldn't tell him," Brayden murmurs, pressing me back against the railing. His hands find my waist, sliding beneath my jacket again, warmer now against my skin. "Though I think the Reverend has made peace with the fact that his daughter is sleeping with a biker."

I laugh softly, tilting my head back as his lips find my neck. "There's a difference between making peace with it and having it happen in his church."

"Mmm, forbidden fruit," Brayden whispers against my skin, his teeth grazing my pulse point. "Isn't that what started this whole religion thing in the first place?"

A moan escapes me as his hands slide higher, thumbs brushing the undersides of my breasts. I lean into his touch, all thoughts of propriety dissolving under his skilled hands.

"We shouldn't," I whisper, even as my fingers work at the buckle of his belt. "What if someone comes in?"

"Then they'll get one hell of a show," he growls, capturing my mouth in a kiss that steals my breath. His tongue slides against mine, tasting faintly of the coffee we stopped for on the ride here.

I'm lost in him, in the way his body presses mine against the railing, in the delicious friction of denim against denim as his hips rock into mine. The wrongness of it only heightens everything—the rebel in me that Brayden has nurtured over the past year flaring to life.

"The choir sits here every Sunday," I gasp as his hand cups my breast through my shirt, thumb circling my nipple until it hardens beneath the fabric. "Mrs. Holloway conducts from right where you're standing."

Brayden chuckles against my throat, the vibration sending shivers down my spine. "Maybe we should move to the pew then," he suggests, guiding me backward until my legs hit the front row of the balcony seating.

I sink down onto the polished wood, looking up at him with what I hope is challenge in my eyes. "Isn't this sacrilegious?"

"Sweetheart, I think we crossed that line when you started unbuckling my belt," he says with that wicked half-smile that still makes my stomach flip. His hands slide to my thighs, fingers playing with the hem of my riding jeans.

I should feel guilty. I should stop this madness right now. Instead, I reach for him, pulling him down until he's kneeling between my legs, his broad shoulders blocking out the twinkling Christmas lights behind him.

"I'm going to hell for this," I whisper against his mouth.

"Then I'll keep you company," he murmurs back, kissing me with a hunger that makes my toes curl in my boots. His hands find the buttons of my jeans, working them open with practiced ease while I fumble with his zipper.

A door slams somewhere in the church, the sound echoing through the sanctuary like a gunshot.

We freeze, my fingers still tangled in Brayden's belt loops, his mouth an inch from mine. Brayden presses a finger to my lips, listening. Heavy footsteps sound in the foyer, followed by voices—plural.

"Shit," I hiss.

Brayden's hand slides up to cover my mouth completely, the pressure firm but gentle. With his other hand, he presses a single finger to his lips, signaling me to stay quiet.

I nod against his palm, my heart hammering so hard I'm sure whoever's down there can hear it echoing through the sanctuary. The voices grow louder, discussing something about the sound system. Church volunteers, maybe? Or the worship team coming in for an early rehearsal?

Brayden doesn't move away. Instead, his hand slides from my mouth down to my throat, then lower, his touch feather-light as it traces the neckline of my shirt. The danger of being caught only seems to excite him more.

"We'll check the wiring tomorrow," one of the voices says. "Pastor wants everything perfect for the Christmas service."

"Fine by me. I could use a beer anyway."

Their footsteps move across the sanctuary floor, heavy boots on polished wood. I hold my breath as they pause directly beneath us, something metal clattering against the floor.

"Dropped my keys," one of them mutters.

Brayden's hand continues its slow, torturous path down my body, slipping beneath the open waistband of my jeans. I bite my lip to keep from making a sound as his fingers find the edge of my panties.

The men below us continue their conversation,

completely unaware of what's happening in the choir balcony. I squeeze my thighs together, trying to control the heat building there despite the danger, or maybe because of it.

His fingers slide lower, brushing against the damp fabric between my legs. I bite down on my hand to keep from gasping. The bastard is actually going to try to get me off while there are people right below us.

"You coming or what?" one of the men calls from the doorway.

"Yeah, just making sure everything's locked up."

There's a click of lights being switched off, plunging the sanctuary into semi-darkness. Only the Christmas lights remain, casting multicolored shadows across Brayden's face as he leans in close, his lips brushing my ear.

"Don't make a sound," he whispers, his fingers pushing my panties aside.

I should stop him. I should absolutely stop him. But the thrill of it—the danger, the forbidden nature of it all—has me wetter than I care to admit. I bite down harder on my knuckle as his finger slides inside me with agonizing slowness.

The church doors close with a heavy thud, and silence falls over the sanctuary once more. Still, Brayden doesn't rush. His movements remain torturously slow, his eyes never leaving mine as he watches every flicker of pleasure cross my face.

"You are so fucking beautiful like this," Brayden

whispers. "Trying so hard to be quiet when I know you want to scream."

His thumb circles my clit as his finger curls inside me, finding that spot that makes my vision blur. I'm trembling with the effort to stay silent, my hips rocking against his hand of their own accord.

"Anyone could walk in," I gasp, the words barely audible. "We should stop."

But my body betrays me, pressing harder against his hand, seeking more of that delicious friction. The knowledge that we're doing this in my father's church, in the choir loft where I sang hymns as a teenager, makes everything more intense, more forbidden.

"You want me to stop?" he asks, already knowing the answer as he slides a second finger inside me. My head falls back, mouth open in a silent cry as he increases the pace.

"No," I admit, surrendering to the heat building. "Don't stop."

"God, what are you doing to me?" I whimper as his thumb circles faster, his fingers curling inside me. The choir loft feels like it's spinning around us, the colored Christmas lights blurring as pleasure builds to an almost unbearable peak.

"Coming apart for me in church, princess. That's what you're doing."

My thighs begin to tremble as he works me closer to the edge. The danger, the sacrilege, the pure wrongness of it all somehow makes everything more intense. I'm seconds away from shattering when we hear it—the unmistakable sound of the side door opening again.

"Shit," I hiss, my body freezing in panic even as it throbs with need.

Brayden doesn't stop. His fingers continue their relentless rhythm as his other hand covers my mouth. "Come for me," he whispers against my ear. "Right now, while they're walking in."

It's too much—his command, the footsteps growing louder, the knowledge that we could be caught any second. I fall apart against his hand, my cry muffled against his palm. My body convulses, inner walls clenching around his fingers.

"That's my girl," he murmurs, slowly withdrawing his hand. I strain my ears, but don't hear any more footsteps. The sound must have come from outside, or maybe it was just the old building settling. After a moment of breathless silence, I relax against Brayden's touch.

"I think we're still alone."

Brayden rises up, pressing his body against mine. "Good," he growls, his lips finding my neck. "Because I'm not done with you yet."

The thrill of almost being caught has left me hypersensitive, every nerve ending firing as his hands slide under my shirt, pushing it up to expose my skin to the cool air. I should feel ashamed, doing this here of all places, but I don't. Maybe it's the year away, maybe it's the woman I've become with Brayden by my side, but all I feel is desire burning through me like wildfire.

"Are you sure?" I ask, even as my hands are working his jeans down his hips. "What if someone really does come in?"

"Then we'll hear them, and we'll stop."

But we both know we're past the point of stopping now. His hands make quick work of my jeans, tugging them down my legs until they pool around my ankles. The wooden pew is hard and cold beneath me, but I barely notice as Brayden positions himself between my legs, the head of his cock pressing against me. I'm still sensitive from before, my body convulsing with aftershocks as he pushes inside me with agonizing slowness.

"Fuck," he groans, his forehead falling against mine. "You feel so good, princess. So tight."

I wrap my legs around his waist, drawing him deeper. The pew creaks beneath us, the sound obscenely loud in the empty sanctuary. I should care—I really should—but all I can focus on is the delicious stretch of him filling me, the weight of his body pressing mine into the hard wood.

"Someone could walk in any second," I whisper against his mouth. "My father could walk in."

"Then we better make this quick," he growls, his hips snapping forward with new urgency.

I bite down on his shoulder to muffle my cry, my nails digging into his back through his t-shirt. He sets a punishing pace, each thrust pushing me closer to the edge again.

"God, I've missed you like this," he pants, one hand

gripping my hip while the other braces against the pew. "Wild. Desperate."

I arch beneath him, meeting each thrust with one of my own. "We had sex this morning," I remind him.

"Still too long," he growls, suddenly grabbing my hips.

With a swift movement, he pulls out and shifts us both. He drops onto the pew, his erection slick and standing proudly between his thighs. "Come here."

I barely have time to process the change before his strong hands guide me to turn around, bending me over the pew in front of us. The polished wood is cold against my palms as I brace myself, my jeans still tangled around my ankles limiting my movement.

"Brayden," I gasp as he positions himself behind me, one hand splayed across my lower back, pushing me down until my chest nearly touches the bench.

"Is this okay?" he asks, his voice husky but sincere, always checking even in the midst of our most reckless moments.

"Yes," I breathe. "Please."

He enters me with a single powerful thrust that steals my breath. From this angle, he feels impossibly deep, hitting places inside me that make stars burst behind my eyelids. I bite my lip hard to keep from crying out, the taste of blood mixing with the forbidden thrill of what we're doing.

"Look at you," Brayden murmurs, his fingers digging into my hips as he sets a relentless pace. "The preacher's daughter bent over a pew, taking my cock so beautifully. I wonder how many Hail Marys we'll have to say to repent for this."

"If God is watching right now, I think we're beyond salvation," I gasp, my fingers digging into the polished wood of the pew as Brayden's thrusts grow harder, more insistent.

"Then let's make it worth the damnation," he growls.

The sound of skin against skin echoes in the sanctuary, mixing with our heavy breathing. The Christmas lights cast moving shadows across our bodies, red and green and gold dancing across my bare skin. I feel exposed, wanton, transformed into someone I never thought I could be.

"Harder," I beg, beyond caring about being caught now. The thrill of it burns through me like wildfire, consuming every last shred of the good preacher's daughter I once was. "Make me feel it tomorrow during the service."

Brayden groans, his grip tightening as he complies, driving into me with punishing force that makes the pew groan and tremble beneath us. His free hand slides around to find my clit, circling it in time with his thrusts.

"I want you to think about this," he pants, rough and breathless, "every time you sit in this church. I want you to remember how you begged me to fuck you right here."

I'm so close, balanced on that exquisite edge when I

hear it—not a door this time, but a sound. My father's call.

"Cecelia? Are you here?"

My hand flies to my mouth, my entire body locking in panic. Brayden stills instantly behind me, buried deep inside me, his breath hot against my ear.

"Cecelia?" The word carries from the foyer, followed by footsteps approaching the sanctuary.

I'm torn between mind-numbing terror and the traitorous throbbing of my body, still desperate for release. Brayden's cock pulses inside me, and I know he's fighting the same battle.

"Don't. Move." The words barely make it past my hand, my heart thundering in my chest, loud enough to betray us both.

But Brayden has other ideas. His hips make the slightest adjustment, pressing against that perfect spot inside me, and his fingers resume their torturous circles on my clit.

"Are you insane?" I hiss, but my body betrays me, inner walls clenching around him.

"Come for me," he whispers, barely audible, "Right now, while he's looking for you."

It's twisted and wrong and absolutely right. The orgasm crashes through me with shocking intensity, my entire body seizing as I bite down on my own wrist to silence the scream building in my throat. Brayden's hand covers mine, pressing harder a wave of pleasure rocks through me, made impossibly stronger by the fear and adrenaline coursing through my veins.

"Cecelia? Brayden?" My father sounds closer now, echoing up from the sanctuary below us.

I'm still vibrating with aftershocks when Brayden carefully withdraws, every movement deliberate and silent. We fumble with our clothes, hands shaking as we try to make ourselves presentable in record time. My legs feel like jelly beneath me, my body still humming with release as I yank my jeans up and button them with clumsy fingers.

Brayden tucks himself away and zips up. He presses a quick, hard kiss to my lips before helping me smooth down my hair.

"Up here, Dad!" I call out, my voice embarrassingly breathless. I clear my throat and try again. "We're in the choir loft!"

I hear my father's footsteps change direction, heading toward the staircase that leads up to the balcony. Brayden and I exchange a panicked glance, stepping apart to put a respectable distance between us just as my father's head appears at the top of the stairs.

"There you are. I stand frozen, willing my face not to betray what just happened. My legs still feel wobbly, my body humming with post-orgasmic bliss that I desperately try to hide as my father's gaze travels between us.

"Sorry we didn't answer right away," I manage, smoothing my hair again just to have something to do with my hands. "We were...admiring the renovations."

My father looks tired, the lines around his eyes deeper than they were a year ago. Still, he smiles when he sees me, genuine warmth breaking through the exhaustion.

"Cecelia," he says, opening his arms. "I'm so sorry I wasn't here when you arrived."

I cross to him, acutely aware of how I must smell—like sex and Brayden and guilt—but my father seems to notice nothing as he wraps me in a hug. Over his shoulder, I see Brayden adjusting his belt, a hint of a smirk playing at his lips even as he nods respectfully to my father.

"How's Mrs. Holloway?" I ask, pulling back from the hug. The genuine concern in my voice helps mask any lingering breathlessness.

My father sighs, worry creasing his brow. "Better now. They think it was just dehydration, but at her age, they're being cautious. She insisted I come back to greet you both." He turns to Brayden, extending his hand. "Son."

Brayden straightens, every trace of mischief tucked neatly behind the polite smile he uses on people he respects. "Good to see you again."

My father shakes his hand, oblivious to the way Brayden's knuckles are still a little red from gripping the edge of the pew a few minutes ago. "You've been taking good care of my daughter, I hope."

"Yes, sir," Brayden answers without hesitation. "Always."

Something in his tone makes my chest tighten. My father seems satisfied, giving a small nod before glancing toward the sanctuary. "We'll have dinner in the fellowship hall in an hour."

"Thank you," I manage.

When he walks away, his footsteps echoing down the aisle, I finally let out the breath I have been holding. My pulse is still racing, my body still warm from what we did, but now it mixes with a rush of relief.

Brayden steps closer, his hand brushing the small of my back. "Think he suspects anything?" he murmurs.

"If he does, we're both going to need to find new identities."

That earns me a quiet laugh. He leans closer, his lips near my ear. "Worth it," he whispers.

I glance toward the sanctuary, where the choir is gathering, and the scent of poinsettias hangs in the warm air. Outside, palm trees shimmer with Christmas lights, and a soft breeze carries the faint sound of carolers from the courtyard. The evening feels peaceful, touched by something good and simple.

Brayden's fingers find mine, his grip steady and sure. For a moment, we just stand there, the hum of laughter and music wrapping around us like a promise.

Some people find faith in hymns and candlelight. I found mine in him.

ACKNOWLEDGEMENTS

After ten years of writing bikers, bad boys, and enough club-related emotional carnage to qualify as its own true-crime docuseries, I have finally fused my two greatest obsessions into one spectacularly chaotic holiday monstrosity: Christmas and biker romance. Anyone who knows me understands that I don't "love" Christmas—I hoard it like a dragon hoards gold. For the longest time, I proudly announced that I had eight Christmas trees. Then, mid-sentence while drafting this, I glanced around my house and thought, "Oh, shit. Nine. Is it nine? WHERE did the ninth tree come from?" At this point, I'm not decorating; I'm spawning them. They're multiplying like festive gremlins and I've lost control.

So of course it made perfect sense to take that level of unhinged holiday devotion and slam it directly into my love of biker romance—leather, loyalty, and men who communicate in a complex language of grunts, forehead creases, and engine revs that somehow express deep emotional trauma. Writing this book didn't feel like crafting a story; it felt like letting Christmas kick down the door of a biker clubhouse, chug a gallon of peppermint schnapps, climb onto someone's Harley, and scream "LET'S MAKE POOR DECISIONS!" while twinkling lights explode in the background.

To my husband, Glen—thank you for surviving another book with me. You were blessed (or cursed?) with nightly questions such as, "Does this joke seal my ticket to Hell?" and "Is this funny, or will I start to sizzle if I leave it in the book?" Your ability to answer with a straight face is nothing short of divine intervention. Truly, you deserve a halo and maybe some noise-canceling headphones.

To Cass and Mads—my PR team and my brilliant editor (Mads), thank you for willingly stepping into the tornado that is my creative process. Cass, you somehow take my chaos, wrap it in a bow, and convince the world it's intentional. I don't know how you do it, but I'm convinced you possess either dark magic or a dangerously high tolerance for nonsense.

And Mads... my editor... the true MVP. Thank you for fixing my unhinged punctuation, deleting my crimes against grammar, and gently letting me know when my jokes crossed from "funny" into "ma'am, that's a felony." You take my unedited brain-soup pages and turn them into something resembling an actual book. If sainthood is real, someone submit your application immediately.

Alicia, thank you for listening to every single unhinged idea I had for this story—even the ones I pitched on zero sleep, too much caffeine, and absolute manic confidence. And thank you for handling my eleventh-hour plot switch like a champ. You're still here, which proves you're braver than most.

And finally, to my readers… you beautiful, chaotic souls. Thank you for embracing the madness, the motorcycles, the mistletoe, the trauma, the healing, and the Christmas trees (all nine of them). Writing for you is the greatest gift I get every year. Your enthusiasm, messages, reviews, and willingness to follow me into increasingly unhinged holiday-biker scenarios mean more than all the twinkle lights in my collection— which, frankly, is saying something.

ABOUT AVELYN

Avelyn Paige is the mischief-maker behind steamy dark romance, gritty mafia love stories, and high-octane motorcycle club tales that have blazed their way onto the Wall Street Journal and USA TODAY bestseller lists. She calls Indiana home, where she lives with her husband and five furry troublemakers who think they're her editors.

When she's not fighting the good fight in cancer research, Avelyn trades test tubes for plot twists and dives into worlds filled with danger, devotion, and deliciously bad decisions. She writes romance because it's the one place where chaos and love can coexist, bullets can fly, hearts can heal, and everyone still gets the kind of ending worth fighting for.

After losing her dad in 2015, she turned heartbreak into creativity and never looked back. Now, she's on a mission to prove that even the darkest hearts can find redemption, and that love—no matter how twisted—always leaves a mark worth remembering.

Join Avelyn's Facebook Reader Group: Avelyn's Angels

ALSO BY AVELYN PAIGE

Heaven's Rejects MC Series

Heaven Sent

Angels and Ashes

Absolution

Lies and Illusions

Resolution

Bad Luck, Hard Love

The Black Hoods MC

Dark Protector

Dark Secret

Dark Guardian

Dark Desires

Dark Destiny

Dark Redemption

Dark Salvation

Dark Seduction

The Bastard Boilers MC

Property of Azrael

Property of Fox

Voodoo City Queens MC

Devil's Queen

Second Sons Duet

All The Pretty Little Lies

All The Darkest Truths

Standalone

The Reaper's Vow

Hogging The Holidays